Entwinements

Copyright © 2023 Caleen J Mettson

This book is a work of fiction. Names, characters, places, and incidents are the product of the author's imagination or are used fictitiously. Any resemblance to actual persons, living or dead, business establishments, organizations, events, or locales is entirely coincidental.

All rights reserved.

No part of this book may be reproduced, scanned, or distributed in any printed, electronic, or audio form without written permission. Please do not participate in or encourage piracy of copyright materials in violation of the author's rights. Purchase only authorized editions.

Printed in the United States of America
First Edition
Original cover art: C J Mettson
Cover Design: RS Ltd.

ISBN 979-8-9899734-0-8 (e-book}
ISBN 979-8-9899734-1-5 (paperback)

Entwinements

By Caleen J Mettson

That life is worth living is the essential message and assurance of all art.

                                                     - Herman Hesse

CHAPTER I

Neva Omaro slowly awakens to the sound of breaking ocean waves emitting from the digital sound cube on her nightstand. She had another restless night. Her sleep disturbed by a sense of wariness. That the answers she seeks are within her reach, but she is still missing something vital.

The soft sunlight streaming into the room helps to allay her unease. She changes into yoga pants and a tee shirt and opens the door to the small terrace outside of her bedroom. Standing briefly with outstretched arms, to let the early sun warm her body prior to beginning a routine of yoga exercises. Later when she enters the shower, her toned lithe body is lightly covered in sweat.

As she turns off the water spray, the warm mist wafts around the bathroom. It relaxes her as she uses the towel for a light massage of her limbs. The pixie cut of her black hair will air dry to frame her angular face, with the asymmetric bangs accentuating her almond-shaped dark brown eyes and full lips.

She is methodical in her dressing, having assembled outfits for the week. They are arranged on a rolling garment rack in the center of her large walk-in closet. It will be five weeks before the current apparel items will be back on rotation. To be paired with other clothing pieces to create different looks. Before leaving the bedroom, she straightens the bed.

Standing in the kitchen, Neva sips a smoothie while preparing a salad with dressing on the side for her lunch. Then gathers snacks - mixed nuts with raisins, and an apple. Placing the food items into a compact lunch bag, which along with her mobile devices are inserted into a fashionable leather tote before she leaves the apartment.

It is a short walk to the bus stop for the commute to work. At this time in the morning, she will always get a seat. Sitting by the window she inserts earbuds and settles back to listen to the Winter Concerto. It is her favorite of the Four Seasons Concertos by Antonio Vivaldi. She gives in to the music. Entranced by the complexities of the musical composition. Fleetingly thinking about Vivaldi, the reluctant priest but passionate musician and composer.

Neva lives and works in Middletown, one of the larger counties in the city of Woodsburne, in Western New York State. Woodsburne is divided into five counties: River Edge, Middletown, Kafton Heights, Brookside Hills and Highlands. Each county has distinctive residential communities and commercial areas.

The city's public transportation system provides a network of bus and street trolley service routes. The trolleys operate solely along Main Street. It is the roadway that traverses the districts of River Edge, Middletown and Kafton Heights. The trolley is used almost exclusively by visitors during the spring, summer and fall tourist seasons. Most locals commute by the buses that travel along Palmer Ridge, a local highway which runs parallel to Main Street and terminates in the Highlands district.

Neva exits the bus on Bessemer Lane and walks one block east to the Avalon Fine Art Gallery located on Main Street. The three-story red brick building is situated along the county's cultural corridor.

The building was once a couture apparel emporium for women. Its interior was facilely converted to the functions of the gallery. There is a walled balcony that partially overlooks the first floor. A wide curving staircase which connects the first and second floors. The second floor has an open loft area that is used for additional exhibit space when needed.

Across and on the right of the loft space are four rooms: one for storage, two for private art showings and sales, and the last one, nestled in a corner, serves as a staff lounge. At the rear, on the left side, are two offices. The largest one serves as Neva's office. The third floor has three meeting rooms and a wide hallway that leads to a rooftop terrace.

Neva takes out the keys to unlock the tall glass and wood double doors, entering quickly to turn off the alarm system. She is the director of the gallery, and manages a staff of ten, which includes four interns.

The Avalon is an exclusive seller of artwork for five principal artists. In addition, the gallery, through a special invitation process, selects four emerging artists for limited exhibits. Each selected artist is assigned a three month period for the exhibition of their works. The gallery will manage the sales for these guest artists during their exhibit cycle; and return unsold works to them.

The advantages of showcasing emerging artists are twofold. It serves to maintain the gallery's reputation as a springboard for new talent, and it ensures an ongoing series of new art exhibits for its loyal and diverse customers. Many of the emerging artists go on to successful careers from the exposure to art critics and collectors connected to the Avalon.

Neva walks to the rear of the gallery's main floor towards the primary art storage room. This is the work area used by the art handlers. She enters the room and looks at new arrivals, including three paintings from Jason Aria, one of the gallery's principal artists. And reviews the intake file for each individual piece of artwork.

The canvasses are hung on a ceiling suspended, pull-out art rack system, installed towards the rear of the spacious rectangular room. Later in the morning, she will discuss display ideas with Matt Bondi, who oversees exhibits.

Mica Ramose, the senior gallery associate, is buzzed in by Neva. She walks into the storage room and leans against a large workbench. Her face still aglow from her early morning workout.

Mica moved to Woodsburne from San Francisco five years ago. The vibrancy of life in a small city still surprises her. At twenty-nine, she has settled into its pace without losing her vivacity. And while she may not be the prettiest woman at a gathering, she will be the one who is remembered. Without missing a beat, she launches into a recap of her previous evening's activities. Neva enjoys these informal morning chats. The energy radiating from Mica replaces any need for caffeine.

Neva briefly thinks about her social life which is centered mostly around her work. Having dinner or drinks with clients, attending exhibit openings, and other events related to the arts. She is forty-three and has had several serious relationships but never married. Reluctant to make a commitment, fearful of losing herself in that societal institution.

Unlike her mother who was never ambiguous about her commitment to family and marriage. A life structured in a cocoon of domesticity. Neva believes that her mother never allowed herself to see an existence beyond what had always been the way of life for women in her family.

However, Neva sees herself forging a different path from past generations, moving beyond the parameters of traditions. The prescribed rules of existence set within cultural boundaries.

Mica goes to the restroom to do a last minute check of her appearance, while Neva completes the preliminary placement sheets. On her return, Mica takes her place behind the front desk. Another business day begins.

The early morning visitors are usually the Regulars, as they are called by the staff. They enjoy walking around the gallery as part of their morning routine. Most of the Regulars are not yet committed to making a purchase. But nevertheless, they appreciate being surrounded by art, if only briefly, each day.

They are important to the gallery not only because some

of them will eventually become buyers. But all of them are unofficial ambassadors, who will readily make referrals to the Avalon.

Mica treats the Regulars as though they are serious collectors. She knows their names and preferences in art. Never pushy, yet subtle in her approach, Mica advises them on the process of how to acquire an admired piece of artwork. She is adroit at keeping people interested in visiting the gallery. Neva is aware of Mica's talent and how attuned she is to their patrons.

Among the morning visitors is Aisa Clare, who just completed an emerging artist exhibit cycle at the gallery. Her unsold works were in the process of being packed for return. She excitedly grabs Mica by the arm and leads her over to Neva. Telling them that the two remaining paintings will be purchased by a marketing firm that is opening a branch office in Woodsburne.

The wife of one of the owners saw her paintings at the gallery last week, and told her husband about them. Now they are discussing the purchase of additional artwork from her.

Neva joins Mica in congratulating her. Aisa asks if the gallery will still manage the sale transaction for her. She also lets them know that she will be hiring an agent to represent her.

"I want to thank you all again for what you have done for me. The exposure from my showing has advanced my art career beyond my expectations. Please keep me in mind for any support needed for the emerging artists program." Aisa tells them enthusiastically.

Aisa is beginning to garner recognition in the art world. She left her teaching career several years ago to pursue her passion for creating art. Eighteen months ago, she met Neva at a locally sponsored street fair for artists. At the time, Neva had offered her the opportunity of a limited exhibit at the gallery when she felt ready to take the next step.

After Aisa leaves, Neva returned to the storage room to look again at Jason's paintings. He had been a successful interior designer before shifting his talent to the mediums of canvas and metal. Jason's crossover was met with almost immediate acclaim. His paintings and sculptures were in homes and offices from New York to Saudi Arabia. With the Saudi among his most avid collectors. His artworks seemingly aligned with their vision of building Utopia in their part of the world.

Neva is struck again by the stark divergence from his previous works. The paintings have a disquieting, almost sinister quality to them. Seeming to exude a dark undertone of message through its color palette and painted images. As if a heretofore untapped rage had been released; given free rein to recast his style of artistic expression. She did not think that two of the three paintings would sell. They made her feel on edge.

Coming to a decision about them, Neva walks over to the packing room to speak with Mona Hastings. She is one of three art handlers on contract with the gallery. They discuss moving the three paintings to a private showroom upstairs. She will inform Matt of Neva's decision to temporarily relocate them.

Back in her office, Neva thinks about the best approach to speak with Jason about the new direction of his work.

CHAPTER 2

Jason had been a coup for Neva when he signed with the Avalon. He was already a rising star, and the critics loved him. He did not need the gallery to boost his career. She knew that Jason had many other prominent galleries vying for him at the time, but he had chosen the Avalon.

Because he wanted a gallery where his art would not be the dominant attraction but a presence within the whole. It was important to him that the visitors be drawn to his artwork by their visceral response to its composition, rather than the lure of his name.

He also endorsed Avalon's support of emerging artists by attending not only the exhibits featuring their works, but participating as a panelist in the workshops that the gallery held for them. Making an effort to attend at least two of the classes during the year. For him, the workshops provided an informal setting to discuss techniques, creative styles, and current trends with the attendees.

But it had been more than four months since he last participated in any of these activities. Through emails, he informed Mica that he was busy working on new projects, which was partially true. Jason did not share with her the real reason for his detachment. His marital problems were overshadowing his artistic life.

It began when his wife, Julie, announced that she wanted to start a commercial art business to sell prints and textiles to be created by him. That pronouncement caused their relationship to morph into toxic warfare. Since then, Jason felt like a soldier entering a battlefield when he stepped inside of his house.

After weeks of bitter confrontation, Jason was at his wits end. Pleading with Julie to explain her reasons for hauling them to the gates of hell. Julie was ready with her response. Her relentless goading was orchestrated to lead him into asking that question.

She spat out her words to cause him pain.

"The entire business plan was a hoax. Everything about it was a lie, Jason. Its purpose was to demean not only your artistry, but also your standing as a fine artist. I wanted to make you feel my pain of being undervalued and belittled. How I felt when a recent a job offer was solely based on me providing access to you. They were interested in your contacts and connections in the art world. I was nothing more than a gatekeeper to them. A side note for their planned expansion into the cultural arts sector."

Julies face was contorted in fury when she paused speaking. Reliving her mortification from the last business meeting.

"When I finally realized that my role would not lead to achieving success in my own right; a seething hatred erupted within me. I could not strike back at them. But you, you Jason, would be their proxy. The perfect stand-in to be given a lesson in humiliation meted out by me. Everything is so easy for you. Opportunities just come your way without any effort from you. Do you even see anyone but yourself anymore!" Julie had shrieked at him.

Jason was stunned by her admission. The way in which she used her fury to annihilate everything they had built during their years together. Her treachery obliterated any sense of remorse he may have felt.

A high moral ground no longer existed for either of them to stand on. That night, when Jason walked out the door, he left behind both his home and a shattered marriage.

Neva's call came just as Jason was leaving the office of the lawyer handling his divorce. He knew that the paintings would prompt a call from her. Those painted images disturbed him as well. He didn't recognize himself in those figurative depictions. Feeling trapped in a place that was not entirely due to his broken marriage. They agreed that he would come to the gallery the next day.

After ending the call with Jason, Neva went downstairs to Matt's office. They discussed ideas for exhibiting the recently arrived artwork. But Matt questioned her decision to put Jason's paintings in a private show room.

"Those three pieces are extraordinary. The nuances portrayed in the foreboding shapes are captivating. The images draw you in to scrutinize them. Like peering into a looking glass, reflecting a momentary glimpse into your innermost self. We must display them."

Neva nods her head hesitatingly.

"It is only a temporary move. To be honest, I had my doubts about whether they would sell. But I see your point. However, they should be installed in the rear section of the gallery. Only because they will probably draw high foot traffic once word of mouth gets out about them. We need to be prepared for that."

"I agree with you. We will deinstall other pieces to clear a space for them. It will be a busy day." Matt said, relieved that Jason's paintings will be displayed on the main floor.

On her way to take the stairs back to her office, Neva is surprised to see Edith Marjoram standing in the reception area. She is a longtime close friend of Neva and loyal patron of the gallery.

She met Edith through a professor during her undergrad years in college. She became a mentor and helped to guide Neva in her career. As the years passed, their relationship evolved into a personal one.

Edith wears her eighty-two years well. She is a vivacious woman who appears taller than her average height and projects a commanding presence.

For over forty years, she and her late husband amassed an

art collection that is eclectic as it is sizable. It is housed in a separate wing of their large stately mansion in the Highlands' historic district.

Edith warmly greets Neva on seeing her. Telling her that she came to Middletown to attend a morning meeting at the Woodsburne Historical Society.

"The timing worked well as Mica called me yesterday to let me know that new paintings from Jason had been delivered. I'm anxious to see them, as she also told me that they are quite a departure from his previous work."

Neva turns her head looking for Mica but does not see her.

"Why are you looking for Mica? She was just doing her job, following the protocol for informing your clients about new arrivals of art from principal artists."

"I wasn't looking for Mica." Neva lied, annoyed that Edith was able to correctly guess her intention.

Neva strived not to appear to give preferential treatment to any of their clients. But in truth, as in most businesses, there is always a short list of select clientele. She would speak with Mica later to ensure that their other patrons were given the same notice.

Edith rolls her eyes at Neva as if reading her thoughts.

"I am simply being the early bird. Now let's go upstairs so that I can see them."

"How did you know where they were?" Neva asks, dumbfounded.

"Matt may have mentioned it to me." Edith replies offhandedly.

"We spoke on the phone before I came here. I had other matters to discuss with him. You know that Matt is occasionally retained as an art consultant by estate agents and private collectors. Well, he was recently hired by a close friend of mine. She suspected that a Matisse painting that she purchased at a yard sale was not a reproduction but an original. As it turns out, she was correct."

Her eyes twinkled with excitement.

"Matt's appraisal made for a historic discovery. The painting had been missing since World War II. My friend's attorney is working with the authorities who are overseeing the return of lost art from the war to their rightful owners. And the intrigue does not end there. Evidently a forgery of the painting has been on display for many years at a prominent museum, on loan from a private collector. Then two years ago, the collector received an anonymous tip that the painting might be a forgery. A discreet investigation was initiated to determine the authenticity of both the painting and provenance documents. Our information provided additional corroboration that both the painting and documents were indeed forgeries."

Edith links her arm with Neva, as they walk to the elevator.

"This little drama is not over yet, and it will be quietly covered up. The scandal and embarrassment would be considerable if knowledge of this affair became public."

"My gracious, what an extraordinary story. Matt never mentioned anything about it to me." Neva said as she looks in stunned disbelief at Edith.

"Surely, you know better than that." Edith replied brusquely. "Matt had to sign non-disclosure agreements regarding this matter. However, I am not under those constraints. As I acted as a friend, so to speak, in advising Hattie on how to extricate herself from this debacle."

Hearing the curtness in her tone, Edith softens her voice.

"And I'm only telling you this much to allay any concerns about your staff. I know that you are the soul of discretion, and can rely on you not to discuss this matter with anyone, including Matt."

"Of course not, you have my word," said Neva. Although she still has questions, Neva understands the ramifications. She would not make any further inquiries. With effort, she regains her equanimity.

"Now let's go upstairs."

Still somewhat unnerved by what Edith had just divulged, they take the elevator across from the storage room.

It is a short ride to the second floor. Edith precedes Neva into the private showing room. Rushing over to the paintings hung on wall mounted art racks. Neva stands quietly at the back of the room.

Straightening up, Edith speaks over her shoulder to Neva.

"They are extraordinary! Who knew that Jason could paint such dark imagery?"

Hearing no reply, she turns around to look at Neva.

"Oh, I see you are troubled. They are not representative of the art that is usually shown here."

Edith sits down heavily on one of the curved low-backed chairs arranged in front of the art racks.

"Do you know what Jason is conveying in these paintings?" Edith asks as she watches Neva cross the room to study them again.

"It is evident that something triggered feelings of self-doubt. Jason is looking for his artistic identity; fearful that he is only capable of painting pretty pictures for rich people. Not a good place for an artist to be in. Jason seems to be at a crossroad in his artistic career."

Neva scoffs at her assessment.

"And you can see all of that from these paintings?"

Edith ignores Neva's sarcasm.

"Knowing Jason and his work all these years, I do see a theme of inner turmoil and struggle represented. And if you were to be honest, so would you."

Neva takes a last look at the paintings before turning away.

"I was concerned at first about whether they would sell. And not because the artwork shown here must be aesthetically pleasing. It's that these paintings embody a feeling of being lost; traveling in darkness. But Matt convinced me otherwise. This is only a temporary placement for them."

"Matt is right. These paintings will appeal to your patrons. If for no other reason than that they are so evocative."

Neva came over to sit beside her.

"They stirred something in me. Somehow, I feel unnerved by

them."

Edith stares intently at Neva, puzzled by why the paintings would have that effect on her.

"Maybe they tugged at something troubling you." Edith said, and tilts her head to whisper mischievously. "Remember these are just paintings, not messages from the dark side."

Coming to a decision, Edith stands and walks over to a small desk and sits down.

"I am going to buy the three paintings."

Neva is utterly astonished, her voice shaded by disbelief.

"I don't understand. Why would you buy them?"

Edith squares her shoulders before responding.

"You know as well as I do that my collection represents diverse points of view. Neither artists or genres are determinants of what I acquire. These paintings are special. Jason may be on to something, but this will not be where he ends his journey. Trust me, these paintings are going to be sought after in a few years and I want to own them."

Rising from her chair, Edith hands the check to Neva, who is now standing in front of the desk.

"You may show them for now, but at the end of the month they are to be delivered to me. Send me the documents for them tomorrow, and let me know if there is a balance due."

She stops before going out the door.

"When will you be seeing Jason?"

"Tomorrow afternoon," Neva replies somewhat guardedly. She is still perplexed by the unexpectedness of the transaction.

"Good, come have dinner with me tomorrow evening. I'll see you at 7PM." Edith said, more as a command than an invitation.

Still standing in the room, Neva looks down at the check in her hand. It covered the full amount for the sale. Jason will certainly be surprised by this purchase, she thinks to herself.

CHAPTER 3

After Edith left, Neva returned to her office to make several telephone calls and check her appointments. Her day will end with an evening engagement. A fundraising event hosted by the local Chamber of Commerce at the Leyden Museum. She will make sure to be seen by the right people and plans to be home before nine o'clock.

The weather had turned chilly by the time Neva arrives at her apartment building. She greets the doorman and takes the elevator to her tenth-floor duplex apartment. Switching on a wall light in the entryway, she sets her handbag on a console table before placing her paisley pashmina in the coat closet. Deciding not to immediately go to her bedroom, Neva lays her suit jacket on a bench and slips out of her shoes.

It is a six-room dwelling, with an open floor plan. The master suite occupies the entire top floor. The living spaces are furnished in a minimalist style, distinctive but not overdone, with most furniture pieces made of wood, metal, and glass. The dove grey hues on the walls harmonized with the pastel textiles used for seat coverings and window treatments. Accent pillows and other décor accessories provide the insertion of bolder colors into the rooms. There is a subtle Asian influence in the overall interior design, which matches Neva's understated elegance.

Going into the kitchen, she placed the lunch bag on the counter. Then prepared a plate of brie cheese, wafer crackers, and three stuffed Medjool dates. She was hungry, having not eaten since late afternoon. A glass of pinot noir completes the small meal.

Taking food and drink, Neva enters the small home office adjacent to the kitchen. She eats while reading her emails. When she finishes, Neva takes the empty plate to the kitchen and refills her glass with more wine.

Going into the living room, she gazes at a large painting hanging above the fireplace as she sips her wine. It is a striking abstract study of color, textures, and subtle shapes. Neva painted it while studying for a master's in museum studies.

The painting is unsigned, and she enjoys telling the story of a young struggling artist giving it to her as repayment for a loan to buy paints and materials.

She never felt any guilt about her subterfuge. And always enjoyed hearing the offered opinions about the painting. The varied commentaries on the artist's intent and meaning; the departure from formalist strictures; the boldness of color and composition; and so forth. Sometimes it was hard for her to keep a straight face as guests prattled on with their pompous critiquing.

For Neva, the most insightful comments came from those who simply expressed their like or dislike, without anatomizing the artwork or artistic intent. After completing her studies, the driving force behind her career goals was to connect people to art. It shaped her work for most of her career.

It was what brought her to Woodsburne. The opportunity to have a larger impact in the art world from a smaller arena.

When Neva accepted the position at the Avalon, she had over fifteen years of experience in arts management. She had been a fine arts consultant and art administrator at prestigious art institutions and galleries in the United States and abroad.

She was at a point in her career where she had the reputation and credentials to choose a position that linked with her interests. One of which was to develop the careers of emerging artists. Another was to create opportunities to collaborate with nonprofit organizations to sponsor community arts programs.

Prior to her hiring, the Avalon Gallery had been well established in its niche for selling fine art. However, its narrow focus limited its positioning for attracting a wider customer base. Novice buyers rarely visited the gallery to either browse or make a purchase. It was known for catering exclusively to established collectors.

When the previous director was coaxed into retirement, the Avalon's Board seized the opportunity to restructure the management of the gallery. They realized that for the business to thrive, it had to expand its outreach and offerings. A committee was formed to search for a new director who could accomplish their next tier growth objectives. After an extensive search, Neva was selected for the position.

The primary objectives for her first year at the gallery were the reorganization of staff, including the addition of two new positions: graphic designer and public relations manager; and initiating an internship program with two area colleges.

In the second year, she launched a digital magazine in partnership with three local arts organizations. Its editorial board was comprised of representatives from each partner.

WNY Arts Mind was an immediate success acquiring over ten thousand subscribers within months of its launch. The success of the online magazine also opened new global markets for selling the artworks available at the Avalon.

Those early successes enabled Neva to inaugurate the emerging artist exhibits and expand the range of services available to artists and art enthusiasts. Gross earnings grew by forty percent during her tenure.

Now after seven years, Neva was considering whether it was time to move on. However, she was planning to make personnel changes that would support gallery operations regardless of her decision. A key move would be to promote Matt to Assistant Director. A role that had become more critical with increased sales and the diverse services being provided by the gallery. Next, the appointment of Mica to backfill the recently vacated position of public relations manager. Those duties were well suited to her skill sets. And lastly, hire Fredericka Martin for the newly created position of digital content manager. Fredericka completed her graduate program in art and technology during her internship there. Her primary role would be to oversee the online presence of the gallery.

Neva was looking forward to her presentation at the upcoming board meeting. But she only had two weeks to reach a decision about her own future.

While she was proud of her accomplishments, her reaction to Jason's paintings stirred a feeling of being unfulfilled. For the first time in a long while, Neva felt a need to confront the loneliness that she kept tightly boxed inside of her.

Her impersonal living space was a reflection of those submerged feelings. It lacked the warmth of a home. Standing there it dawned on her that what she wanted most was a committed relationship, to be married. She trembled at the enormity of that self-revelation. Her knees seem to buckle as she sits. She hugs herself as tears of bewilderment roll down her cheeks.

At that moment, she recalls not only scenes from her childhood; but other life events that bolstered her determination to not become like her mother. Leading her to repress any desire for having a family of her own.

So preoccupied with her thoughts, Neva did not initially hear the chiming of the intercom. Ricardo, the security guard, apologized for the late intrusion. Telling her that she has a visitor who is insistent on seeing her right away. Neva asks him the name of the visitor. It is Jason Aria.

She hesitates momentarily before giving her permission. Glancing at her watch, she notes the time. It is almost 10:00 PM. Running through her mind are various reasons for his impromptu visit. Yet none of them provide an answer for the need to see her before their appointment tomorrow.

Neva goes to the powder room located down a short hallway from the home office. She quickly splashes water onto her face and pats her hair. When the doorbell rings, she is composed.

Jason enters the apartment, and stands gazing at her.

"Am I interrupting something?"

"No, just having a conversation with myself. Your new paintings seemed to have awaken some dormant feelings in me."

"Is that so," said Jason ruefully.

Walking into the living room, they both sit down on the sofa. Neva glances over at Jason.

"So, what brings you here tonight that could not wait until tomorrow?"

Running his hands through his hair, Jason gets up and walks around the room.

"Neva, I feel like I'm out to sea without a compass. He rubs his forehead and sits in a chair across from the sofa.

"I'm getting a divorce. Julie is leaving for Colorado in two days. Our house is already listed with a broker. Honestly, it's been a living hell these past months. It was unbelievable how quickly our marriage fell apart. I thought we were fine, not perfect, but on good terms. Next thing I know, we're at each other's throats. Because Julie not only wanted us to start a new business, but also for me to leave the Avalon and drop Donald as my agent."

Staring unfocused at a far wall, he continues.

"Those demands sparked weeks of bitter arguments. Before she finally told me the cause of our nasty drama. That her identity as an individual had been obliterated by our marriage. That she is not acknowledged as a person outside of her relationship with me."

Jason feels self-conscious as he hears himself speak.

"It shook me. The extreme measures that she took to convey her anger about our relationship. The methods she used to retaliate against me. The whole situation has turned my world upside down. It made me to rethink everything. Have I been so beguiled by my reputation? Unmindful of what I am doing, not only artistically but in my personal life as well. It left me questioning whether I have been fooling myself all these years."

Holding his head between his hands, Jason bends forward looking down at the floor, finding it hard to believe that he is articulating so openly such intimate thoughts to another person. When he looks up, his eyes are tearing.

"Neva, has it all been a lie?"

"Let's pause here for a moment, just for a brief respite."

Neva gets up and walks to the kitchen, with Jason following. Seeing how upset he is, she understands the seriousness of his dilemma. But is flustered by his frankness, unsure of how she should respond.

As she collects her thoughts, Neva opens another bottle of wine and pours a glass for each of them. Handing one to Jason, who takes the glass and drains it.

They return to the living room. Neva sits down on the sofa, while Jason remains standing. She knows that she must be considered in her response.

"Putting creativity aside; let's examine some of the factors that can motivate an artist. Such as seeking critical acclaim, fame, or wealth. And if any or all of these are motivational factors for an artist, does that make their work less worthy? Does the desire for those things diminish their talent, skill, or relevance?" Neva posits before continuing.

"Or on the other hand, those artists who create art for the sake of art. And are dismissive of any critical recognition or public admiration. By taking such a stance, does that make their artwork more profound or significant? You know as well as I do that the nature of art has been an ongoing debate for centuries."

She observes that Jason is attentive. Thinking about what she is saying.

"Consider one of its definitions. That art is the use of skill and imagination in the creation of aesthetic objects, environments, or experiences that can be shared with others."

Jason goes over to the counter and pours more wine into his glass and drinks. He walks over to the fireplace and looks up at the painting. His face is a study of mixed emotions, and his voice conveys those internal feelings.

"I guess what I really want to know is - do you think my work is relevant?"

Neva gets up to stand beside him. Intuitively knowing that physical contact is not needed at that moment. She lightly sets her glass down on a table near the fireplace. And leans her body closer toward Jason without touching him.

"What do you feel when you are creating a piece of art?"

Shaking his head from his reverie, he replies.

"Put simply, it is an instinctive feeling that compels me to express myself through either paint or sculpture."

He stops to think more about the question.

"Sometimes I am inspired by the reflection of light on an object, a rock formation, the movements of bodies, a dream, or music. Whatever the thing is, it ignites a compulsion to convert the essence of that mentally held image or concept into a material depiction."

He closes his eyes as if reliving the spark of creativity.

"During the time when I am creating a piece, I am consumed by it. There is no time. No day or night. No need for food. No need to rest. It is like an out of body experience. As if I am a tool being used by some unseen creative force that is seeking expression in the physical world. Many times, I look at a completed painting or sculpture and know that there was something working through me or with me to create it."

Neva nods her head in agreement.

"What was in your mind when you painted your latest works?"

Jason felt somewhat subdued, gathering up himself before he answered.

"All of my self-doubts about who I am as an artist and as a person. It was an unfiltered rendering of those feelings that streamed from my mind onto the canvases. It was thrilling, and cathartic. When I stood back and looked at the paintings, I saw the portrayals of all that emotional upheaval. My fears, rage, anger, and even regrets."

"Don't you see, Jason? You utilized your creative skill to impart a desired perspective through a specific medium. It was not formulaic, nor done by rote."

His mood is lifted slightly by her words.

"You know all my life I always felt good about whatever I did. Never indulged in 'what ifs.' This situation with Julie and our marriage has caused me to see life, my life, so differently. I'll be fifty next year. This is not how I envisioned coming to that milestone age. Before all this, I felt accomplished. Eagerly looking forward to the upcoming chapters in my life. Now? I don't know what I feel. What is in my future? So many uncertainties."

"But your accomplishments remain the same. That has not changed. Is that why you have been absent these past months?" Neva asked.

"For the most part. I didn't think I was in any position to talk about art to other artists. If I was unsure about my own artistry, how could I speak to them about theirs?"

"Yes, I can understand you feeling that way."

A sense of calm descends upon Jason. He feels more relaxed. Suddenly wanting to be alone with his thoughts.

"Well, let me go. I apologize for intruding on you, making my problems yours. I can't begin to thank you for your wisdom and kindness."

As they reach the door, Neva impulsively gives him a hug. He is touched by her unexpected embrace. That their discussion was more personal than business. His voice is husky when he speaks.

"Ok Doc, I will see you tomorrow at the gallery to discuss business."

He lingers with his hand on the door handle. Unable to leave before he asks the one question that has been on his mind throughout their conversation.

"Neva, why did you stop painting?"

Neva is caught off guard by his question.

"What do you mean?" she stammers.

"The painting hanging above the fireplace, why didn't you continue to paint?"

Neva responds with new insight.

"I didn't feel compelled to express myself through that medium. I took a different path, which brought me to the Avalon. And here to have this discussion with you."

They look deeply into each other's eyes. Jason kisses her on the cheek and exits out the door.

Neva is taking the glasses to the kitchen, when she remembers that she forgot to tell Jason that his paintings were sold. Probably just as well, she thinks. The timing wasn't appropriate. Turning off the lights, she goes upstairs to her bedroom.

Sitting propped up in bed, she calls Edith on a whim.

"Hello Neva, why are you up this late?"

"Jason came to see me tonight. He just left. You were right. He has been wrestling with self-doubts about his art these past months."

"Yes, that was evident in his latest paintings. They will mark a significant transition in his artistic career. I have already alerted Roland to be prepared for the inundation of requests to buy those paintings."

"It's good to know that you are preparing for the onslaught of the wolves." Neva said teasingly.

Edith laughs softly.

"Yes, we are. Okay, let's both get some sleep, and we'll talk more tomorrow evening. Get here on time so we can have a leisurely dinner. Goodnight."

Before she falls asleep that night, Neva's mind is filled with thoughts about the course that her life will take as it wends its way into the future.

CHAPTER 4

Matt was at the same restaurant where Jason had stopped in to have drinks with friends that evening. Fables Restaurant is a favorite gathering spot in Woodsburne for locals and artists who owned homes in the nearby communities. Many famous writers, film and stage actors, singers, and musicians dined at the eatery during their stay in the region.

Fables owners, brothers Leon and Antony Brisbane, worked assiduously to ensure that their famous guests were as undisturbed as any other patron coming to the restaurant.

The establishment is known both for its menu and its themed dining rooms. Matt was attending a birthday party being held in the Brazilian room.

The room replicates a Brazilian carnival atmosphere, including the food, drinks and music found at a Rio Street party. The wait staff wear a variety of masquerade masks. Menu selections include feijoada, Sao Paola churrasco, fish soup with coconut milk, and Brazilian style pizza. Caipirinha and beer are the favorite drinks served. The recorded music of samba, samba reggae, and frevo fills the room with its pulsating beats, and a live band plays there once a month. It is the most popular of the four dining rooms.

Matt was on his phone in the hallway, when he saw Jason heading towards the down escalator. He quickly ended his call to greet him. They chatted briefly, and Matt invited him to join the party for a drink. Jason declined, saying that he had to make another stop before going home. He did not tell Matt that he was on his way to Neva's apartment.

Matt stood watching as Jason descended on the escalator. He ends his silent watch and returns to the party. He looks around for Jack, the friend he came with. Seeing him with a group of friends, Matt walks over to them. And leans in to speak into Jack's ear, telling him that he is ready to leave. But Jack tells him that he is having fun and will be staying. He gives Matt a quick hug, before turning back to their friends.

Until he saw Jason, Matt was enjoying the party. But seeing Jason had reminded him of how lonely he was, despite all the people in his life.

Matt Bondi comes from an upper middle-class family. He grew up in Greenwich, Connecticut, the oldest of three children. At an early age, he knew that he was not like other boys. He always felt more physically attracted to males and was disturbed and confused by his feelings. And dating was a difficult for him. Having to pretend to feel something that wasn't there.

Matt was tall and handsome, with a compact muscular build. His deep-set hazel eyes always looked sad even when he smiled. He had excelled in track while in high school and was a popular athlete.

In college he continued to excel in sports, becoming a star running back on the football team. Girls threw themselves at him all the time. He fended them off by telling them he was taken. Caitlyn had been his girlfriend from high school. She was also the only person to whom Matt told that he was gay.

Back then, she provided the perfect buffer for him. Caitlyn was a beautiful young woman with long silky black hair that framed her oval face. She had a curvy figure suited to her tall frame. However, her demeanor was off putting. Her gray-blue eyes were like beacons, drawing attention to her keen intelligence.

Most of the girls ignored her, feeling inadequate in her presence. Younger boys would gawk at her, at a loss for words, or else utter inappropriate things. However, older boys knew that their usual tactics to get with a girl, would be useless with her. Therefore, to pacify their egos, they resorted to spreading lies and malicious rumors about her in the school.

Matt was her saving grace, sensing a kindred spirit in her. One who was thrusted into a world that would not readily make room for them. They grew to trust each other, able to confide their troubles, fears, and dreams.

Caitlyn accepted who he was, untroubled by his homosexuality. She stood by his side and provided the shield that he needed to come to terms with his identity during those turbulent young adult years.

Their parents took for granted that after college they would announce their engagement. It came as a shock to their families when they announced their decision to go their separate ways. The surprise announcement was made at the joint dinner party held to celebrate their college graduation. Caitlyn was accepted into a graduate program to study ancient archaeology at the University of California at Berkeley. And Matt would be entering the Critical and Curatorial Studies graduate program at Columbia University, in New York City.

Standing close together, they spoke passionately about their chosen fields of study and future careers. And then announced that they would not be getting engaged. They made it clear that their decision was unequivocal. Although both families were disappointed, their parents gave them their support.

What neither family knew at the time was that Matt was about to inform his family that he was gay. He felt ready to face his fears about losing the love of his younger brother and sister. Feeling confident in being supported by his parents.

It was Caitlyn who gave him the encouragement he needed to follow through with his decision. She told him that putting his sexuality aside, he was still the same son and brother that they had known all their lives. He planned to tell them during the upcoming weekend.

Early Saturday evening, Matt gathered his family together. They were eager to hear what he had to say. Speculating that he was going to tell them about his intention to marry Caitlyn after all.

When they were settled in the family room, he spoke to them quietly about the secret that he had kept for most of his life. He spoke movingly about the feelings of anguish and isolation that he experienced. How his pretense to be a "straight guy" was to not let his family down. He told them about his joy in being involved in sports, and how that camaraderie had helped to dampen the constant doubts about not being a good enough person, son, or brother.

He described how running gave him the sense of being part of something larger than himself. It gave him hope that the universe had a place for everyone. He spoke about his faith and his close friendship with Caitlyn. How she kept him sane and helped him to stay focused on his life goals since high school. Like a coach, she advised him not to be fearful of befriending his teammates. Because it wasn't about his sexual preference; but who he was as a person and athlete. Even now, her belief in him gave him the courage to disclose his secret to them. When he finished, he sat down holding his breath waiting for their reaction.

Frank was the first to speak, his voice was thick with emotion.

"From this day, I vow to take my role as a brother very seriously."

"And I as a sister," said Kassie.

With that, Matt felt released from the dread of being rejected by his siblings. It also eased the tension in the room. His father and mother came over to Matt and took him in their arms. They told him how sorry they were that he felt he had to carry this burden on his own, and no matter what he is their son. They all said how proud they were of him and how lucky they were to have Caitlyn in their lives.

Overcome with emotion, they came together in a group embrace. Slowly they sat down, each one reflecting on their own thoughts.

Holding back fresh tears, their mother struggled to speak.

"I want you children to know that your father and I are sorry if we ever conveyed that we were unapproachable and would not listen to any matter affecting you."

The words cascaded from her heart.

"I know that it may seem that all we cared about were good grades, having the right friends, and the other million things that most parents want for their children. But at the heart of all our parenting was an unselfish desire to prepare you to take care of yourselves when you go out into the world. That you understood that happiness was not derived from the accumulation of material things, being powerful, or denigrating the dignity, hopes, and dreams of others."

Kassie throws herself into her mother's arms, while Marv reaches over to hug his sons. Eventually, he corrals his family towards the dining room and the meal that had been prepared for them. Hoping that the meal would bring a sense of normalcy to their evening. But most of all he needed time to process what Matt had just revealed to them.

Having no real appetite, everyone went through the motions of eating. Afterwards, Frank and Kassie asked Matt to talk with them privately. They went outside to sit by the pool.

At twenty, Frank will be entering his junior year of college in the fall. At six feet three, he is two inches taller than his older brother. Like his brother, he is also darkly handsome, with brown hair and hazel brown eyes. There is a mischievous quality about him, which easily draws people to him.

He is the first to speak to his brother.

"I know that this shouldn't be about us, but how do we handle this? Does anyone, other than Cait, know?"

Kassie is embarrassed by Frank's question even though she too was curious, but felt it was inappropriate to ask.

Just turning nineteen, Kassie, like her mother is medium height and has a slim build. However, her physical attractiveness is somewhat overshadowed by her intensity. It can be disconcerting at times. But close friends know her to be a deeply caring person.

Matt looks at his siblings and smiles.

"No, I did not post a grand announcement on social media. And no, I do not have a boyfriend." Answering what he presumed was another unspoken question.

"Basically, Cait and I did everything together while we were in college. The upside, is that we each learned two languages and got impressive grades." He jokes half-heartedly.

"The downside is that neither of us went out much with other people. I mean we had friends and were not tied to the hip, but on campus we were accepted as a couple. In our senior year, we both knew it was time to go our separate ways. Get out of the nest so to speak."

Seeing their anxious faces, Matt tries to assuage their concerns.

"One of the reasons that I did not disclose my sexuality while in high school was to protect you guys from any backlash about me. But now you are older, and hopefully better prepared to accept who I am. You don't have to go around announcing that your older brother is gay, but if the subject comes up, it's up to you to decide how to handle it. My worst fear has been that you would reject me, exclude me from your lives. I couldn't stand it if that was to happen." Both Frank and Kassie affirm that he will always be their big brother.

Matt says more to himself than to them.

"This conversation was hard but having to do again with Cait's parents will be more difficult. I don't want them to retaliate in anger against Mom and Dad. Furious that their daughter had been duped by a gay guy all this time."

Kassie speaks up, feeling protective of her brother.

"Look I think you are putting the worst spin on this. Didn't you tell us that Cait knew about you. So, she wasn't duped into anything. She was standing by her friend. Besides she wasn't 'Miss Popularity' around here. She would be a loner if it wasn't for you. They should be grateful to you for saving their daughter from being a loser outcast."

"Whoa, that's a bit harsh don't you think." Frank said,

unsettled by his sister's outburst.

Matt is momentarily at a loss of how to respond, and noncommittally shrugs his shoulders. He could sense the anxiousness underlying her reaction.

Kassie frowns at them.

"What's the matter? I'm standing up for him," she insisted. Frustrated that her brothers didn't agree with her.

Frank turns to Matt.

"You may be right that Cait's parents will be upset. But in the end, Cait can certainly speak up for herself. And while it might be hard for them to admit, they knew that she had problems fitting in until you befriended her."

"Hopefully, that will be how they see it. They also know that Cait is her own person; and has a mind of her own. Maybe, in time they will accept her friendship with me. You know, she is going to be a brilliant scholar. Already envisioning herself going off on digs and experiencing all the adventures awaiting her." Matt said.

For a moment, their humorous imaginings of Cait on a dig in the middle of some desert, fighting off local bandits, lighten the mood. But for Frank, he mainly felt relief. Matt had inadvertently released him from his guilt. His guilt of loving the girl who captured his heart from their first encounter.

Frank had gone out of his way to help Cait. He was incensed by how cruelly the other students were treating her. And was instrumental in bringing them together. Thinking that if she was accepted by Matt, it would be easier for her to fit in at school. Back then, his older brother was one of the 'popular guys.'

From that time, Frank had carried the guilt of being in love with his brother's girlfriend. This has been certainly a weekend for airing secrets, he thinks to himself.

Kassie goes over to sit beside Matt and hugs him, resting her head on his shoulder. She speaks softly so that only he can hear what she is saying. Looking over at them, Frank realized that she wanted to be alone with their brother.

Matt quietly listens to his sister. Kassie tells him that she loves him. She confides her disappointment in not going to be an aunt to the children that they all thought he and Cait would have someday. But while it may be hard at first, to accept someone else in his life, she will be happy for him when he finds love. With tears running down her cheeks, wetting the front of his shirt, she confesses her selfish gratitude that he did not divulge his secret when she and Frank were younger. That if she was in the same situation, she didn't know if she would have put the needs of others before herself. With her arms around his neck, she murmurs into his ear that they are blessed to have him in their family.

Even before Kassie finished, they were both crying. The tears helping to ease the readjustment of their sibling bond. Feeling the high emotions surrounding them, Frank goes over to the pair. He tenderly reminds Kassie about her date that evening with Jackson. Kassie sits up wiping her eyes and nose on the tail of her blouse.

Still teary eyed, she looks at her brothers.

"Should I tell Jackson about Matt?"

"While it isn't a secret, what would be the point? Frank said. "You just started dating. It's not like you are in a serious relationship with him." He looks over at their brother. "Don't you agree Matt?"

Matt looks at them and suddenly comprehends that coming out as a gay man will have a ripple effect on all their lives and relationships.

"To be honest, I don't know. But I think Frank is right. For now, why bring it up. I still have other people I need to speak to before this becomes widely known. Man, this is unreal, the implications beyond just me and my life."

Matt closes his eyes against the suffering that he has caused his family. The three of them sat quietly. Each contemplating how to adjust to this new reality. But for now, there were no clear answers.

Frank glances over at Matt, sensing his distress.

"Look this is the 21st century, things are different now. We're not going to be branded and forced out of town. And let me be the one to say the most obvious thing. We are not the only family in this entire state to have a gay family member."

They look at each other and giggle, seeing humor in the shock of the day's revelations.

"You are right Frank. We are the same people we were two hours ago. The three of us will each find love, but for me it will be with a man." Matt said, trying to be more upbeat than he actually felt.

While Matt saw love in the eyes of his siblings, there was also sadness and loss. They could not hide that from him. At that moment, he would have gladly plunged a stake through his heart for having upended their world.

This was not how coming out to his family had played out in his head. The stark difference between reality and role play. Matt clenches his jaw, second guessing whether he should have come out to his family. Was it a mistake to upset their lives? What would normal be like from now on? Right then, he did not know. But hoped that time would resolve the unknown.

Kassie gets up and goes into the house. She sees their parents standing at the glass patio doors.

"It's going to be fine," she assures them. "It may be hard on us for a while, but we will get through this. Don't make this into something that is your fault. You did nothing wrong." Her parents smile at her, reaching out to gently hold her hands.

"She's right Jena, we raised our children well. There should be no blaming ourselves. Let's go for a walk to clear our heads a bit."

Opening the patio door, they call out to Matt and Frank; tellling them that they are going for a walk.

"It's a shock man. It'll take time for all of this to sink in, to process it in our brains," Frank tells Matt, feeling anxious again.

"You've really grown up. That's good because I'm going to need your support."

Frank gets up and walks around the pool. Coming back around, he stands in front of Matt.

"I too have a secret. I've been in love with Cait since the first time I saw her. I knew I was younger, and she needed someone her own age. That's why I was glad it was you she was with. I knew you would take care of her, and that I could still be in her life; but in a different way."

He looked down for a moment. "For me, all that mattered was that Cait was loved and being cared for. All I wanted was for her to be happy. I wasn't jealous, even though I felt that I probably would never experience that kind of love again. Life is so funny, right? And now, I need you to tell me what I should do. Should I let Cait know about my feelings or continue keeping it to myself?"

Matt sighs, numbness slowing beginning to take control of his spiraling emotions.

"The only thing I can say is don't rush into doing it. But you should let her know how you feel. You know, I always had an inkling that there was someone else. Nothing specific but a notion that she was giving up something to be with me." Matt said heavily.

"Cait will be here for a week before she leaves for California to attend a summer Fellows program. You'll have time to talk with her about your feelings. If it's mutual, you'll work it out." He looks at his brother. Wondering about this unanticipated twist from his revelation about himself.

Matt stands and grabs Frank around his neck and tousles his hair.

"This is one heck of a tell all session."

Frank meets his eyes.

"Don't say anything, okay. I want to be the one to tell her."

"No problem," said Matt as they headed back into the house. "I could use a beer, what about you?"

Matt goes to the fridge and gets two beers. The bell rings and Frank goes to open the door.

Jackson follows Frank into the kitchen, looking at the

brothers.

"What's up, still celebrating your graduation?" Laughing, they both say something like that.

Frank tells them that he will go and let Kassie know that Jackson is there.

Sipping his beer, Matt studies Jackson.

"Where are you guys off to?"

"The beach, we're going to meet up with friends. It will probably be the last time we can all get together before going our separate ways for the summer. I want to spend as much time as I can with Kassie."

"So, you really like my sister huh," said Matt. His mind in a whirlwind of thoughts.

"Yes, I do," said Jackson. "I know we're young, but I love her. She's so clear about her place in the world."

He blushes at his confession of love for Kassie.

"I just hope that she doesn't go and find someone else at Cornell. But I know better than to stifle her. It would be the surest way to drive her away from me. I'll keep the faith that she will come to realize that she prefers this hometown boy."

Matt wonders if Jackson would still feel the same way for Kassie if he found out that her older brother was gay. Shaking his head to dismiss that thought, he tells Jackson that he is going see what's holding Kassie up.

As Matt passes by him, Jackson lightly grips his arm. He is perplexed by Matt's demeanor, the strange look in his eyes.

"Did I say something wrong? I mean, I was just telling you how I felt about Kassie. Thought you would understand."

Matt shifts his arm, and Jackson drops his grip. He hurriedly explains.

"I've always looked up to you and your relationship with Cait. I wanted the same thing for Kassie and me, though she is a different girl."

He laughs softly.

"She likes spreading her wings and going off on her own to experience the world. I mean she could have gone to Harvard with me. She had the grades. Your father would have been thrilled. I know because he told me. He had hoped that at least one of his kids would follow in his footsteps. No one understood Frank's decision to go to Princeton."

Matt felt stung by his comment about his father.

"My father told you that he was upset with us?"

Jackson backs away from Matt. Holding his hands in front of him, as if protecting himself from the sudden flare-up of anger.

"No, no, nothing like that. It came up when I told him that I was going there. He wasn't complaining. He was accepting of where you all decided to go to school. I mean they are all good colleges. But you know, he'd have liked it if one of you had chosen his alma mater. He knew that Kassie and I were dating. Maybe he was thinking about how you went to Brown to be with Cait."

"I see," said Matt. Feeling the anguish of another disappointment for his father.

Just then, Kassie and Frank entered the kitchen.

"Why so serious guys," asks Frank. He saw how shaken Matt appeared to be.

"Nothing, we were just talking about schools," said Matt. His eyes downcast to avoid looking at them. When he does look up, he smiles wanly. Kassie stares at him, and then glances at Jackson.

Jackson beams at her, oblivious to the current of unease passing between the siblings.

"That's right, just a little man to man talk," said Jackson good-humoredly.

Kassie decides not to probe any further.

"Okay, you ready to go?"

"Yup, good talking to you Matt. See you, Frank."

"Don't be out too late children," said Frank teasingly.

"Yeah, we'll be back when the playground closes." Kassie replies, forcing herself to be lighthearted.

As soon as they leave, Frank turned to Matt with concern

etched on his face.

"Now tell me what really happened?"

"Did you know that Dad wanted us to go to Harvard?" Matt said dispiritedly.

Frank sighs and takes a long sip of his beer, hedging for time. "Ugh, it's warm."

He opens the refrigerator to get another bottle.

"Dad never said anything to me about that," he said after a long pause.

"Uh huh," said Matt. He stands in front of Frank, with his arms folded across his chest.

"So why did you choose to go to Princeton?"

Frank deftly moves around Matt, unnerved by his tone and posture. Already feeling edgy, he wants to avoid being provoked into a confrontation. Resenting his brother for making him feel again the ache that prompted his decision at the time.

"You know why Matt. I wanted to be far away from you and Cait and start a new life for myself. And I have met someone, but we are not in a serious relationship. She is studying mathematics like me. But mainly, I threw myself into my studies. Began doing volunteer work with students in middle and high school who are interested in math and science. That is what I will be doing this summer, tutoring those kids."

They stood staring at each other. Frank is the first to turn away. He opens the bottle of beer and holds it, not drinking. Trying to contol his feelings of betrayal and smoldering rage. He does not want to say something that will ruin their relationship. Or worst, to say something that will drive Matt away from the family forever. He is grateful that he has plans for the evening. As if three days ago, he knew not to be home tonight.

Frank rests the bottle on the counter, becoming aware of how tightly he had been holding it in his hand. He feels the release of tension in his arm when he sets it down.

"Anyway, I'll be heading out soon, and will be staying

overnight at a friend's apartment. I can cancel if you want."

Matt senses that Frank wants to get away from the turmoil that he has caused.

"No need to do that, it's all good. I want to speak to the folks. Make sure they don't think that they failed me or anything. Have fun for both of us."

Frank is relieved and hurriedly walks out of the kitchen to get ready.

Matt tidies up, pouring out the beer bottles and putting them in the recycle bin. He opens the cabinets looking for a snack and finds a bag of pretzels. Taking the bag to the family room and turns on the television. Flipping through channels before settling down to watch a movie.

Frank shouts out that he's leaving, just as their parents open the front door. He tells them Kassie has already left. They have Matt to themselves.

Hearing his parents' voices, Matt turns off the television. His mother tells him that she is going to make coffee. Matt and his father follow her into the kitchen.

"Did you enjoy your walk?"

Matt's mother smiles at him.

"Yes, we did. The exercise is good for us."

"Mom and Dad, I want you to know that you have been great parents. No one could have parents better than you. Like I told Kassie earlier, I didn't want to say anything before because I didn't want to disrupt the family. Or to cause Frank to act out even more, and going off in a whole different direction."

His father, at just under six feet four inches, looks squarely at his son. Marv is momentarily disconcerted by how much they resemble each other. Matt looks just like him when he was that age. He blinks his eyes to dispel the image.

"Matt, maybe that might have happened, but you should have come to us. As a family we would have worked it out. We would have been there for you. What gets to me is that you let Caitlyn shoulder that responsibility. For her to undertake a role that should have been handled by adults."

Unconsciously, he balls his hands into fists, struggling with how to express himself without anger.

"I can't even begin to imagine how her parents are going to feel when they find out. George and Ilysia are going to be devastated to find out that you took advantage of their daughter. I mean think about it. She was just sixteen years old. And was thrust into a situation that many adults would find difficult to contend with. You can understand that right!"

"Marv calm down." His mother said nervously, as she pours coffee for each of them.

Ignoring the coffee, his father bristles, and pounds the countertop.

"I am calm dammit. Did you think about how your mother and I will ever be able to look them in the eye again? Knowing that their daughter gave up a chunk of her life to shield you. How you led us all to believe that you were in love with each other. We went out of our way to support the both of you attending the same college. Did you ever stop to think about Caitlyn, and what she was giving up for you?"

Matt is distraught. His father's words felt like a pommeling to him. He couldn't stop thinking again that this was not how it was supposed to be. From somewhere deep inside came the resolve to confront his father.

"That was not how we saw it. Cait made her own decision to stay with me. I certainly didn't make her do anything. Or force her against her will." Matt fights to control the anger welling up within him at his father's lack of understanding. Only viewing the situation through the prism of his own guilt.

"I told her that I didn't want to prevent her from meeting other guys. Or to be the reason that would stop her from doing whatever she wanted to do. Maybe you're right, I should have pushed her away and gone off on my own. Was that the right thing to do? I don't know."

Matt pauses to gather his thoughts, unconsciously moving his upper body away from his parents.

"Cait told me how hard it was for her when her family moved

back to the States. She was having a terrible time fitting in. She wasn't seen as a prodigy here; a young girl intellectually advanced for her age. Unlike how she was viewed in Australia and Europe. In those countries, her intellectual prowess was admired. Here she was deemed to be strange; difficult to work with."

Matt closes his eyes, remembering the early days of getting to know Cait.

"When we met in high school, we bonded immediately. We saw in each other a kindred spirit. Two people who didn't readily fit in. Believe me, ours wasn't a one-way relationship. I was there for her too. And because we are who we are, our journey of self-discovery had to be on our own terms. Not under the protective umbrellas of our parents."

He stands up and walks around the kitchen, his parents tracking his movements. Finally, he comes to rest against the apron-front sink.

"In our senior year of college, we came to the decision to go our separate ways after graduation. Neither of us wanted to make the other person a lifelong crutch. But in hindsight, I do regret letting you all think that we were a romantic couple. Just so you know, I do love Cait. I'd die for her. But I can't be her husband."

Matt's mother listens to her son, her heart breaking for him.

"I understand what you are saying, truly I do. However, as a parent it still hurts that you didn't tell us. But we'll get over it, won't we Marv."

His father couldn't believe that he had no clue about Matt. Wondering how you can live with someone and still not know them. He is still stunned by the revelation of his son's nature. Fighting hard to make sense of it.

"How do you know that you are gay? Have you ever been in love with another man? Were you having sex with men all this time?"

Jena is horrified by her husband's outburst. She knows how hard it is for him to accept the truth about their son. Having to confront the loss of what they thought Matt's life was going to be. A father desperately trying to forestall the awful pain of having to deconstruct the vision he once had for his first-born child. His son.

"Good gracious Marv!" Jena exclaimed, her hands raising to her chest. It felt like the air was being sucked out of the room.

"Tell me, tell us. Have you or not," demanded his father. His face distorted by anger and heartache.

Seeing his father like that, Matt felt like he couldn't breathe. The room seemed to tilt. He sat down hard on a stool and hung his head down.

Glaring at her husband, Jena goes over to Matt.

"Are you alright?" Even though her nerves were at the breaking point, Jena gently rubs his back.

Matt shakes his head and looks dejectedly at his father.

"In answer your questions, no, I have never been with a man."

His father wrestles with trying to make sense of what he cannot comprehend. Frantically seeking a reprieve from what is, with a longing for what was before.

"Then how the hell can you say that you are gay?" He said in a voice tinged with hope and sorrow.

Matt feels the desperation of the vestigial hope to which his father still clings. But he knows it would be even crueler to support it. He mentally wraps the mantle of his parent's broken dreams around himself. He is filled with remorse that he stripped the joy of who they thought he was from them. At a loss of what to say to make things better, less traumatic for them.

"Dad please, I know okay. I look at other men and am physically attracted to them. But I have chosen not to act on those feelings. I don't need to have had sex with a man to know that I'm gay. I need you to understand that. Even though I'm attracted to Cait mentally: her thoughts, her beliefs, and her desire for making a difference; we could never have a full relationship. Because being mentally attracted is not enough for building intimacy and fulfilment. It is only part of the equation. For us to be a couple, we would need to feel bonded mentally, physically, and spiritually. And although we will be a part of each other's lives, it will never be as husband and wife."

His father slumps forward, defeated by the truth.

"Listen, I'm sorry. I should not have said those things to you. This is all so new for me, for all of us. You've had time to work it out. We have to catch up with you." He said dejectedly.

As an afterthought he asks, "By the way, is there anything else that you children haven't told us?"

Matt shrugs his shoulders.

"Actually, Frank just told me that he has been in love with Cait since they met."

"Good heavens," said his mother. Her hand still clutching her chest.

"I need a drink," said his father. "Think we all should have one."

Marv goes over to a cabinet and takes out a bottle of single malt scotch. He slowly pours the scotch into his coffee. Handing the bottle to his wife who sets it down without pouring any into her mug.

"And I think Cait may have feelings for him."

Marv silently gives thanks that it wasn't something more controversial.

"Couldn't you guys try to make things less complicated for us? Anything we should know about Kassie?"

"Well, Jackson told me this evening that he's in love with her."

His father smiles sadly.

"He's a great kid. Of course, it will take Kassie a long time to see that, if at all."

"Let's make a toast," said his mother, trying to lighten the mood.

"To no more secrets." They all nod their heads somberly.

While his mother is washing their mugs, Matt looks over at his father, and quietly asks.

"By the way Jackson also told me that you had hoped that one of us would have attended Harvard. Why didn't you ever say anything?"

His father puts a hand on Matt's shoulder and forlornly shrugs.

"That's all water under the bridge son, all water under the bridge."

CHAPTER 5

Matt left his parents downstairs and went to his room to call Cait. She answers on the first ring.

"How did it go? Everyone survived the news?"

"Yeah, thanks for your concern about me." Matt replied dryly.

"Oh please, this is not about you. How are your parents doing?"

"Well, they are very concerned about your well-being. How could I have taken advantage of such a sweet innocent young girl?"

Cait giggles.

"I'm sure that you quickly disabused them of that notion."

"They are also concerned about your parents." Matt said, a little unnerved by her levity.

"Well sweet pea, if it will make you feel any better it hasn't been easy for me either. My parents are questioning whether there is more to the story than what we told them at our graduation dinner. They think that you are in love with someone else, and gently letting go of me to save face with friends and family." She laughs into the phone.

"You're enjoying this drama a little too much." Matt said. He knows that she understands how hard it must have been for him to tell his family. But her attitude still nettles him.

As if reading his mind, Cait tells him, "Hey, someone has to keep their feet on the ground. So, when are we going to tell my parents?"

"I don't know honestly. Is it even necessary? Why stir up more confusion."

Matt lets out a mournful sigh.

"Why not let them continue to think that I'm a bastard who is ditching their lovely daughter. You will eventually find love and go off into the sunset to live happily ever after."

"It's your call. But to me it's dishonest. And I'm not being a jerk about this."

"I know. You're right." Matt said quietly, wishing she wasn't.

Cait empathizes with Matt not wanting to out himself to another set of parents. She can guess at his state of mind.

"Look my parents won't be blown away by this. Believe me. They're in the film industry; nothing is going to shock them. When we met, they were so damn happy that I found someone who was kind to me and my own age. I think they were secretly fearful that I would end up dating some dodgy forty-year old."

"This is way different from dealing with an older guy as your boyfriend."

"It's going to be alright. Trust me. So how did Frank take the news, and Kassie too, of course?"

"Frank was okay. Really mature. But he is concerned about you though. Your adjustment to being on your own, without your gay friend." Matt said sarcastically.

"And he is very interested in helping you make the readjustment. Being on your own that is." Matt added quickly, remembering his promise to Frank.

"I see." Cait said simply, not knowing what else to say.

"That's your response?" Matt asked hotly.

He is suddenly overcome with jealousy in thinking about Frank with Cait. The feeling of that unexpected emotion confounds him.

Cait's heart flutters at the thought of being with Frank. But she feels guilty. That she is betraying Matt by her long-suppressed feelings for his younger brother.

She ignores the question.

"What's the plan then? For me to come to your house tomorrow. Let the family see with their own eyes that I'm intact, and have all my wits about me. Then we go to see my parents?"

"Sounds as good as it's going to be. Don't come over too early. I think everyone will probably sleep-in after today." Matt tells her without enthusiasm.

"As you wish my liege," said Cait.

"Get some rest. And Matt, I love you!"

"Yeah, me too," Matt replies softly. Wishing with all his heart that life could be that simple.

Cait sits up in her bed and thinks about the unpredictability of life. She was born in Singapore and lived there until she was three years old. Her parents own a successful independent film production company.

Among their film works were award winning documentaries and short features. Her mother is a renowned film editor and manages the post productions services for the company. Her father is an acclaimed writer, director and producer who has access to the best talent to bring onto their projects.

After Singapore, the family moved to Australia and lived there until Caitlyn was ten. Her parents employed an indigenous caregiver for their daughter. Who came to accept the strong spirited child as one of her own. She introduced Cait to the culture and wondrous geography of the country. And Cait loved hearing the stories, learning about sacred sites and the artifacts left behind by their ancestors. Even at that young age, Caitlyn seemed an old soul. Older people gravitated to her, and she was enthralled by their memories and life stories. It was during this time that her passion for archaeology awaken.

Their next move was to Europe, living in several countries until Cait was fourteen. At the schools she attended, the teachers found her to be an extraordinary young scholar; prodigy was the term that they often used to describe her. They arranged for her to attend university lectures that matched her keen mind and aptitude for learning. Her parents were pleased by her consuming curiosity, in wanting to know the world around her. In some ways, she seemed to be more intellectually advanced than they were.

Just after her fourteenth birthday, Cait's parents made the decision to move back to the States. At the time, they were looking for more stability in both their personal and professional lives. The constant moves were taking a toll on their marriage and impacting the direction in which they wanted to steer their business and careers. They were excited by the move to Chicago and getting into television production.

While the move was successful for her parents it had an adverse effect on Cait. The previous adroitness with which she was able to assimilate into the cultural life of a new country did not work well in the States.

The kids at school found her odd and were not interested in hearing about her travels and experiences. Their immaturity was perplexing to her, and she had no coping skills to deal with this cultural shock. Cait felt like she had been transported to another planet without the benefit of a guidebook.

The school curriculum was considerably below the level of her academic skills. Even the adaptation of course materials did not effectively challenge her intellect. After discussion with school administrators, her parents followed their recommendation and enrolled Cait in a private school with a more rigorous curricula and learning environment.

The new school did not entirely resolve the problem. Cait still found it difficult to fit in. The students were arrogant. Using the cloak of their privilege as a substitute for maturity. She had few friends, and quickly became a loner. Preferring the safe haven of her bedroom to social interaction with her classmates.

Over the next two years, her parents were alarmed to see their daughter deteriorating physically and mentally, becoming painfully introverted. It was like watching an exotic bird trying to survive outside of its natural habitat. She was wasting away before their eyes.

When an opportunity in Connecticut was presented to her parents, they readily accepted the offer. Hoping that a new location would be good for their daughter. Within three weeks of their move, Frank found Cait. Her budding relationship with his family helped to get her back on track to reclaiming herself.

At the beginning of their friendship, Matt seemed as adrift as she was. But he was the one who helped her overcome her social awkwardness. Helping her to understand that social skills were as important as academic ability.

When Matt told her that he was gay, she was grateful that she would not have to deal with the emotional upheaval of a teen romance. Although she felt the stirrings of romantic feelings for Frank, she did not pursue it. Partly because she was self-conscious about liking someone younger than her.

Coming out of her reverie, it occurred to Cait that she should be the one to tell her parents the truth about her relationship with Matt. She gets up to find them.

Matt's parents check the doors downstairs before going upstairs to their bedroom. Marvin sits down in one of the chairs flanking the glass paned doors to a small balcony overlooking their large backyard.

He slouches in his seat, stretching out his legs.

"What a day this has been, full of surprises. Did you have any idea about Matt?" He warily asks his wife.

"No, not consciously, I think. You know looking back there were signs that he was different. Do you remember how he seemed happiest playing with Kassie? Back then, I was so happy to have him occupy her, with Frank being such a handful. It was a relief to have a child who didn't make demands on us or cause any problems."

She closes her eyes briefly.

"Maybe we didn't give him the attention that he needed. It was so much easier to let things drift along. I guess it was convenient to overlook things that were not obvious, not looking too closely below the surface."

Marvin is stung by her assertions. "Are you saying that we

were neglectful parents?"

Jena moves her head to stare at the ceiling, to settle her mind by looking at an empty space.

"No, that is not it. She shifts her head again to face her husband. "We were good parents, maybe not as attentive as we should have been. It's hard to explain. In hindsight, I should have been more aware of what was going on with all of them. Some part of me feels like I failed Matt. As if he knew that I was too busy juggling all the demands for my time and attention. And took it upon himself to not add to the load."

Marv gets up and paces the room.

"Well, what about me. Was I lacking in that regard too? I remember being supportive of their interests growing up. Matt always seemed to be so self-contained, excelling in sports. Dammit, I guess you are right. I did give most of my attention to Frank."

Hearing the despair in his voice, Jena rubs her forehead with one hand.

"This is not about blame. It has nothing to do with what we didn't do for him. This is something that we could not fix. But we could have provided support for him."

Jena sighs softly, gathering herself. She is glad that Marv has his back towards her.

"I'm just trying to understand why he didn't come to us. Were we so removed from their daily lives, wrapped up in ourselves? What troubles me is Cait. A young girl caught in this situation. Matt too, of course. But it's Cait that makes me feel as though I let everyone down."

Marv continues to stare out of the glass doors, not seeing anything beyond it. He is struggling to come to terms with his son's nature. Slowly, self-recriminations creep into his mind; battering his sense of self. He is not fully listening to his wife.

"I guess we should be thankful that everything turned out as well as it did. Those two kids took better care of themselves than perhaps we would have. We must have been doing something right, don't you think? You know what's shameful

Marv? There's a small part of me that is thankful that we did not have to deal with this while Frank and Kassie were growing up."

Jenna gasps at her admission, shocked that she gave voice to this innermost thought.

"What an awful thing for me to say."

The palpable pain in his wife's voice causes Marv to put aside his own despondency. At that moment, it became clear to him that he must take immediate charge of the situation to prevent the breakdown of his family. He goes over to his wife and kneels to enfold her into his arms. Jena sags against him, seeking to draw strength from him.

"No sweetie, it just makes you human. I'm in the same boat as you. The thing to do now is to be there for Matt going forward."

Holding on to each other, Marv tells her what has been bothering him the most.

"How do we face Cait's parents? What do we say to them? What is the appropriate thing to do in this situation? Oh Jena, how does one secret give birth to such chaos?"

Jena pulls away from him, fervently hoping that her words are true.

"You know Marv I think they are a lot like us. Cait was certainly a special child, appearing to need little guidance from her parents growing up. Like us, they were caught up in their careers when they moved here."

She looks at him for his support.

"Cait was happy enough to adopt us as her family, being a big sister to our youngest. Even at times, seeming to be as mature as we were. Do you remember the first time the boys brought her home, how it felt like we had always known her? She blended into our lives so effortlessly. It was as if she was more a family member than just a friend of the kids."

Marv sighs as he recollects meeting Cait for the first time.

"That is true." Standing up, he rolls his shoulders, wanting to shift their mood.

"Alright enough of all this uncertainty and second guessing.

There is nothing that we can do about the past now. Besides it's getting late. Let's get ready for bed and take it on again tomorrow. I think Matt said that Cait is coming over."

Jena doesn't answer right away. She is ruminating on how they went through a lifetime's worth of introspection in the last few hours.

"You're right, we need to sleep on it, and hopefully everything will be less troubling in the morning."

Marv kneels again in front of his wife. He gently takes her face in his hands, staring deeply into her eyes.

"I don't blame you for anything. I don't blame us for that matter. I know with all my heart that we tried to be the best parents we could to our children. You are a wonderful mother." He tells her passionately.

Relief floods through Jena as she whispers back, "And you are a great Dad, and terrific husband."

They help each other to stand.

"Okay it's settled, no more beating up on ourselves." Marv said, wrapping her in his arms.

"I just want to check on Matt, before we turn in."

"You go. I'll be here when you get back."

Jena goes to Matt's room and knocks on the door.

"Come in Mom," said Matt.

"How did you know it was me and not your father?" She asks, going over to sit on his bed.

"Just had a feeling, are you okay?"

"First me," she said gently. "I want you to know that I'm sorry if you feel that I let you down."

Matt sharply cuts her off, unable to stand anymore apologies from his parents.

"Mom, stop it. It wasn't like that at all. I did what I did more for me than for you all. I needed to work things out in my own way and time. Don't you understand? I had to make peace with me before I could confide in anyone."

Hesitantly, but unable to stifle her angst of not being a good mother, she asks.

"But yet, you confided in Cait and not me."

"Because I was still unsure about me, she was a neutral person, not family."

Matt clenches his jaw, resisting the urge to scream. He has had enough. But he looks at his mother and sees her anguish. He wills himself to say more.

"I wasn't ready to speak about it with you guys back then. I don't even remember how it came up with Cait. Unlike today, it wasn't something that I planned to do. We were together for about three months, and I knew that she was wondering why I didn't, well you know 'make a move on her.' It came out one day after we went jogging. She asked me if I liked her, and I said yes. But not in the way that she thought. After we talked, I took her home and told her I would understand if she never wanted to see me again. The next day she walks up to me at school and tells me that she is my girl. I asked if she understood what that meant. She said yes, it works for her."

Matt desperately wanted to get up and walk around his room, to let motion soothe his unrest. Instead, he puts the needs of his mother before his own. Closing his eyes before he speaks again.

"The basis of our relationship remained the same in college. At any time if one of us wanted to break up, it would not be a problem. Sure, I would have missed her, or she would have missed me. But from the start we understood that the relationship could only last so long as we both wanted it to."

Feeling emotionally drained, Matt looks earnestly at his mother.

"In our senior year, we knew that it was time to stop the pretense of being a couple. I was ready to come out to my family; and Cait was more than ready to live life on her own terms."

Wanting to be left alone, Matt resolves to decisively end the conversation.

"Would we go around recommending what we did to anyone else? No, of course not. It was a situation that was unique to us.

I don't know what more I can say. I am sorry that our actions ended up hurting those we love."

His mother looks at him, and comprehends for the first time how hard it must have been for Matt to confide in them. He took the risk of disclosing his secret based on his trust that his family loved him.

"Thank you for talking to me. In time, I hope to make peace with myself when my ego becomes irrelevant, and only my loving acceptance of your truth remains."

Jena takes his hand and puts it to the side of her face.

"Sleep well my dear son, see you in the morning."

Matt reaches out to hug her. Tears well up in his eyes when she leaves his room. Leaning back on the headboard, he is ashamed for not being totally honest with his family.

It pained him to hear their praises for his unselfishness, which was the farthest thing from the truth. If Titus Korsovich had not confronted him the month before graduation, he would still be trying to hide behind his relationship with Cait. Hoping for a plausible break-up story to buttress the illusion of lost love. And for staying single.

Titus was the quarterback of his football team who was also gay and knew about Matt. He saw how Matt grappled with his homosexuality, unwilling to accept who he was. While the two of them were not friends, he understood that Matt was using his relationship with Cait as a cover. Using her to keep away any gay man who was interested in him.

He perceived that Matt needed to believe that he couldn't leave Cait on her own because she depended on him. When in truth, it was Matt who could not survive without her. Because he was shackled to his shame. His self-imposed penance was to remove himself from any chance of a relationship with another man.

Titus and several other players on the team had devised a method to obscure their sexual preference. A stratagem to avoid the pressure of having to maintain the pretense of heterosexuality.

They made sure that their schedules appeared to be filled with academic study, community service, game practices and games. This provided cover for not having time for engaging in serious relationships with women. Going for 'boys' nights to blow off steam seemed natural given how hard they were working. And it didn't raise questions. Any doubters knew it was best not to voice their opinions.

Looking back Matt realized how his attitude laid the groundwork for the fight with Titus. It happened after the last game of their senior year outside the locker room.

Titus had invited Matt to a private party to celebrate the end of their college football careers. But he declined the invitation, saying that he still had a paper to do.

Titus refused to accept his excuse. He confronted Matt about his avoidance tactics. Telling him that he wasn't doing himself, or anyone in his life any favors by denying who he really was.

Matt became incensed, shouting at Titus to go off with his friends and leave him alone. He had nothing in common with them. The argument escalated, each of them going for the jugular with hurled insults. Until unable to restrain his anger any longer, Matt punched Titus, taking him off guard. The fight intensified, each one engulfed in his own rage.

Matt wanted to punish Titus for the audacity to force him to confront what he didn't want to acknowledge. It took five of their teammates to break them apart.

As he was being led away, a bruised and bleeding Titus yelled one final verbal blow at Matt.

"Your problem is that you don't have the balls to come out from hiding behind a woman."

Matt chokingly retorted more to himself than to anyone.

"Fuck you, asshole. You don't know me."

Later in his dorm room, Matt recalled Titus's last comment and began to cry. It was the truth.

The next day, Cait went to Matt's dorm after numerous failed attempts to contact him by phone. She hadn't gone to the game. However out of concern for Matt, several of his teammates told her about the fight.

When Matt didn't respond to her knocks at his dorm room, Cait went to find the dormitory Resident Assistant. She tried charm at first, and then threatened to make a call to security and report that an unresponsive student was locked in his room.

The RA looked at her contemptuously, then reluctantly unlocked Matt's room door. He was lying curled up in bed.

At first, he refused to acknowledge her presence. She told him she wasn't leaving until they talked. After more than twenty minutes of a constant harangue from Cait, he finally sat up.

She moved to sit beside him on the bed, as he told her about what led to the fight. But he did not mention Titus's last remark. Cait was silent for a long time, before quietly asking him what they should do.

They stayed up all night discussing their relationship and its place in their future lives. Both were forthright about their hopes and dreams.

It was from that conversation, that Matt knew the time had come to tell his family that he was gay. Time to be freed from the penalty box that he had locked himself into.

When Jena got back to the bedroom, Marv was lying awake waiting for her.

"Do you feel better? How is Matt doing?"

"He's okay," she said, and went to the bathroom.

She needed a private moment. Standing in front of the mirror, she silently vows that the family will not falter in their love and support of Matt.

Getting into bed, she snuggles against Marv. He tells her that he heard Kassie come in; and that Frank called to check on them. They savor the irony, while waiting for sleep to put an end to the day.

The next morning, they awaken to the smell of brewing coffee and warming pastries. Frank greets them as they wander into the kitchen.

"So how are you all doing? Had a good night's sleep I hope?"

"Yes, Papa Frank," said Kassie.

Frank chuckled good-naturedly, as he placed baskets of hot muffins and croissants and a fruit platter on the table.

"I stopped at our favorite food market on my way home. Thought I'd give Mom the morning off. So did I miss anything last night?"

"No, everything is good. Is that fair to say?" Marv said as he glances across to his wife and daughter.

"We agree with that," they replied in unison.

Nevertheless, Kassie leans over to whisper to her mother.

"Mom, are you really okay?"

"I'm fine sweetie. Time will work out what needs to be worked out."

Matt enters the kitchen and reminds them that Cait will be coming over as he pours coffee into a mug.

"We need to finish breakfast and get dressed before she arrives."

"We will," they said in chorus to him. However, there wasn't any urgency to rush their meal.

They talk leisurely about their plans for the summer. The eight-week urban study internship in Boston for Kassie, Matt's post-grad internship at a museum in Philadelphia, Frank working as a teaching assistant in New Jersey, and the cruise their parents will be taking in July.

They were in the middle of their conversation when Cait strolled into the kitchen.

Matt was the first to see her.

"How did you get in here?" She ignores his question, going around him to give the others a hug. Circling back to Matt, she nudges him off his stool.

"The side door was open. And I knew you all would be in the kitchen." She responded, and pours coffee into an empty mug and reaches over for a croissant.

"Guess I left it open this morning, my hands were full," said Frank sheepishly.

Cait surveys the family scene.

"So how is everyone? You can see that I'm fine, my usual self. But seriously, from the bottom of my heart if you think our actions were wrong, let me apologize for any misjudgment on my part." She said looking pointedly at Matt's parents.

Marv is a taken aback by Cait's demeanor. But realizes that since they have known her, she has been a confident young woman. Aware of who she is, and not someone to be coerced into doing anything she didn't want to do. Not even by his son. The thought gave him comfort. Knowing that their friendship was forged by trust and the mutual acceptance of each other.

"It's just that you were both so young to have dealt with such a matter on your own, without involving the parents."

"In hindsight, you are probably right, but at the time that is not how we saw it. We were close friends who accepted each other for who we were. The fact that Matt was gay didn't change the way I saw him. We had similar interests and enjoyed each other's company. Maybe we should have been more proactive in making it clear that we weren't a 'couple' so to speak. But in all fairness, we weren't the ones encouraging that assumption."

Cait leaned back into her seat and looked thoughtfully at them, before continuing.

"Please don't take this the wrong way. But after a while it was difficult to change how you all wanted to see us. Maybe we were being selfish, but I don't think we did anything wrong."

"It's not a matter about being right or wrong. It is that we weren't given a chance to deal with Matt and his situation." Marv said, his voice rising.

Jena quickly intervenes to stop her husband from revisiting his hurt.

"That is in the past, there is no going back. We can't change what has happened. You are both adults now. We must move forward and accept our new normal." She clutches her husband's hand, willing him to remain silent.

Cait senses the unease and regrets how arrogant her tone was earlier.

"I told my parents last night about Matt. They were, of course, like you surprised. Not what they expected to learn about our relationship. My parents always knew that I was different from most kids. But they have trusted my judgment in most of what I do. In this case though, they were more concerned about all of you. Since this was about Matt. They felt that I should have encouraged him to turn to his family. But also understood that it was his decision to make. And they were pleased that I was there for him."

Cait pauses, looking over at Matt.

"I want you all to know that it was never my intention to cause any harm to your family. For me, I was being a friend to Matt and following his lead in this matter. We supported each other and we also learned a lot about ourselves from going through this experience. Matt is my very best friend. I love him and am proud of him. He will always be family to me. And I hope that you all will allow me to continue to be a part of your family."

Both Matt and his father were elated that Cait had told her parents. But for different reasons. Matt was grateful to Cait for giving him the break he needed before seeing them. And Marv felt as if the weight of the world had suddenly been lifted from him. Her parents understood and held no malice against them.

"You already know that you will always be a part of my life," said Matt. He leaned over to kiss her cheek and squeezes her hand.

"Of course, Cait, you will always be a part of this family. But you must also understand that until yesterday, we had no idea about Matt."

He pauses, wanting to say the right thing.

"We are all deeply grateful for the compassion and understanding of your parents. Frankly, we were apprehensive about their reaction. Looking to the future, we want nothing but the best for each of you. And please know that we are always here for all of you. No matter the situation, we will have your back."

Frank smoothly interjects to end the conversation.

"Okay then, why don't you all go and get dressed while Cait and I clean up in here."

Kassie and her parents leave to go upstairs, each feeling closer to resolving their own inner conflict about the change in their lives.

Matt lingers behind.

"Thanks again, Cait.

She smiles at him.

"You know after we talked last night, it just made sense for me to be the one to tell my parents. Look, they already knew that something was up, and I didn't want them to not know what was happening. They really understood like I said. Even offering to come with me this morning. But I told them that it would made things more complicated than it needed to be."

Matt was so thankful that Cait had understood his pain. After the emotional confrontation with his family, going through it again with another set of parents was overwhelming to him. But he knew that he owed her parents a visit. It was the right thing to do.

However, for the first time in his life, he felt free. Freed from playing the role of being someone he was not. And more resolute for working on his own self-acceptance.

"You know that I leave for Philadelphia in three days," said Matt.

"Yes, I know. When does Kassie leave?" Cait asked.

"She leaves tomorrow," Frank replied.

"What a send-off for her. I'll go up and talk to her, help put matters into perspective if she needs it."

"That's a good idea. If anything is still bothering her, she might open up to you." Matt said, grateful for her thoughtfulness.

Cait turned to Frank.

"You leave next weekend, right? We'll have time to talk."

"Righto." Frank said, keeping his head down to avoid looking at her.

Matt glances at Cait and his brother.

"Okay you two, I'm going to get dressed. I have some shopping to do, maybe we can all go together?"

"Not me," said Frank. "I'm going to get some sleep. I'll catch up with you all later."

CHAPTER 6

Jason arrived at the gallery in the afternoon. Mica was genuinely happy to see him in person after his long absence. She impulsively threw her arms around him.

"Well hello stranger. It's so good to see you in person again. How are you doing? I love your new paintings. Are they part of a series that you are working on?"

"Whoa, take a breath. I'm fine." Jason said laughing. He gives Mica a quick one-armed hug, while smoothly disengaging himself from her embrace. Touched by her ebullient welcome, he invites her to lunch.

"I can't do lunch. I have an appointment with one of our clients. But I'm free for dinner."

"Okay, I'll meet you at Fables around 6:30. Does that work for you?"

"Absolutely, I'll see you then."

"Is Neva in her office?"

"Yes, she is. Do you want me to let her know that you are here?"

"Yes, that would great. Also, is Matt here as well?"

Mica answers while texting Neva. "Yes, he is. Do you want to see him before meeting with Neva?"

"No, I'll do it afterwards."

"I look forward to catching up with you later at dinner. Oh, and Mrs. Marjoram bought your three paintings yesterday." Mica told him excitedly, not ready for their conversation to end.

Jason is startled to hear about the sale of his paintings.

Wondering if Mica was trying to communicate some veiled meaning by sharing that information with him.

"I'm sure that Neva will speak more about it with you. She is ready to see you."

Touching Mica lightly on the arm in parting, Jason takes the stairs to Neva's office.

"Well, good afternoon Ms. Omaro. Did you instruct your staff to give me the rock star treatment today?"

Neva laughs, as she gets up from behind her desk.

"Let me guess. Mica?"

"Among others. I left two of your interns with their mouths open downstairs. Neither of them responded to me when I said hello to them."

"We have hired several new interns since you were here last." They both take seats at a round conference table in a corner of her office.

"I hear that Edith bought my paintings. Didn't think the old girl would find them her cup of tea."

"Don't underestimate her investment acumen when it comes to art."

"Ahh, the ugly side of the arts."

"No, the reality of its business side."

"How come you didn't mention it last night?"

"I didn't think it was the right time or place for discussing a sale's transaction."

"Quite right again, as always," said Jason amiably.

Feeling assured that there was not any implied meaning in Mica's comment about the sale.

Jason quickly scans the room and swivels his chair so that he can rest his arm on the table.

"So, after our discussion last night, and getting the first good night's sleep in months, I've decided to take a sabbatical. I need time to think about my artistic direction going forward."

"I see. If that is what you want to do, I support you."

"You know the *Colloquium of Furies* series intrigued me. It was stimulating to delve into those hidden places in my mind."

"Are you prepared to deal with what you might uncover?"

"That is the big question. How many others have gone there and never found their way back? Honestly, I'm not even sure that it is something I need to explore any further through my art."

"But it's not about doubting your artistic ability though?"

"No, it is not self-doubt. At this juncture I need time to determine the next phase of my artistic expression. Julie told me that my most valuable commodity is my name, that my name sells. However, the one thing that I am very clear about is that I will not exorcise my angst about being relevant through my art. Doing that would be self-indulgent, and egotistical. That is not who I am as an artist."

Jason looks over at her, more certain in his thinking.

"Going forward my work will have a recognizable transition point. My art before the *Colloquium of Furies* and after. It's the after that is now my quest. Determining the future path of my art."

Neva reaches over and puts a hand atop his.

"Listen to me, take all the time you need to work out where you want to go artistically. But Jason, you should not have any doubts that you are a gifted artist."

They both sit quietly for a moment. Jason is the first to break the silence.

"Who knew I was coming for another therapy session today huh?" He half-heartedly jokes to ease the lull in conversation.

"But seriously, thank you for putting up with me and helping me through all this."

He unconsciously swivels his seat to face the table, eager to shift the meeting back to business and away from his personal problems.

Seeing his discomfiture, Neva goes to her desk. She picks up a folder and a large envelope. Returning to the table, she lays aside the envelope and places the folder in front of him.

"It has not been officially announced, but you are among the finalists to be nominated to participate in a new exhibit.

The Leyden Museum received a grant from the Partridge Foundation to mount a permanent exhibition. The working title is: *Contemporary Art: Early Twenty- First Century*. If it is well received and attended, there will be additional funding support for expanding the exhibit. You will receive the formal notification of your nomination from them. I'd advise you not to make any extended travel plans until the nomination process is completed."

Jason sighs deeply as he taps the open folder.

"I really don't know how I feel about this or if I even want to be included for consideration."

"Don't rush into making a hasty decision. You will have time to think about it. I am sure that you know this, but I want to reiterate it. The process for the selection and nomination of the artists to participate in the exhibit was an arduous one. It is a prestigious acknowledgement of your work."

"Yes, I totally understand that my nomination was not made without due deliberation and review. But I am the one who must be convinced about the merit of my work. A jury of doyens cannot make that decision for me."

Jason looks away from her momentarily, reluctant to discuss it any further.

"Change of subject, an artist that I met several months ago at a function. I have seen his work and it is amazing. In fact, when I saw your painting last night, it made me think of him. He called me a few weeks ago to tell me that the leases on both his studio and residence in Buffalo will not be renewed. And Woodsburne is on his list of potential cities for relocation. I told him about the Avalon. That it would be worth his time to meet with you."

"Sounds interesting, do you have his contact information?"

"Sure do," said Jason. He sends it to her.

"Josiah Kipling Summati, what a fascinating name," said Neva.

"Yes, and an even more fascinating artist."

"I'll forward his contact information to Matt. He'll extend an invitation to Josiah to meet with us."

Neva reaches over for the envelope and slides it towards Jason.

"These are the documents for the sale of the three *Colloquium* paintings. We will transfer payment for them into your account by end of day."

"I honestly didn't think they would sell," said Jason contemplatively. He quickly skims through the documents before returning them to the envelope.

"You have Matt to thank really. Honestly, the reason I called you yesterday was to discuss them. But Matt pushed to have them displayed. He said that they would sell, and he was right."

"Yeah, he's my next stop. I ran into him last night before I came to see you. I owe him an apology for my abrupt behavior."

"I'm sure he will understand once you explain what you have been going through."

"Yes, but it is not an excuse. Thanks again, Neva for everything. I will stay in touch. Let you know where I am and what I'm up to."

"You do that. Take care of yourself Jason. Don't forget that you should try to stay in town at least through January. I'm guessing that it will take that long to tie up your affairs here."

"That's true, not so easy to extricate myself from stuff."

He smiles at her.

"By the way I'm having dinner with Mica tonight, join us if you can."

Neva smiles impishly.

"Thank you for the invite, but I have another commitment. Besides, I think the two of you will be fine. No need for a third wheel."

Jason looks quizzically at her.

"I don't get your meaning. Anyway, we'll be at Fables if you have a change of plan. Thanks again Neva for all your support and understanding." Jason says sincerely, before leaving.

He goes downstairs to Matt's small office on the first floor.

"Hey there big guy." Jason said from the doorway.

"Hi." Matt replies, looking up from his computer.

"You have a minute for me?"

"Sure do, come in." Matt clears off a chair for Jason.

"I wanted to apologize for being so unsociable last night. I've been going through some issues lately and was on my way to see Neva to get her advice on a problem."

"No worries. Was Neva able to help you out?"

"Yes, as always."

"That's good," said Matt noncommittally. Not wanting to push Jason into saying more than he wanted to share.

"Listen Matt, I am going to be taking some time off. I have some personal matters to work through, one being my impending divorce."

"I'm sorry to hear that. If there is anything that I can do, don't hesitate to ask."

"I appreciate it. Also, I owe you thanks for getting my paintings sold."

"Not really. They are strong, thought-provoking pieces. Different from most of the work exhibited here. And, there is always an audience for great art. I don't know if this is a new direction for you, but I'm excited to see other works along this line. Clearly, Mrs. Marjoram liked what she saw."

Jason feels gratified by Matt's appraisal of his work. He takes a moment before responding.

"Lately I've felt as if I have not been a contributor to the arts."

Matt scrutinizes him more closely.

"I don't know what's bothering you, but believe me, you definitely have a place in the art world."

Jason sighs heavily. He does not want to rehash his uncertainties with Matt. And quickly changes the subject.

"By the way, I recently became acquainted with an artist that I thought would be a good fit with the gallery. His name is Josiah Summati. I gave Neva his contact information."

"Josiah Kipling Summati?"

"Yes. Do you know him?"

"Not personally," said Matt. "My sister-in-law told me about him and directed me to his website. His work is so original. I have never seen anything like it. From his bio, it isn't clear if he is signed with a gallery. I was planning to speak with Neva about reaching out to him. Ascertain his interest in working with us."

"My thought exactly. What a small world, both of us learning about him."

Jason stands up and Matt follows.

"Okay Matt, thanks for everything. I'll keep in touch." As an afterthought, he tells Matt about having dinner with Mica at Fables, inviting him to join them.

Matt looks at him and smiles.

"Thanks for the invite, but you both will be fine on your own. I'll take a rain check."

Jason laughs at the response.

"What's going on here? That's almost what Neva just said to me. Am I missing something?"

"Not at all. Mica will be the perfect balm for what ails you. Go and have a relaxing evening." Matt stops himself, self-conscious about his remarks.

Jason looks questioningly at Matt, but decides not to say anything more.

"Almost forgot, need your help in meeting the new staff. My greetings to them got awkward."

"Tongue tied, were they? No problem, come with me."

Matt takes Jason to meet the interns and gives him a quick tour of the current exhibits.

"My paintings are still here." Jason said, surprised to see them.

"Mrs. Marjoram has generously permitted us to show them until the end of the month."

Jason wonders whether Edith has any ulterior motives behind her grand gesture. He makes a mental note to call her.

CHAPTER 7

Mica is ecstatic about having dinner with Jason. When she applied for the job at the Avalon, she was impressed by their portfolio of artists and her role in working with them. However, a significant perk was being able to meet Jason Aria.

Six months after she started working at the gallery, Mica was finally able to meet Jason. There was an instant connection between them. In time, he invited her to his studio to see firsthand his work environment. She went to his studio on a Sunday afternoon.

They spent the afternoon talking about his transition from interior designer to artist; early influences; and sharing his world view through his art. It was almost dusk before they realized the time and that they hadn't eaten all day. Jason offered to take her out to eat, but Mica declined saying she had other plans.

At the door, she thanked him for a wonderful day. But on leaving, Mica was thankful that she had declined his invitation. She knew that Jason was married and did not want to start down a road that would lead to nowhere. Been there, done that. She did not want a repeat of the emptiness of promises that could not be kept.

Mica would have been surprised to know that Jason had intended to invite her to accompany him to an exhibit later that evening. But likewise, he too thought better of it. While he felt there was an attraction between them, he did not want to complicate either of their lives.

She often found herself thinking about Jason. It was not

his physical appearance. Although he was handsome. He was average height, with a toned body. The attraction was the way he made you feel. Like you were the only person who existed in that space of time when he focused his attention on you.

Despite the fact that she was acquainted with the futility of being in love with a married or otherwise unavailable man, she could not put him out of her mind. She fantasized about being in a relationship with Jason outside of business.

Even dating other men didn't distract her. After a few months, they would break up. And a another cycle of a meaningless relationship would begin. Family and friends were concerned about her, not knowing the true cause of her rollercoaster love life.

It wasn't until Nina Partridge Colson, one of her closest friends in Woodsburne, invited Mica to her house for drinks and girl talk. It was then that she spoke about her feelings. Relieved to finally be able to talk openly about Jason to someone who knew him.

As Nina listened, she was quietly grateful that Jason had not tried to insert himself into Mica's life. Glad that he understood better than Mica the price of having an affair in a small city. Shrewd enough to not put at risk neither his reputation, nor standing in the community.

It was also clear to Nina that Mica did not really grasp what the personal cost to her would have been. Being ostracized by well-connected art patrons would have impacted her both economically and socially. Mica would have been forced to relocate, with the whiff of scandal trailing behind her.

When Mica finished her story about unrequited love, Nina asked. "Isn't it funny how we sometimes go out of our way to complicate our lives?"

"What do you mean?"

"I'm thinking, here is a young and beautiful single woman, who has a great job, is financially independent, intelligent, has so many opportunities to meet fascinating people, including eligible men. Yet, she is drawn to a situation that is fraught with high personal costs. Does that make sense to you?"

"When you put it like that, it does seem foolish."

"That is not the point, Mica. Have you thought beyond what you want and cannot have?"

Mica takes a breath before answering.

"I haven't acted on my feelings, and I have been tempted. You know that he invited me to his studio months ago. But it was more of a business than a social visit. Neither of us crossed any lines. And while I may sound like a young student crushing on her older, but charismatic college professor, that's not the case either."

Nina rolls her eyes in exasperation.

"For one thing, age has nothing to do with it. It is about using your good sense to avoid a problematic situation. Being savvy enough not to toss away everything in exchange for immediate gratification."

Mica shakes her head, reliving the day at Jason's studio.

"That is not what has stopped me from acting on my feelings. I was simply worried that he would be appalled by me taking advantage of an innocent situation."

Nina nearly chokes on her drink, trying not to laugh.

"What would be your advice?" Mica asked, interested in her opinion.

"For one thing, stop trying to find Jason in all the men you are dating. Release them from having to measure up to this ideal of him in your mind."

Mica sighs and takes a sip of her drink.

"That's easier said than done my friend. But you are right about one thing though. More times than not, we tend to complicate our lives without realizing it.

Nina raises her glass.

"I'll drink to that. That was a hard lesson that I had to learn without benefit of sage advice. My life would have had fewer bumps if I had been more open with the people who cared about me."

"But isn't that how we learn, from our mistakes?"

"Yes, it is. But some of us remain stuck in the lesson, not learning from it and moving on."

"That's true. Maybe Jason is my excuse for avoiding a meaningful relationship." Mica said somberly.

"And if that is true, you are on the way to working out the reasons why. My point is that you are a phenomenal person. And I care about what happens to you."

Mica smiles at her.

"Thank you. And you are right, I need to stop hiding behind my idealization of Jason. Be honest with myself about what I want in a relationship."

"Now you're talking."

Mica studied Nina briefly. She is interested to know more about this woman who was fast becoming more like a sister than a friend to her. They are the same height and have slim builds. Nina's light brown hair is softly curly. There is a burnished beauty to her symmetrical face and features. Her demeanor is reserved. Giving the impression that she has tight control over her emotions.

"What about you Nina? What keeps you centered?" Mica had asked her.

"One conscious raising session at a time. Today it is all about you." She had adroitly replied, deflecting any further response.

Mica recalls this conversation on her way to meet Jason for dinner. She arrives at the restaurant early, stopping to briefly chat with the owners, before being shown to their reserved table in the Library Room.

All the walls are lined with bookcases. A 'Librarian Kiosk' is located near its entrance. Diners typically select a book at the same time as they make their reservations. The chosen book is placed at the reserved table prior to their arrival.

The room has a relaxing atmosphere. Each table has its own lighting control pad. Patrons can brightened the light for reading or dim it for conversation. Soft music plays in the background, providing another layer of privacy to table discussions. It is the smallest dining room at the restaurant, with a seating capacity of sixty.

Mica scrolls through the listing of mystery books and requests a popular detective novel before heading to their table. Vicky, a regular on the wait staff, brings over a small platter of complimentary appetizers. Mica looks hungrily at the various tasty tidbits and orders a glass of Chardonnay. Contented with food and drink, she settles down to wait for Jason. He arrives just as she is finishing the fifth chapter of the book.

Jason walks up to the table and greets her with a smile.

"Hello there. Am I so late that you have almost finished reading a book? He teasingly asks her.

Mica looks up at Jason, as he bends down to lightly kiss her on each cheek.

"Hi to you too, I got here around 5:30. My meeting ended earlier than I expected. Took the opportunity to pass the time with an interesting read."

Jason reaches over for the book, and quickly scans the cover notes.

"Hmm, I wouldn't have pegged you as the crime novel type?" He said mischievously. "Other than solving crimes, how have you been?"

Mica retrieves the book from him and places it in the bin on the side of the table.

"I'm good, unlike you who can disappear for long stretches of time." She says playfully.

"Ouch, that hurts." Jason said, feigning a pained look.

Mica feels her face flushing pink. "Of course, I'm sure that you had good reasons for why we haven't seen you in months."

Jason reaches over and pats her hand.

"Relax, I'm teasing."

Not daring to meet his eyes, she smiles, and fidgets with her silverware.

"Okay, let us start over. So how have you been Mica?"

"I've been fine, and you?" Mica giggles, raising her eyes to meet his.

"Not so fine." Jason truthfully replies.

"Really, you wouldn't know that from our emails," said Mica, her interest aroused.

"That is not how I would communicate about these matters."

"Sounds serious, so what has been happening?"

"I not sure if it is dinner conversation," said Jason.

Just then, Vicky came to take their meal orders. Jason also orders a bottle of wine.

"No, let's talk about it. It might help you to sort through a problem." Mica replies, with concern in her voice.

"You really want to hear about it?" Jason said with some hesitancy.

"Yes, I do."

"Right now, my personal life is a mess."

Mica's eyes grow wide, and her voice catches in her throat.

"What do you mean? What's wrong?"

"Well for starters, Julie and I are getting a divorce."

Mica is stunned, her face shifting through conflicting emotions.

He is surprised by the stunned look on her face.

"You really didn't know? With your connections, I thought someone would have told you."

"No, I haven't heard a word about it until now," she stammers. Reaching for her glass, she drinks most of the wine in one gulp.

Seeing her reaction, Jason regrets bringing up the subject.

"I'm so sorry to have sprung that on you."

"No, please, it's just not what I expected to hear. I was anticipating that you were experiencing an artist block or something."

Mica's mind is flooded with so many thoughts, she struggles to remain calm.

"Mea culpa. I really should not have burdened you with my personal problems. I seem to be doing that a lot lately."

"No apologies needed. It's just such a change from what we usually talk about. We rarely discuss our personal lives."

"Well, hopefully this will be the start of changing that." Jason tells her, still unsure of whether to confide in her.

"So, I'm getting a divorce and will be taking time off to decide if I'm doing what I want to be doing, and to make any needed changes."

Working to control her breathing, Mica tries to quiet her mind, trying to put order to the myriad of thoughts flooding through it. One of the thoughts being that he is in love with someone else. In an instant she feels crushed by a sense of loss of what might have been.

She refills their glasses hoping to quell her unease.

"So, is there another woman involved?" Mica blurts out, before editing her thoughts. She is appalled as soon as the words come out of her mouth.

Jason runs his fingers up and down the glass stem.

"No, there is no one else, at least not on my part. I don't think Julie is involved with anyone either."

"I have been in love with you from the first time that I saw your work." Mica divulges, and is horrified by her admission. Bewildered by her reaction.

Leaning across the table, to touch her arm, Jason knocks his water goblet into his wine glass. The contents of both spills forward, splashing onto his pants. Mica reaches over to give him her napkin, and in the process, overturns her wine glass as well. The dark liquid dribbles onto her lap.

On the way to the table to bring their salads, Vicky sees the mishap. But did not notice right away that Mica's glass had also tipped over. She gives a towel to Jason.

Jason is flustered as he takes the towel. Not sure if he understood what Mica had just told him. His pants are too wet to comfortably sit through a meal. He hands the towel back to Vicky.

"I don't think we will be staying for dinner. My pants have had too much to drink."

Vicky laughs. "Do you want the food to go?"

"No, don't bother." Jason replied. Telling her to put the meal and drinks on his tab, and to add a thirty per cent tip for herself. He is aware of the attention they are attracting from nearby diners, and wants to quickly exit the room.

"That's very generous of you Mr. Aria. Thank you."

Mica stands up, making no mention of her dress. While the attention was diverted from her, she had surreptitiously blotted up as much of the spill on her dress as she could. Thankful that she is wearing a black dress. They leave the restaurant and walk to Jason's car.

Jason opens the car door for Mica. He is troubled by the incident in the restaurant.

"Let's not talk until we get to my studio. Is that okay with you?"

Mica nods her agreement, upset by her reaction. Why did she tell him that?

Jason drives the short distance to his studio and pulls into a parking space in front of the building. He goes around to the passenger side to help Mica out of the car.

She gets out unsteadily and he puts his arm around her waist as they walk up the short flight of steps leading to the door. He holds her as he unlocks it, and switches on the lights.

The studio is an expansive open space with plenty of lighting, both natural and from an intricate system of track lights. It is bare, except for a sofa and two swivel stools, one tall and the other low, against one of the walls. There is a small bathroom at the back of the space, as well as a large stainless steel industrial sink and compact refrigerator. It looks different from the first time she was there.

Jason gently guides Mica over to the sofa and lowers her onto the seat. He pulls over the low stool to sit in front of her. Mica whispers that she would like some water. He goes to the fridge to get a bottle of water for her.

She takes a few small sip of the liquid before breaking down in tears. Unable to control her emotions any longer. Jason takes the bottle from her hand and puts it on the floor. He moves to sit beside her on the sofa, holding her head to his chest.

After a few minutes, Mica takes a breath and raises her head.

"Now look, I've stained your white shirt with my mascara and makeup."

"Yes, it's been a tough evening on my clothing." Jason said, still unaware of the spill on her dress.

He releases her and leans back on the sofa. They both try to laugh.

Mica is unable to find her full voice, and whispers.

"I'm so sorry for ruining dinner. The best thing for me now is to go home."

"Are you sure that is what you want to do? You don't want to talk about it."

She nods her head, afraid to speak again.

"I'll drive you home if you really want to leave. But first let me change my clothes."

Jason walks to an enclosed alcove beside the bathroom. Stepping inside, he removes and hangs his wet clothing on hooks, and puts on a denim jumpsuit that is hanging there.

Sitting on the sofa, Mica mulls over the evening. It did not turn out as she had expected. She chides herself for her behavior, unaware that she is rocking her body back and forth. Jason goes over to her, and gently strokes her hair.

"It's okay Mica. We'll talk more tomorrow, maybe go for coffee if you feel up to it." Jason tells her soothingly.

"Maybe, but I really need to go now." Mica replies, holding herself tightly.

Mica sits quietly during the ride. Not knowing what to say to console her, Jason reaches over and lightly covers her hands which are tightly clenched in her lap. She smiles wanly in acknowledgement of his touch.

When they reach Mica's apartment building, she hurriedly exits the car, not giving Jason time to get out. She quickly walks to the entrance of her building, silently praying that she doesn't encounter anyone. Standing outside of his car, Jason watches until she is inside. The manner of her hasty retreat made it clear that she did not want him to follow her.

While merging into traffic on the return drive to his studio, Jason ponders Mica's emotional breakdown. The evening had not turned out as he expected.

Mica struggles to open the door to her eighth-floor apartment. She lives on the top floor of a renovated factory building. Only the apartments on her floor have terraces. They are secluded outdoor spaces. The brick wall enclosure obstructs a view to the street below.

As she closes the door to her apartment, Mica calls Nina on her cellphone. Nina answers on the third ring.

"Hey there, having fun." She asked brightly.

"Nina, I need you to come over right now," sobs Mica into the phone.

"What's wrong? Where are you?" Nina asked, alarmed by the urgency in her voice.

"I'm home. Please, please just get over here now," pleads Mica.

"I'll be there in twenty minutes."

Nina was on a meeting break when the call came. She tells one of the executives that she has an emergency, and is leaving. Then takes the elevator to the underground parking garage of the building.

Satisfied that Nina is on her way, Mica goes to take a quick shower. Stepping under the spray, the water sluices down her body. It takes a couple of minutes for her to realize that she is still dressed.

She undresses slowly, letting the dress and undergarments fall to the shower floor, pushing the pile with her foot into a corner. She lathers her body with soap trying to wash away the last sixty minutes. With a towel around her, she pads to her bedroom to get dressed in jogging pants and a tee shirt. The doorbell rings as she is towel drying her hair.

Mica opens the door to Nina who looks worriedly at her. Dropping her handbag to the floor, she examines Mica for any apparent injuries. Seeing none, she can't fathom what could have happened to her.

"Tell me what happened. You are scaring me?" Nina

demands, unsure of the situation.

Mica starts crying again and sags to the floor.

"I'm such a fool," she sobs.

"Mica you are scaring me, what the hell happened? Tell me this instant," shouts Nina. As fear takes hold of her.

"It's Jason. He told me tonight that he is getting a divorce and I blurted out that I love him."

Nina is dumbstruck by her admission. Staring at her disbelievingly.

She shrieks in a loud voice. "That's the reason why you call me over here? Are you crazy?"

Nina trembles with anger, wanting nothing more than to shake Mica.

"I tore over here, with thoughts of what could possibly have happened!" she sputters. "Thinking you were hurt or assaulted. Do you have any idea what you have just put me through?"

Nina turns away disgustedly, and heads to the kitchen. Mica follows her meekly.

"Where's the liquor, I need a drink." Nina fumes, her voice thick with seething anger. She bangs open cabinet doors, seeking an outlet for the unused adrenalin.

Crestfallen, Mica opens a lower corner cabinet door and pulls out a bottle of scotch. Nina grabs it from her. Seeing two glasses on the counter, she pours each of them a drink. She stares reproachfully at Mica, while downing hers in one swallow.

Nina pours more scotch into her glass and goes to the refrigerator for ice.

After the second drink, Nina takes a deep breath.

"I didn't know that you drink scotch." Her voice still edged with anger.

"I don't, Ceese bought all this stuff. She believes that every home should have a well-stocked liquor cabinet." Mica tells her miserably.

"Here's to your sister Ceese, a woman after my own heart."

Nina sits down at the small dining table in the adjacent dining nook.

Mica is regrets that she involved Nina in her meltdown. Realizing too late, her overreaction to the conversation with Jason. Letting it override her usual good judgment. She had put her best friend into a tailspin over nonsense. She is profusely apologetic to Nina.

"Look I'm sorry about this. My head wasn't on straight, otherwise I would not have made it into a five-alarm fire. I just needed to talk to you is all. I panicked. Right now, I want to pack my bags and leave town before dawn. I can't believe that I made such a spectacle of myself."

"Oh, stop the pity party and tell me what happened," Nina declares, the alcohol starting to mellow her out.

"You know Jason and I were having dinner this evening," Mica began. Trying to make sense through her narration of what triggered her emotional meltdown.

"Yeah, yeah, fast forward the tape," said Nina curtly.

"Well, I get to the restaurant early, and order a glass of wine while waiting for him. He comes in, sits down at the table we chit chat for a bit, then I ask him how he's doing. That's when he tells me that he is getting a divorce, and I try to be calm. I'm thinking that the man of my dreams is going to be free, and we can be together. Suddenly, it comes into my head that another woman may be involved. Before I can catch myself, I blurt out 'is there another woman.' He looked at me kind of weirdly, and said no. Then, I'm telling him that I love him."

"Uh huh, and so then what happened?"

Nina is incredulous listening to her, dourly noting that it did not necessitate leaving an important meeting and breaking several traffic laws to rush to get there.

Mica continues with her story, painfully cognizant of how ridiculous it sounds.

"Well, Jason leans towards me upsetting his wine glass which spills onto his pants; I reach over to help and knock over my glass which spills onto my dress. Then Vicky comes over to help clean up the mess. He tells her to put the bill on his tab. We leave the restaurant and drive to his studio. I have another meltdown and ask him to take me home. Then I called you."

Mica starts to sob again, more from embarrassment than any other emotion.

"Let me get this straight. This uproar was caused by you declaring your love for Jason, after he told you about his impending divorce?" Nina said sarcastically, unaffected by her tears.

Mica nods her head, as she wrings her hands.

Nina restrains a sudden urge to howl with laughter, but instead bites her lips.

"I don't see a problem here. I mean, it could get awkward if he does not feel the same way about you. And you didn't give him a chance to even talk to you."

"How can I ever face Jason after publicly humiliating myself?"

"Look, I can absolutely guarantee that Jason is not busily posting about this misadventure on social media. However, I can't say the same for Vicky. Your little scene is sure to be talked about among the staff. " Nina said wickedly.

Mica knows that Nina is right.

"How can I go back to Fables again? Everyone there is going to know about this. I'm done, done, that's it I'm done.

"Oh please, stop being so melodramatic." Nina feels a rush of satisfaction at Mica's distress.

"You think too much of yourself dear heart. Okay, so you got carried away in your reaction to Jason's announcement of his divorce. I'm sure that the shock of hearing about it caught you off guard. And I'm sure that his male ego was stoked to learn that a hottie like you has feelings for him." Nina tells her dryly.

"I see now that I acted like a juvenile, but how can I face him after this?

"You are in luck there. In today's world, there are so many ways to apologize for your insane behavior. You can text, post one on the social media platform of your choice. Or you can do it old school. Use your phone to call him."

"You're an idiot." Mica titters, beginning to feel better about the situation.

"And if I'm an idiot, what does that make you?" Nina asks. A smile unwillingly tugging at the corners of her mouth.

"A certified jackass." Mica replied without hesitation. "And you're right, I will call him later."

With the crisis solved, Nina suddenly realizes that she is hungry.

"Do you have anything here to eat. I'm starving."

Mica is curious to know where Nina was when she called her.

"So where were you when I called?"

"I was at a board meeting for the Foundation, which reminds me that I need to call my mother and let her know that everything is alright. "

Mica moans.

"Must you call her? Let her think that I'm lying in an emergency room being treated for a serious injury."

"To be honest, ten minutes ago I had the same thought," said Nina sardonically.

While Nina calls her mother, Mica goes to the kitchen. She finds ingredients to make a salad, and a can of tuna for sandwiches. She prepares the simple meal and brings the food to the table. They eat quietly, chewing the food, as well as their thoughts.

Mica looks over at Nina.

"You know, now that I'm calmer this is an exciting development, don't you think?"

"I certainly would not characterize getting divorced as exciting. Jason has been married to Julie for almost twenty years." Nina said, annoyed by Mica's insensitivity.

"But I had heard rumors that Julie wanted to start a commercial arts business with Jason. Supposedly, that is what drove them apart. They couldn't reconcile their differences. Consequently, the decision to divorce."

Nina didn't mention that most people in the couple's inner

circle did not believe that it was a business proposition gone wrong which led to their divorce. Speculations were rampant. Many of them were vying to be the first to discover the real reason.

Mica looks at Nina with her mouth open.

"You knew that they were getting a divorce and didn't tell me."

Nina puts down her fork and looks sternly at Mica.

"This isn't a topic for frivolous gossip. No one wants to see a long-term marriage end in divorce. Also, Julie is well liked in Woodsburne. So, you better tread very carefully in making any moves on Jason. He is going to need time to get himself together after this. If he leaps into another relationship too soon, you may not get the results that you desire."

"I feel even worse now. As it's so clear that Jason only wanted a friendly ear to talk about his troubles. I can't believe how I acted this evening. Letting my fantasies about him distract me from being a friend."

Nina cannot restrain the exasperation in her voice.

"Dial it back, Mica. Don't go overboard with the guilt trip. You didn't know, and I'm sure that Jason realizes that now. He knows that we are close and probably assumed that I told you about his marital problems. I'm just guessing here."

"What do I do now?" Mica asks again.

"Finish eating and call him after I leave."

"That's it?"

"Yes," Nina replied tersely.

As Mica washes up the dishes, Nina makes coffee, and they take their cups to the living room to relax.

With her legs tucked under her, Mica considers the best way to ask Nina how she manages to keep above the fray. She sips her coffee while thinking about it, finally deciding to be direct in her approach.

"It seems like life has always been so easy for you. You're not much older than me, yet you seem to be able to handle whatever comes your way. Have you never had doubts about anything?"

"Before I answer that, tell me why you didn't stay with Jason this evening?"

"Despite my 'attraction' to Jason, it scared me that he is available. It is one thing to imagine being in a relationship with someone and quite another to know that it could happen. That sudden realization flipped a panic switch in me." Mica answered truthfully.

"Now your turn, how do you manage your life so effortlessly?"

"I'm not perfect okay. Maybe it seems that way to you. But believe me I've made my share of mistakes in my life. My father taught me to look for the solution to any problem. He hammered into me not to waste time complaining or ascribing blame, because that leads to making poor judgements. That advice became my mantra - *think through to a resolution*. In other words, use your intellect not your emotions to find solutions to problems. Even when considering the advice of others, I know that the final decision is mine. My mother is fond of saying that we all have a moral compass. Whether we choose to use it, is our choice."

Mica looks at her thoughtfully.

"So how do we mere mortals do that?"

Nina relaxes into the conversation.

"As a great teacher of mine told me all the time when I was growing up. *Use the good sense that God gave you.*"

"Who was that?" Mica asked intrigued.

"Essie, she was the cook for our family. I would go to the kitchen pretending I was hungry and pour out my troubles to her. She would listen to me. I'd ask her what I should do, and her advice was always the same. 'Child, just use the good sense that God gave you.' Hearing that always made me so mad. I would go to my room, furious at her. Somewhere inbetween fuming and thinking about what to do, the answer would come to me."

Nina fondly recalls those youthful memories.

"That woman drove me crazy, but I kept going back to her, knowing exactly what she was going to tell me to do. The last time I saw her was during Christmas break of my junior year in college. I was in the kitchen chatting with her. When I got up to leave, she uncharacteristically gave me a hug. She told me that she was so proud of me and not to forget to use my good sense as I go through life."

Nina swallows back tears and hugs a cushion to her chest.

"She died later that winter from cancer. My heart broke when I got the news. It was as if a safety net had been pulled out from under me. But looking at her that last time lying in her casket; seeing her peaceful brown face; I knew that she had given me a great gift. I finally understood that there were no magical or instant fixes to life's dilemmas."

Mica goes over to Nina and puts her arms around her. She wipes away Nina's tears with her fingers.

Nina recovers her voice.

"It's been a long time since I thought about that. So my dear friend, use the good sense that God gave you and you'll do fine. And apparently you did just that this evening. You followed your instincts to leave Jason alone and chose instead to scare the heck out of me."

They both laugh. "Okay, I have to get going." Nina gets up and gathers her things.

As they walk to the door, Mica turns to Nina.

"You are a kind and loving friend. Thank you for being there for me, and I hope that I have been as good a friend to you."

Nina reaches for Mica's hand.

"You have been. You've help to keep my head on straight during those times when my compass was going haywire. It's going to be fine Mica. Just call Jason."

"Will do, I'll let you know what happens."

"You better. Kiss, kiss."

Craving fresh air, Mica steps out onto her terrace. She sits on a wrought iron bench that is set against one of the walls. The arrangement of potted plants gives the illusion of a small, landscaped garden to the enclosed space. Leaning back, she looks up at the sky. The cool snap of autumnal air gives notice of the approaching winter season. Mica thinks about her true feelings for Jason. Can true love come from infatuation she thinks? She goes inside to call him. Just as she reaches for her phone, it starts to chirp. It's Jason calling her.

"Hey there," he said in his baritone voice. "How are you doing? Are you feeling better?"

Scenes of the disastrous evening replay in Mica's mind. Feelings of embarassment resurface at the memory.

"Yes, and thanks for putting up with me."

"No worries, I think we were both out of sorts." Jason replies graciously, sensing her unease.

"Listen Jason, I want to apologize for my behavior. I think I was just shocked to learn about your divorce." Mica tells him honestly.

"No, it's me who should be apologizing. I should not have bought it up as a topic of conversation over dinner. I'm like a geyser going off these days whenever I am near any of my friends. I was being selfish and took advantage of your kindness. Matt advised me to have a fun evening. I should have stuck with the plan, and we would have had a great time together." Jason tells her, regretful of how the evening turned out.

"Oh, you told Matt about us having dinner?" Mica asks, somewhat taken aback.

"I invited both Neva and Matt to join us this evening. I thought it would be a good opportunity to tell you all how much I appreciated your support over these past months. But they both declined. Matt told me an evening with you would be good for the soul. Something about how your lightness of being would be sure to lift my spirits."

"Well obviously I didn't live up to the hype," said Mica ruefully.

She had certainly misread the intent of the evening.

"Okay then, let's agree that no apologies are needed."

"So, you have been in love with my work. All this time, I thought it was my charming ways that captivated you."

Mica closes her eyes, silently giving thanks for Jason's gallantry.

"Oh, you caught that one, did you? You know that your work is brilliant. I was looking forward to talking about your nomination. You must be pleased."

"It is an honor to know that my work is being considered for the new exhibition. However, I am but a small fish among other truly outstanding artists. The news hasn't sunk in yet."

"You deserve it."

"Thank you, that means a lot to me Mica."

"Does this change your plans for your sabbatical?"

"Not really. I'll put off foreign travel for now. But I will eventually be going to a villa in Tuscany that a close friend of mine owns there. That's where I'll be doing the heavy lifting in figuring out my future. It's beautiful there. Gives you a better perspective of one's place in the universe.

"That sounds great Jason. Oh, so that's why your studio was nearly empty. Are you planning to move away permanently?!"

"Right now, I'm keeping my options open. I don't think that I will leave the States entirely. But I am selling my house. I own the building where my studio is located. It has an apartment on the top floor."

"Oh, that's good. By the way, I want to thank you for your gracious invitation to meet up tomorrow. Tempting as it is, I have too many appointments at the gallery. I really hope that you will give me a rain check for us to get together before you leave."

"You've got it. However, I think it's your turn to treat me."

"I'll be more than happy to do that. We could do it this weekend, if you are available."

"Unfortunately, I have another engagement."

"No problem, let me know when you are free."

"I'll do that. It will be soon, I promise. And I'll be sure to wear waterproof clothing next time."

Mica giggles. "Seems like I have to redeem myself. Demonstrating that I can handle drinks and conversation at the same time."

"As do I." Jason adds laughing.

"Okay, let me not detain such a dedicated working woman any longer. Just wanted to check on you, make sure you were alright. I'll be in touch. And thanks Mica for being there for me."

"Always. Good night, Jason."

Mica ends the call and relaxes. Thinking back to the conversation, she could see that her comment could have been taken either way.

Letting her thoughts drift, she comes to terms with the crux of her infatuation. In truth, she wanted the bragging rights of dating a celebrity. She had not considered the relationship beyond the glow of winning the trophy. Or the consequences of what do you do after the appeal of the prize wears off. When the thrill of conquest recedes. Did she really want to be burdened with looking for ways to fill the void from making an ill-conceived choice?

She understood now that Jason probably recognized that quandary from personal experience. He shrewdly threw the ball back into her court. Mica had to admit that Nina was right. Recalling the story about Essie. It all comes down to 'using the good sense that God gave you.'

Mica is still thinking about that, as she retrieves her clothes from the shower floor. The dress is made of a washable silk material. It is not ruined. She carries the small pile to the laundry room, putting the garments into the washing machine.

Cleaning up mistakes should be this simple, she muses.

Back in her bedroom, Mica looks at the clock on the nightstand. It was only 9:30 PM, but it felt so much later.

Although it was early enough to call Nina, she decides against it. She had put Nina through enough for an evening. It would be better to wait and see her in person.

Mica sits up in her bed, picking up the remote to channel surf while waiting for her laundry to finish.

CHAPTER 8

Before Neva leaves the gallery for her dinner engagement with Edith, she stops by Matt's office. He's not there, but has the website for Josiah Summati open on his computer screen. Neva sits down at his desk and begins to scroll through the artwork and is immediately enthralled by the images.

When Matt enters the office, she is unaware of his presence.

"Pretty amazing aren't they."

Neva jumps, startled by his voice. "Gosh, I didn't even hear you come in, and yes, they are amazing. They remind me of the artwork of the Aboriginal people."

"There is certainly that influence. From his biography, he was born in Australia and his mother is Aborigine."

"I'm curious? Is he an older artist? I've never seen anything like this."

"He is thirty-five."

"His work belies his age, to have such command of his artistry. He's brilliant."

"I totally agree with you. He would certainly make a great addition to our portfolio. Do you want me to contact him?"

"Yes, of course."

"You won't believe this, but my sister-in-law recently spoke to me about him. I had intended to speak with you about it, and along comes Jason today with his recommendation."

"Great minds," laughs Neva. "Definitely invite him to come to the gallery."

"I'm on it. In fact, I was thinking of arranging a visit to his studio for an in-person look at his work. Followed by a meeting with us here. What do you think?"

"Let's just meet with him. After all, Jason has seen his work firsthand. And we trust his judgment, don't we?"

"We do. I'll call him before I leave tonight."

"I have a good feeling about this artist. Let's hope that he will be interested in joining us."

"We have a lot to offer, and I'm sure that Jason has told him about the quality of services that we provide to our portfolio artists. Although he's successful in his own right, the exposure from signing with us will take his career to the next level."

"Yes, I think so too. There's also something else that I want to speak with you about. I have been so busy lately that I haven't had time to schedule a meeting with you. I want to offer you the position of Assistant Director."

It was Matt's turn to look stunned. The promotion was unexpected. He didn't hear what Neva said next. His mind distracted from the conversation.

"When I came here seven years ago, my immediate focus was on improving operations and strengthening our role in the arts community. We have been exceedingly successful on all those fronts these past years. My current workload is too heavy to manage without help. I need a strong partner to work with me on guiding the future of the Avalon. You have been doing an outstanding job, and I sincerely hope that you will accept the position."

Still processing the promotion offer, Matt doesn't respond immediately.

"Thank you for your confidence in me. And of course, I would be happy for the opportunity to work more closely with you."

Neva smiles at him, pleased that he accepted.

"There are other personnel changes needed to help us to keep pace with our growth. I plan to hire Fredericka to manage our digital initiatives and activities. Also, Mica will assume the role of public relations manager. She'll have increased responsibility for planning and coordinating events and media outreach with our partners."

"Those are good strategic moves. I agree with you on the changes. Do you have anyone in mind to backfill my position?"

"Well, I was thinking about two of our graduate interns, Nora or Bruce. But I want you to make the final hiring recommendation."

"Of the two, Bruce would be the stronger candidate, I think. He's worked with me on several exhibits and was exceptional in performing his duties. Someone else to consider is John. He's a bit laid-back, not your typical artsy type. But he is plugged into the art scene and has a keen eye for exhibiting art."

"John, that's interesting." Neva said doubtfully.

"I would not have included him on the list of candidates for the job. But yes, consider in-house talent first. And cast a wider net, if needed, to find the right person."

Looking at Matt, Neva can already see him in his new role.

"You are going to be a vital asset for what we want to accomplish at the Avalon. I'm glad that we had this talk and that you accepted the job," Neva tells him sincerely.

Neva rises from Matt's desk.

"By the way, you will be moving to an office upstairs. Well, take back your desk for now. I'm off to dinner with Edith."

Matt clasps her hand.

"Good night, Neva. Enjoy your evening. And thank you again, I won't disappoint you."

Neva nods, smiling at him.

"I know that. See you in the morning."

After graduate school, Matt had made strategic choices in his professional career to support his long-term goal of curating a major collection at a leading museum. This promotion will give him key management experience at a well-known and respected gallery. It will be another important step towards achieving his objective.

Looking at the web page stirred up memories of the call from Cait several weeks ago. Josiah is a longtime close friend of hers. She met him while her family lived in Australia, and they became instant childhood friends. At the time, Josiah was already an art prodigy. His mother had been her caregiver.

Even after twelve years, Matt still gets a lurch in his heart when he thinks about Cait. She went on to complete a doctoral program in archaeology; winning awards and recognition for her work. He smiles wistfully recalling the first time he heard the voicemail greeting on her cellphone: "You have reached Dr. Almehudi Bondi……"

During their conversation about Josiah, she also told him about her upcoming trip to Italy. She was going to a conference on ancient civilizations. Frank, Matt's younger brother, would be staying home with their two-year old son, Jacob. Their son was the male look alike of his mother. Frank joked that the only feature his son got from him was his smile. They were married six years ago.

Matt did not attend their wedding, but he did send them an extravagant gift. He had maxed out two credit cards to buy it. His gift was a sculpture by Lizzia Ossie. She had invited him to her studio to look at her new artwork. Among the pieces was *Entwinements*. When he came upon it, he was captivated by the intricacies of its craving. And by the way in which several types of stones were integrated into the sculpture.

"This is extraordinary, Lizzia! How you incorporated the other stones into the piece." He had told her in awe.

She had smiled demurely at his praise. And told him to call her Lizzie. "That's what my friends call me."

He was enthralled by how the sculpture was to him, a three-dimensional representation of his feelings of love for Cait and Frank. And for their everlasting happiness.

Over the years, Matt had not visited his family often. It was too emotionally draining. Having to allay their well meaning concerns about his lack of a steady relationship in his life. The last time he went home was to attend the wedding of Kassie and Jackson.

It was a bittersweet family gathering. His parents were preparing for a move to Arizona. Each sibling returned home with a box filled with chosen memorabilia from their youth. Those memories engulfed Matt as he called Josiah.

After two rings, a woman answers. He is surprised, wondering if he had the wrong number.

"Hello, my name is Matthew Bondi, with the Avalon Gallery in Woodsburne, New York. I'm calling to speak with Josiah Summati."

"Oh yes, Jason told us to expect a call from your gallery. Josiah is looking forward to speaking with you.

"That's great. Is he available?"

"No, he is not home yet from teaching his last art class at the community center. I'm Kathleen, Josiah's wife. I will tell him that you called when he gets in."

"Thank you. And let me also give you my personal cellphone number. He can reach me at either one."

"We are eager to meet you in person. Caitlyn has told us so much about you."

"And I look forward to meeting you both as well. Tell Josiah that he can call me anytime."

"I will. Have a good night, Matthew."

After ending the call, Matt tidies up his desk, and puts the file with information on Josiah into his backpack. He makes the rounds of the gallery before leaving, stopping to speak with the security guard and cleaning service staff on his way out.

He stands outside for a moment, breathing in the cool air, before walking to the public parking garage. He takes the stairs to his car.

Driving past Fables, he briefly considers stopping by to have a drink with Mica and Jason. But decides instead to go to his favorite small restaurant for take out, not feeling in the mood to cook dinner.

He pulls into the garage of his large Victorian-styled house, located in Kafton Heights. It is one of the older neighborhood areas east of the River Edge district. Most of the homes in Kafton Heights were built during the late 1940's. Matt had lucked out on the property. It was an estate sale, the house sold 'as is.' The heirs were eager to dispose of it.

The previous owners had left furniture and crates throughout the house, leaving Matt to get rid of any unwanted items. Going through the three-story house, he was astonished to discover that much of the furniture and décor pieces were of heirloom-quality. And often wondered that if these were the discards, what were the items taken by the heirs. While he kept some, most of it was sold to antique dealers. The leftovers, he donated to charity organizations.

Matt enters the small mud room next to the kitchen. He sets his backpack and food on a kitchen counter, along with the mail. As he sorts through the mail, his phone rings. It is Josiah returning his call. They talked briefly and made plans for him to visit the gallery the following Wednesday.

Josiah also told him that he would be staying until the weekend to look at properties in the area. Matt had ended the call by inviting Josiah and his wife for dinner at his home on Wednesday evening. It would give him a chance to get to know Josiah better and find out more about Cait's relationship with him.

He sends Neva a text message about the meeting and enters it on their shared calendars. There is a conflict on Neva's schedule, but he knows that she will rearrange her appointments to be there.

After eating his meal, Matt grabs a sweater and goes outside to the backyard. This year he plans to complete the final phase of his home projects. Creating an outdoor living space. Hands in pockets, he surveys the yard. Mentally ticking off the essential must haves: outdoor kitchen, dining area, lounge seating, and fireplace.

After buying the house, Matt had gamely made a two-year plan for renovation projects. He divided them into do it yourself and those for which contractors would be hired.

The first year he hired professionals for exterior projects: installation of a new roof, windows, and front door; repairing the walkways and driveway; and overhauling the landscaping in the front yard. While the exterior was being done, he enlisted friends to work with him on interior projects. It took less than three months for him to realize that he was in over his head. The scope of interior work needed was far more than cosmetic fixes.

He hired contractors to do the renovations. The work on the house was completed in four months, and he was pleased with the results. The main floor was filled with natural light that enhanced the updated open floor plan design. Being an excellent cook, he was thrilled with the chef's kitchen.

His favorite space was the living room. It was to the left of the front door, and separated from the other rooms on the main floor by a wide arched hallway. This oversized front room was one of the main selling points for him when he first toured the house. The perfect setting for his art collection. The furniture was arranged to give an unobstructed view of the artwork from any place in the room. As well as to encourage conversation among guests gathered there.

Standing in the middle of the yard, Matt looks at the small stream which flows along the left side of the house. It separates his property from his nearest neighbor. On the right side is a brick wall that ends at a curving stone protective barrier that overlooks a precipitous rocky drop-off at the rear boundary of the property. The steep crag is a natural division between the public preserved land and the homes in the Heights.

While facing the back of the house, he admires the filtered effect of the interior lighting through the large kitchen window and patio doors. An idea occurs to him for the seamless integration of indoor and outdoor living. Something that should have been obvious from the beginning. The installation of folding glass doors across the back length of the house. A perfect way to showcase the majestic natural beauty of the surrounding hills and mountains.

Feeling the chill in the air, Matt saunters back inside. Pleased to be closer to the completion of his renovation project.

CHAPTER 9

Neva is struck anew by the beauty of the property as it comes into view. While they are close friends, she and Edith did not frequently visit each other at home. They preferred to meet at restaurants for a meal, or see each other at social events. In fact, Neva did not know Edith's late husband, Charles, very well. He preferred to stay out of the limelight of his wife's social commitments and friendships. When Neva and Charles did find themselves together, their conversations were casual. But she always enjoyed his company. With his natural wit, Charles had a knack of making you feel like an old friend even if you had just met.

The driver turns the car onto the long winding driveway that leads to the front entrance of the house. He pulls up to the walkway leading to the front door. Neva retrieves the bottle of wine in a velvet bag as she exits the vehicle.

She slowly walks up the short flagstone walkway, taking time to admire the front gardens and breathing in the aromatic evening air. The door to the house opens before she arrives. Mrs. Capers, the housekeeper, is standing in the doorway ready to receive her. As she enters the house, Mrs. Capers takes the bottle of wine from Neva, freeing her to take off her coat. Holding both the coat and wine bottle, Mrs. Capers directs her to the library.

There is a fire burning in the fireplace and it infuses the air with a soft fragrance of jasmine from scented wood chips. It is a welcoming aroma as Neva opens the tall, paneled door into the room. Edith is sitting behind a writing desk. It is placed in front of a pair of floor to ceiling windows that provide a breathtaking view of the back gardens and hills surrounding the property. Seeing the door open, she gets up to greet Neva. Holding out her arms to give a quick embrace.

"You finally made it. I was getting concerned about you. Is everything alright?"

"I'm so sorry for being late, but I stopped to speak with Matt on my way out. It took more time than I intended. Lately, things are so hectic at the gallery that it is getting difficult to make time to meet with staff."

They stroll over to a sofa in front of the fireplace. A chilled bottle of wine is in a ice bucket. Edith takes the bottle and pours wine into two glasses, handing one to Neva. Setting her glass down on the table, Edith presses a button on a handheld pad.

"The wonders of technology, I'm letting Mrs. Capers know that we are ready for hors d'oeuvres."

Within minutes, Mrs. Capers brings in a tray and places it on the cocktail table in front of them. Edith tells Mrs. Capers that they will be ready for dinner shortly. As she retreats from the room, the women lean forward to take one.

"Matt must have been pleased to have had time with you." Edith manages to say around a mouthful of a savory shrimp pastry.

"I think so. And I was even happier that he accepted the offer to become Assistant Director. It will lighten my workload. I will be meeting with Mica and Frederica next, to discuss my plans for promoting them as well. I'm very excited about these personnel moves."

"You've really done wonderful work at the Avalon, Neva. You have proven time and time again that you were the right choice to direct the gallery."

"Thank you, but your confidence in me also played a big part in my success."

"Nonsense, it was your vision and management skills that turned a moderately successful enterprise into a highly respected and profitable business. In addition to becoming a valuable community partner. No, my dear, the credit for all these achievements belong to you and your staff."

Taking a breath, Neva looks at Edith.

"And this may be the right time to turn over the reins to a new leader."

"Hmm, that sounds interesting. But let's wait until after dinner to talk about it."

Edith gets up and walks towards a door at the far side of the room. Neva follows her, their glasses in hand. A trio of tall arched windows gives another spectacular view of the surrounding hills which enhances the tranquility of the room. They stop to gaze out the windows. Edith reminisces about the history of Woodsburne.

"I never tire of looking at these scenic views. When we bought this house, Woodsburne was still a small town. At the time, it was mainly a country getaway for the wealthy. Most of the year-round residents lived in nearby villages. The few businesses that were in town, mainly catered to the needs of the wealthy estate owners and their guests.

You had to travel to larger towns for cultural events and shopping. There were occasional concert, usually held at the church or in the ballroom of someone's home. But soon, due to changes in lifestyles, the wealthy began an exodus from the area. The locals realized that the town was headed for extinction or would have to merge with other townships to survive.

A few of the established families, who were committed to Woodsburne, joined with them to form a town council that would ultimately shape Woodsburne's future.

Over the ensuing decades, Woodsburne grew to include public schools, a community hospital, specialty stores, restaurants, and other businesses. As the economy flourished, municipal services were expanded. Although some of the old families retained their properties, most of the grand old houses and land were sold to developers.

This property was one of the original smaller estates. We

purchased it from a family friend two years after moving here. Charles grew up in the area and knew its history. But like most of the young men during that period, after going away to college, they moved to the big cities to seek their fortunes.

You know that Charles went to Dartmouth and was a financier; employed by a prominent firm that only recruited top tier students. He was very successful and by age thirty-six was on track to be one of the firm's youngest partners. We were married by then. But he was not content and felt his destiny was elsewhere.

Then in our tenth year of marriage, Charles asked if I would support his decision to leave his job. He felt drawn back to the region of his youth. It was a heady decision to make. Taking the risk of giving up assured prosperity for an uncertain future."

Edith looks over at Neva. "I'm sure that you did not come tonight expecting a history lesson. But it's something about the changing of seasons that sometimes gets me nostalgic. Forgive the ramblings of an old woman."

"No please continue. I find it very interesting."

"Once we arrived in Woodsburne, I was convinced of the rightness of our decision. We had a community ready for development. Those early years were tumultuous times. We were among the principal planners and investors, including the Partridge family, to shape the growth of Woodsburne and neighboring communities. We lived here for more than forty-five years before Charles died. His legacy can be seen every day in the continued vitality of the city. I couldn't think of living anywhere else."

Edith pauses, bringing herself back to the present.

"Okay, enough of this. Let's have our dinner."

They enter the dining room through the connecting door. Mrs. Capers and her helper had already set plates of food on the richly set mahogany table.

"Ah, dinner is served. I'm famished. I hope you are hungry too."

"Oh yes, I skipped lunch today in anticipation of having this fine meal."

"No one can roast lamb and vegetables like Mrs. Capers," said Edith.

Mrs. Capers beams at the compliment. They pour the wine and unobtrusively leave the room.

As they eat, easy laughter and banter serve as the accompaniment to the delicious meal. After coffee and dessert, they return to the library to sit in front of the fireplace. Decanters of brandy and sherry, and glasses on a tray are set out for them.

Mrs. Capers asks if they will need anything else. Edith tells her that they'll be fine. However, she sweeps the room with her eyes before returning to the kitchen.

Sipping a brandy, Edith is relaxed as she asks, "Okay Neva, now tell me why you want to leave us."

The question is not unexpected, Neva settles into her seat in no hurry to respond.

"Oh Edith, it's not about wanting to leave you or Woodsburne. For months I have had this sense of not being fulfilled. And being successful is no longer an antidote for my internal unrest."

"I see."

"Last night when I opened the door to my apartment, it struck me how alone I am. For most of my adult life, my career and interests served as proxies for my personal happiness. I have been fighting hard all my life not to be like my mother."

"And what is it about your mother that makes you feel that way?"

"In short, not to make home and family the center of my existence."

"Why is this a problem now? Are you so dissatisfied with your work?"

"I love my work at the gallery, I truly do. It has been a challenging and rewarding seven years. Yet, there is still an underlying desire for me to move on."

"What is it that you want to do, Neva? How are we not meeting your needs here?"

"It's nothing specific. At times, such as when I was speaking with Matt earlier, I felt that I could stay at the Avalon for several more years. However, right at this very moment, I have a desire to be doing something else. I can't explain it any better than that."

"Alright, so you resign and then what?"

"Travel, maybe. I feel like I'm trapped on a treadmill that will not stop. I want to step off, but where will I go and do? That's not clear to me, my next step."

Holding the glass of brandy in her hands, Edith thoughtfully considers her next words. She does not want to appear to be indifferent to Neva's dilemma.

"Maybe this information might be helpful to you. There are plans for a major reorganization of the cultural institutions in Woodsburne. One proposal is for a partnership between the Leyden Museum and the Avalon. You know that Sidney Lacardin was recently appointed to be the new administrator at the museum. He is an extraordinary man. Have you met him yet?

Neva takes a sip of her sherry before responding.

"Yes, at a Chamber event this week. We chatted briefly."

"Well, he is the reason that the Partridge Foundation is funding the new art exhibition at the museum. He's been here for less than six months and already realizes that the museum is on life support. This is a very important investment for the Partridge Foundation. A big change in how grants have been typically awarded to local arts organizations. However, since Nina's appointment to the board, we finally have a strong advocate for supporting our arts institutions. Besides the Foundation couldn't very well refuse Sidney, who was a wunderkind, and still is a major influencer in the art world. You know that he was wooed here by Nina. She promised him a free hand in restructuring a major cultural institution located in the hinterlands of our great state."

Neva nearly chokes on her drink as she bursts out laughing, dabbing at her mouth with a napkin.

"Jeez Edith, give some warning before hurling the zingers."

"I thought you'd recognize that familiar ploy. The same one we always use to lure big talent to our part of the world." Edith said, her eyes twinkling with mirth.

"Yes, very familiar indeed, not unlike the one that hooked me." Neva agrees with amusement.

"Works like a charm every time to entice the mighty to come to us," chuckles Edith.

"I digress though, the partnership was proposed by Sidney. The Avalon has grown to be so much more than a gallery under your leadership. None of us doubt that Jason and the other renowned principal artists would have stayed if not for the services offered by the Avalon. He was captivated by the emerging artist program. As well as the online magazine and blog. He was one of your early subscribers, apparently."

Edith pauses to sip her drink.

"There is a lot of interest in this proposal. It will be a boon for the museum, catapulting it into current art thinking and a new direction. Underlying all of this though, is concern about the continued economic growth of our fair city. As you know, there is a large aging population here. A great many of whom are still caught up in the nostalgia of a pastoral Woodsburne. Its future, however, depends in large measure, on efforts to retain and attract a younger population. This will ensure that businesses will continue to invest in the area. Having strong cultural institutions will not only boost our appeal, but also support employment opportunities for our citizens."

"I understand all that Edith. But frankly what does that have to do with me?"

Frowning, Edith exclaims.

"Oh, don't be so dense Neva! You would be the best person to lead the proposed partnership. I should also mention that the Cellous Group will be setting up headquarters in Woodsburne. They have high expectations in bringing their businesses here. From their market research this is a prime location for their industry."

Edith pauses dramatically before continuing.

"They have put in a bid to acquire the Avalon's location. The plan is to renovate the building and use it as a flagship showroom for their products. And, they will be building a manufacturing facility, probably in Brookside Hills. They are also considering opening a Green Arts gallery. It will feature artists who use recycled materials in their artwork. The Board is considering leasing space at the Atrium building for the Avalon."

"I heard about the Cellous Group coming here, but not that they would be taking over the Avalon's location. My goodness, this is too much to take in at once." Neva said, unconsciously kneading her forehead with her fingers.

Her mind is whirling, trying to absorb all the information she just heard.

"Well, I'm giving you a heads up of the agenda for the next Board meeting.

"I don't know what to say, this is overwhelming. Are there any recommendations for my replacement?"

"Currently it is between Matt and Nina. Nina wants a more hands-on position and has tossed her hat into the ring for consideration. But Matt is the front runner. He certainly is well qualified for the job, wouldn't you agree?"

"Of course, absolutely, he is very qualified for the job. Mica's public relations role will be even more pivotal now."

"I agree with you on that, and all the other personnel changes mentioned earlier."

"So how is all this going to be rolled out?" Neva sits with glass in hand as she runs through possibilities in her mind.

"First things first. Will you accept the new position?"

"Oh Edith, how naïve of me to think that this was just going to be a quiet dinner with my very dear friend." Neva said, genuinely astonished by the turn of the conversation.

"You should have known better. There are no free meals in this town," replies Edith humorously.

She slowly rises to her feet.

"I have a very special bottle of champagne ready to toast this occasion. Please say the right words so that we can open it."

"I don't know what to say. Wait, you have champagne ready?" Neva stammers, also rising from her seat.

"I always have champagne. Just say yes, we will work out the details of your title, compensation and so forth later. Your acceptance will set into motion a ripple effect of very positive and progressive changes."

"Edith, I'm sure that you understand that this was not my expectation coming here this evening. Yes, I knew that we would talk a little about business, but nothing like this. This is not something for which you make a rush decision."

Edith turns to face Neva, looking searchingly at her.

"Neva, I know that you did not come here this evening expecting a job offer. But think about it, a short while ago you yourself said that you wanted a change. This is exactly what I'm offering – a new challenge. It will be a good move for you. It will give you a vantage point from which to map the next stages of your career."

Turning aside, Neva looks through the windows at the night sky. As if searching for the answer in the stars. No doubt they will be entering uncharted territory with this proposal. Perhaps this is the next step that she needs to take.

Neva turns back towards Edith.

"Let's open that bottle of champagne."

"Is that a yes, you'll take the job?" Edith asks joyfully.

She is also secretly pleased that her personal motives for Neva's acceptance have been achieved.

"For now, it is a tentative yes," replies Neva. She wants to have an exit option if needed.

"You won't regret it. I promise you."

Linking arms, they leave the room and walk to the glass domed conservatory. It provides a panoramic view of the magnificently manicured gardens beyond. At the center of the room, inscribed with a poem, are twin black onyx stone slabs, set upright on a thick marble base. With mother of pearl inlaid into the exquisitely carved lettering. It renders a three-dimensional quality to the etched words. The craftsmanship is awe inspiring in its power of projection.

The back of the conservatory has a waterfall that flows over a slab of roughhewed granite. It provides soothing water sounds within the room. At night, the room's lighting intensifies the dramatic effect of these prominent features. There are two marble benches in front of the rendered stone slabs, providing a place to sit in quiet contemplation.

Edith waves her hand around the room.

"The conception and design of the conservatory was one of Charles's last projects. He was like a young man again during its construction. And it was completed a year before he died."

She wistfully shook her head.

"I asked him about the poem, but he couldn't recall how he acquired it. During the planning of the conservatory, he found it among old rolled papers and drawings in a cabinet drawer. I visit here to find peace and imagine my loving reunion with Charles when the time comes."

The women stand together, each silently reading the words of the poem.

Chorus of the Universe

The woman feels as if she is sitting
at the top of a mountain.
Giving her a clear view from which to gaze upon
the gentle unfurling of her life's journey.

As the montage of her life scrolls before her,
she is pleased that she had not been inflexible.
Nor fearful of change,
and had been blessed with the serenity
that comes from spiritual transformation.

When the montage comes to its end,
she is prepared to embrace
the revelations of wisdom sought.
Those grand cosmic truths.
And steps peacefully
into the Nothingness.

At once, she is filled with the joyous
rapture of tranquility and love.
Encircled by the all-knowing.
She ascends to the heaven
of which we all dream.

Her mind's eye slowly closes.
The solitary witness
to the divine reunion of her soul
with the chorus of the universe.

        - Tenaj

Edith's voice is thick with emotion when she resumes speaking.

"I always experience a renewal of purpose when I come here. Inspired to continue the work we started for one more day. Standing here I can see beyond the present to Charles's vision of what could be."

In a low voice, Edith talks as if to someone unseen.

"Charles and I were partners in our marriage. He believed in me and did not disparage my intelligence or ideas. We worked well together in our endeavors and were equals in making decisions regarding our finances. Able to be honest in expressing how each of us wanted to spend or invest our money.

You know, when I was growing up, it was not typical for a woman to control her own money. Even for those who did, they usually had a man to front for them in most business matters or investments.

My mother died giving birth to me. She was a very wealthy heiress, and her estate was wholly inherited by my father. He decided not to remarry after her death, raising me on his own; assisted by nannies and servants of course.

As a child, I was always curious about his work. Interested in knowing what kept him from spending time with me. It was my interest in his profession, I think, that made him decide not to send me away to boarding schools.

He was a banker, an executive vice president. His duties included the stewardship of the inheritances and trust funds bequeathed to young and middle-aged women. They came to him for advice, and to request funds for personal needs or other expenditures.

In my mind, it was not unlike how I had to go to him to make a case for an increase in my allowance or some such. My father was honest, yet it bothered me that he held that power over those women.

From age twelve, I was determined to learn about the field of finance. In preparation for being able to control my own inheritance when the time came. Not to passively accept the perceived expert advice from others.

At first, my father merely indulged my interest. Soon he realized my resolve to attain this knowledge. He became more considered in his teachings, providing more in-depth information about the tools of the trade, so to speak.

He was pleased that I was mastering the workings of finance. So, when he died unexpectedly, killed in an automobile accident, I was well prepared to manage my wealth. However, his real legacy was not the money that I inherited, but the knowledge that he had imparted to me.

From those beginnings, came my commitment to support programs that teach women about money management. And now, my work is being continued by people much smarter than me."

All of a sudden, Edith stops speaking. Standing rigidly, her arms at her sides. It had been decades since she spoke so openly about her past. She is momentarily frightened. That by talking about these long buried memories, her imminent passing was being portended. She struggles to recover her composure.

Unaware of Edith's distress, Neva waits silently, not wanting to intrude on her thoughts. Edith walks over to one of the benches. She glances up, as Neva sits down beside her.

"I'm babbling again. Don't know what has gotten into me."

"You were not babbling. Your story is compelling. Revealing a side of you that I never knew about. Like getting to know you all over again. That's a good thing."

Edith closes her eyes and takes a deep breath. Feeling centered again, her tone is more conversational when she continues.

"I was very fortunate to have married the love of my life. We accepted our fate of not being able to have children. Instead, taking pleasure in being the doting Aunt and Uncle to the children of Charles' two siblings. We built a good life for ourselves, always generous in giving back. While Charles is no longer physically here with me, he dwells in my heart."

Listening to Edith, longing washes over Neva. It sparks a heartfelt desire for finding her soul mate.

"I'm sorry that I didn't get to know Charles very well. But on the few occasions when I did spend time with him, it was evident that he was a remarkable man and loving husband. And he certainly was right that you are a wise woman. I want to thank you for all that you have done for me and so many others. You are a treasure to me." Neva tells her tearfully, hugging Edith.

"As are you, my dear." Edith once again closes her eyes briefly, to release any lingering ghosts from her mind. "But we still have plenty to do."

CHAPTER 10

On arriving home, Neva goes upstairs to her bedroom to change out of her clothes. She slips on a silk kimono and returns to the living room. The evening has left her in a pensive mood. She turns on the music system and selects a playlist before going to sit on the sofa.

With the music in the background, she replays the conversation with Edith in her mind. It felt like a whirlwind of change had occurred since she left for work that morning. There were many things to consider about her future. However, Edith's musings had also stirred up memories from her youth.

Those memories were not poignant ones. Tonight, she gained a keener insight into her relationship with Edith. Why she had clung to her from the first time they met. She realized that Edith has been a surrogate mother for her. A source of consolation from the hurt that encased her heart since childhood.

Her mind wanders to one particular memory. The week before she left for France.

She had recently graduated with her master's degree, and was one of seven American post grads selected to work on coordinating a special exhibit at the Louvre. The posting would be for a year. Neva's mother had come to her apartment to give her a farewell gift. They chatted briefly and her mother soon left.

Neva had been more preoccupied with getting ready for a dinner date with Edith later that evening, than being attentive to her mother. It wasn't until later that night that she opened the gift from her mother. Nestled inside the box, wrapped in soft tissue paper, was a beautifully hand-knitted mauve sweater and scarf set. There was also a letter.

It was no secret that Neva bitterly resented her mother for consenting to have the two children from her father's extramarital liaison to become a part of their family. And then, being embraced as 'rightful offspring' by the entire family. She had been estranged from her relatives since childhood. Exuding a cold tolerance and politeness towards them.

After seeing the contents, Neva had thoughtlessly consigned the items to the bottom of her trunk. She habitually placed things of unimportance on the bottom half of the trunk and things she valued at the top.

Neva rediscovered them when she was packing for the move to Woodsburne. There was the sweater set, lying at the bottom of trunk, forgotten from all those years ago. And lying on top was the unopened letter. She finally read it.

My dearest Neva,

Please do not summarily disregard this as another of our ongoing attempts for reconciliation with you. Your father and I accept that you are in control of 'if or when' that will ever happen.

However, I would like for you to consider that sometimes you don't get the desired answers to the 'whys' behind the things that occur in our lives.

This is my way of saying that you have imposed obstacles for gaining any understanding of the family issues that are of concern to you. And you have been dismissive of accepting any answers that could provide clarification or insight. Preferring instead, to stand in your own truth.

I must admit that this was a difficult letter to compose. I spent days writing and rewriting it. Not wanting to alienate you by its phrasing. Yet striving to be clear in conveying my thoughts and feelings. That its overall message is one of our wanting only the best for you. With that said, these are the things that, given the chance, we would want to tell you.

Do not let your heart become entombed by disillusionment. Do not let anger and resentment be the thieves that rob you of your hopes and dreams. The denial of living a full and happy life.

We beseech you to open up your heart to finding joy, happiness, and love. Do not let your profound disappointment in us distort your worldview. Rejecting anything outside of your preconceived assumptions. And please, please, do not make us the excuse for not becoming the person that you want to be. That would be the most cruelest thing to do to yourself. Living your life as an impostor. While the real you watches from the sidelines.

The takeaway from these entreaties is this: do not become your own enemy. And hopefully, the next time we see each other, you will be willling to have an open discussion with us. That is our wish. Our hope.

And lastly, please never forget that your father and I love you. Never forget that we believe in you. Never forget that we are here for you. You are our daughter. And will always be a part of us. Always.

After finally reading the long forgotten letter, Neva remembers how her body had trembled with shame at the memories of her cruel acts of indifference. How her estrangement must have weighed so heavily on her parents and relatives. Her arrogant dismissiveness of the many attempts by Eduardo to reason with her. Impervious to all of his entreaties.

But the most staggering realization was that her parents knew, had to know, that she never read their letter. During those handful of times that she went home over the years, her behavior had given proof of that to them.

And what had been their crime? That her parents loved two children whom she had rejected as being part of their family.

Within days of reading the letter, Neva had scheduled a trip to visit her parents. It was ironic that she turned to Eduardo for advice on how to seek their forgiveness. They talked on the phone for hours, and true to his empathetic nature, he offered to accompany her. He lived in California with his family. A professor at the University of California at Davis. She declined, knowing that it was something that she had to do on her own.

When she arrived at her childhood home, she stood momentarily on the sidewalk to gather herself. Her mother opened the front door; and unable to hold back her tears, Neva had collapsed crying into her mother's arms. Her father, behind them. Her parents stood in their foyer transfixed as they listened to their daughter. Not understanding the torrent of words that poured from her, like a rushing river after a big storm.

Slowly comprehension came to them, their daughter was asking to return to her family. The readiness of their forgiveness had pierced her heart. As if it was her, and not them, who had been so unjustly mistreated. Making her wish to go back in time to be the daughter that they truly deserved.

Pushing those memories aside, Neva goes to her home office. She turns her attention back to Edith's job offer. Not totally convinced that the new role would serve her best interests. She considers planning a short vacation to mull over her options.

While she is well traveled, most of the countries where she lived or visited were connected to work. She would be at a loss to describe the daily life of the inhabitants of those locales. It struck her then, that she had gone through life as a spectator, not attentive to the world around her. The thought brings her up short, as another sequence of past mistakes are stirred in her mind.

Sitting in near darkness, Neva stares blankly at the computer screen. A notification sound for an incoming email brings her back to the present. She clicks on it.

Hi Neva,

I will be attending a medical conference next week Monday in Rochester. I would love to plan a stopover in Woodsburne to visit with you the preceding weekend. I can book a flight to arrive on Saturday. Let me know. Hope you will be available.

Love, Arizzia.

Neva looked at the message as if an unspoken wish had miraculously been answered. The unexpected visit from her sister would be another step towards exorcising some hurts from the past.

CHAPTER 11

ZAIEDA

Neva was six years old when her mother suffered a nervous breakdown. It was after her infant sister, Illiana, died in her sleep from Sudden Infant Death Syndrome (SIDS). Her parents, Francisco and Mora, were told by their doctor that the baby's death could have been caused by a congenital heart defect. His explanation was unconvincing to her mother. She was inconsolable. Blaming herself for the death of the child.

After six months of not showing any signs of improvement in her condition, Francisco arranged to send their mother to Florida. Her older brother owned a large farm there. Everyone thought that a respite from caregiving would be beneficial for her recovery.

Her planned visit was for a two-week stay. But soon after arriving in Florida, she had to be hospitalized. Remaining there for more than a year.

During her absence, the children went to live with their paternal grandparents in Queens. Their father remained in the family's home in the city's Greenwich Village neighborhood. Picking up them on weekends to stay with him. He was a master stone mason, and the co-owner of a consulting firm that collaborated with architects on restoration projects of historic buildings. He frequently traveled for his work. His job provided a very comfortable lifestyle for the family.

It was during this prolonged separation from his wife, that Francisco met a young woman. She was a thirty-one year old graduate student from Egypt, studying for a doctoral degree in economics at Columbia University. She lived in a brownstone apartment in the Morningside Heights area on the Upper West Side of Manhattan.

They met when he got lost on the way to a meeting being held on campus. His company had been recently hired as consultants for a major restoration project at the university.

Concerned about being late, Francisco had randomly approached her to ask for directions. She was on her way to the library and volunteered to accompany him to his destination.

During the short walk, they talked about major restoration projects around the world. Their brief conversation was a pleasant distraction from his troubles. He invited her to have coffee with him later that afternoon. She agreed to meet at a nearby coffee shop. Her name was Zaieda Saddat.

She was the middle child of five children, two sons and three daughters, from a wealthy Egyptian family. The family owned a major import and export business among other holdings. When her two older brothers were killed in a plane accident during a military training exercise, Zaieda, by default, entered the family business.

Her father, Abaan, devastated by the loss of his sons, was forced to rethink the future of his business conglomerate.

He began preparing Zaieda for an executive position. Abaan knew that of all his children, Zaieda was the only one who had the talent and leadership qualities required for commerce. And he also knew, that even with his support, Zaieda would still encounter antagonism from male colleagues and other partners, resenting not only her gender but her acuity for business.

Even though Zaieda held two post graduate degrees, in business administration and political science. Her father counseled her to go abroad to study for a doctoral degree in economics. He felt that this advanced degree would further enhance her already impressive credentials. They chose Columbia University in New York City.

Initially, the relationship between Francisco and Zaieda was platonic. Staying within the parameters that they established for their friendship. They were contented with exploring the city by walking through neighborhoods that piqued their interests. The Cloisters, in Fort Tryon Park, was one of their favorite places to visit. They talked for hours while roaming its grounds.

Francisco enjoyed Zaieda's quick mind and wit. He admired her knowledge of world history and economics. She was tall, with slim hips and long legs. Her light caramel coloring accentuated her large brown eyes and long wavy hair. Her manner was determined, but not dogmatic. She had a dash of arrogance mixed in with a generous measure of humility.

Her demeanor hinted at a lineage of nobility from an ancient era. This perception was reinforced by her husky voice which imbued sagacity in her manner of speaking.

Francisco's attraction to Zaieda was not based on her being more beautiful, charming, or smarter than his wife. The allure was that she communicated with his heart in a way it had never been touched before or would be ever again.

Zaieda admired Francisco's extensive knowledge of stone craft and architecture. She liked the confidence he projected in his posture and the movement of his body. The way in which he emanated a sense of strength without being imperious. That he seemed unaware of his physical attractiveness. It pleased her that he was not intimidated by her intelligence, but appreciated it. His acts of thoughtfulness and kindness captured her heart. With him, she was free to be herself. Able to exit from the stage of a scripted life.

Neither of them was aware when their feelings shifted from friendship to love. They were unconcerned with the reasons why destiny brought them together at this point in their lives. Accepting, without question, the now of it. Neither of them yearned for forever.

One night after intense telephone conversations with doctors and his wife's family, the mental strain of the situation overpowered Francisco's inner resolve. He sought physical comfort from his despair. They came together in a night of lovemaking. Surrendering to the powerful attraction that they had managed to suppress.

The intensity of their coupling shattered the established boundaries for going back to being just friends.

Days later, because of those unleashed feelings, they mutually decided to end their relationship. Even though they both longed for more, neither of them was in any position to fulfill those desires.

They both knew that their love could not survive outside of the bubble in which it now existed. For Zaieda, the experience of first love unlocked within her a new level of consciousness. While Francisco understood that his love for Zaieda was a keepsake to be cherished. A gift from an alternate life that would never be.

Two months after they ended their relationship, Zaieda found out that she was pregnant. She chose not to tell Francisco, upholding their decision to move on with their lives. Confiding in her family was out of the question.

Aside from university acquaintances, Zaieda's only friends were Kathleen Radnorth, whom she affectionately called Radi. She was the owner of the building where she lived and treated her like a daughter. As did Elsie Mallardy, the longtime best friend of Kathleen. She was the other tenant in the building.

The women were in their mid-fifties. Both of them had substantial annuity incomes. Kathleen's was from her late husband, and Elsie's from a divorce settlement. But despite this income, they continued to work in their chosen careers. Kathleen, a successful author of romance novels, and Elsie a registered nurse. They would provide the emotional support that Zaieda would need as she decided her future.

Seven months after the affair ended, Mora was well enough to return home. Despite the rainy day, Neva and Eduardo stood guard outside their home to await her arrival.

In no time, they were back together as a family. The fear

of their mother leaving again had receded from the children's minds. The house was once again filled with the smells of cooking and furniture polish when they came home from school. Their parents seemed to be happy, and friends and relatives started visiting again. Everything was back to how it had always been.

Zaieda spent those seven months shifting between exhilaration at becoming a mother and being mindful of the approaching life altering change. Returning to Egypt with a child would force her family to denounce both mother and child. Even if she was able to contrive some way of having the child near her, there would always be the fear of exposure.

A significant portion of their business dealings were with corporations in countries that would sever all ties with them should her predicament become known. Mixed in with those concerns was the guilt she felt in regards to her two younger sisters. She had to protect them from any hint of scandal. Their prospects for a good marriage would be at risk, if not ruined, because of her pregnancy. No, there was too much at stake to even consider returning home.

These thoughts left Zaieda longing to be with Francisco. Wanting to let him know that she was pregnant with their child. But she never did. Even though she had opportunities to do it. Francisco had called several times to check on her.

During their last conversation, Francisco told her that his wife was coming home. On hearing this, Zaieda told him that she too would be returning to Egypt. A family emergency required her to leave sooner than planned.

They ended the call by wishing each other to have a life filled with all good things and much happiness. Based on this last conversation, Francisco genuinely believed that Zaieda had returned to her country. He had no reason to disbelieve her.

With only a few months away from her graduation, Zaieda was in a panic about how to inform her parents. Her father was planning to attend the graduation ceremony.

Unable to put off the unavoidable any longer, Zaieda finally wrote a letter to her father. He was distraught by the news of her pregnancy, sure that his life must be cursed. But grateful, that she was abroad. He traveled to see her soon after.

Abaan was intent on making sure that Zaieda fully understood the consequences of having a child outside of marriage. He would emphasize that her intemperate action consigned her to spinsterhood, unable to accept any future proposals of marriage. Because a previous pregnancy could not be concealed from a doctor or husband.

Yet, he also saw a strategic advantage in the situation. None of his associates would know the real reason behind Zaieda's decision to forgo marriage. It would appear to be a demonstration of her utmost commitment to the company.

Still, it could be a double edged sword. Some would be pleased at the personal cost required for being a female executive. Others would be offended by the decision. Regarding it as unnatural behaviour for her gender. Abaan concluded that the risks were manageable.

Over the next three days and nights they discussed her future. The tone of the discussions were not unlike tense negotiations between opposing sides. In the end, Zaieda's arguments prevailed. She would seek a fellowship position and remain in the States. The justification would be for her to acquire practical experience that will support the company's planned expansion into growing markets.

Abaan reluctantly agreed. Still hoping that Zaieda would come to accept his judicious advice to give the child up for adoption. For Zaieda, the additional time in New York gave her an opportunity to determine her best course of action.

She knew that she was not the first unmarried woman from her country to have a baby. And had heard rumors of brokers who made discreet adoption arrangements for the babies of unwed mothers. There was a lucrative market for these infants. They were sought after by wealthy families looking to adopt newborns. This would be a plan of last resort.

Zaieda did not attend her graduation, no longer able to

disguise her condition. A month later, she gave birth to twins. Radi and Elsie accompanied her to the hospital and sent a cryptic telegram to Abaan, informing him of the birth of Ahnan and Arizzia.

Her father quickly arranged a trip to see her. He had every intention of insisting on a plan of adoption. The birth of twins made it quite a different situation from raising a single child on her own. But to his astonishment and dismay, he fell in love with the infants at first sight. And spent a week with his daughter and grandchildren.

Six months later, Zaieda travelled to Egypt to attend a company meeting. A segment of her presentation was an update on her fellowship experience. She also provided a synopsis of recommendations for expansion into new lucrative markets where their goods and services would be profitable, with less competition. The directors readily approved the plan. With that approval, Zaieda saw a way to tactically disengage from the company. A win/win for both sides. But for her in particular, as she would be able to have the life she wanted with her children.

On her return to New York, she eagerly began to prepare her exit proposal. The key components included the promotion of Asif Gamal to replace her. Given that he has informally been functioning in that role. Zaieda would assume the newly created position of Global Operations Consultant. Under the proposed arrangement, she would no longer be a direct employee of the company; but linked through a contract agreement.

As she reached this point, Zaieda stopped typing and gasped. How had she not seen it before? Asif had already replaced her. They wanted her to remain living abroad. Pursuing any business experience that aligned with their interest, benefiting from her ideas and strategies. And her absence was a convenient way for not acknowledging her contributions to the success of the conglomerate.

She also realized that her role had been restructured into

one of being a hidden asset. A useful tool. Her father had to have known, and made the choice to protect his interests. He has been walking a tightrope to appease all sides. From these insights, it was clear that she did not have to waste time strategizing an exit. The door had not been opened for her. She was never inside. Therefore, her father would be the one responsible to end the charade. And for her exit payout package.

Zaieda was nearing the end of her tenure in the fellows program when the headaches began. Initially, she ignored them as being caused by her demanding work schedule and motherhood. However, Elsie became concerned about Zaieda's health when she noticed her weight loss and tiredness. She was persistent in urging Zaieda to see a doctor.

The doctor prescribed medication for migraines and advised Zaieda to reduce her workload. A month later she was back at the doctor's office, intending to ask for stronger medication. But this time, he referred her to a specialist.

A week later, Zaieda sat speechless in his office She had a brain tumor. She was only partially listening to him as he informed her of recommended medical options. He told her that she had only days to decide on her choice of treatment. When she left his office, rather than going home, she went to the Cloisters. A place of refuge for her.

Sitting there she promised herself to be purposeful in how she spent her remaining time. Thoughts about her children eclipsed thoughts of her mortality. It was wrenching to realize that the twins would not remember her. They were so young. The idea of writing a memoir occurred to her. A written chronicle about her life and philosophy for her children and grandchildren. She took comfort in knowing that her 'second mothers' would ensure the well-being of the twins. All of these thoughts gave her the inner strength to not mourn the years of life that she would not have.

Elsie was in the sitting room, off the entryway, waiting for Zaieda's return. She was anxious to hear about the test results.

Radi was upstairs on the third floor with the children. At first, Zaieda tried being evasive. She was not ready to discuss her diagnosis. The ramifications of which she was still processing. But Elsie refused to be put off.

Zaieda began by talking about the irony of her day. In the morning, she received a job offer from the corporation that sponsored her fellowship. The job would be at their Chicago headquarters. She had felt elated that a new chapter in her life was about to begin. Then in the late afternoon, she was told that she did not have long to live.

"The doctor told me that if the operation is successful, I might live up to three years. Today I thought about my brothers, and had they lived, my life would have turned out so differently. But their deaths altered my destiny. In ways that I could not have imagined back then."

A stream of memories causes her to stop speaking. Memories of her adolescence inundated her mind. Time stopped for a moment.

In a contemplative voice, she resumes.

"Can you imagine, that since I came to this country, I have lived a lifetime. I gained knowledge and self-awareness; found two second mothers, in you and Radi; met an incredibly special man; fell in love; became a mother of two children; and will die surrounded by the people whom I have come to love and cherish. While it may seem counterintuitive, I feel blessed. Because I received everything that I needed to be happy. Think about it. In a condensed period of time, I experienced a well lived life."

Elsie was moved by the poignancy of Zaieda's words. She marveled at the wisdom and fortitude of this young woman and reached out to hug her.

"I just wish that you had many, many more years."

"That is my wish as well. But it is not to be." Zaieda said wistfully, and promptly dismissed the thought from her mind.

Less than two years later, feeling the accelerating decline of her health, Zaieda knew that she did not have long to live. The weeklong stay, at a friend's home in the Adirondacks, would probably be her last trip. She and Radi were sitting in rocking chairs on the back porch. They could hear the laughter of the children in the background.

Zaieda took the opportunity to discuss the legal provisions she had made for her affairs. And the letters, for Francisco and Mora, that were in her dresser drawer at home. Asking Radi to deliver them upon her death.

"I wrote the letters soon after my diagnosis, when my mind was clear," she confided quietly.

"You already know that you will become the guardian of the twins, in the event that they decide not to take them."

They shared a long meaningful look. There was no need for further discussion.

It was a late Friday evening, when Abaan arrived at his daughter's apartment. It had been an arduous trip and he wanted to freshen up before heading to the hospital. But after a call from Radi, he immediately rushed to get there. He arrived shortly before Zaieda died.

The next day was bleak for the three of them. The miracle they had wished for did not materialize. Sorrow swirled in close but did not overcome them. They had to remain strong for the children.

Making the phone call to Francisco compounded their anxiousness. So much depended on his reaction to being told about Zaieda and the twins.

At first, Francisco was confused. He did not understand what Radi was telling him. But as it became clearer to him, the momentous disclosure hammered at his sanity.

The call came just as he was leaving his office. When he hung up, he was too shaken to drive. Instead he had his assistant call a car service. On the ride over, he realized that he had forgotten to call his wife.

When he arrived at their home, the women took him straightaway to meet his three year old children for the first time.

Francisco fell to his knees at the sight of them. Getting to his feet, he staggered to the side of the bed on which they slept. He wrapped his arms around their warm sleeping bodies. Crying silently, grief shrouding him. He vowed to make everything right. It was heart wrenching to witness his anguish.

Abaan had left earlier to stay at a hotel. Determined to avoid meeting the man whom he blamed for his latest tragic loss. And kept himself occupied with making the arrangements for the transport of his daughter's body to Egypt for burial.

Eventually, Radi took Francisco downstairs to her apartment to give him the letter from Zaieda. He could hardly read the pages, his tears blurring the written words. When he finished, Elsie gave him a sedative and took him back upstairs to be with his children.

She was also the one to call his wife to let her know what was happening. Mora took the news calmly, asking that Francisco call her when he was able.

He called early the next morning, asking Mora to come there, so that he could explain the situation. She rushed next door to ask a neighbor to stay with Eduardo and Neva until a relative could come to their home.

When Mora arrived, Francisco gave her both letters to read, and placed his fate into her hands. He left her alone in the room to read them. She sat silently afterwards, holding a photograph in her hand. Thinking about the events that led up to that moment.

She did not come to her decision from any sense of moral obligation or duty. Or the poorly disguised looks of pleading in her husband's eyes. It came, in part, from Zaieda's written request. That she should only agree to take the children if she could love them as her own.

Mora studied again the recent photograph of Ahnan and Arizzia, that had been tucked inside of her envelope. How it captured their childhood innocence and ebullience. They were playing outdoors on a sunny day. Arms outstretched, heads tilted back, being sprayed by water from a garden sprinkler.

From that image, she felt a visceral connection to them. A dormant fissure of love reopened within her. Eradicating any uncertainty about bringing Ahnan and Arizzia into their family.

Returning to their home later that night, Francisco looked as though he had aged ten years. Mora sent Eduardo and Neva to their rooms. Simply telling them that the adults needed to speak privately about an important matter. The sounds of crying and raised voices reached them from downstairs. It grew louder as other family members arrived.

The next day, they did not get ready for school as usual. After breakfast, their parents spoke to them about the little brother and sister, who would be coming soon to live with them. Neva did not understand. It did not make sense to her.

How could a little boy and girl suddenly appear in their lives? Where had they been all this time? Later, when their father left the house, she still had many unanswered questions. Fearful of what it meant for them. For she and her brother.

This time, when Francisco arrived at Radi's house, Abaan was there. Radi had convinced him to meet Francisco, even though his anger had not subsided towards him. Meanwhile at home, Mora was busy preparing a room for the twins. As well as coaching the two older children, as they helped her, on being a big brother and sister.

The next day, when Eduardo and Neva came home from school, the twins were sitting on their mother's lap in the living room. They walked over to look at them. Their mother told them that Arizzia was the girl's name, and the boy was named Ahnan. They were beautiful children, but Neva did not see any kinship in those little foreign faces.

From that day, her parents said nothing more about the sudden insertion of the twins into their lives. Neva was alone in her resentment towards them. The only one who understood that they did not belong. But she kept those feelings to herself.

As she grew older, Neva barely tolerated their existence.

Outraged by the devotion shown to those creatures by her family members. As if it was perfectly normal to love these outsiders and give them a place in their hearts.

And so, from a young age, she swore an oath to herself. She would never be weak like her mother. A person ruled by their heart, and not by their head.

Abaan continued to pay rent for Zaieda's apartment, staying there when he came to visit his grandchildren. But he kept his distance as he watched them grow. He usually saw them when they came with Francisco to visit Radi and Elsie. As they got older, he attended their school plays and recitals.

He never formally introduced himself to them, beyond being known as a distant relative. Despite protestations from Francisco, he sent money every month to help with the care of the twins. Francisco opened a savings account for each child. The funds to be used for their college education.

On their sixteenth birthday, Ahnan and Arizzia were finally told about their birth mother. Francisco took them to Radi's house, and the apartment where they had lived with Zaieda. It was also the first time that Zaieda's parents traveled together to New York. A special gift awaited the twins that day.

The memoir that Zaieda had written for them. *'A Mother's Story: The Life of Zaieda Saddat.'* It was a comprehensive tome covering Zaieda's life from childhood to just before her passing. Among its many chapters were those that described: her decision to be a single parent; how she met their father; and the pivotal role that Radi and Elsie had in their lives.

She had two copies of the book professionally printed and bound in fine leather. The front covers had the title embossed in gold leaf lettering. The twins were overwhelmed with emotion on receiving their copy of the book.

Ahnan and Arizzia did not feel upset by what they found out that day. Or felt betrayed by the adults in the room with them. If anything, they realized that most of the people in their lives had worked tirelessly to provide them with a good life.

They were also relieved to get confirmation of their intuitive observations through the years. Receiving the answers to unspoken questions. The reason why Neva had treated them as not being equals. The identity of the foreign grandfatherly figure. And why he had maintained a distance between them.

One of things that stood out most to them was gaining a deeper understanding of the depth of Mora's love. Her love for them was unequivocal. Not tainted by pity or disapprobation. This realization was both powerful and consoling.

And finally being reunited with their birth mother, Zaieda, through her memoir and the memories shared that day. Bringing to light a part of themselves that they always knew existed. But did not know how to claim. The knowing of her made them feel whole. Because now, in addition to their parents, they had Zaieda. Their Umi. An angel to watch over them.

In the present, Neva composed her response.

Arizzia,

Book your flight, can't wait to see you... Love, Neva

CHAPTER 12

The next day, Neva felt happier than she had for a long time. She was looking forward to seeing Arizzia, thinking about how they would spend their time together. She sent an early text message to Matt asking him to open the gallery. There were errands that she wanted to do before coming to work.

When Neva arrived at the gallery, she went to Matt's office. She was eager to brief him on her conversation with Edith from the night before. Matt stared at Neva with total disbelief.

"Unbelievable. I always thought I was in the know about the doings around town, but I never heard anything about this. What astounds me is Nina wanting to manage the Avalon. And that you weren't made aware of any of this beforehand!"

Neva understood Matt's reaction. It was analogous to her own when she heard it from Edith.

"For some reason the boards wanted to keep their plans under wraps. We will know soon enough the full scope of their thinking." Neva said, still trying to come to terms with not being included in the initial planning.

"The Avalon and Leyden Museum that is some pairing, certain to raise eyebrows once the news gets out. I can understand the advantages for the museum: a partnership for mounting exhibitions; and additional revenue from a percentage of profits from our workshops and lectures. However, what is the equivalent advantage for the Avalon in the proposal." Matt said, still thinking through the proposed plan.

"That is a good point. Unfortunately I don't know that

either. But let's talk about you becoming the director. I can promise that you will have input in structuring the partnership."

"Honestly, I can't agree to it right now. There are too many unknown factors. But I'm pleased to be considered for the job."

"Your concerns are valid ones. As far as I know, which isn't much, there have been no final decisions made on anything. But I wanted to give you a heads up on the matter."

"And I appreciate that. But you should know that I have no interest in being a director if it entails having limited autonomy under a new organizational structure."

Neva nods her head.

"Believe me, I understand. And to be honest, I would have the same misgivings."

Matt brings up another concern.

"Neva, I don't know if this is the right time to discuss Josiah. I spoke to him last night. We have an appointment with him for next Wednesday. While I don't want to miss the opportunity to sign him, this might not be the best time to do it. Maybe we should postpone the meeting until we know more about our situation. What do you think?"

"Well, our meeting with him isn't until next week, which gives us time to learn more about the plan. It's out of the box now, so I can be aggressive about obtaining more detailed information. For now, let's not cancel the meeting. The partnership, notwithstanding, we are still a business. I will give Edith a call to get her thoughts on whom to contact to get the answers we need. Let's meet again today at 4:00 PM, if that works for you."

"Not a problem. I have a 2:00 meeting with the magazine staff at Leones, but I should be back by then.

"Great, we'll continue our discussion later."

Leaving Matt, Neva goes to her office, and reviews her schedule. She has a meeting with Sidney at the Leyden Museum at 1:00 PM. Was this meeting a coincidence? Or had Sidney intentionally scheduled it for this week. Either way, she intended to leave the meeting knowing more about the proposed partnership. Next, she calls Edith.

Edith answers the phone immediately.

"Good morning, Neva. How are you today?"

"I'm fine Edith, thank you again for a very provocative evening."

Edith chuckles mirthlessly.

"So how can I help you? You haven't changed your mind, have you?"

"No, not that. But I spoke with Matt this morning about the partnership, and he raised some important concerns. Do you have any suggestions for whom I should contact? Basically, to have an informal chat about this? Give me more pieces of the puzzle."

"Give Carter a call, he knows that I spoke with you about the plan. My role is very limited in this matter. I was asked to be a neutral broker so to speak, since I am not a member of either board. You may not believe it, but I am trying to be objective in all of this. I want what is best for all of us. Keep me in the loop."

"I will, take care."

Neva ends the call and swivels her chair to look out the window, thinking about what Edith just told her. She found it interesting that the boards had selected Edith to present the proposal to her and not Carter, the board chair for the Avalon.

Neva makes the call to Carter.

"Good morning, Neva, glad to hear from you. I know that Edith gave you a briefing on the partnership we are considering. She also told me that you have agreed to oversee the project. That's great news."

"My agreement is not definite yet. There is still so much that I don't know. I was hoping to meet with you to get a better understanding of it."

"I'm available this Friday, at 6:30 PM. Why don't you come to my office. We can have dinner here and I will try to answer any questions you may have."

"That works for me, I'll see you then." Neva smiles as she

ends the call, recalling Edith's remark about 'there are no free meals.'

Neva sends a text message to Mica to come to her office when she returns to the gallery. Mica was at a meeting with the staff of Arts At Large, a grassroots organization that operates art education programs in the area.

One of its main activities is an annual art competition for program participants. Mica not only serves as a judge, but also organizes a one day exhibit of winning artworks at the Avalon. It is a major perk of the competition.

Mica arrives back at the gallery just as Neva is on her way to the meeting with Sidney Lacardin. They step into the storage room.

"Neva, I'm so sorry to be late. The meeting ran over due to the number of entrants this year. We are elated about the increasing level of participation and quality of the work being submitted. I was thinking about pitching the idea of featuring the program in an upcoming issue of *Arts Mind*."

"Sounds good, the team is usually open to filler articles for each issue. Now, let me give you some good news, which was the purpose of our meeting. I am promoting you to the position of public relations manager. You have excelled at performing David's duties these past months. Think about it and we'll talk more when I get back."

"Neva, thank you. I would love the opportunity to do the job. I have so many ideas, this is great. Goodness, I can't wait to discuss them with you."

Mica practically runs into Matt's office. He is on the phone, but motions for her to come in. Matt barely ended his call before Mica blurts out her news.

"Matt, Neva just told me that I'm being promoted to Public Relations Manager. David was good, but I see the role so differently. In my opinion, there was so much more he could have done to better publicize what we do at the gallery."

"It is not without reason that Neva gave you some of his responsibilities when he left. She notices excellent work. And you're right, David was great for when she first got here, working with her to rehabilitate the image of the Avalon. This is a good move for you."

"Yes, it is." Mica responded, feeling slightly guilty about her last comment. Her intent had not been to disparage David's work at the gallery.

"By the way I might be taking on a new role as well. There are going to be a lot of changes at the gallery in the coming months."

"Like what? We are becoming more of an arts institution and will need more space for all the activities that we have going on now." Mica jokes.

"You're not too far off the mark in your assessment. But Neva will talk more about it with us. Okay, now on to something much more important. How was dinner last night with Jason? Did you two have fun?"

Mica groans. "It's a long story. We'll need lots of drinks to discuss it."

"Well, that sounds intriguing. I'll cook dinner for you on Friday and you can give me all the juicy details."

Mica laughs. "How can I refuse such an offer?"

"Okay back to work with you, we do have to earn our keep."

Neva arrived early for her appointment and is greeted by the front desk staff. One of them messages Sidney to inform him of Neva's arrival. He is with two of the curators in the great hall on the first floor.

Sidney strides across the floor to the front desk. He extends his hand to Neva. She grasps it in a firm handshake.

"Neva, I'm so glad to see you again and hopefully we'll be working together. You have done extraordinary work in Woodsburne for the arts."

"Thank you so much." Neva said, smiling at him. A little put off by his enthusiastic greeting.

"And I am pleased to perhaps be working with you, one of the superstars in the art world."

Sidney chuckles good naturedly at her compliment. "Well, enough flattery. I can see both of our heads getting inflated as we speak. Let's go to the conference room. I ordered lunch for us."

Before going to the elevator, they walk around the first floor as Sidney points out changes that he plans to make. He briefly mentions the annex buildings in the elevator, before they exited on the fourth floor. The administrative hub for the museum divided into two wings. Offices are located in the west wing, and meeting rooms are in the smaller east wing. Sidney leads the way to a meeting room at the end of the east corridor.

A walnut oval table and deep tufted upholstered chairs dominate the room. The back wall has a built-in screen for presentations. The food has been placed on a small serving cart that is plugged into an outlet near the door.

Sidney switches off the heating element on the cart before lifting the metal lids covering the plates. The aroma from the blackened grilled salmon, roasted red peppers over penne pasta in a white wine cream sauce wafts in the air, whetting their appetites. There are place mats laid out on the table, each one set with a linen napkin, silverware, water goblet and a chilled bottle of sparkling water. A small oval glass bowl filled with lime wedges is within easy reach. Sidney takes his seat after serving the meal.

"This pasta dish is delicious," Neva exclaims. She pours water into her glass and adds two lime wedges.

"Yes, it is a sample from the menu of the soon to open Fables Bistro. I have become a big fan of the restaurant. I find myself eating there at least twice a week. It was a 'no brainer' to reach out to the owners to discuss opening a smaller venue on the grounds of the museum. Luckily for us, Leon was interested in the opportunity for expansion."

Neva nods her head in agreement.

"That was a very astute move. Fables is regarded as an extension of the local arts community in the area."

They make small talk while enjoying their meal, exchanging bits of personal information about themselves. When they finished eating, Sidney gets up to place their plates on the cart.

Sidney eyes Neva as he settles back in his chair.

"I know that Mrs. Marjoram spoke to you about the proposed partnership with the Leyden. I am very interested to hear your thoughts about it."

"At this point, I have too many questions. I would prefer to hear from you, how you envision the partnership to work."

Sidney takes his time in responding. He does not want Neva to know that he is the chief architect behind the idea.

"Well in a nutshell, the museum is on life support. Our exhibits are outdated, we are losing members, attendance is low, our endowments cannot fully support us, and donor contributions are dwindling. Therefore, we are not well positioned to obtain capital resources in our current condition. However, on the plus side, we have an amazing space which is underutilized. When I learned about the range of classes offered at the Avalon, I thought that is what the museum should be doing. We should be the leader in learning programs, showcasing emerging artist, and utilizing technology to disseminate information about the rich art offerings in our region."

He smiles at Neva before continuing.

"Did you know that I visited your gallery several times since I've been here? I took care to disguise myself, not wanting to be easily recognized by your staff."

Neva looked genuinely surprised by his disclosure. But looking at him, she could see that it would not be difficult for him to disguise himself. He is tall and lanky, with longish dark curly hair, and at age fifty-two, still has his boyish good looks. He would easily blend in with their patrons.

"It was an opportunity for me to not only see the gallery, but to speak with your visitors about their reasons for coming there. I also had informal conversations with several staffers, one in particular: Mica Ramose."

Sidney is enthusiastic as he describes their conversations. Emphasizing, Mica's knowledge about the art on display and art appreciation in general.

"She is an excellent spokesperson for the gallery. After my visits, it became quite apparent that the Leyden is on the path to becoming an anachronism. While the Avalon is poised to be one of the most dynamic and influential art organizations in this part of the state."

Relishing the small victory of his undercover exploit, Sidney is somewhat patronizing as he articulates the merits of the proposal.

"The partnership will be advantageous to both institutions. Particularly for mounting joint exhibits, expanding the scope of the online magazine, increasing the number of classes offered, and collaborating to obtain funding for special exhibitions. In short, I want to bring to scale what you are providing at the Avalon but without the duplication of effort. Together, we can provide exciting cultural experiences for the community and visitors. I want Woodsburne to become known as a vibrant center for arts and culture by art devotees everywhere."

Neva is irked by Sidney's attitude. And her response is tinged with acerbity.

"Let me understand correctly, you want us to hand over exhibits, learning programs, and our online magazine to you. As well as to support your fundraising and community outreach activities. Basically, you are proposing to relegate the Avalon to solely being an art purveyor."

"That's a harsh summation." Sidney said, stung by Neva's barbed reply.

"When you put it like that it portrays us as seeking to take over your highly successful initiatives. The truth is the museum is in jeopardy of closing, and even the Art Society won't be able to save it. Frankly, we don't have the benefit of time to plan and launch new programs. Your activities have already been proven. The demand for them demonstrated.

I know that you have waiting lists for your seminars. Working with us can eliminate that problem. We have the space to accommodate additional sessions and to increase the categories of courses offered."

Sidney tries to restrain his annoyance at Neva's brashness. Her silence forces him to continue.

"And no, I am not suggesting that you don't have any activities, just to consider the broader reach of your educational services by collaborating with us. Also, we can provide permanent office space for the magazine. And assign dedicated staff to provide a more structured operation. And yes, I am very much aware of the subscription numbers, and how successful it is."

He pauses to take a sip pf water.

"But imagine the potential for other online publications. Believe me, our intention is not to marginalize the Avalon. But rather for the gallery to collaborate with us to better serve our constituencies."

Neva hears the thinly disguised irritation in his voice. She had swatted his pride.

"And what is your thinking on what my role will be in this partnership?" She is unsuccessful in modulating her tone of voice, still irritated by his earlier arrogance.

Sidney had not expected to have a confrontation with Neva, certainly not at this early stage in the process, if at all. He was prepared to match wits with a very savvy arts administrator and had looked forward to it.

But obviously this was a side of Neva that none of his backers had anticipated – the lioness protecting her turf. He could easily identify with Neva's position. An executive seeking an advantage in a business negotiation. Sensing that his reply could prematurely pull the plug on the proposed partnership, he carefully enunciates his thoughts.

"To be a neutral broker. You shouldn't be encumbered by your loyalty to either entity: the Avalon or Museum Annexes. Your role would be to look at the big picture and facilitate strategic decisions on which partner is best suited to implement new or established programs, or other undertakings."

Studying her face for any hint of antagonism, Sidney continues.

"Neva, let me be very clear here. We are not wholly reliant on the Avalon to save the museum. The Annex project and the new Contemporary Art exhibition are examples of some of the initiatives being undertaken to restore the museum's standing with its benefactors. We envision that a partnership with the Avalon will be a catalyst for accelerating that goal. Our objective is not to undermine the success of the gallery, but to enhance its achievements through a connection with us."

Neva had to give credit to Sidney. He came through with persuasive points for consideration. She understood now that the main purpose of the meeting was to jump start a working relationship between them.

"Please do not misconstrue my previous remarks as being hostile. That was not my intent. My objective was to better understand not only your standpoint on the partnership, but also your perspective on how we can all work together under this new business paradigm."

As he listened to her, Sidney suddenly realized that there was a serious misunderstanding.

"Neva, you do know that what we are talking about are the annex buildings?"

"What do you mean?" She asked confused.

"We're talking about a partnership for launching the Leyden Museum Annexes. The four newly renovated buildings that are located on the far side of the museum grounds. The programs and activities that we have been discussing will be housed in two of the buildings, not here in the museum. The name of each building will be associated with the activity to be sited there."

Sidney gives a concise overview.

"Leyden Museum Annex: Centre for Arts Education; Leyden

Museum Annex: Centre for Emerging Artists. And the third building: Fables Bistro at the Leyden Museum Annex. The overarching marketing theme is *'Feeding body, mind, and soul.'* With a catchphrase such as: *Eat at the Bistro. Participate in activities at the Annexes. Visit the Leyden Museum. Get inspired at the Leyden Museum and Annexes.* It's a little trite, but remember this is early days. The fourth building, which is the largest, is being considered as a venue for cultural events. Again, keep in mind that these are preliminary working ideas. It is all subject to change with input from our partners."

At first, Neva is flabbergasted, barely listening to him. Her thoughts focused on one critical question. Why had Edith neglected to mention such a crucial detail in their discusion last evening?

Looking at Neva, Sidney is convinced that she did not know about the Annexes.

"Believe me I know this plan may be a bit unorthodox. But the annex buildings are the perfect space to do everything we have been discussing. In terms of risks, this venture will be under the auspices of the museum. We have a unique opportunity to maximize our resources and talent. In the end, it will benefit both of our consumers and supporters."

Sidney paused, to give Neva time to absorb the new information. He also made a quick decision to put all his cards on the table.

"There is one last thing that you should be aware of. The end game for all of the proposed changes is the acquisition of the Marjoram Art Collection. Edith has decreed that the Leyden must demonstrate its revitalization within the next two years, or otherwise the collection will be going elsewhere."

Neva exhales a short breath, her posture becoming taut.

"Then let me be equally candid with you. If the impetus behind the proposal is to use my personal relationship with Edith to accomplish that outcome, you have made a grievous error. Believe me, this alliance is over before it has even begun."

Neva's sharp response unnerves him. Realizing too late how

poorly he had articulated both the need for the acquisition of the collection and Edith's financial support. He had allowed his enthusiasm to override discretion.

"I seem to be doing a very poor job of conveying my thoughts to you."

Modifying his approach, Sidney leans forward to stare directly into Neva's eyes. He knows that he is invading her personal space but is determined that she is unambiguous about his motivations in the context of her influence with Edith.

"Trust me, my intention is not about exploiting your personal relationship with Edith. I was merely voicing my personal aspiration for acquiring the collection for the museum. And to be honest, a big part of this effort is to convince Edith that we will not mismanage it. Please be clear on that point. This endeavor is not a nefarious plot of some kind. I swear to you in that regard."

Neva breaks away from his stare.

"I can understand your desire for the collection. I too have often thought about its disposition by her estate."

At that moment, Neva perceives Edith's ploy. How she had adroitly maneuvered the idea of the partnership to achieve her own objectives. Getting Neva to leave the Avalon, so that she will have a role in guiding the management of her collection by the museum. As these thoughts race through her mind, she is fighting hard to resist the urge to laugh. Thoroughly enjoying Edith's clever manipulation of circumstances. Deciding that for now, she will keep herself in the game.

Neva abruptly rises from her seat and stretches out her hand to Sidney.

"I look forward to working with you on the partnership. And that we begin the planning process immediately."

Sidney is mystified by her sudden change in attitude. He too stands, and shakes her hand.

"Yes, of course. I will also schedule a tour of the Annex buildings for you and pertinent staff from the Avalon."

"That would be great. I'll get back to you with dates and times for meetings."

Sidney walks with Neva to the elevator.

"I am very excited about this project and look forward to working with you. I'll be sure to keep my schedule flexible."

He stays with Neva until the elevator arrives and the doors close.

Sidney turns and walks to his office, replaying in his mind the last part of their conversation. Trying to pinpoint the moment when the tide turned in his favor.

Entering his office, he goes to stand in front of a large window overlooking the front entrance. He catches sight of Neva walking towards the parking lot. Sidney tents his fingers as he looks down at her. Yes, this partnership is going to be an interesting one.

Mica is escorting a customer to the door as Neva arrives back at the gallery. She steps aside so that the customer can exit before she enters. Mica tells her that the "Cosmos" sculpture by Lizzia Ossie had just been sold.

Lizzia Ossie is a renowned sculptor who signed with the Avalon last year. The gallery only exhibits her smaller bas-relief stone carved sculptures made from alabaster, soapstone, chlorite, or marble. The artist handles the sales of her large-scale works in limestone. Since her signing, collectors have been avidly acquiring the smaller pieces sold at the gallery.

"The buyer came from Canada to see the sculptures in person. I am going to miss the Cosmos."

Mica furtively glanced at Neva.

"I was secretly hoping he wouldn't buy it. Is that awful to admit? He's coming back on Friday to complete the purchases of the Sea Urchins, and Faces."

Neva too feels the loss of the Cosmos. It is a well-guarded secret that staff do get attached to artworks sold at their galleries.

"Honestly, I would need a warehouse to store all the artwork that attracted me over the years," she confided to Mica.

"Give me five minutes to get settled, then come to my office."

Entering her office, Neva puts down her bag and listens to her voicemail. She is in the middle of listening to a message from Sidney when Mica walks in.

Mica sits in front of Neva's desk. Admiring, as always, the décor of the office. Her mind drifts briefly to decorating ideas for David's office, when the time comes. She is sincere when she tells Neva how much she appreciates her promotion. That she will work hard to demonstrate that she was the right choice for the job.

"I am confident that you are a good fit for the role. However, what I want to discuss with you is the new direction being considered for the gallery. The board is supporting a plan to enter into a partnership with the newly established Leyden Museum Annexes."

Mica audibly gasps at this information, her eyes growing wide.

"I will be leaving the gallery to oversee the partnership. So, you can see how important your position will be during the transition and afterwards."

Mica involuntarily puts a hand to her throat as if her breathing has become constricted. All thoughts about office decorating vanishes from her mind.

"Wow, when I spoke with Matt earlier, he hinted at changes at the gallery. But Neva, it never entered my mind that you would be leaving. To be honest, I was so excited about the position because I wanted to work more closely with you. I don't know what to say now."

Neva gets up and moves around her desk to sit beside Mica.

"Believe me, it is going to be fine. We will be working closely together to coordinate public relations activities aimed at the public and other stakeholders."

Mica feels overwhelmed by the reshaping of a role that she hasn't even begun. Her earlier self-confidence waning as the reality of the new position becomes clearer to her.

"Do you really think that I'm the right person to do this job? I mean it is a lot larger in scope than promoting the gallery. The level of expectation may be more than I can deliver."

"Mica, if I did not think you could do this, I wouldn't be making the offer. You are selling yourself short. You have the skills required to do this. So yes, you are absolutely qualified to do this job." Neva firmly tells her.

Mica is filled with both apprehension and exhilaration. She begins to feel a bit giddy about her new job and its potential for her career. And decides immediately to confer with friends who have experience in working on public/ private partnerships. They will be invaluable in providing practical advice for tackling her new responsibilities.

"Neva, I am sincerely grateful for your confidence in me. Do you have any objections to me reaching out to colleagues that I know in the field? I'd like to get their thoughts on best practices for managing this type of initiative."

"No, that might be helpful. However, I am trusting you to be discreet in sharing information about the proposed plan. Nothing is finalized yet."

"Understood." Mica replies as she gets up from her seat.

"Don't leave yet, Matt is on the way to join us."

They move to the conference table. While they are waiting for Matt, Neva asks Mica about her dinner with Jason.

Mica dodges providing details, simply saying that they had a nice evening. Just then, Matt enters the office. Saving her from further conversation on the matter. He is eager to tell them about his meeting with the magazine staff.

"It's going to be our biggest issue yet," he proclaims enthusiastically. "Leading with an article on the Cellous group and their move to Woodsburne, and two in-depth profiles on Sidney and Lizzia Ossie."

Neva's interest is piqued by the article on the Cellous group. She asks Matt who did the interview.

"Kurt Marins, the executive director of Janus Arts. It turns out that Kurt is a friend of Celia and Reynard Louson, the founders of Cellous."

Mica asks if there is room for a filler article, pitching her idea for Arts at Large and the annual art exhibition.

Matt tells her that the November issue is full. But an article can be considered for the December publication.

Neva redirects their focus by summarizing her luncheon meeting with Sidney. Beginning with the clarification that the partnership is with the Leyden Museum Annexes. Informing them that they will be included on the planning team. Together they prepare a tentative schedule for planning meetings to send to Sidney.

"Matt, I want you to work with Natalie to review the emerging artist project and art education courses. And to reach out to some of the presenters to obtain their input on the proposed transfer, and opinions on any potential downside to the move. This information will help us to be better prepared in making recommendations."

"I can tell you right now that of the twelve seminars, five are proprietary, created by in-house staff; and four were developed jointly with the presenters. We act as co-host for the remaining three seminars, for which we receive a fee. The bigger question is whether to sell the proprietary seminars and transfer the rights to the Leyden; or retain them and negotiate fees for their usage. I suggest that we submit written recommendations on both options to the Board for their review. Then based on their input, make the final recommendations to the larger group. Do you agree?"

"Absolutely, you are right. That's an excellent point. Prepare a spreadsheet on attendance, costs, fees, earnings, etc., for the last three years."

Neva is reminded again that the transfer of educational programs is not simply a matter of a change in location. There are many other factors to be reviewed and considered.

"I have something to add along those lines. There are two workshops that I created for emerging artists which should be included in this assessment. They are highly regarded perks for exhibiting here. And although the emerging artists are not directly charged for attending the workshops, the costs are offset by the handling and sale transaction fee charged for the exhibition cycles. Additionally, the classes generate positive word of mouth for the gallery. These endorsements are value-add to overall associated cost. We should be able to determine a dollar value for the classes by using these and other metrics."

Matt looks over at Mica with approval. Those two workshops might have been overlooked by them.

"Consider it done," he tells her.

"We have a lot of work to do. Thank you for your ideas and input. I'm beginning to feel that this collaboration can be advantageous for us." Neva said. Appreciating the impact that the gallery has had on the local art community over the years.

Before the meeting ended, Matt asks Neva whether she was able to confirm that the gallery will be relocating to the Atrium building. She tells them no, but she is having dinner on Friday with Carter Reynolds and should learn more about it then.

Mica is surprised to hear about the move. Neva apologizes, telling her that the Board is also proposing to move the gallery to the Atrium.

"The Cellous Group has submitted an offer to purchase our building. Which coincidentally, provides a fortuitous opportunity for putting a positive spin on all the upcoming changes."

Mica nods in agreement. Thinking that it will also provide a blank slate for to begin her role as public relations manager.

Matt hangs back after the meeting to speak with Neva privately.

"Neva, based on what you just told us, it is even more critical for the gallery to have a strong leader to represent its interests."

"Matt, I agree with you, I do. And to be honest, it wasn't until my meeting today with Sidney that I accepted the new position in my head. You know that you are my first choice for leading the gallery. But the Board has the final say. In thinking about it, I can't see Nina wanting to work here. It doesn't make any sense. It's more likely that she is angling for a more senior position within the Partridge Foundation.

"I hope that you are right." Matt said, willing to concede the point for the time being.

"Time will tell. But I don't think that anyone is going to let a highly profitable business like this be mismanaged." But for the first time, Neva felt unsure about the future of the gallery.

On Friday, Neva arrived for her meeting with Carter Reynolds. A man who is both very ambitious and vain. He is medium height, with the beginnings of a paunch. A result of having too many expensive meals with clients and associates, and not enough exercise. He is aware that he must get serious about managing his weight before it becomes a problem. His image is a big part of his brand.

Lately, he has began to consider more benign options for managing his weight, other than dieting. One option was to follow the example of his wife. She moved the food around on her plate, like chess pieces. And ends up eating very little of it. But from its arrangement, she has created an illusion that most of meal has been consumed. He then realized that many of his meal companions also did something similar. They ate only half of the served meal. Unlike him, who devoured the entire serving.

For him, focusing on the food was preferable to paying attention to table discussions. The thought of having to be engaged, listening to others, almost made dieting the lesser evil. So when, in a follow up call, Neva suggested that they forego having dinner, he readily agreed. A dry run of experiencing active participation in a meeting.

"Let's get right into it shall we." Carter said brightly, after greeting Neva. They went to the seating area of his office. It has four club chairs and a coffe table, on which a tray with a carafe of water and glasses was set.

"The Avalon is one of the main hubs for culture in the city. Its exhibits and services have filled a void unmet by other institutions for several years. And although the Board has in the past, approved and supported the direction of the gallery, we are concerned by the outsized focus on its ancillary activities. That these activities are beginning to overshadow the primary business mandate. With the hiring of Sidney Lacardin, Avalon's Board agrees that the gallery should pull back from its art education programs. And redirect its attention to sales and artist services."

As she sat there listening to him, Neva was utterly stunned by the Board's justification for the proposed partnership. Throughout her tenure, the board had never questioned her management of the gallery. Recovering herself, she is barely able to restrain her anger.

"If the Board was so concerned about the operation of the gallery, why am I only learning about it now? Is that the reason why I was excluded from the discussions about the proposed partnership?" She wills herself to calm down, and stares stonily at Carter.

He squirms uncomfortably in his seat. It suddenly felt too small for his body. He knows that he can't afford to antagonize Neva. They need her to achieve their plans. He nervously clears his throat before speaking again.

"Okay, let me back up a little. First, we are thrilled with your work and the diversified activities that you have implemented at the gallery. You have provided the Board with numerous opportunities for boasting about it. And while it has been great to bask in our successes, unfortunately the unintended effect has been the diminution of the Leyden Museum. I'm sure that you are aware that in many circles, the Avalon is known as being much more than a gallery."

Carter pauses before continuing. Reminding himself to be cautious, as he articulates the underlying impetus behind the proposed plan.

"And frankly, we cannot allow that opinion to continue. The museum must remain the linchpin of Woodsburne's arts and cultural projects. Towards that end, a coalition of key stakeholders made some hard decisions to ensure this outcome. The first step was restructuring the museum board, which opened the way for hiring its new director. By the way, you were on the short list of candidates. But in the end, we went with Sidney."

Carter shifts in his seat, uncomfortable in this type of discussion. The need to be mindful of his words.

"I'm sure that you can understand why. He has a superb reputation in arts management, and many years of experience in leading world class museums. I am not ashamed to admit that we wanted his star power in leading the renaissance of the Leyden."

Neva calms down, but is still on guard.

"I totally understand and agree with a smart business decision. But with Sidney on board, why is there a need for a partnership between the Avalon and the Leyden? We, meaning you and I, could have arranged for the shifting of targeted activities to the Leyden, if the intent was to attract visitors and appease benefactors."

Carter smiles at her.

"You would be right if those were the only reasons. We need to have, let's say some leverage, to make sure that our 'star player' remains laser focused on meeting our expectations."

"So that's the plan? I am to be the designated watchdog over Sidney." Neva asks, her anger rising again. Noting that he has yet to explain the real purpose behind the changes and her proposed role.

Carter gazes thoughtfully at her, considering how to answer without alienating her support.

"Come on, you know that's not it. We need Sidney to keep his mind on the big prize, which is the acquisition of the Marjoram Art Collection. Recently, Edith has begun to express her desire to find a permanent home for it. And for us, the only appropriate place is the Leyden."

All at once the pieces came together for Neva.

"Are you saying that the real motive behind all these machinations is to obtain Edith's collection?"

Irked by Neva's bluntness, Carter responds sharply.

"Don't be so smug. You know Edith as well as any of us. She wants assurances that her collection will be expertly managed before even considering handing it over to the Leyden."

Carter pauses briefly, letting his last statement linger.

"While it may come across as a convoluted approach for achieving a goal, it's the best course of action to placate our backers. I'm sure that you know that it will not be an easy matter to overcome public perception of the Leyden. It is viewed as a vestige of the past, failing to maintain its relevance in today's art world."

Feeling more in control, he makes his last point.

"Even money will not be enough to save it, and I do not say that lightly. We must give both the supporters and visitors reasons to be excited about the Leyden. And quite frankly, the Marjoram Art Collection is exactly what is needed to make that happen. It is our golden ticket. People will come in droves to see it. So, can we count on your support?"

"Before I answer that, tell me why I was not included in the meetings regarding the Leyden."

Carter sighs and his shoulders droop slightly. He had been foolish to think that he could avoid answering that question.

"Because the talks centered on the acquisition of the Marjoram Collection. And the discussions were blunt, and not very flattering to Edith or her demands. We didn't want to put you in an uncomfortable position, given your closeness to her. Nor for you to feel pressured into using your influence to obtain her acquiescence."

His response leaves Neva speechless for a minute.

"Okay, so after the 'ol' boys' confab, why wasn't I still not included in subsequent meetings."

Carter exhales a sigh of annoyance, displeased with the direction of the conversation. He knew what she was doing. Cornering him with her questions.

"Sidney came up with the brilliant idea for repurposing the four unused buildings on the museum grounds. Turning them into activity centers. He dubbed them the Annexes. And provided a sound rational for relocating the educational programs and emerging artists exhibits from the Avalon into two of the buildings. Such a move would further support the ongoing efforts to revamp the image of the Leyden."

Sweat begins to bead on Carter's forehead, and Neva hands him a glass of water from the carafe on the table. He takes a few sips before resuming.

"Even though we agreed with his ideas about the Annexes, we didn't want him to take on another project that would compete for his attention. Running the risk of his bandwidth being stretched too thin."

"I still don't understand what my role is in this." Neva persisted in her questioning. Forcing him to be truthful and give her a full explanation of the plan.

Carter stares at her and realizes that his only recourse is to be honest.

"The truth is that we needed a proven administrator for the initial rollout and management of the Annexes. As well as someone whom Sidney would trust to discuss concerns that he wouldn't express to us. In essence, a means to an end. An adjunct who would provide not only support, but help Sidney to keep his eyes on the prize. And also of utmost importance, was that the job offer would neither appear to be an undervaluation or an underestimation of your considerable skills and talent. That was a key concern of ours."

"Enter Edith to feel me out on leaving the Avalon." Neva said, her earlier conclusions almost confirmed.

"It's not as cut and dried as that. There's no harm in telling you now that the suggestion for hiring you came from Edith. The idea was a game changer. All our plans fell into place. The perfect solution was right there in front of us." Carter reluctantly admitted.

"Listen Neva, I cannot stress enough the importance of your role. This is the only chance for the Leyden. We cannot miss the mark on this. Sidney has been working hard to bring in additional corporate support. He has gotten the Cellous group to fund a facelift for the front exterior of the museum and other improvements. Everyone has skin in the game so to speak. And while the partnership is writ small with the Avalon, it is primarily with you. There is no doubt that you are the best partner for Sidney to have at this time. Can we count on your support?"

"Yes, but with stipulations. First, I want Matt to replace me as the gallery's director. You can negotiate with Nina for another role elsewhere. But the Avalon is not the place for her. Second, I want wide latitude in my management of the Annexes and hiring of staff; and I will not report to what I dub the investor cohort. But to the Leyden Board and indirectly to Sidney. Third, now that we agree that this is not a partnership per se, I will consult with key staff from each organization on the activities to be provided at the Annexes. Lastly, my tenure will end in one year. As part of my exit plan, I will submit recommendations for its ongoing operation."

Carter smiles thoughtfully at her.

"We were thinking the same thing, regarding the lines of reporting. And this is a good time to let you know that I will be stepping down from my position on the Avalon Board. I will be the new Board President for the Leyden. My term begins in three months. It was important to me to be personally involved in the transition of services from our end."

Neva nods her head knowingly. A slight smile lifting the corners of her mouth.

"Why am I not surprised by your announcement. It will certainly make things easier. And congratulations on your appointment."

Carter smiles too. He felt sure that she had guessed it from the gist of their conversation. That he was moving on from the Avalon.

"Thank you, Neva. I sincerely mean it when I say that you are an extremely talented and astute executive. This is an excellent start for all of us. And rest assured that Matt is our choice as well. He has the experience and skills needed to lead the Avalon in its next phase of development. But we had to acknowledge Nina putting herself forward for consideration. To be fair, I think that Nina knew that even with her considerable skill sets, helming the Avalon was not in her wheelhouse."

"Well, I'm glad to hear that." Neva said, relieved that Matt's appointment would not be an issue. And feeling assured that her other requests would be approved. It was apparent that all parties involved were intent on making this undertaking a success.

"I will have James Noblesse, from the Leyden, contact you regarding the contract for employment and financial compensation. However, I'm not completely convinced about the timeframe for your tenure. Let's agree to include an option to extend if needed. There is something else that I would like you to mull over. The possibility of working with me after your contract ends. Just keep it in the back of your mind for a future discussion."

"I have no objections to the contract term." Neva agrees, not seeing any advantage for arguing the point. And chose to ignore the offer made by Carter. It was far too soon to even contemplate.

Carter escorts Neva to her car. She uses the walk to ask about the proposed relocation of the gallery.

"The purchase agreement will soon be signed. Apparently, the Cellous Group has gotten over any concerns about buying a location so tied to its previous occupant." Carter told her jovially. Overall pleased with the outcome of the meeting.

"Thanks for a most interesting evening." Neva tells him as they reach her car.

As he heads back to the building, Carter takes out his phone to call Ross Ebbers. The interim Board President for the museum.

"Hello Ross, I just finished meeting with Neva. She's on board. I'll be in touch with more details later."

Back in his office, Carter makes another call to John Markum, the general counsel for the Avalon, who is in London on a business trip.

CHAPTER 13

On the drive home, Neva sifts through all the information she learned. Taking great pleasure again at how Edith had so shrewdly maneuvered Carter and his cohorts. Getting them to unknowingly accede to all of her preconditions. She parks in the garage of her building and walks up the short stairway to the lobby door. Greg, one of the security guards, is sitting at a desk watching the security monitors. She waves to him on her way to the elevators.

After changing her clothes, Neva went downstairs to her office. She reads her emails including one from Mica. Reminding her about the last committee meeting that she will be attending tomorrow. It is for selecting the winners of this years's art competition. And is sorry about missing the opportunity to meet her sister.

Finishing with her mail, Neva writes a summary of her meeting with Carter. She makes sure to include brief comments next to her requirements. Also drafts a budget outline for staff and other administrative need. She makes a note to inquire about the work location. Her preference would be the fourth Annex building.

In thinking about the actions required for the museum to be on track to acquire the Marjoram Art Collection, Neva prepares another outline of a plan. This document will be for her personal use only. A progress assessment tool that can later be shared with Edith.

The thought of curating Edith's collection briefly crosses her mind. But in her heart, Neva knows that when the time comes,

Matt would be the best person for the job.

Her interests are elsewhere. She wants to establish a Folk Arts Gallery. It is a unmet arts niche in Woodsburne. The gallery will not have signed artists, instead it will be organized as a cooperative. Exhibiting the works of local and global folk artists selected by its members.

Neva owns two properties in the River Edge section of the city. A once thriving mercantile commerce district until the turn of the twentieth century. Now its shorelines are where tour boats dock during the months of April through December.

The Wharfs, as it is known by the locals, is a compact community of dozens of narrow interconnected streets, and tall arched alleyways. Its layout imbues a bazaar-like atmosphere to the rows of small shops.

Adjacent to the waterfront are eight large warehouses and six smaller ones. The larger buildings have been converted into residential lofts and studios, occupied by local artists and craftspeople.

Of the six small warehouses, she owns two. One of which has three floors, divided into multiple storage units. The units are rented by seasonal vendors to store their inventory. This is the building that Neva will use for her gallery.

As tiredness from a long day overcomes her, Neva goes upstairs to her bedroom. The itinerary for the next day runs through her mind before she sleeps.

- Drive to airport to pick up Arizzia at 9:00 AM.
- Drop off baggage at apartment before going to gallery.
- Lunch at Fables.
- Tour downtown Woodsburne and River District.
- Return to apartment to cook dinner or order takeout.

CHAPTER 14

After a long day at Arts At Large, Mica was glad to have a relaxing Saturday evening at home. She listens to her voicemail messages while reheating leftovers for her dinner.

The first one is from her friend Jolene Olmstead. Calling to confirm next weekend's get together to celebrate the promotion of their sorority sister and best friend, Haliah Barrows, to the rank of Detective Sergeant, in the Major Case Squad of the NYPD. Jolene also mentions that due to a family matter, she will not be able to join them.

Mica fondly thinks about how they all met in high school and remained friends ever since. All of them have successful careers, and are always ready to celebrate the achievements of each other.

For most of them, marriage and having children are in their future. And looking forward to the time when the group will be expanded to include spouses and children.

But for now, they will continue their tradition of taking annual group vacations. Last year's trip was to Thailand. Mica is sure that at some point during the upcoming weekend, they will begin to plan their next getaway.

She smiles at the memory of some of their past vacation jaunts. And thinks of suggestions for their next destination.

The last message was from her older sister Cecelia. Asking her to come to Boston the upcoming weekend to help with the planning for her wedding. Their mother had readily agreed to host the occasion.

Her fiancé was also happy to manage the photography studio

while she is away. Being delighted that she will begin working on their soon-to-be nuptials. She is looking forward to a break from her busy work schedule and being with everyone.

Mica immediately called Ceese back. Explaining that she already had plans for the same weekend with her friends in New York City.

Although disappointed, Ceese agreed to postpone her trip for two weeks. She knew how close Mica was with her friends. And that it would be unfair use the 'sister' card to guilt her into changing her plans. They spent an hour chatting, catching up each other on the latest in their lives. Mica was proud to share the news about her recent promotion.

After the call with her sister, Mica fondly remembers how she got her nickname. When they were kids and got into trouble over some mischief, the reprimand always began with *'cease and desist your tomfoolery!*' For Cecelia, the nickname of *Ceese* was adopted by family and friends. Fortunately for Mica, the pet name of *Desiss* did not stick.

CHAPTER 15

On her way home from the airport on Sunday, Neva stops at a favorite scenic overlook. She enjoys the quiet peacefulness of the area as other motorists seldom stop there. Reclining her seat to get comfortable, she replays the visit with her sister in her mind.

Arizzia had enjoyed the tour of the gallery. Matt was the perfect guide, expertly describing the exhibited artworks and providing background information about the artists. The conversation with him continued at lunch. He went with them to Fables. Afterwards, the two sisters visited several places of interest on their own.

At the end of their busy day, they decided to stay in for the night and order takeout from Fables. Arizzia had loved the resturant's menu choices. After dinner, they went to Neva's bedroom with a bottle of wine to have a sisterly chat.

Arizzia had confided to Neva details of her conflict with their brother Ahnan. Explaining that the cause of their disagreement were the casual clothes that she was so fond of wearing.

"He keeps insisting that I need to dress for my role as an executive whenever we are going to meet with potential donors. My usual counter argument is to point out that a medical degree; Dr Ph in Public Health; and field experience is all the dress code required. Our confrontations always ends with him saying that it is not about me, and to get over myself." Arizzia had fumed.

"This thing about image is particularly sensitive for me.

Several years ago, I was approached by an older woman, a senior executive of a major corporation, who advised me that an investment in my appearance would make my presentations more impactful. I was incensed by her judgement of me. It was a ludicrous thing to say. Totally missing the point for why we were meeting. Anyway, her company gave a boatload of money that year, fearful of backlash over her comments. A contribution that was made more to soothe any ruffled feelings, than for the genuine support of our initiatives. It still bothers me to this day."

Arizzia had taken a deep breath to calm herself.

"After that incident, I told Ahnan that I would no longer attend events that were aimed at making donors feel self-satisfied about giving. Going forward, I would only meet with practitioners who were interested in learning about our methodologies for developing processes adaptive to the health care needs and available resources in any given country. Or to meet with those parties who were eager to learn about our metrics for measuring success. The importance of creating infrastructures to ensure the continuation of services after we leave. For goodness sake, isn't that the point? The sharing of relevant information with donors and partners?"

Arizzia had laughed self-consciously at her tirade. And rather than responding, Neva had gone to her closet. Her sister had been puzzled.

When Neva returned, she was holding three suits on hangers and a pair of shoes.

"We're about the same size. Try on one of these suits."

Arizzia had needed no coaxing to change. When she turned around to look at herself in the mirror, she gasped.

"My gracious! The magic of clothes. Granted, the look is sophisticated and polished. But this is not really me. I don't feel like myself."

"Yes, you may look different, but you are still the same person. That was the point that Ahnan was trying to make about dressing for the audience. Think about it from that perspective." Neva said, as Arizzia looked dubiously in the mirror.

"Dressed in this outfit you are projecting an image of being a trustworthy administrator. One who is capable of effectively utilizing donor funding to provide described services. While you may personally believe that 'dressing up' is superficial, foolish even, it is a factor in connecting with certain audiences." Neva had told her unaffectedly.

"So, it's image and not competence that matters the most?" Arizzia had asked sarcastically.

Seeing the smirk on her face, Neva knew that the question wasn't being posed seriously. But decided to answer it in that manner anyway.

"I get your point that intelligence and competence should be valued more than image. That being said, time usually unmasks the practitioners of smoke and mirrors. And to answer to your question; image and competence should be the two sides of the same coin."

"Well said! Truth be told, I do understand Ahnan's viewpoint. And thank you for sharing your insights on the matter. But I must admit to enjoying being stubborn. Taking my time to come around." They had both giggled at a shared trait.

Looking at Arizzia's reflection in the mirror, Neva had observed how the meticulous cut of the suit had molded to her figure, like a bespoke garment. When she put on the shoes, she was striking. The clothing would work to accessorize her presentations. Helping to maintain audience attention on the message.

"Take them as my gift to you, Niza. Really, as a favor to me. Not to have them hanging unworn in my closet."

Neva had surprised herself in calling Arizzia by the childhood nickname used by her parents and brothers.

"Neva, I couldn't. They are brand new."

On seeing a price tag that was tucked into a slit pocket inside one of the jackets, she had exclaimed at its price.

"Oh, my goodness, a truckload of basic medical supplies

could be bought for what you paid for these outfits." She had looked at Neva with her mouth open.

"A truckload really, that's an exaggeration. Well then, think of it as a contribution to support your important work."

Neva had blushed at her sister's comment, the suits were expensive. But when she bought them on a trip last year to New York City, she had intended to have her seamstress make the needed alterations on her return home.

"You crazy woman, thank you so much. Ahnan will be over the moon when he sees my upgraded attire. Be prepared to get a very gushy phone call from him." Arizzia had said gleefully.

"Don't worry about packing them. I will have the outfits delivered to you. And I have some dress pants that you can take with you now, if you are interested."

"Oh my gosh, I would love that, thank you! Poor Ahnan, I can just imagine his face when he sees me on Tuesday, the last day of the conference. He might have a coronary. Not to mention my other colleagues. I'm going to have to rethink my position on wardrobe expenditures." Arizzia had said with wry amusement.

Neva also had in mind other unworn clothing pieces residing in her closet. Imagining Arizzia's surprise when the packages arrived. Another step toward becoming a better big sister.

Their conversation then segued into talking openly about their shared childhood experiences. Neva had been the first to speak. Trying to explain her feelings when Arizzia and Ahnan had come to live with them.

"I have never admitted this to anyone, holding it in all these years. But when Eduardo and I were told about your existence, I was terrified that we were being replaced by 'new children.' That for some reason our parents didn't want us anymore. As I got older, I became resentful of how seamlessly the both of you were assimilated into the family."

Although her admission made her feel ashamed, Neva continued.

"Then, in my late teens, when I discovered information

about your Umi, I was envious at what an accomplished and educated woman she had been. She was everything that I wanted our mother to be. What I hoped to be. But looking back, it is apparent that I did not embrace her core philosophy."

Arizzia followed, sharing her own thoughts about their childhood. She accurately captured what it must have been like for Neva and Eduardo, two young children caught in a complex situation. Both of them trying to understand their connection to siblings born outside of their parent's marriage. Without there being a set of rules to follow. Leaving the people involved to determine for themselves the manner of their response.

Sitting there, Neva comprehended for the first time the profound effect their mother had on the twins. Arizzia tearfully admitted that her love and devotion saved them from a lifetime of shame.

"Through her love, our mother empowered us to be our better selves and to manage with dignity all that life had dealt to us."

Neva learned more about their Umi and her family. However, there was one question that had nagged Neva since childhood, an unvoiced dread. As if reading her mind, Arizzia answered it. Telling her that their Umi had no desire to take their father away from his family. And had she lived, her intention was to build a life for the three of them in Chicago.

"We probably would have never known about the existence of each other if Umi had lived." Arizzia told her sadly, trying to fathom how differently their lives would have turned out.

She went on to speak candidly about the wealth that she and Ahnan had inherited. Their main inheritances came from their Umi and as the primary beneficiaries of the estates for Radi and Elsie. Explaining that the largest of the estates was that of Nana Elsie. She had been the sole beneficiary of her ex-husband's fortune. He had been a renowned cardiologist, whose patent holdings and other assets were worth hundreds of millions of dollars.

"We were so blessed by the people that Umi had placed in our lives. We felt compelled to use our wealth to help those less fortunate; to use it in a meaningful way. As she would have done. But we are not saints. Just two people who found their purpose in life." Arizzia had said earnestly, and then smiled at some private thought.

"And lastly, Grandpapa Abaan. He had wrestled for many years with the fact that we would be excluded from any direct inheritance from him. His solution was to form the Abillah LLC. Through this entity, he made it possible for us to discreetly have a share of his estate."

The irony of his action was not lost on Neva. From Abillah, they received what was denied to them at birth.

"Serendipity," Neva had said softly.

"Perhaps," Arizzia replied ruefully with a shrug.

"Abillah and our own personal financial contributions comprises almost half of the annual budget needed for our global healthcare initiatives."

For a moment, Arizzia had been quiet, stilled by some inner thoughts. Touching a pendant that hung from a fine gold chain necklace around her neck. It had belonged to her Umi.

"Grandpapa Abaan was a complicated man, who did the best he could given the circumstances of his life. He told us, when we were older, that he came to truly know his daughter after her death. Going through her personal possessions and reading her writings, both personal and academic. It showed that although her life was short, it was well-lived. He continued to pay the rent on the apartment until Radi died. It was a shrine to her. The place where she found love and happiness. By the time we inherited the building, Grandpapa Abaan was ready to let her rest in his memories. Leaving it to the next generation to accomplish what the previous one could not."

Arizzia had smiled lovingly at Neva and reached over to clasp her hand.

"We cannot go back in time to make fond childhood memories. But we can make new ones by growing closer together. And committing to seeing each other more often, not just on holidays or special occasions. Doing more of what we did this weekend – visiting each other at our homes. Seeing how we live our lives. And to grow closer by sharing our innermost thoughts and secrets. Next trip should be to my home in Chicago. You have yet to visit me there."

"Yes, I will come to Chicago next time. And it will be soon, I promise." Neva had replied tenderly. Holding tight to Arizzia's hand.

In looking back over her weekend, Neva was pleased with its outcome. She had finally confronted her shame about being envious of her two younger siblings. And had truthfully admitted her feelings of inferiority to them because of their Umi and her wealthy family.

And for the past several years, she had begun to feel humbled by the selfless ways in which they used their wealth to address humanitarian issues. Living their lives in alignment with their calling. Not contented with the mere act of charitable giving.

As she moved the seat into an upright position, a new thought crossed her mind. "What would she have done if she had their wealth?"

It troubled her that she could not readily answer the question. And she reflects on it during the drive home.

CHAPTER 16

On Monday, Neva met with Matt and Mica to brief them on her meeting with Carter. They ended it with a brief discussion about Josiah's upcoming visit to the gallery.

It was going to be a busy week for everyone. The first meeting of the 'Annex Workgroup' was scheduled for that afternoon. The purpose of these meetings had been revised. Now they would be working on a transition plan for the Annex project.

On Wednesday, Josiah arrived at the gallery earlier than his scheduled appointment. He wanted to tour the gallery on his own. A way for him to get a sense of the environment and see the staff at work.

He was not concerned about being immediately recognized. He had shaved off his beard and trimmed his hair. The transformation was dramatic. His face was more open, adding depth to his eyes.

Josiah was surprised to see the number of people browsing the gallery at that time in the morning. A striking young woman came over to him, introducing herself as Mica.

Mica did not recognize Josiah, and he adeptly avoided telling her his name. She asked him about his art preferences and led him around the gallery. Leaving him briefly to greet other customers who were obviously regulars. He observed how at ease they were with her, and the obvious respect in which she was held.

Josiah was studying Jason's latest paintings when Mica came back over to him. She found him to be different from the individuals who normally visited the gallery at that time of day.

"Ah, you found Jason Aria's paintings. Are you familiar with his work?" Mica asked, coming up behind him.

"Yes, I am," Josiah replied. He turned his head slightly to glance at her. "But these are quite different from his other paintings."

"You are right," Mica said affirmatively. "But it is expected that an artist will explore other styles to express their artistic vision. Wouldn't you agree?"

Josiah turned to look more closely at her.

"You appear to be knowledgeable about what drives artistic expression."

"It comes from being passionate about art and having the privilege to work at a great art gallery." Mica replied evenly, somewhat taken aback by his comment. The remark seemed to have an undertone of condescension.

Just then, Matt came over to them. He extends his hand to Josiah.

"I almost didn't recognize you. You shaved off your beard. I see you have already met Mica."

Mica looked from Matt to Josiah. Stunned by her failure to recognize him.

"I should have known. I'm so sorry that I did not recognize you right away." She said stammering, chagrined by her faux pas.

"We are very excited by the prospect of you joining us." Mica said, getting back her composure.

Matt smiles reassuringly at Mica. He knows that she is upset about not recognizing Josiah. Together they walk to the elevator. Neva is on the phone when they arrive at her office. She hangs up quickly and comes over to greet them. Matt makes the introductions.

Without preamble, Josiah describes his first impressions of the gallery. He makes sure to warmly thank Mica for her time and attention.

"We are pleased that you have come to such a favorable opinion," said Neva.

Studying Josiah, she is struck by the difference between his in-person appearance and the photo posted online. It was more than the shaving of his beard and trimmed hair, he was shorter than she expected. He was medium height, and had a lean muscled body. His full lips were sensual, making his narrow nose more prominent in his face. And his rich baritone voice gave depth to his spoken words.

However, she was drawn to his eyes. They were mesmerizing. They seem to peer into you, not just look at you. As if to dissuade you from being pretentious in your interaction with him. It was disconcerting. His magnetism was palpable. Yet, he seemed unaware of the effect that he had on people.

Mica quickly left, thankful that she did not have to stay for the meeting.

When they were seated at the conference table, Josiah continued to share his feedback.

"The staff is very observant of the artistic preferences of your clients. You have some remarkable artworks on exhibit. I only hope that my work will measure up to the quality currently featured at the Avalon."

Neva was gratified by his comments.

"You are being too modest. From what I have seen of your work, you will certainly hold your own here."

"Thank you, for your appreciation of my work," Josiah replied. He removes two thumb drives from his jacket pocket and gives one to each of them.

"A precis of my work and curriculum vitae," he explains.

"Thank you. As you know we are somewhat informed about your work. But we look forward to gaining more insight on your point of view from this meeting."

After Josiah finished speaking about his art and influences, Matt took the lead in describing the services provided to portfolio artists.

Neva followed up with a brief overview of the impending changes at the gallery, and her new role. And gave Josiah the opportunity to ask questions.

Afterwards, thinking the meeting to be over, Neva tells Josiah to get back to them with any additional questions, and hope that they will soon be working together.

But instead of standing up to leave, he remained seated.

"When I came here today, I was not fully prepared to sign with the Avalon. Even though my research showed that the gallery has an excellent reputation. But what has been most impressive to me is the environment that you have created for artists and patrons. I also appreciated your candor in letting me know about the forthcoming organizational changes. Lastly, the lack of a hard sell to sign with you. For these reasons, I believe that I will be in good hands here."

"We are so glad that you feel that way. We'll send the contract to your lawyer." Neva said. She is thrilled by his decision to sign with them.

"I'm not that complicated. Just send it directly to me."

They all stand and Neva walks with them to her office door.

"Not a problem. I will leave you in the capable hands of Matt."

Josiah bows slightly to Neva.

"Thank you, Neva. I am honored to be the last artist that you signed for the Avalon."

Neva is struck by the truth of his statement. He will be her last signing. At that moment, Neva felt emotional about leaving a job that she has loved.

CHAPTER 17

It was almost closing time. Matt and Mica were standing near the reception area discussing the dinner party he would be hosting later that evening. Mica was grousing about having to miss it. She was on her way to attend an event on behalf of the gallery.

Matt beams at her.

"I guess we will have to become accustomed to scheduling time to be with you."

"Yeah right." Mica said sourly. "Next week everything will return to normal, and I will be hounding you for invitations."

Just as Mica is leaving, Nina enters the gallery. They stop to briefly talk about Nina's unannounced visit.

"I think that's for the best," Mica said, ill at ease. She is worried that Nina's feelings have been hurt by her quick agreement. She had not bothered with going through the motions of trying to dissuade her from her decision.

To fill the awkward silence, Mica tells Nina about her promotion, who is relieved by the change in subject.

She had noticed Mica's discomfort. Being torn between her loyalty as a friend and to the Avalon. They made plans to meet for dinner the following week.

Nina takes her time walking up the stairs to Neva's office. It will be another awkward encounter. She knocks on the door before entering. Neva is baffled at seeing her.

"Oh, I didn't realize that you were coming here first. I thought that we were all going directly to Matt's house."

"Bit of a change of plan. I wanted to speak with you

beforehand. If Matt is still here, I'd like for him to join us." Nina tells her as she sits down.

"This sounds serious. What's up?" Neva asks, trying to discern a hint from Nina's demeanor.

Nina smiles coyly at her.

"I'd rather wait until Matt gets here."

Matt arrives, and is taken aback at seeing Nina. Neva had not mentioned that she was there in her text to him. Both were perplexed by her unexpected visit. Their faces reflecting the apprehension they were feeling.

"Don't look so concerned, it is good news." She squares her shoulders, before making her announcement.

"I wanted to tell you personally that I am no longer a candidate for the director position. I know that Matt is the frontrunner, and I am confident that the Avalon will continue to be successful under his leadership. Lastly, I hope that my actions have not caused a breach of trust between us."

She ends her short speech by telling Matt that he has her full support.

Matt and Neva struggle to repress any outward show of relief at the resolution of her candidacy. It also meant that any undercurrent of estrangement at dinner later was also eliminated. It will be a pleasant evening.

Neva is the first to speak, saying that she knows that Nina had only the best of intentions in seeking the job. Nina nods her head and apologizes for having caused a kerfuffle over what should have been a straightforward choice.

"No need for apologies, and rest assured that my trust in you has not been affected." Neva said, seeking to end any further conversation about the matter. It was neither the time nor place for having an in-depth conversation regarding her reasons for doing it. And her decision just cleared the path for Matt's appointment.

"I never took it personally, and same here regarding our relationship," adds Matt, failing to suppress his elation.

Nina's eyes glint with canny amusement at their reactions.

"You are both being way too kind," she said sardonically. The three of them laugh with relief.

She left the gallery soon after, relieved that they had not questioned her decision to withdraw. Or, for that matter, ask about her reasons for initially seeking the position.

Her purpose in doing it was to force Carter into including Neva and Matt in the discussions for the proposed changes at the gallery. It had infuriated her that Carter and the investors viewed Neva, Matt, even Edith, as set pieces to be moved around without any regard for their best interests.

Carter had been furious at her request to be considered for the job. He accused her of making the process more difficult. But Nina held firm, demanding that either she be given the job, or they be informed of the plans.

"Neva and Matt will bring more to the table than most of those already there. You are acting like a kid who thinks he can swim with the sharks." Nina had seethed in response.

Abashed by her retort, a compromise was reached. The plans would be discussed with Edith, and she would then have an informal discussion with Neva.

Nina had been incredulous when she learned that Edith had agreed to do it. Having expected that she too would have insisted that Neva, at the very least, be included. She went to see Edith to ask why she agreed.

"Because it is much better for them to underestimate us than to realize that we have the upper hand."

Nina had howled with laughter at Edith's reply. Her faith restored that things would work out as they should.

Matt was the first one to speak after Nina left.

"Saying how glad I am, doesn't even begin to cover it. But if I don't leave now, there won't be any food to eat for dinner." Inwardly, he was rejoicing. The job was his.

By the time everyone arrived, Matt had dinner ready. At the end of the relaxed meal, everyone helped to clear the table in the dining room.

Neva and Kathleen stayed in the kitchen with Matt, helping

to make coffee and plate the dessert. Nina offered to accompany Josiah to see Matt's art collection.

They were standing in front of a cubist painting. Josiah was telling her his point of view on art.

"For me, art is a complex form of expression through which an artist communicates with others. Regardless of the format, be it painting, sculpture, film, music, etc., that is the method selected to convey a unique creative perspective. A material depiction of a vision that is held in the artist's mind."

Nina followed up by asking how he would define a masterpiece. He bows his head slightly, contemplating his response. And does not immediately look up as he speaks.

"Let me begin with this. A masterpiece is essentially an agreement among a group of people that a common form as depicted by an artist, through their imagination, has touched their souls. Making them realize that there are forces that exists greater than themselves."

As Josiah continues with his explanation, Nina admires his eloquence. As he spoke, it occurred to her that the right people were in the right place for achieving the desired outcomes for the future of the arts in Woodsburne.

Neva leading the Annex project; Matt as the director of the Avalon; Edith's shrewd approach in managing her collection; and her own small part in making it all come together. Her thoughts were interrupted when Neva came to the doorway to tell them that coffee and dessert were ready to be served.

Nina was grateful for the interruption. Her mind needed a break. She was fatigued from the day's events. Wanting nothing more than to go for a drive to unwind before going home.

"None for me. Unfortunately, I have another commitment. It's been a privilege to have had this tête-à-tête with you Josiah. My best wishes for continued success here in Woodsburne."

With disappointment, Josiah thanks her for keeping his company. He had enjoyed their conversation. Hoping to continue it over dessert. He felt more at ease discussing art, than making small talk with people he hardly knew.

As he heads back to the kitchen, the two women stand watching his retreating back.

"He is something special."

Neva nods in agreement. "The Josiah Effect, it certainly is powerful."

"It's been a rough day. I need to leave and clear my head." Nina said tiredly.

"You know what, I'll leave with you. If you don't mind. We can stop for coffee or drinks on the way home. Of course, you know that we are missing out on a fabulous dessert."

"Then Fables it is, to make up for our lost." Nina said, her mood lifting.

"And give us the chance to exchange information on all the latest shenanigans at the Ivory Towers." Neva said mischievously.

They went to the kitchen to say their goodbyes. Matt looked questioningly at Neva. He will call her later to get the scoop on their early departure.

"Do you want us to leave also? You must be tired, working all day and coming home to prepare such a delicious meal." Kathleen said to Matt when he returned.

"No, this works out. It gives us a chance to catch up on Caitlyn and family." The couple smile at him, easing back into conversation.

"Are you also on Team Baby Girl?" Kathleen asks him.

Matt looks at them in surprise. "Cait is pregnant?"

"Oh, I'm so sorry. I thought you knew already. We did not intend to be the ones to tell you the news." Kathleen is effusive in her apologies.

"She just found out a few weeks ago. They are so happy." Kathleen explained further. Still chagrined about being the one to have told Matt.

"Please, don't feel bad at all. No apologies are needed. It's not your fault." Matt tells them sincerely.

It occurred to him that he hadn't spoken to Cait, since the

call about Josiah. He was doing a poor job of keeping in contact with his family. Just to avoid talking about his personal life. Too much was being lost because of his obstinacy. He made a mental note to call them over the weekend.

Not wanting Josiah and Kathleen to leave feeling upset about disclosing Cait's pregnancy, he takes them outside to the back yard. Discussing with them his quandary on a final design plan. In surveying the outdoor area, Josiah tells Matt about a landscape designer that he knows.

"We worked together on an estate garden project. I provided some ideas on the layout of botanicals to enhance the sculptures in the gardens. Frankly, my contribution was minimal. The man is a genius with outdoor spaces in my opinion. Your property would be especially appealing to him. You'll work well together, I think." Josiah said. He was relieved that the evening would end pleasantly.

Returning to the house, they take their leave. Thanking Matt once again for a lovely evening.

Standing in the kitchen afterwards, Matt enjoys the solitude of the moment. It had been an eventful day. The promotion will be an auspicious step in his career.

And he thinks again about his family. They are right. He needed to stop making excuses for ignoring his desire for happiness. For love. What is success without having someone to share it with? His heart was ready for love. But was patient in waiting for him to take the next step.

These last thoughts stayed in his mind as he turned off the lights in the house.

CHAPTER 18

The following week was a busy one at the gallery. With the signing of Josiah, Mica issued a press release about the newest artist at the Avalon. There was another planning meeting with Sidney and his staff, who were shocked by the intricacies for shifting programs and services to the Annexes.

Sidney admitted to Neva that he was grateful that she would be leading the project. It was much larger in scope than he had anticipated.

"I would have been drowning in all this if you weren't here." He had confided to her. Chastened by his underestimation of the task during his discussions with the boards. Grateful for being rescued from his hubris.

Neva also initiated her transition. Working closely with Matt to begin shifting her duties and responsibilities to him. He felt beleaguered several times during their meetings.

"How were you able to do all this by yourself, and for such a long time." Matt said, already feeling overwhelmed by the demands of the job. Marveling at how Neva was able to manage her workload. "No big secret, I did not have a life outside of work. It was my choice though, and I strongly advise you to not follow suit. In hindsight, the personal sacrifice is not worth it. But at the time, I didn't fully recognize its cost."

"I agree with you on that point; and already making notes to reallocate staff to keep up with this strenuous work schedule."

"That makes sense. But the good news is that with the reduced activities, you will have the time to explore new options for maintaining core customers and attracting new ones." Neva said. Glad that Matt will have the chance for a better balance between his personal life and work.

On Wednesday, at an editorial meeting, Matt obtained approval to include a profile on Josiah Summati in the upcoming November issue. The story on the Cellous Group moved to the December edition.

He also gave an overview of the collaboration with the Leyden Annexes. While there were many questions, out of their respect for Matt, the attendees did not press for more definitive answers. He promised that as soon as plans were finalized, they would be among the first to be informed. Ending the meeting with the announcement of the relocation of the gallery to the Atrium. Carter had called Neva to confirm the sale of the building.

By Friday, everyone at the gallery was glad to see the end of a hectic work week. Mica was leaving to go directly to the airport for the short trip to New York City. She would arrive in time to relax before meeting up with her friends. Matt had a meeting with the landscape designer, recommended by Josiah, later that evening.

When Matt opened the door to Quintin Mathers, he had only arrived home a few minutes earlier. He had little time to prepare for the consult, having left later than he intended. In darting around his study to gather various design drawings, he appeared to be muddled.

He was constantly stopping to apologize to Quintin for not being more prepared for their appointment. The drawings he reasoned would facilitate the conversation about his ideas. He hurriedly arranged several sketches on the draft table that he used as a desk.

Noticing Matt's agitation, Quintin took charge of the situation. He ordered Matt to stand still and take a deep breath. And walked behind him to gently knead his shoulders. He was the taller of the two, with an athletic build. And wore his shoulder length black hair tied above the nape of his neck. His chiseled face would be austere, if not for his friendly mien and good humor.

At first, Matt accepts the gesture, relaxing as the tension in his shoulder muscles eased. But in mid-discussion, he began to feel self-conscious. Reaching up to stop the massage, he feels a mild electric shock when their hands touched.

"Thank you, I'm good now. Do you give massages to all your clients?" Matt asks, trying to be nonchalant.

"No, only to the ditzy ones." Quintin jovially responds. He gives a brisk slap to Matt's shoulders before coming around to stand beside him.

Unsure of how to respond, Matt leads the way to the backyard. Quintin grabs a sketch pad from his bag, and leaves Matt standing by the patio doors.

Matt found it pleasing that Quintin was drawing on paper. It seemed more personalized. Watching Quintin as he pace the grounds; losing sight of him when he walks along the side yards.

After his second walkaround, Quintin appeared to be talking to himself. So engrossed in his thoughts. Overtaken by curiosity, Matt strolled over to him.

"So, what do you think? Can you design the space that I want?" As soon as he said it, Matt felt foolish for asking such an insipid question.

Quintin stops short to glance at Matt.

"Ah yes, I have some ideas. But I'd prefer to prepare a project proposal before I discuss it with you."

"Of course, not a problem." Matt said haltingly, feeling flummoxed by his reaction to Quintin.

"There is one thing I can share with you though. A fire element will tie the outdoor spaces together."

"I agree with you on that." Matt said, still feeling out of sorts.

"Okay then, I'll contact you as soon as I complete the plan."

Matt turned to walk back to the house, assuming that Quintin was following behind. He asked a question and when there was no reply, turned his head. Quintin was still standing where he left him.

He sat at the kitchen island to wait for him. When Quintin finally came in, he smiled at Matt.

"Sorry, I just needed to take in some last impressions. I like how the diffusion of interior lights harmonizes with the starlight in the night sky."

"Huh, I never thought about it in that way," Matt replied.

Finding it hard to express his thoughts, he offers Quintin a cup of coffee or a drink.

"No thank you, its late. I need to get going."

They walk to the front door and shake hands. This time it is apparent that both of them felt a connection.

Matt was never so glad to see a guest leave his home. He leaned against the back of the front door, feeling out of breath as if he just finished a vigorous workout. It confuses him, as he tries to figure out what just happened. For a split second, he is terrified that he is experiencing a heart attack. But rationally dismisses the thought.

What he didn't know was that Quintin was also sitting in his truck experiencing a similar reaction. Both men having experienced the kinetic attraction between them.

Quintin called Matt early the next morning. Asking to come over to see the property in daylight.

"I guess I left my head in the stars yesterday evening. I apologize for the short notice. If it is inconvenient today, we can schedule an appointment for next week."

Matt tells him that he is leaving to go to the gallery, but will leave the side gate unlocked for him.

Neva arrived at the gallery shortly before Matt. They had agreed to meet before she went to the airport for an overnight trip to Syracuse. She will be accompanying Jason and Nina to an arts event that evening.

After reviewing Matt's plan for the relocation of the gallery, and preliminary exhibits schedule; it was evident that vacant positions needed to be promptly backfilled.

They sent an email to Mica asking her to prepare a work plan for the next three months. And were surprised to get a call back from her.

The call became a lively brainstorming session on ideas for publicizing the relocation to the Atrium; the holiday sales events, special sales of selected inventory before the move; and laying the groundwork for the announcement of the collaboration with the Leyden Annexes. And lastly, how to capitalize on Matt's promotion and Neva's new job.

Neva's last words to Mica were to enjoy herself for the rest of the weekend. Ignoring that friendly suggestion, Mica continued to work on the plan that she had been preparing prior to the call with them.

Last night, the group had decided that Saturday morning and afternoon would be free time. Most of the women wanted to spend the time shopping. Giving Mica time to work on job related tasks.

And her host, Haliah Vilamieux, Hal, as she was known to friends, was using the time to do errands not done during the week.

Mica completed the revised copy which included many of the ideas they had just discussed, and sent them the document. Pleased that a big item on her 'to do' list was completed.

Sitting there, she hoped that her friend Jess would be able to meet with her on Sunday. She did not want to extend her trip thru Monday. Jess had years of public relations experience. And could provide prudent advice on the different approaches for doing her job.

Since the offer of promotion, Mica had begun to feel more confident about her new role. Even seeing a future beyond it. Becoming a director of an arts non-profit organization within the next three years.

Mica was sending a text message to Jess to confirm their meeting on Sunday, when Hal returned to the apartment.

They took their time getting ready for the evening. Enjoying the lighthearted sharing of confidences. Things that they weren't ready to tell the other women in the group.

CHAPTER 19

On Saturday evening, when Matt returned home, Quintin was sitting in the backyard.

"Jeez, you're still here! I thought that you would have left already." Matt said, pleased to see him.

"My truck parked outside didn't give you a clue to my presence?" Quintin replied teasingly.

"Oh, you got me there, big guy." Matt said, with a wide goofy grin. Not at all embarassed by having overlooked the obvious.

"Anyway, thanks for giving me access to the property. I've rechecked measurements and finalized my drawings. It was so relaxing to work here that I lost track of the time."

"Actually, I think it should be me thanking you for giving up your day to come over here. I didn't expect to hear from you so soon, but I am glad that you called."

"No worries. If you have time now, I can go over my plan with you. And if you do decide to hire me for the project, I will be able to begin immediately." Quintin said, looking expectantly at Matt.

"Absolutely, I'd love to hear your ideas." Matt quickly responded.

They walked around the backyard as Quintin gave his presentation, pointing out features from paper drawings. As they walk the property, Matt could visualize the layout of the outdoor space. Quintin had understood what he wanted.

On their return to the patio table, Matt requested some minor changes to the plan. He sat back in his chair and admired the approaching dusk as it settled around the landscape. Pleased that his final home project will soon be completed.

"I noticed that you sketch your ideas on paper. That's a bit old school. But I can totally appreciate your reason for doing it." Matt said, looking at the drawings spread across the table.

"Well depending on the job, I like to sketch preliminary design ideas on paper. But have no fear, my good man. For I also use the wizardry of technology in doing my work. Very observant of you, Sherlock."

Matt could not suppress his laughter at Quintin's jocular reply. He enjoys his quick wit and invites him to stay for dinner.

While Matt prepares a meal of asparagus, mashed red potatoes, and pan seared ribeye steak; Quintin opens a bottle of wine. He pours a generous glass for each of them.

"How did you come to live in this part of the state." Matt asks as he cooks the meal.

"I'm originally from New Mexico. I was a partner in a landscape architecture business there. We were very successful and had high profit margins. Then a large company made an offer to merge with us. At the time, it seemed to be a good business decision. But after a year, I was restless. I missed being at jobsites. Working in an office wasn't for me. So, I took a severance package and started my own business. My former partner, Gerald Albrecht, often sent jobs my way. The smaller projects that the company were not interested in doing."

"Okay, that still doesn't answer how you came to be in New York," queried Matt. He was eager to learn more about Quintin.

Quintin takes his time with his story. He snags a couple of roasted grape tomatoes from a small skillet pan that Matt had taken out of the oven, and pops them into his mouth; savoring their sweetly acidic taste.

"Don't be impatient, I'm getting to that. But first I had to give you the back story."

"Of course, excuse my interruption of your saga." Matt said with a chuckle.

Licking salt and olive oil from his thumb and forefinger, Quintin continues.

"Then, I received a referral for a job in Canandaigua to landscape the grounds of a renovated boutique hotel. I loved that job. From that project, I received more bids for work in the Finger Lakes region. Which lead to a job in Buffalo, to work with a team restoring the gardens and exteriors of three landmark grand estates."

Quintin pauses to take a sip of wine.

"Buffalo is where I met Josiah, while working on one of the estate projects. Then, we both got invited to some swanky party. We were like the 'nerds,' and neither of us could figure out how we got on the guest list. Let me rephrase that. It was more me, not being able to figure out how I got an invite. Anyway, we clicked and became friends. Eventually I moved to West Seneca. It was a good location for traveling to different project sites in the region. And that is the very abridged version of how I came to live in upstate New York."

"Interesting story, and lucky for me that you stayed here," Matt said. Immediately blushing at his comment.

"For me too. But it was hard adapting to the winter weather here. I'm not going to lie. It was difficult in the beginning, getting adjusted to the change in climate. It was so different from the winters I had known. There were quite a few times that I thought about moving back to the southwest." Quintin said, recalling those early winter experiences.

"Do you miss being with your partner, uh Gerald?" Matt asked, more anxious than he realized about wanting to know Quintin's status.

"You mean Jerry? Oh no, he is very happy living in New Mexico with his wife and three kids. The merger was the best thing for him and his young family. He was ready to settle into an upper management position."

"Oh! So you are here on your own?" Matt asked him. Beads of perspiration on his forehead.

"Yes, I am. Free as a bird." Quintin replied laughing.

Matt looked like he was about to faint. Quintin goes over to him.

"Are you okay there. You look wobbly all of a sudden."

"It's nothing. Just feeling a little lightheaded. The smell of the food, I hadn't eaten much all day." Matt said breathlessly. The singular thought that Quintin was unattached reverberating in his mind.

"Aaah, the wine got to you; drinking on an empty stomach."

Quintin picks up a piece of steak with his fingers and feeds it to Matt. He almost choked on it, spitting it out into his hand. It felt like fire in his mouth. Not from the temperature of the meat but from the touch of Quintin's fingers on his tongue.

"Some water would be best I think." Matt said, as he quickly moved over to the sink, filling a glass with water from the faucet. He barely sipped the cool liquid.

"What's wrong Matt? Did I say something to upset you?" Quintin asks anxiously.

"No, no, I'm fine now. Just a little hyperventilation. I think the steaks may have been overcooked." Matt said, still feeling a little shaky.

Quinton throws back his head and laughs heartily.

"What a drama queen!"

Matt bristles at the comment at first, but then joins in the laughter. "I guess so. You're right."

"The food smells great and I'm starving. I only had a handful of nuts all day." Quintin said mischievously.

"You really can't help yourself." Matt said, chuckling.

They decided to eat in the kitchen, preferring its informality.

"Best meal I ever ate, and superbly prepared in under an hour. Cheers to the chef." Quintin said, raising his glass in salute.

Matt gets up to clear the plates and Quintin helps him. They work in tandem. One loads the dishwasher, while the other cleans the stove top and wipes down the counters.

With the clean-up completed, Matt goes to the wet bar for a bottle of Scotch and glasses.

Eying the bottle, Quintin nods his head in appreciation at the single malt.

"Very nice, Glenfiddich 18 Year Old. You have any music to go with it?"

"Do I have music you ask? Follow me my good man and I'll show you." Matt said playfully. He tugs at Quintin's sleeve while juggling the glasses and Scotch bottle in his other hand.

They go up a wide three step stairway to the entrance of Matt's sweeping music room/library. There are built-in cabinets along the length of three walls. Books are stored in the open-face cabinets of two walls. The third wall of cabinets houses compact disks, LPs, and a music system.

A baby grand piano dominates the right side of the room. The wall housing the recorded music and audio system its backdrop. The natural light in the room comes from two large, tall windows that provide a panoramic view of the back of the house.

Quintin lets out a long low whistle.

"Big Papa got swag."

He saunters over to the piano and plays random chords. It is well tuned. Quintin sits down and begins to play.

Matt sets the glasses and Scotch on the top of the instrument, violating his own rule of not placing anything with liquid on its closed surface. He pours them each a drink, sipping from his as he watches Quintin play.

Looking up, Quintin pats the seat beside him, and Matt sits down. They begin to play show tunes. Each trying to outplay the other, until Matt calls for a truce.

They move from the piano to sit in leather club chairs grouped around an oval marble and brass coffee table in the center of the room.

"This is a beautiful room Matt." Quintin said, admiring his surroundings.

"Oh right. You haven't really seen the house." Matt leaps up and beckons Quintin to follow. Taking him on a tour.

Quintin is fascinated by the attic and the things that Matt

has stored there. Several photo albums are stacked on a table in the middle of the room. He takes a seat on a trunk and flips through the album on top. It contains photographs of Matt and Caitlyn.

"Beautiful girl, who is she?" Quintin asks quizzically. Matt looks over his shoulder, suddenly feeling his stomach tightening.

"A very dear friend of mine," Matt replies simply.

Hoping to end further inquiry, he reaches over to retrieve the album. Dreading having to explain about Cait. With memories of the fight with Titus resurfacing in his mind.

"I can see that from the pictures. Is she the woman that got away and stole your heart?" Quintin asks. He notices that his question is upsetting to Matt.

Matt lets out a deep sigh and sits down on the floor. He draws up his knees and hugs them to his chest. The time had come for him to explain his past and his difficulty with self-acceptance. A divide which had to be crossed in order to finally free himself to finding love.

The conversation continued as they returned to the more comfortable music room. They spoke unreservedly about their innermost selves until the early hours of the next morning.

The soft light of dawn was filtering into the room, when they finally fell asleep. Lying on the floor, bottles of Scotch between them. In the background, a Cole Porter song was playing on repeat through the speakers.

CHAPTER 20

Although she was having a good time, Mica decided to leave the club before her friends on Saturday night. She found it hard to admit that she no longer had the stamina for back-to-back nights of partying. No, that wasn't true she corrected herself. It no longer held the attraction it once had for her. Also, her mind kept drifting to ideas for her new job.

She didn't want to spoil their fun by constantly writing notes on her phone. This was supposed to be their weekend. But she wanted to be prepared for her dinner meeting with Jess on Sunday evening. Promising herself to be more attentive at brunch the next day. It was going to be a busy one for her. Brunch in the morning, dinner that evening, and then off to the airport for the return trip home.

As she sat there, on impulse, Mica ordered gift baskets of spa items for each of her friends. She did it more as a gesture of love; to show that she did not take them for granted, than as an apology for her current distraction. The gifts were scheduled for delivery on their return home.

Before leaving the club, Mica went around the table and hugged each of her friends. She was hardly out of the door before they began to scheme about bombarding her phone with meme messages. Giggling as they planned their prank.

"What, we're back in high school now. Pulling silly stunts." Hal said with amusement. She knew that Mica would not find it funny for long. Anticipating a group text message from her begging them to stop.

Ignoring Hal, they eagerly searched their favorite sites for memes.

"Oh, come on. We don't have much time left to act silly. Sandy is getting married in two months. Most of us will soon follow. Then, just like that, we are catapulted into the stratosphere of maturity and sensibleness. The mantle of our youth folded away forever." Juliana told them dramatically. Her assertions sparked jovial banter among the women. Enlivening the conviviality of the gathering.

When Mica did not immediately text back, everyone was surprised. Rianne dryly noted that she was doing the mature thing by ignoring them. With their concern brushed aside, they resumed enjoying their last night out in the city.

But Mica's departure did not go unnoticed. He had seen her with her friends. Something about her had caught his eye. She would be his next kill. For some reason she had separated from her group, no longer protected by a herd. When she left, he followed her outside and stood in the shadows of the building.

As a predator, he locked onto the movements of his target. Ready to seize the first opportunity to get near his prey.

Mica, exasperated with the wait times for car service from her two ride app accounts, was about to download another one. When she spotted a taxicab coming down the street.

She sprinted to the curb to hail it. As the vehicle stopped, he moved in quickly. Asking to share the ride with her.

"This is a dead zone for getting ride service. Wherever you are headed works for me. It will get me out of the area."

He was tall and muscular with cropped sandy brown hair. His dark eyes held no hint of warmth, his face attractive but unreadable. She remembered seeing him in the club, next to the bar, surveying the crowd. Mica hoped that he didn't think of her as a mercy pick-up. But his smile disarmed her, and she agreed.

They chit-chatted as they sat in the back seat. The polite exchange between two strangers in a chance encounter. However, on reaching Mica's address, he casually told her that he would also get out. To show that she wasn't interested in being with him, Mica paid the full fare.

He put up his hands in a gesture of surrender. Telling her to relax, he got the message. Putting one hand to his chest, he swore that his sole intention was to make sure that she got safely to her door. A way of thanking her for letting him share the ride. His own destination was only four blocks away. He will walk the rest of the way.

A departing pizza deliveryman held the door open for them to enter the building. Mica was still fumbling in her small purse for the house keys, having admitted during the cab ride that she was not sure whether she had them.

He followed her inside, riding with her in the small elevator. She repeatedly told him that she was fine and thanked him firmly, but politely, for his concern.

Something about his demeanor disturbed her, but Mica pushed it aside not wanting to offend him. Her mind more occupied with her aching feet. Desperate to get rid of him so she could finally take off her shoes.

It was so innocent the way they walked to Haliah's apartment. She opened the door, her hand on the doorknob, ready to tell him goodbye. From the look on his face, she knew instantly that she was in danger. But it was too late.

After pushing her into the apartment, he thought that she could be quickly subdued. It was the first time that he had social contact with a victim. He wanted to increase the challenge of his practice kills. Bored with his usual methods of random abduction and killing in a transient lair.

He swiftly realized that he had misjudged Mica's self-control. She maintained her composure and made a valiant effort to defend herself. For a few minutes, he was amused and toyed with her.

He knew that the door was not completely closed. Somehow, she had managed to wedge a shoe into the doorway. He calculated that there would be sufficient time to lock down the apartment once she was under his control.

His full attention snapped back when she cut his face with

a shard from a broken decorative bowl. The surprise of her attack made him flinch. He drew back his fist and punched her hard on the side of the head. Momentarily dazed, she managed to grab hold of his quilted vest to keep from falling backwards onto a toppled chair.

The move put him off-balance. She stumbled sideways as he fell forward, striking his chest forcefully on the legs of the upturned chair. Shoving the chair aside, he sprung up determined to punish her for his humiliation. His fury overtaking his usual tactical discipline. The attack became personal.

Mica was trying to run toward the slightly ajar door when he grabbed her roughly from behind. He firmly clamped his hand over her mouth, dragging her backwards, forcefully restraining her movements.

He slammed her onto the living room floor. The force of his thrust knocked the breath out of her. He pressed his foot heavily in the middle of her chest to not only keep her immobilized, but for the broken shards on the floor to be dug deeply into the flesh of her back. The pain was excruciating.

Looking up, Mica saw him remove his wig and stuff it inside his vest. She saw now that he was bald, and his facial features changed as he removed some of his prosthetic makeup. He would look like a completely different person when he exited the building.

In the club and later outside, she had not paid much attention to his clothing. It was military styled, and the fabric was expensive, custom made clothing. The footwear was above the ankle boots. And the black boot pressing down on her felt weighted.

While he was reaching into a pocket on his pants leg, she heard someone passing in the outside hallway. She yelled for help, but he swiftly stuffed a cloth deep into her mouth. Taking hold of her left ankle, he violently twisted it, breaking the bone. The pain was agonizing, and she realized that he intended to sadistically kill her. Every part of her body was throbbing with pain.

He knew that he was taking too much time. But felt compelled to prove his complete dominance over her. Unable to stop himself from boasting about his previous kills. Determined to make her torment both physical and mental. The sacrificial lamb, made to bear witness to his confession about the multitude of lives snuffed out by him.

Mica was transfixed by the scope of his horrific acts. She fought now, not for her physical survival but for her sanity. Regretful that a momentary lapse in judgement had resulted in the defilement of Hal's home. It was her fault.

As soon as that thought arose, it was dispelled by a sense of knowing that she was not to blame. Making her more resolute in protecting her soul from the monster who was destroying her body.

He made a show of putting on a fingerless glove onto his right hand. It had a row of steel inserts across the knuckle line. A more refined version of a brass knuckles weapon.

Looking down at her face, he expected it to be contorted in terror. Instead, he saw calmness in her eyes. He was fractionally puzzled, the usual surge of adrenaline was lessened. Nevertheless, he whispered, "It's time to send you on your final trip."

His voice is raspy, thick with anticipation of the kill. He steadies his breathing by mentally reviewing the methodical cleanup of the site. And positions her head for the lethal blows.

Hal began to be concerned about Mica. She hadn't messaged anyone. It was so unlike her to ignore them for this long. Almost an hour since she left. Her instincts were telling her that something was terribly wrong. Particularly, if Mica had forgotten the house keys, she would have definitely called or texted her by now.

This sudden change in Mica's behaviour prompted Hal to take action. But she didn't want to let on about her concerns. She had to remain outwardly calm. And casually told the group about her decision to go to her apartment.

"Clearly, Mica is locked out and being too stubborn to let us know."

The others asked if they should come along. But she told them to stay, in case Mica was on her way back to the club. Either way, she would keep in contact with them.

A neighbor on the way to a parking space had seen them entering the building. He lived on the same floor as Hal, and had to pass her apartment to get to his own. After parking his car, he made a quick stop at a deli to buy bread and coffee for his breakfast.

On passing Hal's apartment, he heard sounds of a commotion. He was not sure what was happening inside, and moved on to his own apartment. It was not a matter for him to personally deal with.

At first, he was only going to call Sonny, the building super, to report his concerns. But then, he decided to also call Hal. He felt it was the right thing to do. It was seeing her friend bringing a man home with her which caught his attention. It seemed to be out of character. Not something to do as a guest staying in your friend's house. In any case, he would let Hal know about it. She was a good neighbor to him.

When Hal saw the name of the caller, she was already sitting in a car, the driver speeding to her address. Mr. Norsebrook told her about seeing Mica with a young man, and the noises that he heard coming from the apartment.

"It sounded like some sort of disturbance. The door wasn't fully closed. But I didn't knock. I thought it best to let you and Sonny handle the matter," he dutifully informed her.

Hal tried to keep the apprehension she was feeling out of her voice.

"I appreciate you calling me Mr. Norsebrook. I'll take care of it. And thank you again for your concern."

With her suspicions confirmed, she called Timothy Manneh a colleague and friend in her division. He lived less than two blocks from her building. She told him bluntly that an assault was in progress at her apartment.

Timothy knew that Hal was getting together with friends over the weekend, and that Mica was staying with her. She gave him as much information as she had, which was little.

Next Hal called for police backup. Her last call was to Sonny, the building super. Telling him that she was on the way, but that Timothy would get there before her. He should be on the lookout for him.

Sonny was anxious about whatever the trouble was upstairs. None of the other tenants had complained about a disturbance or loud noises. He was pacing the entrance hall when Timothy arrived at the door. He assured Sonny not to worry, as they walked to the waiting elevator.

With his gun drawn, Timothy slid against the wall leading to the apartment door. At the doorway, he could hear faint noises coming from the interior. He kicked open the door.

"Police! Freeze! Stand! Hands behind your head, fingers interlocked! Walk slowly to me!" he shouted.

He had been poised to deliver the fatal blows to Mica's face and skull. The sudden intrusion perplexed him. How could the police have known to come there? Who was this woman?

He released his tight grip from around Mica's throat. In two rapid moves he slid a knife from the inside of his boot and scooped up a handful of broken fragments from the floor. It would give him a strategic advantage, forcing his opponent to be on the defensive. He arose into a combat position.

He flung the shards as airborne projectiles into the face of the man confronting him. Timothy was forced to dodge the hurled objects, giving his adversary the opening to land a vicious sidekick to his forearm. Knocking his gun from his hand.

The attacker rapidly advanced towards him, with slashing knife movements. He sustained gashes to his upper arm as he tried to recover his gun. They fought for possession of the knife.

Timothy managed to push him backwards with a hard knee thrust to his abdomen. Forcing the assailant to release his hold on the knife. As Timothy moved to retrieve his gun, the assailant kicked his legs out from under him. He landed hard on his back.

In an instant the assailant sprung onto him. They grappled in close combat, each defending against the other's offensive strikes. The assailant's punches were more injurious because of the weighted hand covering.

Timothy was focused on deflecting the punches to his face and head. The fierce fight was exhausting him. His opponent seemed to be superhuman in both strength and agility.

The assailant was dominating the confrontation, when Hal burst through the door with her gun drawn.

"Police! Freeze! Hands up where I can see them!" She commanded.

He delivered a blow to Timothy's nose, as he leapt off him. In a half crouch, he launched his body at Hal, aiming to knock her off her feet. Sure that he could get to her before she could squeeze the trigger. So fixated on his attack move, he failed to see the other police officers outside of the door.

His body was mid-air when they fired their weapons. As the bullets pierced his body, in those fleeting moments before death, came his final thoughts.

'He had committed the tactical error of letting his pride usurp the mission. He should have surrendered, when commanded by the second police officer. His arrest would have triggered the protocols for protecting the organization. His failures had now left them open to exposure.'

These mistakes costed more than his life.

As Mica lay on the living room floor, she knew that her attacker was in a fight with someone. Her body started to shut down the nerve centers that were transmitting pain signals to her brain. Momentarily feeling a diminution of the torrent of pain. She sensed that parts of her body were no longer responsive.

She was unable to get up from the floor or move her right shoulder and arm. Her left ankle was broken. She had trouble breathing because of fractured ribs. Her jaw felt dislocated, the lips split. Her vision was blurred, the left eye swollen.

Still clutched in Mica's left hand was a small shard of glass. With the last of her strength, she had intended to cut his hand before he took her life. Leaving her mark on him. A permanent reminder of his vulnerability.

The raging battle at the entryway came to her in dull drifts of sounds. It was unclear who was winning the battle. Distantly, she heard Hal's voice and knew then that the monster would not escape. The monster would no longer be free to hunt the innocent again. Still, she needed confirmation.

With the assailant no longer a threat, Hal left the other officers to rush over to Mica. She knelt beside her and gently removed the cloth from her mouth. Mica steeled herself against the onslaught of jarring pain. Managing to whisper, "Did you get him?"

"Yes Mica, he's dead." Hal replied. Her eyes welling with tears, as she frantically shouted for medical assistance.

All of Hal's training and experience did not prepare her for the appalling carnage in her apartment. It was surreal. This was not her home, but a crime scene. The bloody body on the floor was a victim of a brutally vicious assault, not her best friend. The perpetrator lying dead by the door was a beast, camouflaging as a human being.

Mica made guttural sounds, trying to soothe Hal. Her hand opened to reveal the piece of glass. With great effort she murmured, "I knew you would save me."

Tears ran freely down Hal's face. "I'm so sorry, I was too late."

Mica's last words were cryptic. "No, you saved many."

At the time, Hal did not understand the significance of that statement.

Mica felt herself drifting into a haze. She was safe. She could rest. Later, when she was wheeled into the hospital emergency room, she felt rather than heard the doctors saying that they did not have much hope for her survival.

She knew that was true. But she was not ready to let go of life just yet. She yearned, for however briefly, to feel the presence of family and friends.

    Transporting her to an operating room, the doctors would do all they could to save her life.

CHAPTER 21

Hal braced herself to inform the other women about Mica. Still staggered by the visions of the crime scene, she was operating on automatic pilot. She was not ready to talk to them just yet. And sent them a group text.

The four friends had returned to the hotel after not hearing from either Hal or Mica. They were tired and knew that the story of whatever had occurred would be recounted later at brunch.

On reading the text sent by Hal, they gathered in Maronna's hotel room, in shock. They sat around the suite trying to comprehend the turn of events. Maronna was the first of the group to recover. She took charge, instructing them to go get ready to leave for the hospital. Mica needed them to be there for her. Shortly after, they were on their way.

When they arrived at the hospital, Hal was waiting at the entrance to the emergency room. Mica was already in surgery. Juliana looks around at the others, dazed by her grief.

"What have we done? We shouldn't have let Mica go home alone. Because of us, she may lose her life."

Hal goes to her. She hugs Juliana's slumping body to her side.

"Stop that way of thinking. There is no blame here. We were all celebrating and having a good time. I live in a very safe neighborhood, none of us would think that Mica would be in any danger." Hal said firmly. Trying to prevent their emotions from spiraling out of control.

Wielie's face was masked in misery.

"But Hal, you knew something wasn't right when you left us

at the club."

Hal looks at each of the woman.

"Listen to me, all of you," she sternly commanded. "I was only checking that Mica wasn't locked out. That's it. I did not know the situation when I left."

Her words gave little consolation to the group. The feeling of guilt was beginning to consume them. Starting with letting Mica leave alone. Then their nonchalance in dismissing her lack of response to their text message. And continuing to enjoy their night out. It was all gnawing at them now.

Wielie breaks their silence. She asks Hal whether Mica's family had been contacted. Hal informs them that her parents and sister will arrive by early afternoon.

Finally, Rianne asks the one question they all had on their minds.

"Hal, is Mica going to pull through?"

Letting go of Juliana, Hal crosses her arms around her body. Her eyes are downcast, to avoid making direct eye contact.

"I don't know. It's very serious though. We will know more after her surgery."

Maronna begins to sob. "Mica is not going to make it, is she."

"Let's not give up hope on her pulling through," Hal replied somberly. Her voice was filled with the sorrow that they were all feeling.

The group sat together holding hands to support one another. It weighed heavily on Hal that she alone knew the extent of Mica's injuries. She could not bring herself to tell them. They had to remain strong for Mica and her family.

When the women appeared to be somewhat calmer, Hal told them that she had to go check on Timothy. He was at the same hospital being treated for injuries sustained in the fight with the assailant. Although he took a severe beating, his injuries were not life threatening.

An investigative team, from the NYPD, was also at the hospital. Waiting to debrief both Hal and Timothy on the incident.

It seemed like days had passed, not hours, before a doctor finally came to the waiting room to inform them that Mica was out of surgery and in the recovery room. Telling them that her condition would be closely monitored for the next forty-eight hours. He would say no more despite their desperate pleas for more information.

When Hal returned, they told her about the update they received from the doctor. She curtly nodded her head and together they waited for Mica's family.

Mica's sister, Cecelia, came to see them before going to her sister. She thanked them all, on behalf of the family, for staying with Mica.

Cecelia left them with a heavy heart; astonished at how quickly everything had changed. Her thoughts were occupied with the plans that she and Mica had just made to see each other. They had so much more experiences to be shared together. Cecelia refused to think about Mica dying. At a loss of knowing how to prepare for losing a part of yourself. Someone you love. Your baby sister.

Joining her parents in the room, the three of them stood huddled together. Fighting hard to recognize their beloved Mica. Her bodily form obscured by bandages, splints, and attachments to IV lines and other medical apparatus.

The doctors were straightforward in delivering their prognosis. They did not want to mislead the family by encouraging false optimism. Explaining the details of the grievous injuries that she had sustained. They were doing everything medically possible to keep her alive. That the outlook for her survival did not look good at this point. And the next forty-eight hours would be a critical period for the chance of recovery.

The family heard what was being said to them. They could see for themselves that her condition was grave. But they fervently prayed that the will to live would be stronger than the injuries.

CHAPTER 22

It came at her in waves. The sadness; the grief; the guilt; and the anger. Hal felt that she too was a victim of this appalling crime. Having to bear witness to the heroic efforts being made to save a life that ultimately, she knew, could not be saved. Her tough professionalism could not shield her in this situation. In this instance, her grief had nullified its protection.

Even as an officer of the law, the randomness of the crime shocked her. The circumstances of which were churning in her mind. What nagged at her the most was how could anyone have imagined something like this happening. To them. To one of their own. How could she have possibly foreseen the unimaginable? The turning upside down of what you thought the lives of you and your friends would be like. These people who had become a second family to you.

Or how their ordinary plans for a Sunday morning would be obliterated by this unanticipated tragedy.

They would not be having brunch. They would not be talking over each other to raucously recount details of their weekend escapades. They would not be eagerly planning their next group gathering. They would not be experiencing the bittersweet moments of goodbyes as each of them left to return home. And this time, they would not be leaving feeling secure about their future.

Instead, their lives were altered forever because of this one Saturday night. The night that Mica fell through the safety net.

She didn't know how she had been able to make the call to Mica's family. Her heart felt like it was being ripped out as she spoke to them. Their anguish was also hers. As was the question of - why? Why had Mica become a victim of such a shocking crime? The answer to which was beyond their collective understanding.

Even though she had not rested for over twenty-four hours, Hal took on the responsibility of making another difficult call that Sunday. She did it so that Mica's family would be spared the ordeal. With effort, she called Neva.

Neva was stunned, not grasping what was being told to her. She had to ask Hal to hold on so that she could pull over to the side of the road. Hal closed her eyes in regret. She should have realized that at that hour, Neva may not have been at home. With her composure shaken, she quickly provided the hospital information, and ended the call.

After the call, Neva's head was reeling. She was trying to come to terms with the information she just heard. Her hands started to tremble so badly, it would be unsafe for her to resume driving. She had been on her way home from the airport. Fortunately, she had the presence of mind to call Matt.

As it happened, Matt was not alone when she called. He and Quintin were cleaning up after an early dinner. The phone was still held tightly in his hand when the call ended. He was inarticulate in his explanation to Quintin of what had happened.

But Quintin understood enough to know that whatever it was, Matt had been deeply upset by it. He did not hesitate to drive him to Neva. When they arrived, he parked behind her car. Matt jumped out to go over to her. Neva was sitting inside, clutching the steering wheel, staring straight ahead in a daze.

Matt tapped softly on the window. "Neva, I'm here."

Turning her head, she looked at him bewildered. He helped her to get out of the car.

"Breathe deeply," he tenderly instructed. Instead, she sank to the ground sobbing.

"I know it is a shock, Neva." Matt said as he cradled her in his arms, trying to calm her as well as himself.

"Let's get you back into the car and I'll take you home."

Quintin had initially not intruded, but now came over to them. He assisted Matt with getting Neva onto the passenger seat. With Neva settled, Matt tersely told Quintin to go home. Assuring him that he was okay to drive.

He started to protest but acquiesced. Because he perceived the motive behind Matt's reaction. In his despair, Matt had reflexively retreated into himself, unsure about trusting his budding relationship with Quintin.

As he sat in his truck, Quintin took deep calming breaths. He realized that he was probably being unfair to Matt. They had just met. How could he expect to be so quickly ensconced into his life. And in all honesty, was he ready to do the same.

They were off to a good start for building a relationship. He didn't want to ruin it. Taking another deep breath, he sent a text message to Matt.

"I'm very sorry about your friend, and what you must be going through. Let me know if there is anything I can do to help. I mean that. Anything that you need to get through this. I'm here for you. Just a call or text away."

Matt drove the short distance to Neva's apartment building. Somewhat recovered, she was able to walk unaided into the building and elevator. But Matt unlocked the door to her apartment, and gently guided her to the sofa. Leaving her to go to the kitchen for water.

"It was such a shock Matt," Neva said in a low voice, clasping the glass of water with both hands. "The last thing I would have expected to hear about Mica."

"Is she going to be alright," Matt asked apprehensively. He was desperately trying to reign in his own emotions as he sat beside her.

"I don't know. I really didn't hear anything after she told me that Mica was in the hospital," Neva said. She sighs heavily, trying hard to recollect what the caller had told her.

"Look, I'll go to New York tomorrow, take the earliest flight out. You stay here and let the staff know. We are going to get through this Neva. Mica is going to be fine, don't worry. Do you have her friend's phone number?" Matt asks anxiously.

"Yes, it should be in my recent calls." Matt gets up to bring Neva's handbag to her. She reaches inside for her phone and gives him the number.

"We have to tell Nina what happened," said Matt.

Neva groans softly.

"Nina. She is going to be devastated. The three of us just left each other at the airport," she said.

Unconsciously she raises a hand to her throat as if choking on the words. She starts to tremble again, thinking about how swiftly life can change.

"Don't worry about Nina. She will be able to handle it." Matt said, hoping that was true.

"I know it's hard, but you must be strong. There are a lot of people in Woodsburne who care for Mica, and they will need you to be there for them."

Neva wraps her arms around herself. Her voice is unsteady.

"Matt, right now I don't know if I can do that. I feel so distraught, you know."

"I understand, but we can't fall apart, for Mica's sake. We must be optimistic, that she is going to recover and come home to us." Matt's eyes fill with tears, and they cry softly together.

Neva collects herself first, and reaches for Matt's hand, squeezing it.

"You're right of course. We need to think of Mica now. Help me to make some tea and figure out what to do next." They walk to the kitchen, arms around each other for support.

Neva pours water into their mugs, while Matt leans against the kitchen island, too jittery to sit.

"I just feel that more than anything, sending our thoughts of love and prayers to Mica and her family will help us all get through this crisis."

Matt looks at Neva in surprise, but somberly nods in agreement.

With his tea mostly untouched, Matt gets ready to leave for

Nina's house. They had agreed that it would be best to tell her in person. Neva had tried to convince Matt to let her drive him there. But he emphatically refused her offer.

"Right now, it is better to let someone who is not affected by this situation do the driving. I'll call you later."

"Matt," said Neva with a catch in her voice.

"I know," said Matt. Giving her a hug before leaving.

Standing outside the building waiting for his ride, he inhales the cool air. Letting it relax him. He checks his phone for messages and sees the text from Quintin.

Reading it, he felt so much better. Quintin was there for him. He wouldn't be so easily pushed away. It made him feel less anxious about telling Nina what happened to their dearest friend.

He texted back his reply.

"I'm so sorry for the way that I acted earlier. The news about Mica put me in a tailspin. I'm relieved to know that you understood that. It means a lot to me. I really could use your support. Someone to lean on. I'll call you later."

CHAPTER 23

Mica sensed the presence of a tall slender man in the recovery room after her surgery. He was also with her when she was transferred to the Intensive Care Unit. She assumed that Hal sent him to guard her as a precaution. But it seemed odd to her that no one coming into the room acknowledged him, nor did he speak to anyone. Nonetheless, his company was comforting to her.

She was aware of her family and friends when they are in the room with her. And attempted to communicate with them. It was Hal who observed the faint movement of the fingers on her left hand. Surmising that could be Mica's way of responding to their voices or touch. Letting them know that she was aware of their presence.

It was remarkable how at peace Mica seemed. The attitude of her body belied the grave injuries inflicted on it. Her brain was primarily working to maintain the organs necessary to sustain life for the time being. Its primary function now was to let life ebb away in a predetermined sequence.

Matt and Nina arrived at the hospital early Monday morning. Hal was alone in Mica's room. They had been keeping vigil in rotation. It was too emotionally charged for any of them to constantly be in the room with her. Their high emotions unintentionally infusing the room with stress.

The medical staff gently, but firmly, ordered that it was in Mica's best interest to take brief turns at her bedside. Hal turned her head on hearing the new voices at the nurses' station. Going over to introduce herself and letting them take her place.

They were totally unprepared to see the figure lying in the hospital bed. Nina moaned and slumped against Matt, who struggled to hold her upright. He was transfixed in place by the thought of how it was possible that Mica was still alive. With all his heart, he silently prayed that she was not in agony. The sudden chirping of a machine jolted him out of his thoughts.

He half carried Nina as they departed from the room. Hal had stayed by the nurses' station. She knew how distressing it was to see Mica in her condition. Wordlessly, she stepped forward to help him. Guiding them to the family waiting room.

The starkness of their anguish was etched on the faces of everyone gathered there. The two newcomers took seats beside Maronna. And were seamlessly enfolded into the solemn vigil.

As Tuesday arrived, it would be the last day for the group of friends to be at the hospital. Most of them had existed on little sleep and food since the assault on Mica.

In the early afternoon, everyone went to the cafeteria. Over coffee and sandwiches, family and friends told their favorite stories about Mica. The laughter and shared memories brought a measure of comfort to them.

Her friends knew that the period of vigil was coming to a close. It was time to let Mica's family have their private moments with her.

When they got back to the hospital room, each one quietly waited their turn to stand by Mica's bedside. Saying their personal goodbye to her. Then they hugged in turn her parents, sister, and Hal before taking their leave. The family instinctively knew that the end was near.

The afternoon round on Wednesday, had just finished. Mica's mother was by the nurse's station speaking with the doctor about the medical treatment plan he had just briefed them on. His discussion about a treatment plan had sparked a sliver of hope within her. Perhaps Mica would survive against all odds.

Cecelia was sitting alone in the family waiting room talking on her cellphone with her fiancé. He was trying once again to convince her that he should be with the family in New York. But he understood that for Cecelia, him being at work gave her a sense of normalcy. The hope that everything will turn out fine. But things had changed, the group of friends had left. He wanted to be by her side.

Her father was sitting by Mica's bedside talking softly to her, very gently stroking her hand. Suddenly, Mica's eye fluttered open, gazing at him.

He jumped up, shouting for the nurse, who together with his wife and doctor rushed to her bedside. But before they could get there, Mica began to convulse. It stopped shortly after onset. The life force had left her body.

Immediately, the tall slender man was by Mica's side. He leaned in close to murmur that he would be escorting her to where she was going. She was confused at first, and then understood. Concurrent to that understanding, came a sense of perfect love and peace. A gentle caress to vanquish all fears of the crossing.

Hal arrived after Mica's body had been taken to the morgue. The clerk left her alone in the cold room. She was grateful for the solitude. Looking down at Mica's covered remains, Hal softly prayed that she was at peace in her passing. Then strode resolutely from the room.

The news of Mica's death spread rapidly through Woodsburne on Thursday. On Friday, the Regulars filled the gallery with flowers and cards. Mica's funeral was held in Massachusetts the following Wednesday.

Three weeks later, on a Saturday afternoon, a memorial service was held in Woodsburne. The outpouring of love and the esteem in which Mica was held was consoling to her family. The attendees filled to capacity the great hall of the fourth Annex building. Everyone was moved by the many tributes that spoke of how lives had been changed by Mica through her love of art.

The December issue of the *WNY Arts Mind* magazine was dedicated in memoriam to her. It had its highest circulation, online and print, for the entire year. The printed edition was sought after by many subscribers. For most, it would become a framed memento that honored the life of a young patron of the arts. One who was gone too soon. But left an indelible mark on all those who knew her.

CHAPTER 24

From the subsequent investigation into Mica's death, law enforcement investigators uncovered the network of contract killers to which the perpetrator was affiliated.

At his modest condo, located in the city's Williamsburg neighborhood area, they found a hidden room. It was filled with encrypted evidence of his trade craft including: a database of crimes; names of organizational leaders and associates; and their site locations in the United States and abroad. It was aparent that he had held an upper level position in the criminal organization.

A review of the data showed that he was meticulous in gathering intelligence from hacked databases and other sources to create threat analysis reports for eluding investigative agencies.

He was also at the forefront for developing innovative techniques for disguising operatives, and planting false leads for the misdirection of authorities after the committal of crimes.

Behind the false front of a bookcase, they discovered stacks of notebooks filled with descriptions and drawings of his personal forays to test new weaponry and methodologies.

The victims of these kills were randomly selected. Most were ordinary people going about their everyday lives. Only to end up being statistics in databases for unsolved crimes.

Based on the gathered intelligence, the investigators were able to determine that he was responsible for more than a hundred killings over a period of sixteen years. Many unsolved criminal cases would finally be closed. Including the thirteen year old case of the brutal slaying of a well known minister and his wife in Charleston, South Carolina.

While the investigators were able to compile a basic profile of the perpetrator, they would never know all the details of his life.

❖ ❖ ❖

Like most women in her situation, his mother did not tell anyone about the domestic abuse. She was ashamed to confide in others the details of her torment. It started during their second year of marriage. Her husband began to blame her for everything that went wrong in his life.

Vehement in asserting that his aspirations for success were being hindered by her modest upbringing and bland personality. Thereafter, she became the convenient scapegoat for his inability to realize his ambitions.

This line of reasoning was much more preferable than having to admit that he had an unjustified opinion of his intelligence and skills. Or that due to his insecurities, he habitually squandered many opportunities for upward mobility.

The escalation in violence worsen when her husband no longer cared whether their six-year old son witnessed the merciless beatings. He beat her with his fists or any other objects that were accessible.

Her head and body was a storyboard of her abusive existence. The healed scalp lacerations, bone fractures, and scars each told a story of the undeserved rage directed at her. Paying for infractions of non-existent rules. Rules that were made up as she was being assaulted.

When she suffered her third miscarriage, due to another savage beating, she began to suspect that he found it thrilling to snuff out a life growing inside of her. He could kill without facing any consequences. And now it seemed that he was preparing to include their only living child in this circle of violence. It would not be long before their son would be punished for the shortcomings of his father. They would never be able to leave. He would kill them first. His death was the only way to escape from him. And so, she began to devise a plan for ending their torment - permanently.

Her husband was a diabetic, who was careless about his condition. His doctor constantly warned him that he was heading towards an untimely death by ignoring medical advice for medication, diet, and exercise. She researched the disease and learned how to utilize her husband's indifference to her advantage. In her mind, she was merely putting him into the early grave that he was already digging for himself.

It would have to happen after a period of not taking the medications required to regulate his blood sugar level. That would make him susceptible for slipping into a diabetic coma. Towards that end, she would prepare all his favorite foods for dinner on the chosen night. Food he would not balk at eating. Not unlike serving a last meal to a condemned prisoner.

It has been over a week without him taking his meds. She decided to cook the meal on the Friday. Because he would also stop at a bar before coming home. He was having problems at work and faced the possibility of losing his job. His anger and resentment from that situation made him even more dangerous to her and their son.

She was nervous when Friday arrived. But knew that she had to concentrate on preparing the food. It had to be cooked perfectly. There could be no mistakes with the seasoning or presentation.

The meal consisted of fried pork chops smothered in onions and gravy, fried okra, creamy mashed potatoes, and cornbread. With a tall glass of beer beside his plate. On a corner of the table was an unopened bottle of whiskey that she bought the day before.

When he finished eating, she meekly asked if he wanted to take his medication. He generally ignored taking it except for when he was drinking heavily, which lately had become a daily routine. But the more he drank, the less important it became to adhere to his regimen.

His red bleary eyes were glowering at her as he picked up the whiskey bottle and took a long swig.

"Who do you think you are to tell me what to do?" He growled, moving menacingly towards her. Stopping midway when he remembered that she was working that night. He turned abruptly, and went into his den. Slamming the door shut behind him.

She knew that would be his reaction, he wasn't going to hurt her, not then. Not before she had to go to work. He had not protested when she took the part-time job at a 24- hour convenience store. Liking the idea of her finally earning her keep. After all, why should he be the only one to work so hard to provide for them.

Getting a job was also part of her plan. She started it three weeks ago, working the late-night shift. So that she would not home to call for medical assistance on the night that he ate the special meal. Her son would be sound asleep upstairs in his bedroom. She had been giving him a mild sedative nightly. A precaution against him waking up before she returned home. He would be defenseless without her there as a distraction. Becoming a fresh new victim for his father's failures.

Five hours later, she returned from work. She crossed the hall to the den, and quietly opened the door. His body was slumped in the chair. The nearly empty whiskey bottle was lying on the floor under his dangling hand. There was a foul stench in the room, despite the open window.

She entered the room warily, needing to get a better look at him. He didn't move when she stood next to the window, casting a faint shadow across him. There was vomit caked on his mouth and nostrils, and no discernible signs of breathing. His eyes were half closed.

But she was uncertain if he was dead, and afraid to get any closer to the body to make sure. She left the den, and went upstairs. Checking first on her son, before going to their bedroom.

She changed into a nightgown and pulled back the covers on the bed to lie down. But became fearful that he might come upstairs. She decided instead to put on a heavy robe and sit in a chair opposite the bedroom door.

Startling awake after dozing, she went back to her son's room to check on him, before creeping downstairs again. Silently peeping into the room to make sure that he had not moved and was sitting in the same position.

She went to the kitchen to call for an ambulance. While awaiting their arrival, she mentally rehearsed her answers to questions about finding his body.

The cause of death was asphyxiation, his disease noted as an underlying factor. Three months after the funeral, she sold their house and furnishings.

She used a portion of the money to buy a new car. Nothing fancy, and priced to be paid in full. They needed a reliable vehicle to transport them to a better life. She shouldered the burden of her actions, but was not unscathed by it.

It took until four years after her husband's death before she felt ready to have a relationship. She had recently begun to date a minister. They met while standing in a checkout line at a local grocery store.

But in truth, he was attracted to the son, not her. Even though her son was older than the boys that the minister usually chose.

They were the young children of drug addicted mothers. His ministry revolved around drug abuse and addiction. The mothers in his program were not going to complain about him, so long as he provided them with drugs and other small favors.

But even with this available supply of young innocents, the pleasure was unsatisfying for him. Their hollow eyes were devoid of any emotion. They were rigid, like little statues. Stoic, as another predator came to ransack the remnants of their childhood.

It had been a while since he last felt such excitement. This ten year old boy was healthy, with a more fully formed body. And he had intelligence, making him a challenge.

The minister had no problem in gaining the confidence of the mother. The ache of her need to provide a loving home for her son was heart wrenching. He almost decided to leave them alone. Almost. In the end, he had to have the boy.

When the boy was months past his eleventh birthday, the minister knew he had to stop seeing them. He began to gradually withdraw from their lives. Making excuses for calling infrequently and not coming to their home as often.

Seeing how distraught his mother was at the unexpected ending of the relationship, he told her about the molestations. But refrained from telling her the real reason for his silence until then. He had withstood it for her. He wanted her to be happy.

His mother was devastated. She did not doubt that he was telling the truth. She knew the way in which the abused spoke about their pain. It unsettled her that she had missed all the signs.

How she had accepted, without question, that the charming and caring minister was a godsend to them. How she had blithely encouraged the minister to be alone with her young son. Overjoyed for him to have a positive male role model in his life. It was agonizing to realize that her ardent desire for having the ideal family had made her so gullible. Causing her to unwittingly invite another disguised monster into their life and home.

She briefly considered reporting the minister to his church and the police. But decided against doing it. They would have an uphill battle to be heard and believed. The outcome uncertain. She doubted that justice would be served.

Afterall, he was a respected clergyman at a highly regarded local church. Those in authority at the church would chose ignorance over confronting inconvenient truths. Turning a blind eye to any situation that would require action. Preferring hollow platitudes and making promises rather than to upset the status quo. No, the best course of action for them was to flee from this horrific situation.

Within forty-eight hours, they were ready to leave. Packing only the clothing and household items that could fit into four suitcases and three large boxes.

Since they left Ohio, she had only rented furnished housing. Moving was the easy part. The hard part was having to suffer the guilt of failing to protect her son.

On the morning of the day that they were leaving, she called the minister. Informing him that her mother was sick, and she had to leave immediately for Des Moines, to take care of her. It was a proactive measure of protection for them. Providing the minister with peace of mind that they were no longer be a threat to him.

The minister seemed almost gleeful during their brief conversation. Making little effort to seem caring about her situation. He didn't even ask her to keep in touch with him.

Hanging up from the call, the minister was ecstatic. His dilemma was miraculously resolved. More importantly, she gave no indication of being aware of his sexual abuse of her son. It never occurred to him that she was safeguarding her family from further harm or retaliation.

Her telephone call gave him exactly what he wanted. He had been thinking for weeks about how to make sure that the boy would not tell anyone about their special relationship. His mother was not some drug addict who was pimping out her child.

She could have caused him trouble. And derailed his future in the church. But now, he could accept the offer of promotion recently made by the deacons. And further advancement would be contingent on him getting married and starting a family.

He already knew the woman who would fulfill this role. She was a new congregant, ambitious, pretty enough, and skillful in using her physical assets. He had started dating her two months ago.

On their last date, she told him that her main life goals were wealth and status. That the lifestyle she envisioned for herself did not include having children. They would prevent her from pursuing the life she sought.

To his surprise, he had agreed with her. It would free them from having to go through the motions of being parents, and portraying the happy family. It was much better for their union to be a business partnership. One devoid of amorous feelings.

Best of all, they would be able to keep they private life private. And he would keep her in line by using her greed and desire for status. By dangling "shiny objects" in front of her. That thought made him chuckle. The power of manipulation. The art of which he was very talented, and quite skilled in its techniques.

Since that night at the restaurant, an idea had began to form in his mind. After being married for a year, they would sorrowfully disclose their problem with fertility. Being unable to have children. It was the perfect cover story to conceal their decision to not have children.

His mind was filled with all the money to be made from that declaration. The first step would be to launch a new ministry to help couples going through the same situation. A demonstration to the elders of his ability to create lucrative revenue streams for the church. Then all he had to do was sit back and take advantage of the opportunities sure to come his way.

His other lucky break was a invitation from a 'brethren,' to become a member of a private club. It was located in a small town near the Tennessee border. A safe place for indulging in his other appetites, and be protected from the threat of exposure.

He tilted back in his chair, sighing with deep self-satisfaction. The vision of a long and prosperous life playing in his mind.

It took her by surprise, when the minister's secretary pulled up alongside their car. They had just finished packing the trunk. The secretary rolled down the front passenger window to call her over.

"I'm so glad that I got here in time. Minister thought you could use something extra for your travels." Handing her an envelope, and promptly driving away.

She waited until the car had turned the corner before opening it. It was an unexpected windfall. The amount of the check was enough to finance their expenses for months. Clearly his intent was to buy her silence. As if money could pay for what he had done to them.

But his day of judgement was coming, she prayed. And quickly pushed aside the thought to concentrate on their trip to Florida.

The road trip was like a vacation. They were able to stay at decent hotels, eat at restaurants, and purchase new clothing. But she was troubled.

For years, she knew that her mental health was slowly deteriorating. The situation with the minister caused a setback. She began to feel more acutely the sensation of being lost in her own mind. Her mind rapidly becoming an overstuffed closet. Soon the door would no longer be able to close.

But during the drive to Florida, all the voices in her head were silent. Miami would be their permanent home. She did not have the mental stamina for any more moves. When they arrived, she was able to quickly rent a furnished apartment and find a job.

For the first three years, she was able to cope. In the fourth year, she sold their car, unable to drive anymore. Her mind too easily distracted.

By the fifth year she came to a fateful decision. She was no longer able to control the decline of her mental health. And she did not want to burden her son with her care. Nor did she want him to witness the last stages of her breakdown. She wanted him to have good memories of her.

They were standing outside on the terrace of their apartment, just before sunset one evening. Holding her son's hand, she told him that she couldn't hold a job any longer. But now that he was eighteen years old, he could find work and be able to take care of himself.

She told him that the rent was paid for three months in advance. Giving him time to find a job and rent a studio apartment from the manager of the complex. He knew them to be good tenants. Next, she handed him a keepsake wooden box.

Inside was a total of eight hundred fifty dollars, divided into four rolls. Each one wedged along a side of the box. Nestled in the center were three pieces of jewelry wrapped inside a piece of cloth: two gold chain necklaces and a ruby ring. These were all her worldly possessions.

His inheritance from her.

He sat there, sadly listening to his mother, saying nothing. He was aware of her worsening mental health. At his age, he understood more than most about the cruelties of life.

His mother left while he was sleeping. She took a long lingering look at her precious son, comforted by her belief that he was prepared to make a good life for himself. But sadly, in her present mental state, she did not realize that her son was only sixteen years old.

He met Kiko after living in the streets for seven months, learning quickly how to survive in his new environment.

His few possessions were kept in a sports sac. Hanging from his neck was a small leather pouch. Folded inside was a newspaper clipping about the body of an unidentified woman found under the piers of a local beach. From the brief description of the woman, he knew that it was his mother. He had been searching for her since she left. But never saw her again.

The initial meet ups with Kiko were casual and not overly friendly. They talked while walking the streets, sipping bottled sports drinks that Kiko brought with him.

He liked the way the older teen handled himself and accepted his offer of a meal two weeks later. He didn't know then that Kiko was a spotter for the Branch Cell, an organization of contract killers. His job was to recruit street youths for them.

Kiko took him to a big house. As he sat in the large kitchen waiting for his food, he was introduced to a tall imposing man, the owner of the home. The man expertly elicited information from his teenage guest as he ate his meal.

Later they observed how he played video games that were modified to evaluate his potential for cunning and violence. The leaders tagged him a trainee. Otherwise, he would have ended up as a practice kill for the others in the room with him.

Instinctively he knew that to exist in this shadow world, his humanity had to be buried forever. He could never backtrack to where it was hidden. When he was alone, he threw away the wooden box and amulet and flushed the torn pieces of the newspaper clipping down a toilet.

On that day he extinguished forever, Lucius Matthew Reynolds. The person he had been. He chose the name of Demone. A name that he felt was more fitting for the entity he was destined to become.

They taught him the art of killing. He was a fast learner and was soon assigned as a decoy to a lead assassin. His superior held the rank of General within the organization. It infuriated him that the General used him as bait for certain targets. His reward was to witness the General's varied techniques for dispatching their marks. He would watch mesmerized, pleased that his impassive face was the last thing that they saw before dying.

By his eighteenth birthday, he made his first solo kill.

The General wanted him to become his lover. Reeking of death and high on drugs, he lewdly suggesting that the teen was well acquainted with such desires. Lying beside the General, he leaned over as if to kiss him. Instead, slitting his throat with a slim short blade that was hidden between his legs.

He knew how to dismember the body, tossing the parts into two coated steel drums containing a chemical solution formulated to dissolve its contents. The next day, he contacted their affiliated Waste Management Company for a service collection.

Demone was fearless in reporting to the Operations Chief the death of the General. The Chief saw in him a rare talent among their kind and allowed him to leave with his life. He had unknowingly solved a problem for them. Lately, the General had become incautious and flamboyant. Rumors were spreading about his Staged Death Shows, which were attracting unwanted attention, endangering their clandestine existence.

They reassigned him to a unit in Seattle, Washington. He rapidly rose through the ranks, and eventually leading his own special unit in New York City. From a warehouse building in Queens, he oversaw special operations for the organization.

He was fearless, never questioning his ability to eliminate a target or adversary. Never feared being captured. Always confident in his ability to overcome any obstacle.

He was invincible. Until he wasn't.

It happened one Saturday night. When he encountered a force greater than himself. The deep bond between two close friends.

CHAPTER 25

A year after the death of Mica, Haliah Vilamieux resigned from the NYPD. She could no longer tolerate the constant praises and accolades of heroism. It made her feel like a fraud.

When she was recruited to join the International Crimes Task Force (ICTF), she immediately accepted the job offer. It would be a fresh start for her. A chance to leave her past behind.

The ICTF is a covert special intelligence agency, that is headquartered in Geneva, Switzerland. The agency is not bound by the jurisdictional laws and protocols under which most law enforcement agencies operate. The Office of Special Tribunals, which has linkages to judicial and intelligence agencies globally, acts as the quasi oversight agency for ICTF.

The high value criminals who were taken into custody by the agents under the command of ICTF were confident of a quick release. In their mind, they were facing a detention of forty-eight hours, at the most. They knew there was a divide between being charged and getting convicted.

What they didn't know was that this time, there would be no release. They had already been convicted.

Under ICTF custody, the 'subs' would undergo a series of psychological interviews and be monitored around the clock. Every aspect of their daily movements recorded and studied. After five months of observation, the 'subs' were injected with a drug that induced a hyper dream state. The drug primed them to enter a Virtual Reality Experience (VRE).

The VRE was designed to enhance the effects of the drug

which stimulated memories of the 'subs' lives prior to their custody. In this state, they were reliving their everyday lives in familiar environments. Engaged in doing their criminal and personal activities, with no discernible changes in behavioral patterns or tendencies during the simulation sessions.

Upon extraction from their term in VRE, the 'subs' retained no memory of it. Believing their confinement to have been continuous, without change in daily routines.

After another three months of additional assessment and observation, they were summarily terminated. Their disappearance generally accepted as an inherent risk in their line of work.

All VRE data is downloaded into a behavioral analysis database system. From which customized behavioral blueprints, mind mapping profiles, and other analyses are generated. Access to this highly classified information is granted through special security agreements with ICTF.

Arnot Descourt, is the chief commander of the Special Investigation and Apprehension Division (SIAD), within ICTF. It is the division tasked with the apprehension of identified targets. He will be Haliah's new boss. A man in his forties, of average height and stocky build, with an avuncular face. And an expert in various fighting styles of martial arts. However, it is his high intelligence and deductive reasoning abilities that are his key assets. The cornerstones of his career success and achievements.

Hal's training for her new position started with unlearning the training from her previous law enforcement career. The senior training officer in charge, had an unique approach in his teachings.

One of the most provocative theories was on the topic of killing. Declaring that categorizing the acts of taking lives in terms of: contract killings, spree killings, serial killings, terrorism, and the myriad other labels was to mollify society. The simple truth is that irrespective of motivations, ideologies, or methodologies, these individuals were simply killers.

Indifferent to terminating human life in order to achieve either their own objectives or those of others.

Nor can these crimes be effectively managed through law enforcement. That is a perpetuation of the belief that the capture and incarceration of criminals is a "fix" for it. But that is another illusion.

Prisons and incarceration are not solutions to crime. The main function of the penal system is to keep hidden an aberrant society that exist among us. Its other critical task is to maintain a secure barrier between them and us, the "normal" society.

He was forceful in telling the trainees that they had to discard the notion of acting for the greater good, or being self-righteous in the performance of their duties. Because over time these thought processes would make them act amorally. Not unlike the criminals they were apprehending.

Another favorite maxim was knowing 'when to leave their line of work.'

"There is no dishonor in getting out when you feel that you have reached your limit." He had advised them knowingly.

Hal stayed behind after the class to speak with him.

"What did you mean about knowing when to leave the job?"

"Just what I said. If you ever feel the need to walk away, do it. This organization neither wants nor needs heroes. I did it myself, years ago, when I was battle fatigued. I wanted a normal life. A family. Fortunately for me, due to my experience and knowledge of field work, I was reassigned to my current position. ICTF prefers to redeploy staff to other roles, if possible."

He looks at her thoughtfully.

"We put a lot of time and effort into training our agents. It is much more expedient to retain talent, if an agent is interested."

As she turned to leave, he said, "Just so you know, I was Arnot's second in command."

Hal nodded her head and smiled at him. She knew then that

the meeting with Arnot could no longer be avoided. The next day, she scheduled a meeting with him.

She had been with SIAD for four months. Arnot had been patient in giving her the time she needed to come to him. He knew that her decision to resign from the NYPD was due to issues connected to the death of a close friend; and that there were still issues which were difficult for her to deal with and discuss.

As Arnot sat in his office with Hal, he once again observed her. She had an edgy elegance about her; tall and long legged, with chin length brown wavy hair. Her movements had a feline grace. A mixture of constrained sensuality and physical prowess. Though her face just missed being beautiful, her eyes were its best feature. The deep emerald green color appeared almost black depending on the lighting. The lighter green pooling around the pupil, and the darker shade filling the outer edges of the iris.

Hal attempted to lead the meeting. And began by explaining her decision to make a career change.

She spoke candidly of her displeasure at being hailed a hero for the takedown of an infamous criminal. The heavy shame she felt every time she was given an award or accolade. That her promotion to a higher rank felt undeserved. How her protestations were disregarded. Mainly because the aftermath of the incident had been a boon to the department.

As she faced Arnot, Hal once again tried to make the case that the night of the incident was an ordinary one. She was an off duty cop enjoying the company of a group of close friends. That it was only the unusual behavior of one of those friends that led to her subsequent actions.

Arnot listened patiently as she spoke. Then he leaned towards her when she stopped speaking. Taking back his control of the meeting.

"But, in truth, it was not an ordinary night. And your reaction to your friend's change in behavior was decisive. No matter how you choose to frame it, you acted immediately on your instincts. And that led to significant outcomes for everyone involved that night."

Hal attempted to interrupt, but he stopped her.

"Let me review that night for you. First, you saved your friend's family from the horror of being informed that her identification would have to be made through DNA testing. And imagine if they had insisted on seeing her body. It would have broken them. Being shown her pulverized body and obliterated face at the morgue.

Secondly, how would you have handled finding her body in your apartment later that night. The mental toll of making that discovery. Not only on you, but on all those connected to her. Once again, it would have been another grievous scenario had you not acted as you did.

Thirdly, the ensuing investigation. The forensic evidence would have been little to none at the scene. And the descriptions of the perp by witnesses would have led nowhere. Her murder was not going to be solved despite your best efforts. You would have been chasing a ghost. Would you have been able to live with that result? To move on with your life?"

Hal's body went rigid. She was fighting for self-control. They both knew that she would have become another casualty stemming from that night.

"Due to your actions, her family was saved from that nightmare. They got the time to say their goodbyes. And more importantly, your friend received dignity in her death. Her body was not left behind as detritus by the killer. A set piece at a crime scene."

Arnot locked eyes with Hal. Forcing her to keep her head up.

"Having said that, you must get it out of your mind that you could have saved her. She left the 'group' that night and that action made her a target for the perpetrator. He was on the prowl for his next kill. It didn't matter who it was." Arnot told her callously, his hands firmly clasped on his desk.

"Don't you think that I have tried to come to terms with all that? But my feelings of blame won't go away. I didn't save her.

Don't you understand? I didn't save her!" Hal wailed. Her voice choked with anguish, reliving once again the events of that awful night in her mind.

Although sympathetic to the emotional pain she was experiencing, Arnot was unequivocal in his response.

"You must let it go. This mindset of seeking atonement is dangerous. It will get either yourself or someone on the team killed. I cannot let that happen. Leaving me with no choice but to dismiss you from SIAD. Which would be unfortunate, because you are an excellent investigator, with great instincts."

Hal sat there, immobile. His words coming at her like jabs to an open wound.

"The death of your friend was tragic, a senseless loss of life. But it did lead to intelligence which enabled SIAD and other agencies to hunt down and dismantle a network of highly organized killers. Think about this for a moment. On that night, you had no idea that a killer was in your midst. If you all had left together, he would have chosen another victim. And still out there, undetected, killing at will. I'm only saying this to give some context to her untimely death. It is true that you were not able to save her life. However, in the end, you saved many."

Arnot sighed heavily. The bluntness of his assessment was unsettling even to him. Always the deliverer of hard truths. Which at times was more a burden than a skill.

Hal froze when she heard Arnot say those last three words. Suddenly recalling the final words Mica had said to her, 'No, you saved many.' Instantly, Hal's eyes filled with tears. She tried in vain to hold them back, but they slowly rolled down her cheeks.

Unclenching her fists, she roughly wiped them away. A shuddering breath escaped from her. Oddly experiencing a sense of relief from her brief vulnerability.

"The events of that night changed the trajectory of all your lives. Don't get mired in guilt and self-reproach, and to lose sight of your purpose. I will give you three days to think about your next step. Your will return either ready to work or to submit your resignation." Arnot said, in a softer tone. Still watching her closely.

Hal internalized his analysis as she sat there. His words were the stimulus needed to reset her psyche. By the end of the meeting, she was genuine in thanking him for not only his counsel, but the time off to think about her future.

Later at her apartment, Hal stood looking out the living window. It overlooked a small park across the street from the building. She decided to go there to do some thinking.

As she reviewed the meeting with Arnot in her mind, she realized how lost in grief she had been. And being in denial about it. She had pushed away everyone who cared about her. Running away to Geneva so that she could stay trapped in her own prison of guilt. Untroubled by leaving everything and everyone behind.

In a new place, she was able to reinvent herself. Be someone she was not. No one would know the difference. Outwardly, she conveyed the image of an accomplished law enforcement professional. While inwardly her mind was embroiled in conflict and dissonance.

It became apparent to her, that Arnot saw through the facade. He saw the inner turmoil. Her fear that she had lost the capability to do policing without having the backing of an augmented law enforcement organization. Being terrified of leading, preferring to be lead.

Moreover, the last four months with SIAD had been more therapy than training, she realized. Arnot's way of assisting a fellow officer in need. But one in whom he saw ability and talent. And a future with the organization if she wanted it. She had three days to make a decision. Not only professionally but personally as well.

As she got up to walk back to her apartment, she felt a sense of closure.

Coming to terms with the circumstances which shaped that tragic night. With this acceptance came a sense of peace.

Laying to rest not only her guilt, but the harrowing memories as well.

She was on her way to recovery, but not completely there yet. A portion of her time off would be used to reconnect with her 'sister group' of friends. She needed them back in her life. They would welcome her return with open arms. No questions asked.

Going forward, her thoughts of Mica would no longer be eclipsed by the manner of her death. But replaced by the memories that she had been unconsciously suppressing. Those of the vivacious and intelligent woman that Mica had been in life. Mica deserved to be remembered in that way.

And she would finally begin to unpack the boxes in her apartment and buy furniture for it. Making it a home. No longer a way station. Finally ready to reclaim the life that she had buried because of one Saturday night.

PART II

The source of most conflicts in the world stems from one groups 'truth' being another groups 'lie'. And this stalemate will continue until one of the sides begin to consider whether 'their truth' or 'their lie' has the basis of logic to support their assumptions.

-Tenaj
The Untethered Mind (Excerpt)

CHAPTER 26

Neva was sitting in her loft office, reviewing proposed ideas for folk art exhibits. She had moved to the River Edge building after her contract ended with the Leyden Museum Annexes.

On the wall opposite her desk, hangs a mixed media collage on wood panel. From afar it appeared to be an abstract. But up close it is a depiction of the activities held in three of the annex buildings, and the exterior of the Avalon Gallery at its former location. The artwork is titled *Quadrants in 'A' Major.* But she called it *'my resume in pieces.'*

It was commissioned by the board of the Leyden Museum. The chosen artist had had her artworks exhibited in the inaugural exhibition held at the Leyden Annex for Emerging Artists.

Neva received it in recognition of her achievement in establishing the Leyden Annexes. Since its launch, the initiative has garnered statewide, national, and some international recognition for being an innovative cultural enterprise.

It amuses her, the attention that she has been getting lately. Suddenly in the limelight for work she has been doing for decades.

Neva glances at yet another invite for an upcoming award ceremony. It occupies the left side of her desk, an acrylic hexagonal shaped invitation.

She will be the recipient of an award honoring her contributions to the arts in Woodsburne. The Partridge Foundation will be hosting the event. Sidney will also be honored for his outstanding leadership of the Leyden Museum.

An hour later, Neva leaves her office. She is on her way to visit Edith, who recently suffered a heart attack. This will be the first time that she is seeing Edith since it happened. On her arrival, Neva is escorted upstairs by Mrs. Capers, the housekeeper.

Edith is reclining with closed eyes on an upholstered chaise lounge placed near a window in her sitting room. The room is bright and airy and has a grand view of the back gardens. A patio door is slightly ajar, letting in a late afternoon breeze that gently ruffles the pale blue silk curtains. The air is lightly scented by early blooming spring flowers.

Neva walks tentatively over to Edith not sure if she is asleep. Edith opens her eyes unexpectedly at Neva's approach, startling her. Recovering quickly, she bends over to kiss her dearest friend on the forehead. Edith smiles up at her and clasps her hand.

"So how was your sister's wedding in Morocco? I want to hear all the details." Edith said, her voice is a bit unsteady. Not her usual imperious tone.

"It was wonderful. But first, I want to know why I wasn't told about your medical condition until after I got back." Neva scolds her mildly.

"Because being with your family was a lot more important than worrying about an old lady in a hospital." Edith retorted firmly, putting an end to any further discussion.

Neva draws up a nearby chair to sit beside her. She observes how fragile the stalwart of Woodsburne appears to be.

"It is ironic that it took almost dying to see what is really important to me," said Edith. "And to look back on some of my past mistakes." Her voice is quivering with emotion.

"There are two reasons why I asked you to come see me today. I want to sincerely apologize for cajoling you into leaving the Avalon and taking on the Annex project. I saw an opportunity to get you to do what I wanted. I am ashamed of having used altruism as a guise to achieve my objectives. And in doing that, I abandoned my own personal mores in the process. Making my actions not very different from those crass investors involved in that maladroit situation from two years ago."

Neva starts to interrupt, but Edith holds up her hand.

"Let me finish please, before you speak. I must say this to you." Reluctantly, Neva complies.

"How foolish I was, I see that now. Charles would never have condoned my actions, nor wanted any recognition for anything that he did for Woodsburne. That was not what motivated him. He simply wanted to be a part of making this city the best it can be for its residents and visitors."

Edith expels a long slow breath. Before she can resume, Neva interjects.

"There is nothing to forgive." Neva said emphatically. "Do you remember the discussion that we had about Jason's paintings at the time?" Edith nods her head affirmatively.

"How those images made me rethink what was important to me. Was I doing what I really wanted to do?" Neva pauses, looking into Edith's eyes.

"The offer to take on the Annex project was a lifeline that I needed more than you could ever know. Whether I was conscious of it or not, I needed to leave the Avalon. To gain the perspective of what I needed for the next chapter in my life. Being able to move forward confidently in doing what I really wanted to do."

Neva's voice is heavy with emotion.

"Therefore, it is I who owe you a debt of gratitude."

Edith snorts in derision, feeling more alive than she has in awhile.

"You always had the flair for the dramatic. What a pair we are! All of what you just said may be true. But more than anyone, I knew how hard it was for you to leave the Avalon. I also know that you did it for me, Neva. You understood that I wanted a permanent home for my art collection."

As Neva starts to protest, but Edith raises her hand.

"What I just said is the truth. And I am thankful for your loyalty and devotion. It is important to me that you know how very grateful I am for all you have done not only for me personally, but also for Woodsburne. You have been both a revered friend and a consummate patron of the arts."

Neva sits silently, flattered by the accolades, but the words have a sense of foretelling. She rises from her chair and kneels beside Edith.

"Thank you. But know this also, I have no regrets about my decision to leave the Avalon. I need you to believe me."

"We'll leave it at that." Edith replied somberly, closing her eyes momentarily.

"My second reason for asking you here today is that three days ago, I signed all the legal documents to bequeath my collection to the Leyden Museum. The collection will be transferred to the Leyden over specified time periods. The first of which is in about six months and the final phase is after my death."

Edith looks at Neva before continuing.

"I also named you as the executor of the collection. However, your appointment is not etched in stone. If you decline, I will have to find someone else to do it."

Neva gasps in amazement. At the enormity of the trust bestowed on her. Rendered speechless, Neva rests her head on the side of the chaise.

"Neva are you alright, I thought you would be pleased with my decisions."

"My goodness, I never expected this. I don't know what to say."

"Hopefully, you won't say no. I know that you are working on the start-up of your gallery. But I have hired excellent people to do most of the administrative work. Your role will principally be oversight. Making sure things happen when they are supposed to; and that promises are kept."

"Is this another Machiavellian plan of yours? Is there

something more to it that you are not telling me?"

Edith laughs heartily.

"You know me too well. No, this is not part of some devious plan. I simply want the eyes and ears of someone whom I completely trust to direct the process."

Edith pauses briefly to take a breath.

"And frankly, I want to keep Carter in line. He has a track record for underhanded moves. Let's not forget the partnership ploy. All done, at the time, to portray himself as a 'shaker and mover' in the art world. And it worked. He got the leadership position on the board of the Leyden Museum."

Edith looks intently at Neva. Making sure that she understands the seriousness of what she is saying.

"Now, with the official bequeathment of the collection, I don't want him to start planning how to leverage it for his next big career move. Even though there are strong legal safeguards in the documents, it is not possible to cover every contingency. Bottom line, I don't trust his intentions. And Sidney will need a strong ally to keep him in check."

"Yes, I see your point. Neva sighs heavily. "The fox in the hen house."

"My point exactly. However, you should not feel any pressure to take on this role. You can say no. I mean that. I will make other arrangements." Edith tells her sincerely.

Neva looks up at her, and smiles.

"I will do it. I'll make it work."

Edith sighs contentedly.

"You are like a daughter to me. Certainly, you must know that. And the only person to whom I can entrust my life's work." Edith tells her emotionally.

"You are also very dear to me." Neva replies, and gets up to retake her seat.

"Now then, the last time that you asked me to do your bidding, you served an excellent meal to go with it." Neva quips, to lighten the mood in the room.

Edith looks at her, and they both chuckle.

"Quite so. Well, this time, it is not a meal I'm serving. It is something different. I am bequeathing my house to you. I'm confident that when the time comes, you will put it to good use."

Neva stares at her, mouth agape.

"Edith, that is unnecessary. I don't need any compensation. The management of your art collection is important to me as well."

"That is a most utterly preposterous assumption. How could you conclude that this is my feeble attempt to pay you back for anything. That is certainly not the manner in which I conduct my affairs!" Edith replied hotly.

"Edith, please I apologize. I'm so sorry. That is was not my meaning. It's so unexpected. Quite frankly, this is all a bit overwhelming."

Neva looks abashed by her gaffe, her hands tightly held in her lap.

"No, you are right. I shouldn't have rushed to tell you everything all at once. But since my heart attack, I just want everything to be in order."

Neva looks searchingly at her.

"Take that concerned look off your face. I'm fine. Just being mindful of my own mortality." Edith smiles warmly at her.

Neva reaches for Edith's hands.

"I am very honored by your trust in me. And will do everything in my power not to disappoint you."

On the drive home, Neva had a tough time concentrating on the road. Her mind occupied with the implications of Edith's decisions.

Her life no longer seemed so simple and direct. Edith had thrown a curve ball into her plans. As though she knows what I need before I do.

CHAPTER 27

Months later, on the day before the awards ceremony at which Neva would be honored, Edith had an accident at home. After cutting flowers in her garden, she tripped going up the stone steps leading to the covered patio. Bumping her forehead on the edge of the top step. Although the scrapes and bruises were minor, her doctor nevertheless confined her to bed rest for three days.

On the evening of the event, the venue was filled with a sense of high energy and expectation. It would be the last function for which Reginald Partridge will preside as President, and Chairman of the Partridge Foundation.

In addition to the award presentations, there was the anticipated announcement of his successor. The audience was eagerly awaiting this part of the program.

When the time came, he introduced his nephew, Chandler Partridge. Everyone in the audience was stunned by the announcement. It had long been assumed that his daughter, Nina, would succeed him. The first female to lead the foundation. Making her appointment a historic milestone in its long history.

Perhaps knowing this, Reginald was unstinting in praising his nephew. Taking the time to enumerate his experience and achievements which qualified him for leading the future of the Partridge Foundation.

"I want everyone to join me in welcoming Chandler Partridge, our new President, and Chairman of the Board of Directors for the Partridge Foundation."

After shaking hands, Chandler stepped forward to give a short speech. When he finished, there was little disagreement about his suitability to fill the leadership role of the organization.

Jason came up quietly behind Neva.

"Aaah, close your mouth, you are drooling all over yourself. Not a good look for an admired personage."

Neva snapped back from her trance-like state and whirled around.

"What are you doing here?" she said on hearing Jason's voice. Her face reddening at being caught ogling Reginald's nephew.

"While I'm no match for the Greek Adonis standing up there, it's good seeing you too."

Neva giggles girlishly, still surprised to see him. Jason steps in closer to give her a hug. Releasing her, he takes her by the arm and ushers her next door to a smaller gathering space.

The room is arranged with round cocktail tables covered with white tablecloths. Making it easy for the guests to move around to chat with other attendees. There were a few small table with chairs on one side of the room. The wait staff was ready to serve hors d'oeuvres and take drink orders as the guests began to drift inside. Eager to gossip and exchange information about the new Chairman.

"I got in two days ago. You are looking at the poster boy for a local artist who did good. And is included in a major art exhibit at the Leyden Museum. So, it is to be expected that I should suck-up to the recently anointed champions of the arts and all things Woodsburne." Jason said tongue in cheek. But he is genuinely happy to see Neva.

"Wow, only here two days and already clued into the doings." Neva said, with a touch of discomfiture about her new position, especially among peers.

"Lighten up Madame Dowager." Jason said, snickering at his own joke.

Despite herself, Neva chuckles at the mental image.

"Not so fast buddy, I'm a long way from being a dignified

elderly woman. Give me another thirty years to grow into it. But to your point, people I've known for years, are treating me differently now. I'm not use to it."

"Edith could not have chosen a better person to succeed her. I mean that. We are lucky to have you." Jason tells her seriously.

"But that's the thing, Jason. I'm not taking her place. Edith may be frailer these days, but she is still very much in charge of her affairs. Make no mistake about that."

"Understood, but you are the heir apparent. Relax and enjoy your status. Don't downplay its importance." Jason counsels, clasping her hands on the tabletop.

"Thank you, and I am truly grateful for the recognition. But there is a downside to all this. I have very little time to pursue my own projects. I'm so busy working with the company that Edith hired to document and catalogue her collection and papers." Neva grouses in an unfiltered moment of frustration.

"Oh gosh, I didn't mean to say it like that. I just feel pulled in so many different directions right now."

"No worries, I completely understand the feeling. So then, you are no longer working with the Leyden?" Jason asked her.

"No, my contract ended months ago. But I was nominated to the Board prior to leaving. I'm sure because they thought it would be in their best interest to keep me tethered to them."

"Tsk, tsk. Who is being cynical now." Jason said mockingly.

"Yet, it is true!" Neva replies laughing.

"I have since resigned, given my new responsibilities for the Majoram Art Collection." Neva said more soberly.

Their conversation shifts to Jason and the working farm that he bought in Umbria. He feels a swell of pride in speaking about the wine and olive oil produced from his land. Although the products are not widely distributed, they are well known in the nearby towns and villages. When he purchased the property none of the workers lost their jobs, nor did he try to change its way of operation. That move, gained the respect of the locals. His willingness to assimilate into their way of life rather than trying to impose his way on them.

"It's done wonders for me," Jason gushes, extolling the virtues of a simpler way of living.

"My whole outlook on life has changed. I feel so much more alive. I know this sounds crazy, but creating art is more joyous, it literally springs from me. I'm doing my best work yet, in my opinion." He catches himself.

"I do tend to get carried away sometimes, but really Neva, you should come visit. You'll thank me."

Neva smiles at him affectionately, causing him to blush slightly.

"Thank you for the invitation. I just might take you up on it. Matt is over the moon about your work, and I concur. I'm purchasing the *Woman in the Mirror.*"

"Are you really. What drew you to the painting?"

"The attitude of introspection in the female figure. The sense of her grappling with making the right decision for herself. It resonated with me." Neva said, somewhat disconcerted by the candor of her reply.

Jason flushes with pleasure, as he looks wonderingly at Neva.

"We have to toast this moment!" He exclaims, looking around for a waiter to take their drink order.

As they wait for their drinks, Reginald Partridge stops by the table with Chandler. During the introductions, Neva is tongue-tied. Barely articulate in responding to their proffered congrats on her award.

She is smitten by Chandler Partridge. He is strikingly handsome with piercing blue-grey eyes, sandy brown hair, and warm olive skin. He looks much younger than his thirty-seven years. Although slightly over six feet tall, his toned body makes him appear taller.

Her distraction continued when she is asked about her experiences in establishing the Annexes. The responses were inane. Seeing her befuddlement, Jason deftly steers the conversation to the newly reopened performing arts center. One of the last projects under Reginald's tenure.

But Reginald is nettled by Neva's inexplicable behavior. And hurriedly withdraws from the uncomfortable encounter.

When their drinks arrive, Jason gives Neva her drink with a flourish. Her hand trembles slightly as she takes hold of the glass stem.

"Don't say a word, just let the floor open up and swallow me." Neva said through clinched teeth.

Jason tries to be sympathetic, but could not hide his amusement at her discomposure. Unfortunately for Neva, Matt joined them at that moment.

Both men are nattily dressed in dark suits. Matt is wearing a tie, and Jason has on a collarless shirt.

"Oh brother, you just missed it. Neva getting shot by Cupid's arrow." Jason laughs into his drink to muffle the sound.

Matt quickly glances over at Neva, who appears to be frazzled. Jason's mirth is contagious, and Matt is unable to stifle a chuckle.

Neva gives both men a venomous look before leaving the table. She goes to the restroom and checks to make sure that she is alone.

Assured of her privacy, she begins a breathing exercise to center herself. And pats her face and neck with cold water on a paper towel. Feeling less flustered and back in control, she exits from her temporary sanctuary.

In the corridor leading back to the tables, Neva literally bumps into Chandler. Her head bumps against his upper chest.

"Whoa, a penny for your thoughts," said Chandler. He holds her securely by the shoulders.

Neva looks up at him feeling weak in the knees, and is again bewildered by her reaction to him.

"I'm so sorry. I was not paying attention to where I was going." Neva replies, with a hand raised over her left eye. The gesture making her appear to be disoriented.

"Are you okay?" Chandler asks with concern in his voice.

Neva awkwardly pulls back from him.

"I'm fine, it's the excitement of the evening getting to me." She answers lamely, unable to think of anything else to say.

"Well, I am glad that we ran into each other, no pun intended." Chandler said jovially, but seeing the look of consternation on her face, immediately changes his tone of voice.

"I'd like to invite you to have lunch with me. To discuss your thoughts on how the foundation can improve its support of community arts in Woodsburne."

"Yes, I would like the opportunity to discuss that with you. Give me a call once you are settled. And again, my congrats to you." Neva said hurriedly, in a rush to get away from him. His dazzling smile seared on her brain.

"Thank you. I'll call next week to schedule it." Chandler said. He couldn't stop smiling at her.

Neva moves around him and makes her way back to the table. Jason and Matt were watching her approach, their eyes mischievous.

"We saw your run-in with the Hunk." Jason said, laughter coloring his words. Matt was not even trying to hide his own amusement.

"You are both acting like juveniles." Neva hisses at them. Not that she is angry. She too sees the humor in the situation. But people were beginning to look over at them.

"Guys, enough. Carter is walking over here." Neva said, looking over their shoulders.

There is a trace of panic edging her voice. With effort, Jason and Matt rein in their merriment. They are poised by the time Carter arrives at their table.

"Well, this seems to be the fun spot. Fill me in on the joke." Carter said, looking at each in turn.

"Matt and I have simply been making sure that our awardee here, doesn't get too swell headed on us. Just merely interjecting a touch of humor into the evening's proceedings. And Neva has been a good sport about it." Jason said effortlessly, with Matt guilelessly nodding in agreement.

Carter considers his reply. But is not convinced that is the cause of Neva's unusual behavior. Surreptitiously, trying to assess her demeanor for himself. Did she have too much to drink? The thought crossed his mind.

"So that's the reason why she seemed so out of sorts when Reginald stopped by to introduce Chandler. Good to know that you all are enjoying yourselves. Working as hard as you all do, a release of the pressure valve is needed occasionally." Carter said with forced affability.

Neva groaned inwardly, mortified at the memory of the conversation with Reginald. She smiles wanly, not trusting herself to speak.

"I came over to request that you all circulate around the room, mingle with the other guests. We cannot have our luminaries keeping to themselves." Carter said in a tone of voice that conveyed that it was not a request.

He turns his back to the men.

"And, Neva, there are some people who would like to meet you. You don't mind, do you?"

Not waiting for a reply, he grasps her by the elbow and leads her away.

Walking alongside Carter, Neva turns her head to look back at the table. Both men raise their glasses in salute, wide grins stamped on their faces.

Neva quickly swivels her head forward, suppressing an urge to laugh. Thinking about how out of character she has been acting all evening. She must get her mind back in the game.

"Think she'll speak to us again? Jason asked, as they watched Neva being ushered away.

"Neva will be alright. She knows that it was all in jest. A little ribbing among friends." Matt replied with more conviction than he felt.

"Hope so," Jason said. "Do you think we went too far?"

"We're fine, don't worry." Matt said, relieved by Jason's concern.

Jason sighs deeply, then asks. "So where is Quintin?"

Matt's face lights up as he replies.

"He left for a job yesterday. Even if he was here, he probably wouldn't attend. It's not his thing – hanging with the artsy crowd."

Jason chortles, nodding his head in understanding.

"Oh man, I feel his pain. I'm counting the days until I can return to Italy."

"Missing home so soon? Why didn't you bring Sylvia with you?"

"Her teaching schedule at the university, she couldn't find anyone to cover her classes. Truthfully, this is not her thing either."

Both men are silent for a moment, pondering the distaste their respective partners had for attending required social functions with them.

"Well, I guess we can't put it off any longer, we had better circulate," Matt declares reluctantly.

They finish their drinks, and go in separate directions to work the room.

At the end of the evening, Matt and Jason were walking to the valet parking kiosk. Seeing them a short distance ahead of her, Nina calls out. Both men stop mid-stride and walk back towards her.

"I didn't get a chance to speak to you guys alone, all evening. You were always with someone or some group. Aren't you bushed?" Nina said, stopping to take off her shoes. Relief coursing through her body on being released from her crystal slingback pumps.

Matt bends down to retrieve her shoes and holds them for her. Jason stands on her other side, and she takes his arm for support.

"I couldn't wait to ask about what was happening at your table. Why were you giving Neva such a hard time?"

Matt and Jason traded a look above her head.

"Were we that obvious?" They asked in unison.

"No, it's only because I know you both so well that I could tell something was up. Okay come on, give!" She demands, looking at them.

Noticing their hesitation, she answers for herself.

"It was about Chandler! I knew it! That was the reason for the teasing." Squealing in delight at the expression on their faces.

"Slow down Momma Mia. Don't go making assumptions." Jason said firmly. He did not want to cause Neva any embarrassment.

Nina looks askance at Jason, and then breaks into a wide grin. Forgetting about Neva for the moment.

"We haven't announced it yet. How did you know?"

"How did I know what?" Jason asks, giving her a questioning look.

Before she could reply, Matt blurts out, "Oh my gosh, you're pregnant!"

Jason is astonished, staring at her.

"My gracious, is it true?"

She nods her head.

"I'm in my fourth month, we're so excited. We've been trying for over a year and were about to give up hope. And consider other alternatives: IVF, surrogacy," Nina gushes enthusiastically, and then stops talking.

She giggles at the expressions of uneasiness on their faces. Jason is clinging to her arm and Matt is clutching her shoes to his chest.

"I know, TMI." Nina said gaily.

Matt is the first to speak.

"Congratulations, I'm so happy for you and Jeff."

"Ditto for me, I'm very happy for you both," said Jason warmly.

Matt bends down to help Nina slip back into her shoes.

"Well, this has been one very interesting evening." Jason tells them, as he hands over their parking ticket stubs.

CHAPTER 28

Neva is running late for a meeting with Sidney Lacardin at the Leyden Museum. Rushing from a meeting with the Folk Art Selection Committee, or the 'Cadre' as they called themselves. It had ran longer than planned.

They had been reviewing the last three portfolios of artists they wanted to invite to exhibit at the Artem Folk Arts Gallery. The name for the gallery that Neva and her group of advisors had chosen after months of deliberation.

Although Neva had called Sidney's office to let them know that she was running late, it still bothered her. She knew that Sidney's schedule had to be as tight as her own. But she also knew that it was harder for him to shift around appointments than it was for her.

She is profusive in making her apologies for arriving fifteen minutes late.

"I understand that you have a lot of demand for your time right now. And veterans like us, know how to manage our packed schedules. I'm just glad that we didn't have to cancel." Sidney said, taking a seat across from Neva at the conference table in his office.

"Thank you for being so understanding. These last few months have been beyond hectic for me. But I have no complaints." Neva said, after quickly checking her phone and putting it on silent.

"How is the gallery coming along? Are you on track to open this year?"

"It is going well, thank you. And without the Cadre, my

group of dedicated art mavens, I would be lost. Barring any hiccups, we should open this year, but perhaps on a smaller scale. We finished the artist selections today. So that is a big accomplishment. I'm very pleased with our progress so far." She enthusiastically informs him.

Sidney smiles at her, thinking how much has changed since they met almost three years ago. Neva is now the executor of one of the most prestigious art collections in the country. And he will soon be its custodian on behalf of the museum.

Once word got out about the Marjoram Collection bequeathment, there had been a tremendous surge in funding support from benefactors and sponsors to the museum. All of them were eager to be included on the list of supporters for the exhibitions to be mounted in the coming years.

"I don't want to seem brusque, but do you have any objection if we proceed directly to the meeting objectives?" Sidney asks, mindful of the shortened timeframe.

"Not at all. Again, I am so sorry that we have less time to meet. There won't be a problem in the transfers of historical research papers, rare manuscripts, and essays on ancient art history. As most of the cataloging processes have been completed. We can release the documents on the Renaissance, Baroque, Romanticism, and Neoclassical periods." Neva said, pleased that his request could be granted.

"That will be great. Many of those academic documents are not generally known or available for study. The left wing of the third floor will be a perfect interim space to house them. We are in the process of contracting with security specialists and other experts to manage both the materials to be downloaded on our website and available for study on premises. We have also identified a small cohort of influential art historians to grant preliminary review access. The word of mouth from this group will generate excitement for the eventual unveiling of the Marjoram Art History Collection."

"I like it, that's a good plan." Neva said, looking thoughtfully at Sidney.

"I aim to please," he teased, getting up to go to his desk to retrieve his laptop.

"Along that line, I have two recommendations to discuss with you regarding the papers."

Sidney moves to sit closer to her and opens his laptop.

"On reviewing the extensive listing of written materials, we have been brainstorming about effective ways to maximize their use."

He clicks on a file. "One idea is to invite a select number of universities to submit proposals to obtain, on loan, some of the documents for academic study at their institutions. We are still working on components of this recommendation. But you can see from the chart, where our ideas are headed"

He moves the mouse to click on another file.

"These are preliminary sketches for the Marjoram Art History Pavilion at the Leyden Musuem. It will be located in a building that you are familiar with, Annex Building Four. With some renovations, the site fits the requirements for housing this part of the collection and more. The space on the ground floor is ideal for lectures and small conferences; the second floor for the display of the sketchbooks and drawings; and the two upper floors can be divided into secure rooms for accessing both digital and original documents."

"These are excellent suggestions. I'm sure that Edith will be very interested in receiving more information on them. The timing is perfect for obtaining input from her specialists regarding these ideas. This can work."

"I am so glad to hear you say that. It will be a major step for increasing ways for sharing this knowledge. Which I'm sure was the purpose of acquiring these artifacts."

"Yes it is. Over the years, they have loaned some of the items, but I feel certain that this is how Charles Marjoram envisioned their eventual use. He would approve." Neva said.

She was thrilled that Sidney was the one proposing these ideas. Because his suggestions coincided with her own thinking about the papers. It pleased her that they had both arrived at similar conclusions.

"Now, for the last piece of business. I don't know if you were aware that Edith provided start-up funding for the construction of the new wing about two years ago. Shortly after you agreed to manage the Annex Project. In the beginning, she was very involved. Inserting herself into the design process." Sidney said, recollecting those early meetings. He eventually came to appreciate Edith's involvement, particularly for controlling budget costs without forfeiting quality.

"We are on target for completing construction next year. The grand opening is planned for the spring of the following year. My dilemma though is finding the right curator for the collection. There is no question that I have very talented people on staff. And ever since word got out about the collection, resumes have been pouring in. Some stellar people among the submissions. But they all lack the characteristic that I think is most crucial for the success of the exhibitions."

"Passion," Neva said. Surprised that she had spoken aloud.

"Yes, absolutely. It will take more than professional skill and knowledge to curate this collection," Sidney replied emphatically.

He abruptly gets up from his chair and walks to stare out the office window. Hands behind his back, he stands there for a moment in contemplation.

"It seems like we have been here before," he said, coming back to retake his seat.

Neva looks at him, unsure of his intended meaning.

"True confessions." Sidney tells her, smiling self-consciously.

"When I accepted this job, I was looking for a posting to be the capstone of my career. One that would have a lasting impact on the art world. The Marjoram Collection was the drawing card for me. Through its acquisition, I would restore the stature of a declining institution. Giving it new life and relevance. An achievement that would ensure my legacy. But that is no longer important to me."

He settles back in his chair, thoughtful, before continuing.

"Let me explain. When the idea for a permanent exhibition of contemporary artists was proposed, my passion was reignited. An exhibition of the works of artists who were still active, and not at the end of their careers. The concept captivated me. My vision for it was not only to showcase their artwork, but also to provide insight into their creativity. A look at the thought processes behind the creation of their art. And plan the exhibition in a way that other artists and genres could be included in coming years."

Sidney stands again, as if made to move by a surge of energy.

"I believe that the Marjoram Collection presents a rare opportunity for creating a dynamic audience experience. For viewers to have an instinctive connection to the art they are seeing. Letting the art speak to them directly. And not influenced by the exhibit's design layout." Sidney tells her ardently. "

"I totally understand what you mean." Neva said, nodding her head knowingly. "The Regulars at the Avalon taught us that lesson well."

"And the curator I want for the Marjoram...."

"Matt." Neva said, not waiting for him to finish.

"Yes, Matt. Do you think he would be interested? More importantly, do you agree?"

Neva smiles briefly, an unreadable look on her face.

"Yes, I agree with you. He was always my choice if the collection stayed in Woodsburne."

"We're not so different in our thinking, I see. Any suggestions for how we approach Matt about taking on this role? Sidney asked, genuinely interested in her advice.

"The best approach is to be candid about the reasons you want him to curate the collection. I also know that curating a major collection is one of his goals."

"But the timing is what concerns me. He's still young and

can set the pace for achieving his goals. And he is thriving as the director of the Avalon. His move to partner with the Prints Limited Collective was genius. It filled the gap of not having the emerging artist exhibits. Their limited print editions are not only affordable, but of high quality. Bringing attention to a new genre of artists. His bold ideas have attracted a younger audience not only to the gallery, but here as well. He reminds me of my younger self." Sidney said pensively.

"Meet with him, Sidney. Don't do Matt's thinking for him."

Neva advises him kindly. And rises from her seat.

Sidney shakes his head as he also stands, smiling at her.

"You always know how to end a meeting. And you are right. I'll reach out to Matt this week."

Neva had just gotten into her car when her cellphone chimed.

"Hey there, didn't expect to hear from you today. What's up?"

"I was thinking maybe we could get dinner later. Are you free?" Chandler asks her.

"Yes, I would like that very much." Neva smiles as she answers. Feeling aglow with anticipation of seeing Chandler later.

CHAPTER 29

Julie was walking through the lobby of the Woods Hotel. She was back in Woodsburne for the first time in more than two years, to visit a close friend recovering from knee surgery. Nina was stunned to see her.

"Oh my gosh, Julie! What a surprise! It's good to see you! What brings you back to Woodsburne?"

Julie smiles and leans in to embrace Nina.

"It is good to see you as well. Jeez, I thought I could quietly slip into town to visit an old friend. I didn't think I would meet anyone I know by staying at this hotel."

Nina laughs. "Well, I come here for the spa service. It's the best kept secret in town. Do you have time to stop for coffee with me?

Julie hesitates, not seeing a way to genially decline the invitation.

"Sure, why not."

Nina links arms with her, as they stroll out of the hotel.

"Let's go to the Blue Platter. We shouldn't run into anyone we know there, and can have a quiet chat."

During the short walk to the eatery, Julie talks about her job in Colorado. She is a senior producer on a popular local political talk show. They settle into their booth and make their order.

Julie looks over at Nina.

"Shall we cut to the chase and talk about the elephant in the room?"

"Julie don't be so defensive. I'm a friend remember."

Julie shrugs her shoulders.

"I'm sorry. But I guess that I have been subconsciously bracing myself for the possibility of running into friends of Jason."

"As I recall, we were friends of both you and Jason." Nina said, bristling slightly at her careless comment.

Julie looks contrite at Nina's soft rebuke. She sighs deeply.

"Let's start over. I'm happy to see you. But I am also still embarrassed by the way I left. I was so angry at everyone. I couldn't get away fast enough."

Nina nods understandingly and reaches over to pat her hand.

"We all understood that your divorce was difficult. No one judged you. We were there for you both. You could have reached out to any of us."

Looking at her, Nina could see that Julie had changed since she left. Her body was more toned and relaxed. The lines around her eyes and mouth were reduced. She had cut her hair to neck length, layered around her face, which softened it. Her facial expression appeared more open, although her eyes still had that sharp look of seeing everything at once.

"Oh Nina, it was a mess largely of my doing. For the first half of our marriage, we ran a very successful business together. Each of us had a distinct role in the operation of our company. But when Jason decided to quit interior design to focus on his art, I was set adrift. There was no longer a defined role for me. Then, when Jason signed with the Avalon, they did everything for him. My minor tasks were no longer required."

Unexpectedly, Julie's eyes fill with tears, and she dabs at them with her napkin.

"I kept myself busy being the surrogate for Jason at social functions and events. Many of those invitations were extended in the hope that Jason might accompany me. While I sometimes felt used, I too was complicit in the sham. Fast forward to two years ago, when a marketing company reached out to me with an offer to join their team. I was elated to be asked to do something in my own right."

Julie's voice chokes up, her mind besieged by memories of the emotional upheaval in the aftermath of that failure. She closes her eyes to steady her breathing, while their food is being served.

Nina intuitively understood Julie's need to talk and for her to listen. They chew in silence, not really eating with any interest.

After a few forkfuls of food, Julie pushes aside her plate.

"But I soon realized that it was Jason, they really wanted to work with. They saw me as the gatekeeper to him. They were rolling out a new business concept for partnering with cultural arts institutions. And wanted Jason to be their ambassador, opening doors for them through his contacts. I was devastated and wanted someone to pay for my hurt. And Jason was the perfect stand-in for venting my rage."

"But why didn't you just tell him the truth about what happened? Nina asked. She is somewhat taken aback by the realization that Julie just told her the real reason for their divorce.

Julie shakes her head as she stirs her coffee.

"Because at the time that is not what I wanted."

Propping her elbows on the table, she rests her chin on her folded hands.

"After all those years, I had knowingly linked my identity to Jason's success. And being confronted with the reality of that choice, it infuriated me."

"The conundrum of how to balance our sense of self within the framework of a marriage." Nina remarked.

"I often wondered if things would have been different if we had children. But truthfully, I'm glad that we did not. Can you imagine the upheaval in their lives that I would have caused, due to my own fears and insecurities. Not to mention the lies that I allowed everyone to believe about Jason." Julie said ruefully.

Nina looks at her in disbelief.

"But things might have turned out differently. You may not have found yourself in the same situation. Don't you think?

"Not really. If we had children and got divorced, they would be involved. There's no way to keep them isolated from the situation. And the emotional state in which I was in at the time, they would have become pawns in the process. I would not have been able to put their interest above my own. From being totally unconcerned about how they would be affected by the fallout."

Nina stares at her, astounded by the frankness of her admission. Realizing the truth of what she said for many people in similar circumstances. Being on a rollercoaster of emotions that can lead to unintended consequences.

"I'm not proud of admitting this. That I would not have been a noble parent in such a situation." Julie said sadly. Reflecting on the hurt that an unhappy person can cause.

"I understand what you are saying. But it is hard to hear it being stated so bluntly. Nina responded plaintively. Shaken by how her own previous thinking about having children was not so different.

Julie closes her eyes briefly, her upper body resting heavily against the back of the chair. She shook her head imperceptibly.

"Luckily for me, I spoke with a friend about my actions. The same one I'm here visiting. She nonchalantly asked me why was I so aggrieved? That one simple question!" Julie said, with a faint smile.

"Then she, very calmly, preceded to point out that I had been trading on my relationship with Jason for years. So why was I so mad? Was it because their offer wasn't tied up in a pretty bow? Or because they were upfront in wanting to buy what I was selling. Or was I offended by being treated as an experienced player in the game of gatekeeping?"

The conversation was as fresh in her mind as though it had just taken place.

"Hearing her say those things to me, I felt so small. All the air was let out of me. Because she was right. Being brutally honest in a way that only a true friend can be. It wasn't malicious, or intending to hurt. It was simply the unvarnished truth of the matter. And it stopped me in my tracks. Made me rethink everything. To put things into perspective. Because of her tough love, I was saved from becoming an embittered woman for life."

Julie looks directly into Nina eyes.

"It all came down to my anger over Jason being able to grow and change. And I didn't. I didn't put the same effort into myself." Julie finishes in a hushed tone.

"I'm just glad that you had someone you trusted to help you through that difficult time." Nina said solemnly.

"And I also need to tell you one more thing. That Jason is an honorable man. Given everything that I put him through, you would think that he would have used the currency of payback in the settlement process. But he didn't."

Julie looks wistfully into the distance.

"And after all of the lawyers' negotiations to reach a settlement, the outcome didn't matter much to me. A battle fought without a sense of winning. There was no victory. The check amount represented an impersonal valuation of my time spent in our marriage. Based on some contrived algorithm for quantifying the value of a partnership in that social institution."

A look of sadness washes over her face.

"Anyway, after much consideration, I decided a year ago to donate most of the money. This happened after I retrieved my better self from the attic in my mind. I didn't do it as an act of pennance. But rather giving back on behalf of the alter ego that I had created. The one who had profited from the fame of someone else."

Her perspicacity struck a chord with Nina.

"I gave more than half of it to the three arts organizations that Jason worked closely with here. And contributed to several art scholarship funds in my state. It is satisfying to know that the money is being put to good use."

Sitting there, Nina maintains her equanimity on learning

the identity of the anonymous donor. There had been a lot of speculation about the benefactor who had made those substantial donations.

"You should know that your support has been a game changer for those three organizations. They have been able to expand their programs to serve more community artists." Nina said.

"Thank you for telling me. That was my intention, to help to make a difference. Part of my journey to find my way back to happiness."

"Yes, finding our path." Nina said, as parts of their conversation replayed in her mind.

Making her think of how carelessly she had treated her marriage in the past; leaving Jeffrey to do the heavy lifting. Delaying having children because she wanted an uncomplicated exit should the marriage fail. Pursuing career success to feel validated.

How the death of Mica, had finally made her take the time to examine her life. Clarifying what was important to her. Reaching the conclusion that her marriage and starting a family were what mattered most. Everything else was secondary. Which led to her decision to not seek the leadership role in the family's foundation. When she informed her father of her decision, he understood and was supportive.

"Well, I've had my rant. Guess I had a lot on my chest that I wanted to unload. I'm sorry for taking advantage of your kindness, Nina." Julie said sheepishly, although not entirely regretful for doing it.

Now at ease, she stares into Nina's face and takes an inward breath. Until that moment, she hadn't really looked at her.

"You're pregnant!" Julie said excitedly. Her face reddened, ashamed of the prior conversation.

"I'm so sorry for not recognizing that sooner. It seems that I still have work to do on myself. My goodness, what an inappropriate conversation to have had with you."

Nina reaches out to take her hand.

"It's fine. I'm glad that you felt comfortable with me to express your feelings. No harm done. We are all works in progress. And yes, I am in my second trimester. We are so happy."

"That's fantastic. You and Jeff are going to be wonderful parents." Julie tells her with heartfelt emotion.

Returning to her hotel room later, Julie felt upbeat about her future. Feeling closer to living a life without lingering shame. An unanticipated perk from her trip to Woodsburne.

Settling herself in the room, she recalls her therapist recommendation to start journaling about the dissolution of her marriage.

At the time, she balked at doing it. Stating that it was ridiculous, not worth doing. Giving excuses when asked about her progress. Until she realized that it was really an exercise for her to analyze her motives and motivations.

Giving her a new blank slate for building a life on the foundation of her own identity. Its construction under her name. No longer needing or wanting to take anything that was not rightfully hers.

Before drifting off to sleep, she thinks about Nina's parting words. "Self-love is the best salve for old wounds."

CHAPTER 30

Neva and Nina were at Matt's house relaxing on the patio, enjoying the warmth of the first sunny day after a week of rainy weather. Nina is wrapped in a woolen throw, comfortable after a satisfying meal. In her ninth month of pregnancy, she was big and couldn't wait for the baby's arrival.

The brunch with Neva and Matt would be her last public outing. The next three weeks, before her due date, would be devoted to planning the homecoming for their newborn son or daughter. Early on, she and Jeff had informed their obstetrician that they did not want to know the gender of their baby.

Nina snuggled into the deep cushions of the chaise, the sun caressing her face. She opened one eye and stole a furtive glance at Neva who was curled up in a club lounge chair. Matt sat opposite them, lost in thought. No doubt pining for Quintin who was away in the Berkshires, at a worksite.

"So, Neva, are you and my cousin serious about each other?" Nina asked mischievously.

This was the first time that the three of them had gathered socially in months. She wanted to be updated on their private lives.

"We are moving slowly towards a relationship." Neva answered evasively.

"But I have a question for you. Were you and Chandler close growing up?"

Nina moved against the cushions on the chaise lounge. Getting herself into a more comfortable position before answering.

"My most memorable childhood memory of Chandler is when I was about nine years old, and he was six. He and his parents came to our house. Chandler's father, Uncle Ryan, had business with Grandfather. And Grandmother had asked him to bring his wife and youngest son.

She was hosting a tea party for out of town relatives. They wanted to see his family while they were there. I was excited because this was the first time that I wouldn't be the youngest child at a family gathering. My uncle's two older children were away on a trip with other relatives.

Uncle Ryan was the first one through the door leading to the outside patio. He held Chandler's hand, who was such a beautiful child, so composed. It was also the first time that I really paid attention to his wife, Margaux. She was stunning.

I was captivated by her. She reminded me of a royal princess. Tall and regal in bearing, a sensuous curve to her mouth, warm beige skin, and golden brown hair, worn in a chignon above the nape of her neck. Her exotic eyes, light hazel with flecks of green, blue, and grey. Their color changing with the light, like a kaleidoscope. I stood there gawking at her.

My mother was the first to go over to greet them. It's funny, that was always the same reaction whenever they came around. Treating his family as if it was your first time seeing or meeting them."

All the while, my uncle had a faint smirk on his face, with his wife standing demurely by his side. A soft smile on her lips. By their nonchalance, it was evident that they were used to being goggled at. Chandler looked bored and scowled at us.

One thing stood out to me that day. I overheard my Aunt Louise talking to my grandfather's older sister, about Uncle Ryan's wife.

'Look at the problem he has brought to us. Marrying that woman. Ryan never knew how to stay within boundaries. Father lets him get away with anything. Now we're stuck with his mess. He needs to be taught a lesson.'

It was apparent that Aunt Louise was upset by Uncle Ryan's

family, particularly by their two older children: Jack and Paulina. Jack was a mini Uncle Ryan, both in looks and demeanor, and Paulina resembled her mother, but had a much lighter skin color.

Truthfully, they looked like any of us. Only Chandler was an admixture of both his parents. It was apparent that Uncle Ryan's family made some of our relatives and friends feel uncomfortable."

Nina abruptly stops talking. All of a sudden aware that those childhood memories should not have been spoken about outside of the family.

"I'm so sorry Neva. That was not an answer to your question. I haven't thought about those memories in years. A chapter in our family history that never gets aired out." Nina said, troubled by her reply to the question. Unable to fathom why she had answered in that way.

"Anyway, Uncle Ryan was aware of their feelings and infrequently attended family gatherings through the years. And when they did come, it was usually he and Aunt Margaux. Sometimes with Jack, their eldest son. Their daughter flatly refused to attend family functions.

So, although I wasn't close to Chandler growing up, I do know that he is a good person. You will not be making a mistake by letting him into your life." Nina told her sincerely. The last thing she wanted to do was derail the developing relationship between Neva and Chandler.

"Thank you for being so honest. My goodness, I don't know what to say. Not what I expected to hear when I asked you that question. I guess Chandler and I will have a lot to talk about as we get to know each other." Neva said, feeling uncomfortable by what she had learned so unexpantantly.

She feels that that information should have come from Chandler. And was unsure whether to tell him about it. The last thing she wanted to do was to cause a problem between the cousins. Or more worrisome, that it could end their nascent relationship.

The doorbell rang and Matt gets up to answer it. He returns with Jeff.

"Just coming to pick up my wife." Jeff said jovially.

Nina manages to direct a smile at him. And Neva goes over to give him a hug.

While Matt and Jeff assists Nina to get up from the chaise, Neva is busily gathering the bags of gifts that she and Matt bought for baby and Mom.

"The bottle of aged scotch in the blue canvas bag is for you. Something to keep handy for the next three weeks." Matt whispers to Jeff.

Jeff is both surprised and pleased with his gift. Telling Matt cheerfully that he hopes it lasts that long.

"Okay, Momma, let's get going." Jeff says to Nina, taking her arm as they walk to the car. Matt loads the bags into the trunk. He and Neva waving as they leave.

On their return to the kitchen, Matt takes a pitcher of homemade Sangria and salsa from the refrigerator.

"I was saving this for when were alone. Do have time to stay?" He asks Neva, assembling bowls of chips and salsa, and glassware on a large tray.

"Yes, I do. I could use a real drink." Neva quickly replied.

She carries the pitcher, and Matt takes the tray as they head back to the patio. Matt pours a glass of Sangria for each of them. They take their first sip in silence.

"Well, that was some story," Matt said. Looking at Neva, who is seated across from him.

"Indeed, it was. I feel so awful now about asking her that damn question. I should not have done it. Chandler and I haven't talked much about our families." Neva said worriedly.

"Please, don't get stressed over it. Your question was innocuous. How could you have possibly known that it would have elicited such a response from Nina. I guess she was trying to put her best foot forward for when you do have the talk about families with Chandler." Matt said, perplexed himself about Nina's response to the question.

The story about the prejudice Chandler and his siblings experienced from their father's family goes through his mind.

He can relate to being treated unfairly by others. He sighs to force these thoughts from his mind.

"I also know about treating family members unjustly." Neva tells him. Picturing Arizzia and Ahnan in her mind.

"I am certain that when you speak to Chandler about today's conversation, he will understand." Matt tells her with conviction.

Yet, he sees the worry on Neva's face. She is no longer relaxed, but is upset by the incident.

"Listen, you haven't known each other long enough to start sharing family histories. It's not a priority at this point. The discussion will happen when the time is right." Matt said, trying to put her at ease.

Although Neva nods her head in agreement, she is still bothered. Concerned that she had acted imprudently by questioning Nina about her cousin.

Matt waves his hands in the air. As if the movement will dispel the tension around them.

"Okay, change of subject. I have some big news. I have accepted the offer to curate the Marjoram Collection." Matt proudly announces.

He wants to distract Neva from her thoughts.

"That is great news. I'm so happy for you." Neva says, grateful for the change in topic.

"But I must admit, I never imagined that the position would be at a museum in Woodsburne. The cosmos has its jokes."

"You are the best person for the job. I'm thrilled that you are going to be part of this endeavor. When do you start?"

"Unofficially, I'll be starting next week, reviewing plans with Sidney, getting to know the other assistant curators. Edith has also invited me to dinner that same week. I'm looking forward to having an open discussion with her regarding the management of the collection."

"While I can't speak for Edith, I do think that you will have the autonomy to make the exhibits successful. And most likely, I will be her point person for most decisions regarding transfers and so forth." Neva tells him.

"That is exactly what I was hoping for." Matt said with relief.

"I'll be officially leaving the Avalon in a month. It will be a bittersweet departure. Sad about leaving the gallery, but elated for this new opportunity." Matt said somewhat dolefully.

"This will be a very exciting and demanding project for all of us. Trust me, the collection will be impactful. Until recently, I had not fully realize the magnitude of it. I feel so humbled by the dedication shown by Edith and her late husband Charles in the acquisition of these artworks." Neva said truthfully, as she considers how the love of art inspired their endeavour.

"It is mind boggling when you think about it. For not being trained art professionals, not only did they understand details and techniques, but appreciated the subtleties of every acquired piece of art. Not to mention the sketchbooks, manuscripts, and other items. That was a considerable undertaking, and one for which we are truly indebted to them." Neva said, overcome with admiration and affection for Edith.

"I totally agree with you on that." Matt replied dutifully.

But his mind was preoccupied with what he was about to say.

"And I have something to say to you. Its off topic, but it is important. I'm asking you. No, I'm begging you, to not let what happened earlier be more than it is. Do not let that spoil the chance of having a relationship with Chandler. He will understand that you weren't prying into his private life. Stay focused on the joy and happiness that he has brought into your life. If Chandler is the one for you, please, please do not let your fear chase him away." Matt tells her passionately.

Neva reaches out to hug him, tears springing into her eyes. "Oh my goodness, that is exactly what I needed to hear right now. Thank you so much, for your wise advice. It means so much to me, Matt. It really does."

"It comes from my heart. And from my own experience. I want you to be happy."

They sit in silent companionship. Each one lost in their own thoughts.

CHAPTER 31

Two days later, Neva and Chandler were driving back to her apartment after dining at Fables. He was telling her about a new project that he might have to lead temporarily.

"It will involve a lot of travel initially, to meet with the senior management and other affiliate partners. It's more for public relations. A way for us to demonstrate our commitment to the project." Chandler said casually.

He glances over at Neva when she doesn't respond.

"A penny for your thoughts."

Neva stirs herself and looks at him.

"I'm sorry, just preoccupied with things at work."

"I thought everything was going well. Is there anything that I can do to help?" Chandler asked with concern. Noting that Neva had also been subdued at dinner.

When they were seated comfortably in her living room, Neva tells him about the conversation with Nina that took place at Matt's house.

Chandler leans towards her and smiles.

"Don't worry about it. Nina already called to tell me what she said to you. She blames pregnancy hormones for her lack of discretion. I want you to feel free to ask me anything and vice versa. This is how we will get to know and trust each other."

Neva heaves a big sigh of relief.

"I just felt so bad about the whole thing. It wasn't my intention to snoop behind your back or look for gossip. I was only interested in knowing about her relationship with you."

"Okay then, let's talk about our childhoods and growing up

in our families. Me first." Chandler said.

"I'll begin with my mother and her family. That side of our family is not complicated.

My mother is an only child, born in Haiti to a Creole mother, Marcella, and French father, Jacques Perviliere. He was a very successful businessman and landowner. In Haitian society, her family was considered to be upper class. Her father died when she was ten years old. Soon after, she and her mother moved to Louisiana to live with relatives.

While my mother has a loving relationship with her paternal relatives, she is much more closer to relatives from the maternal side of her family. As are we. These relatives are kind and loving, not perfect, but good people.

They have worked hard to achieve their wealth over generations. Each succeeding generation builds on the wealth passed down from the preceding one by continuing to invest in the family's three main business interests: real estate, healthcare, and telecommunications.

Her side of the family is likewise involved in philanthropy. Generous in their giving; and actively involved on select boards. Their wealth is not used as a shield to separate them from the world, but as a tool with which to make a meaningful difference globally.

My father is the youngest of four children, three sons and a daughter, born to Maximillian and Catherine Partridge.

My father's eldest brother, Maximillian Jr., died in a boating accident when he was sixteen years old. The family was out sailing when the boom of a sail suddenly got loose. As it swung around, Maximillian was able to push his mother and sister out of its way. However, he was hit with the full brunt of its strike, knocking him overboard. By the time they reached him, he was dead.

The family was never the same after the accident. Soon after, my grandparents decided to move from New York City and live permanently in Woodsburne. The manse on Riverside Drive was sold, but my grandfather kept an apartment on Fifth Avenue. A place for them to stay when traveling to the city.

My Uncle Reginald became the next in line to head the family empire. When he retired from his CEO position, he succeeded my grandfather as executive officer for the Partridge Foundation."

Neva interrupts him.

"Chandler this is not necessary, we can talk about our families over time. I'm satisfied knowing that you understood my motives for asking Nina about you. Let's just enjoy the rest of the evening together."

Nina felt uncomfortable. She was concerned about her turn to speak about her family and childhood. Knowing that her actions in the past will be difficult to explain. She once again regrets asking the question about Chandler.

"No, this is an important conversation to be had. I want you to understand what made me the person I am today." Chandler tells her, unaware of her discomfiture.

"My father never aspired to have a leadership role in the family business. After the death of his older brother, he did not want to be tied to the family business. He wanted to have a life of his own choosing. After finishing college, he travelled through Europe. That is where he met my mother, at a party in Paris.

She is two years older than him, and at the time was studying for an advanced degree in European literature at the Sorbonne. My father is an economist, and my mother is a professor of literature and cultural studies.

A year after my parents met, they got married in Paris. Soon after, they relocated to Louisiana. Six months later, my brother Jack was born. Shortly after the birth of my brother, my paternal grandfather came to visit them. He was hoping to persuade my father to dissolve his marriage.

My grandfather had mistakenly believed that my mother was a poor, uneducated Caribbean woman who had trapped his son into marrying her. He was intent on rescuing my father from the clutches of a conniving woman. However, when grandfather met my mother, he knew that his son would never leave her. She was a highly intelligent woman, and a classic beauty.

On that day, I think that my grandfather envied his son. Because he had married for love. In my grandfather's social class, it was custom for marriages to be more like a business contract. An arrangement to solidify the financial futures for both families. And he took for a wife, a woman who came from the right family and understood the tenets of their social position.

If my grandfather had to be honest, he would admit that he cared for my grandmother, had affection for her, but was not in love with her. And to be fair, she would probably say the same thing about him. And while this may seem to be impersonal, these practical pairings have worked for many families, across many generations. With most couples finding their own way of maintaining the marital union.

But I digress. It's just that in talking about this out loud, it explains so many things which occurred in the past. Things that never entirely made sense to me before."

Chandler moves away from Neva and crosses his legs, before continuing.

"The wife that my father chose to marry dismayed his family. Because she and their children did not fit the racial stereotypes that they had of black people. We frightened them. Placed alongside their children, my two older siblings did not outwardly look any different. They blended right in with them.

They were obsessed with Paulina. Treating her like some new species to be gawked at and touched. But Paulina stood up for herself, which made her more of an object for their resentment.

When Paulina complained about their behavior, my mother believed her. As my mother had also experienced similar treatment. Which led to the talk with my father. At first, he denied their concerns; and implied that they were being overly sensitive. Stating that his family was merely trying to get to know them. But my mother insisted that he pay attention to their behavior on our next visit. He came to accept that they were right."

Chandler's tone of voice began to harden, and Neva felt both uneasy and absorbed by his narrative.

"As a result, my siblings and I were no longer required to attend most family functions. Of course, my father was angered by the

prejudicial conduct of his family, particularly by his sister, and older relatives. However, through his own growing self-awareness, he began to understand what his children had to contend with in the broader society. Where we did not fit neatly into societal categories of ethnicity.

His growing understanding of this issue brought us closer together as a family. And he became a better person and father from facing his own prejudices. And although my paternal grandparents were kind to us, I don't know if they loved us. At least, not in the same way that my mother's family loves us."

Chandler pauses to sip his drink. Gathering his thoughts for the next part of his narration.

"But my paternal grandparents did not want to lose their son because of whom he married. Gradually, grandfather came to admire and respect my mother. She was an asset at formal dinners, especially with foreign business leaders.

They were impressed by the ease with which she was able to fluently converse with them in their language. As well as her understanding of their cultures. Her prowess made these executives more inclined to do business with our family.

My grandmother also grew to like my mother. And began to introduce her as 'my beautiful daughter-in-law' to friends and acquaintances. Thereby, curtailing inquiries about her racial origins.

However, Aunt Louise and other relatives were not pleased by these acts of acceptance. Looking back on it now, I think that Aunt Louise was jealous of my mother. In her mind, my mother was usurping the position that she felt was rightfully hers.

When Uncle Maximillian died, the family had coalesced around the two surviving sons. While she became the living proof of her deceased brother's bravery. And to be sure, Aunt Louise probably had unresolved issues stemming from that childhood trauma. However, she chose to use her displaced anger to fuel the flames of prejudice and discontentment. Eventually causing the splintering of the family."

"What did she do?" Neva asked. Wanting to know the

answer, yet also knowing that she will be repulsed by it.

"She devised a scheme to have my brother accused of sexual misconduct. The young daughter of her close friend would make the claim against him. It was to take place at a birthday party for one of our teenage cousins. Jack and my parents had planned on attending the event.

However, their real objective was to humiliate my father and discredit him within the family. Jack was just collateral damage.

It was only by chance that the scheme was averted days before the party. The husband of Aunt Louise went to my grandfather and told him about their plan.

My parents were summoned by my grandfather, and from the way they left the house after his phone call, we knew that something bad had happened. They went straight to the airport where the family plane was waiting for them.

My grandfather took swift action against Aunt Louise. She was removed from her board seats and divested of all stocks, rights and privileges in all family businesses and holdings, including the Foundation. Her two children were similarly excluded from these rights. But grandfather did eventually arrange for them to receive a cash settlement.

Richard, who was my aunt's soon to be ex-husband, had to sign legal agreements which precluded him from doing business with Partridge Industries and its affiliates. His penalty for having known about their plan, and not exposing it sooner. Turns out, that he only reported it because my aunt reneged on key sections of their pending divorce agreement. The other relatives involved were similarly dealt with."

"How awful. Going to such an extreme to defame her own brother and nephew." Neva exclaimed, outraged by their actions.

"It was reprehensible. The entire family was shaken by it." A look of sadness came over Chandler's face. Those memories were still painful.

"And your brother Jack, how did this affect him?" Neva asked, deeply concerned.

"My grandparents came back with my mother and father. They wanted to be the ones to explain the situation to Jack and answer his questions.

He was seventeen years old at the time. Afterwards, Jack simply asked that the matter not be discussed again. But he was a changed person. Frankly, we were all changed. Some of us for the better, others not so much.

And I think that was the first time that my grandfather realized that his wealth could not erase the emotional pain caused by the egregious actions of his daughter. The rift caused by that incident, to this day, has not been fully mended within the family."

"I'm so sorry Chandler, how awful it must have been for you all. But you seem to have come to terms with it. I mean, to the extent possible given the matter." Neva said soothingly, at a loss for the right thing to say.

"My parents never allowed that experience to overshadow our self-esteem. That we did not have to prove our worth to anyone other than ourselves. Honestly, we took our lead from Jack, who vowed not to let that incident define him.

As he rightly pointed out, we were the ones in control of our future. Currently, Jack is a congressman. He is preparing for a senate race next year. And Paulina is a prominent neurosurgeon, married and the proud mother of two children." Chandler sat silently, his mind back in time.

Neva looks questioningly at him.

"Sorry, just thinking about when we were kids." His voice is husky with emotion when he continues.

"Before my grandfather died, he asked me to come to see him. One of the most surprising things I learned during that visit was his feelings about Aunt Louise.

He told me that disinheriting her was not a problem for him. But making sense of her indefensible act was more difficult. Because he felt it was his fault.

After all these years, he still hadn't come to terms with the death of his eldest son. And as illogical and unfatherly as he knew it to be, he couldn't overcome his resentment that Max had lost his life for *someone to whom his sacrifice meant nothing.*

Louise had not gone on to accomplish or do anything constructive in her life. Remaining as selfish and entitled as she had been from childhood. And raised her sons to be like her. Both of whom are out of touch with the world outside of their privileged lives.

There was so much pain in grandfather's voice as he said this to me.

'For decades I couldn't stop myself from thinking about what Max would have achieved had he lived. I would probably have gone to my grave stuck in that mindset. But a month ago, an old friend visited me. He said something that opened my eyes to how apathetically I have been living my life. A shadow of the man that I had once been.'

Chandler stops speaking briefly, needing time to collect himself. The image of his grandfather on that day, vivid in his mind. The way he looked, so vulnerable and unsteady. An old lion who could no longer roar.

"*From that friend's visit, came another painful realization. That in addition to Max, he had also lost touch with two of his other children.*

Louise to his indifference and resentment; and his selfish behavior had caused my father to leave the family for the life he wanted.

On that day, my grandfather asked me to return to the family fold. He knew that it was probably too late to make amends with Jack and Paulina. But he hoped that through me, they would eventually come to realize his deep regret for any harm he had caused them.

I can still hear his last words to me. 'Learn from my mistakes, Chandler. I have lived a good part of my life encased in bitterness for something that could never be undone. And in so doing, I wasted so many precious years catering to the longings of a fool.'

My grandfather died two years ago. Ironically, his funeral provided an opportunity for family members to renew ties, particularly among the younger generation.

And then late last year, Uncle Reginald approached me about succeeding him at the Partridge Foundation. Prior to making the offer, he had discussed it with several family members, including my father and brother.

It didn't take me long to accept the job. And as it turned out, it was a very propitious move for me. I found you."

"And the same for me. I met you." Neva said, smiling fondly at him.

"And I am honored that you so openly shared your family history with me. Your story has shown me how much our lives are shaped by the people that are in it. Whether we are aware of it or not. Although my family dynamic is very different from yours, it has also shaped the person that I am. But fair warning, I am still a work in progress." Neva said thoughtfully.

She gets up and holds out her hands to Chandler. He also rises, and they share a long embrace. She leans away slightly to glance up at him.

"It has been quite an emotional evening talking about family experiences. Let's end the evening by giving ourselves some downtime to process what was said and heard. For reflection, in our own way. We can see each other tomorrow, maybe go for a stroll along the walkway by the river. Introduce you to another gem of our city." Neva tells him soothingly.

She sensed his disquietude. And knew that he needed to be by himself. To put to rest those revived memories.

Chandler brings her in for another close embrace.

"I think you are right. This has been a deeply emotional experience for me. Letting out the ghosts from the past. But it is a good thing too. And like you, I too am a work in progress. I like your idea of meeting for a walk tomorrow. Thank you." Chandler murmurs quietly.

He was grateful that she understood. His need to be alone to shake off the aftereffects of talking about his family. But he did not want to offend her by leaving too soon.

Neva breaks away from him and puts her arm around his waist. They walk slowly to the door.

"I'll text you the time and location of where we will meet."

"Perfect. I'll see you then." Chandler kisses her gently on the lips before leaving.

CHAPTER 32

After Chandler left, Neva felt drained. Yet, tired as she was, her mind drifted back to the day before her sister's wedding in Morocco. Her mother had complained about having leg pains and Neva had volunteered to stay with her. The others had gone to attend a luncheon hosted by a relative of the groom.

At the time, Neva did not know that her mother had feigned her malady to have some private time with her. For while Neva had reconciled with her family, she wasn't emotionally close. A barrier of distance, a lack of intimacy, still existed in her interactions with them. Her mother knew this. And she wanted to help Neva to finally bridge that gap.

Neva was also aware of her disjointed connections to the family. She observed how the relationship between Arizzia and her mother, our mother she corrected herself, was so different. The deep love and affection that they had for each other was demonstrated in the subtle ways in which they communicated, through glance or touch.

A fleeting spark of envy flared up as those images came to mind. But she knew that her past resentment had stifled the forming of such bonding ties with their mother.

Neva quickly broke away from those thoughts and refocused on the revelatory conversation that she had with her mother that day. How a snippet of family history changed the course of her life.

"You look ready to open yourself to love." Her mother had said to begin their conversation. Her remark had caught Neva off guard.

"That's what weddings do to you. Open you up to the possibility." She had replied tentatively, not sure how to respond.

From there, they segued into having the most personal conversation the two of them ever had. Her mother spoke about her early life in Sardinia and her first love, Gilberto. This was before she was introduced to Francisco by a close relative on her father's side of the family.

She wanted to marry Gilberto, but her parents would not give their consent. In their mind, Francisco was a far more suitable choice for their daughter. He was already a skilled craftsman and would be able to support her and a family. They were married and soon after immigrated to America.

"Come, sit closer to me," her mother had instructed. "I have something to tell you that I think you need to hear."

Intrigued, Neva did as she was asked. She was curious about what her mother had to say. With her legs folded beneath her, she sat attentive as her mother began to speak.

"It's as if everything that happened back then, took place centuries ago. As if such a span of time was needed in order to understand the course in which life would take us. It began with a chance remark from a cousin about Gilberto.

She told me that she had seen him recently in New York City. He was a merchant marine, and his ship often docked there to deliver cargo. He rented a room on the city's West Side during layovers.

I found out his address and over the next two years, would visit him whenever he was in the city. Leaving you and your brother with a babysitter on those days.

It was a platonic relationship, based on our shared love of cooking. There was never any thought between us of trying to revive a love affair. We had long outgrown those romantic dreams of our youth.

For me it was a chance to be my own person, not linked to the identities of wife and mother. Able to freely discuss and exchange ideas on food and cooking techniques. Without having to be concerned about hurting someone feelings about their perceived cooking skills.

And Gilberto was glad for the company of a close friend from the old country. One who understood his passion for cuisine and creating recipes. The last time that we saw each other, he told me that he and his fiancé had recently bought a bar/restaurant business in Portugal from her uncle.

He was proud of becoming its owner and to be working with his wife. We parted ways being truly happy for the good fortune in our lives."

Her mother had taken a deep breath, as if preparing herself to talk about what came next.

"Soon after, I became pregnant with Illiana. I was joyful for a new addition to our family. But it all fell apart, when she suddenly died. I thought that I was being punished for having selfishly renewed my friendship with Gilberto.

Even though it was innocent, that I had somehow betrayed my marital vows. And her death was my punishment. But I kept those thoughts to myself, unable to talk about it with anyone. So deep was my shame. My guilt almost wrecked our family."

With her eyes closed, she continued.

"The state of my grief led to the decision to send me to Florida, and ultimately to being hospitalized there. During my hospitalization, the psychiatrist were able to help me to understand the reality of my relationship with Gilberto. That there were no hidden desires for rekindling what might have been. We were simply two friends who could talk about a shared interest in food with appreciation and enjoyment. And slowly, I came to accept that the loss of Illiana was not a judgement against me."

Her mother stopped to take a sip of water.

"During my hospital stay, I was fortunate to have Rosa assigned as my aide. She was like an angel. Because, while the doctors concentrated on healing my mind; she helped me to heal my heart.

Without her, I would have remained trapped in recurring cycles of despondency. Never fully recovered, going through the motions of living. Being emotionally detached from all whom I had once loved.

Rosa showed me that since the death of Illiana, all my thoughts of her were centered on loss and guilt. In essence, transforming her into an object of despair and sorrow. Being obsessed by the shortness of time she was with us. Ignoring the joy that that beautiful infant child had brought into our lives."

Her voice trembled, filled with the emotions from the remembrance of that time.

"Those private conversations with Rosa led me to the awareness of rather than mourn her, I should give purpose to my love for her. Let that love restore me, empower me, and work through me. In time, I began to understand the power of unconditional love. I will always miss Illiana. But now, when I think of her, it no longer causes me anguish. She is forever in my heart, and I'm at peace. Do you understand?"

"I do." Neva had replied simply.

"So, when your father asked me to make the decision about bringing Arizzia and Ahnan to live with us, it was not a difficult one to make. I realized that they too were conceived in love, and therefore, were no lesser than the ones born to me. And that those innocent children needed a home; to be cared for; and most of all, to be loved. And it was within my power to provide all of that for them, without any misgivings. An expression of my unconditional love."

As she said this, there was a faraway look in her eyes. As she remembered the letter that Zaieda had left for her.

"I also believe that the power of unconditional love was awakened within your father through his relationship with Zaieda. For when he learned about the twins, he too was able to love them unreservedly, without self-reproach."

Neva had been spellbound as she listened to her mother's story. The things she learned was like finding the lost pages of a book. A book consigned to the back of a shelf because it was incomplete.

This new knowledge shook her. Making it apparent how little she knew about her parents. Growing up, she was never interested in knowing anything about them. If asked, she could only provide basic information about their lives.

A question came to her mind as she sat with her mother. She asked about the love that her parents had for each other.

"In the beginning, we were two people who came together through arrangement. Gradually, we came to love each other. By accepting the other person for who they were, not who you wanted them to be. Adding to that a generous measure of humor. A secret ingredient that makes it easier to put in the effort for making a relationship work. And in so doing, the payoff is that you are thankful for all the good years and able to withstand the difficult ones. That's how your father and I have been able to endure and prosper in our marriage." Her mother had said with a broad smile, while gazing thoughtfully at Neva.

"Are you thinking about getting married?"

"I only asked the question to understand how you made your marriage work. As for me and marriage, you never know what the future has in store." Neva told her with a smile.

"Yes, that's good. Keep yourself open to finding love. And it will find you." Her mother had gently advised.

That surprising conversation in Morocco had caused a seismic shift in Neva. On that day, she was finally convinced to let go of all her past judgements. The ones still buried deep within her. It completely altered her outlook on life, particularly about her mother. Her mother, she came to accept, was neither unwise, unintelligent, nor weak in character.

This belated understanding was crucial. For it exposed the falsity of a woman conceived from the assumptions and half-truths of a child. An image that had resided somewhere in her mind ever since. The adversary against whom she had sought to prove herself superior for most of her life.

With this comprehension came the opening to finally rectify all the other erroneous suppositions about her childhood and family. To see more clearly the reality of that time period.

As Neva sat quietly in her living room, she became calmer. The recollection was like a talisman. Soothing her anxiousness about speaking of her past.

To be sure, her story will be very different, but no less complex or compelling. She imagined telling him about her immensely wealthy younger siblings. The thought of which made her giggle.

And with a deep sigh, she was once again grateful for that afternoon in Morocco. For when she met Chandler, she was not apprehensive about falling in love. There was no lingering fear of turning into her mother. Because she finally understood that she would simply be a woman in love.

CHAPTER 33

It was a bright, November afternoon. The day was warm but seasoned with the colder weather to come. Neva was sitting in her office at Artem. She had an appointment with Merjanh Bandar, an eminent motivational speaker that she met at her sister's wedding. Her company also worked with women entrepreneurs globally. They will be discussing a joint venture with the gallery.

As Neva awaited her arrival, she listened to a recording of a recent seminar presented by Merjanh on *'Love and Life.'*

Merjanh: "Two women have each recently experienced a break-up of a relationship. One goes on to find love again, and the other doesn't. Why? The difference is that one of them remained locked in her failed experience. Adopting a pattern of negative thinking which will influence her life choices going forward. While the other has moved on. Choosing instead to understand the lessons learned from the situation. Her attention is focused on her well-being. She does not let herself become mired in the emotions of anger, blame or self-doubt."

Some audience members vociferously objected to her premise. One woman strenuously asserted that the examples given were oversimplified. An extremely narrow interpretation of self-growth and relationships.

Merjanh: "Is it because it could not be that simple? That there must be a more complex explanation based on some unknown factors? Because you are not ready to accept that happiness is a matter of choice. Is that the objection? Trust me, I totally understand that choosing a mindset of positivity is not easy. It is a choice that must be made every single day. Because negative thoughts and emotions don't just disappear. I also know that it is much easier to point a finger at anyone or anything rather than at ourselves. Placing the blame for your problems and inaction on abstracts. To conveniently forget that in the end, the only given is how you choose to use the time you have on earth."

Neva skips to the next segment.

Merjanh: "How many of you think that having wealth is the answer to everything that you feel is lacking in your life? Imagine that you just won a billion dollars from a lottery. What would change? Will it make you a better person? Will it solve all your problems? Will all your worries disappear. Maybe. Now, I want you to think about this question. And be honest with yourself. *What do you really need to live your best life?* By looking inward, into your innermost self, you may be surprised by the answer. Your inner voice will help you to put into perspective what you need to be happy, aside from a certain lifestyle or the acquisition of material things. Let's explore this topic more in depth."

Looking at the time, Neva skips ahead in the recording.

Merjanh: "We've come to the last circle in the diagram, the Atlas Syndrome. Wouldn't life be easier if we took ourselves less seriously. How did we become a society of Atlases? Think about that for a moment. And I am not going to ask for a show of hands here. But how many of you think that if it wasn't for me, things would fall apart? Let me tell you this, that even with all you do or try to do, things will sometimes fall apart. We need to change this way of thinking. It begins with a simple affirmation of intent. Start your day by saying: *'Today I am going to do the best that I can, in all aspects of my personal life and at work.'* (Audience question.)

Merjanh: In answer to your question. The reason that I did not say 'work life,' is because working is a part of life for most of us. But in this part of our lives, we are paid for the work that we were hired to do. We can come back to this subject later. But right now, let's continue where we left off.

Merjanh: Our affirmation of intent is to do your best each day. Over time, this daily affirmation will become a part of your way of thinking. Gradually you won't get stressed out by the things that you feel need your attention. Because you will come to realize that if it matters, it will get done. And eventually all those mental prompts in your mind will be silenced. The ones that make you feel that: *you need to do better; you are not doing enough; or you are failing at doing what needs to get done.* The second part of this change process is also very important. When you begin to feel stressed or frazzled, pause for a moment. Place your right hand over your heart and repeat this mantra: *'Through my touch and with each deep breath, I become centered in my core.'* Let's practice doing this together."

Neva forwards to the final segments of the recording.

Merjanh: "So then, love is not fearful; but fearless. Love is not a game. It is not a prize to be won. Love is not blind, it is all seeing. It knows when it is being mistreated or dishonored. But it does not judge. Love does not wither nor die. It slumbers, cradled by the soul, until reawaken. Love is often confused with lust, or obligation. That is not the way of love. For love is a gift that comes from the heart. It is given by choice everyday. And if you are honest with yourself, love will show itself to you as a tapestry. Giving you insight into how you used its power in your loving. Before, we move on to the conclusion, I will answer a few questions. [Break to answer questions.]

Merjanh: In preparing how to end the seminar, my initial thought was to conclude with a few brief statements on life. But my mind kept returning to thoughts about art. Which was strange, because while I love the arts, in all of its forms, it is not a main focus of my life. But the more that I thought about why this idea kept coming to mind, an answer occurred to me. That living life can be thought of as an art form, the art of how we live it. In this context, your knowledge, experiences, decisions, and choices would be the base materials used to depict: its imagery and depth; the background and foreground; the shadows and light; and the mental process guiding its composition. So, I will leave you with this thought. Be an artist. Make good use of your materials. And let self-awareness be your color palette to shade in the peaks and the valleys of living an authentic life. And as you look at the development of this artwork, through your mind's eye, you will see an unfolding portrayal of your life.

❖ ❖ ❖

The recording was ending when Merjanh came into Neva's office. She gets up to greet her. Pleased to see her again.

"I was just listening to the audio of your seminar on 'Love and Life.' I was so moved by your teachings. In fact, I'm in a fairly new relationship and was struck by your comments on love. For most of my life, I have shied away from commitment. And now at age forty-five, I am unable to stop the feeling of wanting this person in my life." Neva stops talking, stunned by her remarks.

"Oh, my goodness, please forgive me for that outburst. Clearly, my thoughts are still wrapped up in the seminar. I'm so sorry, that is not why you are here today." Neva looks at Merjanh feeling embarrassed.

She realizes how desperate she has been to talk about her feelings with someone outside of her small circle of friends.

"No, it's fine. Don't worry about it. I can understand wanting to discuss what you just heard. As you know, Ewanna is usually the lead for handling the business to business dealings for our organization. But since I was going to be the area, I offered to make a side trip to meet with you. Get a sense of whether our organizations are a good fit for working together."

"Well let's start by giving you a tour." Neva said, as they leave her office to go to the first floor of the gallery.

"This is an incredible space. I really like how the rooms are setup to be individual exhibit spaces, but yet it is all cohesive. In fact, many of your paintings look like fine art to me. They could be hanging in a museum or fine arts gallery." Merjanh said, impressed with the layout and quality of the works being shown.

"You are right, Neva replied, pleased by her observation.

"Most people tend to think that folk art is less refined in composition and technique. Less intellectual. But, I beg to differ. For while many folk artists may not have had formal training, nevertheless, their approach to creating art is the same. Which is to communicate with others through their creations. Without being bound by any strictures for how to depict their artistic vision. And in all honesty, it is the ordinary people who view their work who are the real judges. They are the ones who will say whether it has moved them or not."

"That is very true. And I appreciate your point of view about this type of art. We ran into prejudice about the quality of the art being offered through MerNa. It was hard in the beginning to get showings for the artists connected to our organization." Merjanh said, recalling her discussions with Ewanna about those early rebuffs.

They continued the tour of the gallery. Stopping at the two rooms where the works of the four artists, who were selected by Neva and the Cadre, would be displayed.

"Yes, I think we can work together. Your gallery has shown that it recognizes the artistic value of the artwork that it displays. Let me text Ewanna to see if she is available for a video chat with us. Save time for all of us."

The call lasted for more than an hour. By the end of it, another meeting was scheduled to finalize agreements.

Satisfied with the outcome, Neva and Merjanh went to a nearby restaurant for dinner. Afterwards, Neva invited Merjanh to her apartment to continue their dinner conversation.

"Your apartment is beautiful and suited to who you were before. But now, you are changing. More open to the world." Merjanh said, viewing with interest its layout and decor.

She is a voluptuous woman with large brown eyes and short black hair. The firmness of her skin makes her look much younger than her fifty-six years.

Merjanh reclines on the sofa, using the decor pillows to make herself more comfortable. Neva smiles at the small fortress of pillows that Merjanh erected to support her upper body. The first time that any of her infrequent guests, herself included, used the pillows in that way. Making the sofa more functional than form.

Neva burrows into a deep armchair, having removed the décor pillow, and tucks in her legs. The first time that she sat like that in the chair.

"Let's continue our conversation where we left off. You were saying that until your mid-thirties you harbored deep seated anger towards your mother and two younger siblings. But now you understand the reasons for the decisions made by your parents during your childhood." Merjanh said thoughtfully.

"It seems so foolish now when I look back on that period. And my parents, my mother in particular, made every effort to help me to understand, but I rebuffed their every overture. If I had listened then, I would have saved myself years of pain and unhappiness."

There is a brief silence in the room.

"But at the time, I did not realize how cavalierly I was tossing away opportunities for having a different type of life, from the one that I ended up making for myself. Which was not the life that I really wanted. All because I was so determined to not be like my mother."

Neva pauses, amazed at her unflinching truthfulness.

"For so many years, I found solace in my professional achievements. And acquiring things. My life would probably have continued that way, if not for the conversation that I had with my mother while we were in Morocco. And shortly thereafter, I met Chandler. Now, my world has changed. I have all the pieces needed for making a good life for myself. And yet, I am hesitant about putting it all together."

"Are you happy that you have met someone that you want to share your life with? Merjanh asks gently.

She can hear the pain that Neva's past has caused her.

"You would think so. But all I can focus on is the age difference between us." Neva sighs sadly.

"My mind keeps thinking about him leaving me for a younger woman. Isn't that crazy? I have him leaving me already."

Merjanh stares at Neva intently.

"What do you think is driving that fear?"

"Because there is still some part of me that thinks I don't deserve to be loved." Neva quietly replies, as tears fall from her eyes.

Merjanh quickly gets up and goes over to hug her. She brings Neva over to the sofa.

"Neva do not retreat back into being that frightened little girl from your childhood. Cut the final cord to that pain. You have learned the reasons for what happened back then. You have done the heavy lifting in confronting your past." Merjanh tells her.

She lets Neva compose herself before speaking again. Wanting her to pay attention to what she is saying.

"You are prepared to make informed choices for the life you want. Because you now know, that you are in control of the narrative for your story. You have the writer's pen in your hand."

"But I am still fearful of messing it up. I want to get it right. Since Chandler came into my life, I have been so happy. For me, he is everything that I want. However, I can't stop thinking about: Am I the right person for him? Is he making a mistake by being with me? Can I make him happy? All these doubts keep swirling in my mind."

"Pushing those doubts aside, what else is troubling you?"

Neva shifts herself to face Merjanh. She is astonished by not only the question, but also her insightfulness.

"How did you know that there was something else bothering me? Neva asked wonderingly. Taking her time to reply.

"I'm worried about the children that he has from his previous marriage. They are twins, aged eleven. I am petrified to meet them. To be a part of their lives."

"Do they live with Chandler?" Merjanh asks, sensing Neva's real concern.

"No, they don't. They live in England with their mother, stepfather, and younger brother. The twins, Henri and Collette, spend summers and holidays with Chandler. The prospect of motherhood, even a quasi-maternal role, frightens me. And I know you don't want to hear this, but I am older than both sets of parents. I will probably meet his children during the upcoming holidays. And I can't stop thinking about their reaction on seeing me for the first time. That their dad is dating a grandma!"

Merjanh burst out in laughter, her whole body shaking with it.

"Oh Neva, what a theater you have going on in your head," she said between gasps of laughter. When she is composed, Merjan gets up to go to the powder room.

Neva also gets up and goes into the kitchen to refill her glass, bringing the bottle of wine back with her.

She retakes her seat on the chair. And is perplexed by Merjanh's reaction. Not seeing the humor in what she said. She is still thinking about it when Merjanh returns.

"Oh, I see that you are not pleased with me. You have put distance between us. I did not mean to offend you with my laughter. It was the image of you as 'grandma' which struck me as humorous. And you should not view me as this person who has all the answers. One who does not have human emotions or reactions. That is not realistic."

"You are right. Forgive me. I am treating you as if you are an Oracle. The wise and unemotional dispenser of wisdom."

They both chuckled at the idea.

"An oracle, I'm not. And for me, humor and laughter are like reset buttons. It gives you a different perspective on things. I'm not saying that all humor is like that, but in general."

"I guess I'm feeling vulnerable and inexperienced right now. This is the first time in my life that I feel I am in love. And I don't want to lose him."

"Okay. Let's talk briefly about age and aging. Starting with age. I think of age as a mental process. The process for observing, understanding, and learning how to use and apply the information obtained through our interactions in the world around us. Therefore, the number of years that a person has lived is not a true measure of their attainment of wisdom, knowledge, and understanding." Merjanh pauses to take a sip of her wine. Giving Neva time to think about what she just said.

"And so, a person at age eighty may not be any wiser than someone half their age. Or a thirteen year old may seem wise beyond their years. Take yourself for example. You had been locked into a certain thought pattern since childhood. But upon reading a long lost letter, a desire for self-discovery was awaken. Opening your mind to recieve truths that that were either hidden, ignored, or misunderstood. And that awareness has helped you to perceive the world around you differently. And since then, you have continued to evolve."

"Age is just a number." Neva said softly in agreement.

"Aging on the other hand is the physiological changes in our bodies as we get older. Which may be your primary concern regarding the age difference between you and Chandler. How he will perceive you as your body ages." Merjanh said thoughtfully.

"Yes, you are right. That is concerning to me. And it's not

about me being vain. I can't imagine putting myself through an endless pursuit of cosmetic intervention to appear younger. My chief concern is that I don't want to become a burden to Chandler." Neva said dolefully.

"I agree with you about not seeking the proverbial fountain of youth. For me, being comfortable in your skin is how you remain attractive. And your mindset is a valuable tool for maintaining vitality and well-being. As to your concern about becoming a burden, don't forget that Chandler will also be getting older. He doesn't remain at his current age. And as long as you are both healthy, it should not be a problem. Give Chandler the benefit of knowing that the both of you will be undergoing physical changes in the coming years. Don't let this fear overshadow the life that you want to have."

"Can I tell you that I feel so relieved right now. Just being able to talk freely about it. It's like you read my mind."

Merjanh smiles at her.

"It's not mind reading, just being attuned to the person I am with. But I do want to go back to your statement about your relationship with Chandler's children. You are right to think about a suitable approach for when you meet them. However, you implied that your status with Chandler isn't a committed one. Therefore, you should have time to discuss your feelings with him. Or do I have that wrong?"

Neva blushes deeply before replying. Chandler's marriage proposal going through in her mind.

'Neva, I want to marry you. Can I promise you that our marriage will last forever? No, I cannot. You change, I change, things happen. Just know that I love you! My heart yearns to be with you. Let's make our own infinity. There is a beginning, but not a known ending. And not knowing its ending will become our commitment. For us to cherish our love, so that it will last forever.'

"Actually, he has asked me to marry him."

"Oh, I see. Are things moving too fast for you then? Are you feeling overwhelmed?"

"Not so much feeling overwhelmed. I never saw myself as

a domestic goddess. The one responsible for housekeeping, cooking, cleaning, and taking care of someone other than myself. It will be a monumental shift for me."

"Is that what you think marriage is all about?" Merjanh asks incredulously.

"No, no, I'm not articulating my thoughts cogently. I do want to get married. My concern is that I don't want to feel pressured into changing into someone who is not me. My self-awareness keeps me moving forward not backward. The genie cannot be put back into the bottle." Neva said, and sighs heavily.

Finally expressing the last of her fears for making a commitment. Her body slumps into the chair, as if resting after a lengthy battle.

"That's a great point. And not only for you, but for Chandler as well. I highly recommend that you have a candid conversation about life as a married couple. Covering the full gamut from doing chores to finances. All the little things, the nitty gritty, that is so often overlooked or taken for granted. This should be the next step in preparing for your marriage."

Merjanh gazes at Neva for a long moment. And realizes that this will be her first marriage. She will be a first time bride.

"Let me also say this to you. All the things I just said about having the nitty gritty conversation is important. It will help to build a solid foundation for your marraige. But the other part of the marriage equation is this. For the both of you to reach a mutual agreement on how to balance the Me/We in your marriage. So that neither of you will feel that you are losing 'the Me' in being part of 'the We.' And it is also crucial that you both recognize and accept that 'the We' is the linchpin in your marital life."

Neva is overcome with emotion as she listened.

"That has to be the best advice that I will ever receive about marriage. You understood what I needed to hear and know. I thank you, from the bottom of my heart, for that."

Merjanh gets up, smiling at Neva.

"You are welcome. I'm glad that I could be of help. But it is getting late, and Granny needs to rest these old bones."

"Okay, you are never going to let me forget about that comment." Neva laughingly tells her, as they walk arm in arm to the door.

"Call me anytime you need to talk. I'm here for you."

Merjanh caresses Neva's cheek, before leaving.

CHAPTER 34

Three days later, Neva received a package from Merjanh. Her curiosity peaked by its shape and weight. Opening the large outer box, Neva finds an envelope, taped onto a blue cardboard tube with a twist off lid on one end. She takes out the note to read.

Dearest Neva,
After our dinner on Tuesday, I could not stop thinking about our conversation. I often turn to a favorite author of mine for guidance – Tenaj. Who was also my second great grandmother.
I find that her written thoughts and observations provide perspective whenever I am grappling with a problem.
As I own the copyrights to most of her literary works, several years ago I published an anthology entitled: 'A State of Being/ In the Words of Tenaj/ Collected Poems and Short Stories.' I wanted to share her knowledge and wisdom with a new generation of readers.
Enclosed is an excerpt from that book. A story about love between an older woman and a younger man. And although it is not an actual representation of your relationship with Chandler; its core message is about the gift of love.
It is my hope that her words will help you to take a leap of faith into the promise of what can be.
Love,
Merjanh

Neva twists off the end cap of the tube. A copy of the story, printed on fine art matte paper, slides out. As she unrolls it, her hands begin to tremble.

Her breath catches in her throat as she begins to read. And for a moment, she stops breathing.

The One Love

An older woman meets a younger man one day. The younger man proclaims that he is the *One Love* she has been seeking.

The woman does not believe him.

For years she had been praying for her *One Love*. As she grew older, she had begun to despair of ever finding him. When she met the younger man, it never entered her mind that he could be the 'One' that she has yearned for most of her life.

"How can you be my *One Love*?

"Because God sent me to you. He heard your prayers," replied the younger man.

"But I want a man who will give me all that I want. The perfect man of my dreams. How could that be you? You are too young." She said to him in disbelief. Unable to discard the image of the man she had desired for so long from her mind.

"God knew that you needed time to be prepared to receive me. For I am the man that you would have rejected in your younger years. Because you have been seeking something nonexistent on this realm. I am here to guide you back to the path of love and happiness. The path that you strayed from for a long period of time. When you were lost. And was wandering in the wilderness of insecurity, doubt, anger, jealousy, and sadness. I am the fresh eyes through which you will see love again, and relearn its ways." He told her earnestly.

The older woman takes his hand and looks searchingly into his eyes.

"Show me."

Years later, the younger man and the older woman are at a beach watching the sunset. She is nestled in his arms as they sit on a blanket covering the sand. With her head resting on his chest, she tilts up her face to gaze at him. A feeling of contentment courses through her body.

In the past, that feeling would have provoked her subconscious mind. Unleashing its cruel tirade. 'He will leave you!' 'He will hurt you!' 'Only heartbreak will be your companion forever!' 'You are unlovable!'

Her ongoing battle with this unbidden voice continued until she was able to silence it forever. It happened on the day when she finally realized that she was unbreakable. On the day when she found self-love.

It was then, that she understood that if he did leave her, her heart would not go with him. It would stay with her. Resilient. She would remain whole. Her body and soul would not wither away. Nor would her mind be imprisoned by desolation.

Dismissing these thoughts, her mind returned to the present. The light had already begun to fade on the horizon. He stands up and holds out his hands to help her to her feet. She clasped his arm as they walked the short distance back to their home.

She knows that her time is near but is unafraid. Grateful for the thousands of days, in all the years, that they have been together. Thankful for all of the spiritual gifts that she received from being wedded to him. Her one love. The finder of a once lost soul.

Neva slowly places the print on the counter. Her eyes filled with tears. She is shaken by how deeply the story resonated with her. That she too had once wandered in a wilderness of her own making. And that now, she too wants to be fearless in pursuing her heart's desire.

She sighs deeply as she leaves the kitchen. Wanting the cleansing of a shower before reading it again.

Later, after reading it for the third time, she reaches for her phone to call Merjanh, but stops herself.

What more is there to discuss? I'm the only one who can decide what to do. What's next. The artist holding their brush above a canvas.

With this thought in mind, Neva gets up. She goes to stand in front of Jason's painting. The painting of a woman poised to make a decision for herself.

CHAPTER 35

Neva was turning into Matt's driveway to attend the 'adult catch up,' as the gathering was called. She had been intrigued by Matt's tease of sharing news about something she absolutely would want to know about. He also promised that the elusive Quintin would be there. She had jokingly told him that how could she decline such an enticing invite. While she was parking, she received a call from Chandler.

"Hey there! Are you at Matt's house yet?"

"Yes, I'm parking in his driveway as we speak. Are you on the way?

"No, I won't be able to make it. I got pulled into a last minute board meeting to resolve a hiccup with one of our partners. Please give my apologies to Matt and Quintin. Let them know how sorry I am about not being there. I was really looking forward to it. And I'm also sorry about not being able to spend time with you. Love you, and I'll see you later."

"Love you too."

Neva sits in the car for a moment. Thinking about how easily she has adapted to hearing and saying, "I love you."

Matt comes out to greet her as she closes her car door.

"Is everything alright? I saw you on the phone. The doorbell camera sees everything." He laughs at her look of confusion.

"Never mind, just come inside." Matt said cheerfully, they link arms for the short walk to the house. Quintin is placing a tray of hors d'oeuvres on the coffee table as they enter.

Seeing Neva, he rushes over to hug her.

"Hello, so good to see you. And don't you look all glowy!

Where is your handsome boyfriend?"

"Hello to you too. Unfortunately, Chandler won't be coming and sends his apologies to you both. He has to attend an emergency board meeting. And he is my fiancé now. We are engaged." Neva tells them beaming. Unable to hold back her announcement.

"Wait! What! When did this happen?" Matt and Quintin asked in unison.

"Two weeks ago. I'm still getting used to saying it." Neva replies, seeming to quiver with happiness.

"Congratulations! We're so happy for you. For both of you. Group hug." Quintin said enthusiastically.

"We were going to make the announcement at Nina's get together next week. You are getting the early edition of our news." She tells them, her eyes sparkling.

Matt and Quintin look at each other and laugh.

"This is too funny. And the timing. You can't make this stuff up!"

"What are you talking about?" Neva asked, looking at them perplexed.

"We invited you and Chandler over to announce that we got married two weeks ago. Around the same time, it seems, that you got engaged."

"What! Oh my gosh!! Matt!!" Neva rushes over to hug and kiss Matt. Tears stream down her face.

"She would be so happy for you," Neva whispers in his ear. Matt clutches her close, his eyes tearing.

"Umm, hello, I'm the other part of the happy couple. I got married too." Quintin said, his eyes also tearing up.

Neva turns around and walks over to Quintin, hugging him tightly. "I'm so happy for you both."

"Oh my gosh" Neva repeats, tears still streaming. "My heart is full of love for both of you. And may you have a long and happy marriage."

Matt comes over to hug her again. He is deeply touched that

Neva had mentioned Mica, who would have been elated for all of them. Matt looks over at Quintin, he nods his head. He understands the connection that the both of them share in remembering Mica.

"Now a toast all of us!" Quintin says, with a brisk clap of his hands.

The effervescence of the light golden wine seemed to change the mood in the room. The momentary sense of loss, is quickly replaced by thoughts of happiness and the excitement for their futures.

"Tell me everything, beginning with what happened to my invitation." Neva demanded teasingly.

"Alright, we left for California on Thursday, over a week ago now. For what I thought was a private screening of a documentary on archaeology that Cait, my sister-in-law, and her parents had made. However, unbeknownst to me, Quintin and Cait had been working on our wedding. In fact, probably my whole family was in on it with them. Anyway, we arrive in Cali, and land at Santa Rosa airport in Sonoma County. When I asked him about our landing destination, having taken it for granted that our tickets were to Los Angeles. Well, this sly fox quickly responded that it was the location for the private showing. That close friends of Cait's parents owned a winery there and offered to host the event. I accepted the explanation like an innocent lamb, not having a clue to what was being planned. At dinner, everyone was extra cheerful and happy. Which I ascribed to their being hyped about the documentary." Matt stops to smile and take a sip of his wine.

"The next day, after a late breakfast, Quintin takes me to the Sonoma Overlook Trail and proposes to me. I am a little confused because we did the proposal thing months ago. But I put it down to his enthusiasm for the weekend. When we arrive back at the hotel, my brother Frank is waiting in the lobby. He informs us that the film showing had to be postponed due to some last minute technical problems. But we will all meet up later at dinner."

Quintin interrupts him. "This is the best part!"

"We had barely entered our room, when Quintin calmly announces that we will be getting married the next day. *'Why wait he tells me. Everyone is here. Let's just do it.'* I am flabbergasted, completely speechless. And going through my mind are thoughts of how we are going to pull off a wedding ceremony without any preparations." Matt looks over at Quintin, who is smiling with self-satisfaction.

"Later when we arrive for dinner, there are new guests seated at the table. Quintin's family had arrived, also Josiah and his wife, and others. I look at Quintin and ask him, *'How are they here? How did all they know?'* That is when he tells me all about the secret planning that has been going on for weeks."

"The only question that I could think to ask was: How did you know that I would go along with your plan?"

His reply was: "How could you say no to this face."

Neva bursts out laughing, clapping her hands. Her head thrown back in boisterous laughter.

"This is such a great story." Neva said gleefully. "So was the documentary also part of the ruse?"

"Oh no, that part was true. They did make one. But the film was in post-production, and months away from being ready for release. They took a chance on me not knowing that." Matt replies humorously.

"Okay, back to our wedding story. It takes place the next day, and everything is ready. I mean - tuxedos, venue, guests, food, drinks, flowers, and wedding officiant. It was beautiful. It was magical."

"And we got a marriage license about a month before. I told Matt that it was a practice run. Getting him accustomed to the idea of taking the next step." Quintin interjects.

Matt rolls his eyes.

"I know that I appear to be a dunderhead in this little drama. But Quintin put into motion what should have happened much sooner. I knew he was the one for me from the first time we met."

"Same for me. Also, we would never have had time to get married once Matt descended into the catacombs of the Marjoram Art Collection."

The truth of his last statement brings on another round of laughter from the group.

"Back to the wedding. We had maybe fifty guests, mostly family. Josiah and his wife had to be there. Because without them there would be no us, and Quintin's longtime friend Gerald and his wife are like family to him. My brother and brother-in-law were my best men, and Quintin's brother and Gerald were his."

Quintin chuckles, remembering their wedding day.

"I wanted Matt to be flanked by the best men so they could tackle him if he tried to ditch me at the altar."

His remark caused hearty laughter and quips. Quintin waited until they had settled down before continuing.

"The biggest surprise was my older brother, Victor, showing up. Did not expect that. For him to leave the Bat Cave. He is a leader in the field of AI. The 'mad scientist' as he is known in our family. But it was fantastic to have him there. He's a big guy, over six feet tall, with long hair and a ripped body from his passion for rock climbing. Oh man, it was so good seeing him. And he wore his hair in a man bun!" Quintin exclaimed. The memory still poignant to him.

"We were surrounded by love and well wishes. It was perfect. I felt so blessed looking around the room. You did good." Matt said, as he affectionately squeezes Quintin's hand.

"I like the idea of a small, intimate wedding. You're right, the focus should be on giving loving support and well wishes to the newlyweds. Without all the hoopla and stress of making it a social event." Neva said thoughtfully.

"On that note, another reason for this gathering today, is to let you know that Nina already knows about us. She sent a private plane to fly Quinn's parents to California. We didn't want to tell you about us getting married when we all go to meet Baby Aiden next week. It wasn't the way we wanted to let you know."

Quintin immediately adds.

"And the only reason I told Nina is that I was trying to figure out how to get my parents to our wedding. My mother dislikes air travel. So, when Matt's brother had jokingly asked me if I knew anyone with a private plane, I reached out to Nina. My mother forgot about all her fears of flying when I told her how she would be traveling to the ceremony. She couldn't pass up the opportunity for a ride in a private jet."

"I'm touched that you wanted to share your wonderful news with us personally. Thank you." Neva said warmly, captivated by their story.

"You and Chandler are special to us." Matt tells her affectionately.

"Okay, enough about us. Have you begun to think about your wedding?" Matt asked. He knows that Neva will have to find a balance between having a society wedding and a simpler affair.

"After hearing about your wedding, I want that same small and intimate feel for ours. Although we will probably have more than fifty guests. But I do want the attendees to be mainly close family and friends."

As she replies, Neva is wondering how will she manage the planning of a society wedding. Edith and Nina will be invaluable resources to help her navigate the dictates of that social echelon.

Quintin gets up to refill their glasses.

"I think another round of champagne is needed."

"Here's to us, our futures, and may both of our marriages be long and happy."

CHAPTER 36

Once the official announcement of their engagement was made, Neva started the search for both a wedding dress and wedding planner. However, finding a wedding planner, soon became the top priority for her.

The gallery was keeping her busy, as were her duties for the Marjoram Art Collection. Leaving little personal time for herself. Chandler's time was even more constrained due to his 'hands-on' leadership style. Sometimes they only got to be with each other for a few hour a day. A pace that they both knew was unacceptable and could not be permitted to continue.

Two weeks into her online browsing for gowns, Neva felt overwhelmed. She did not see the style or silhouette of a wedding dress that was to her liking. Her ideal dress was a combination of several styles that she had bookmarked.

She soon realized that a custom design dress was the only way to get what she wanted. And began a search for wedding dress designers.

Her list was narrowed down to three designers when she received a call from her niece Adrianna. She was the eldest of her brother Eduardo's four children. And she was also a clothing designer. Recently launching an upscale women's ready to wear clothing line under the brand name of *'Adi.'*

"Hello Auntie, how are you doing? I was just thinking about you and wondering if you could use some help in selecting a wedding gown."

"Adi, how good it is to hear from you. And yes, quite frankly

I do need help. It is a daunting task." Neva told her, glad for the offer of assistance.

It also dawned on her that Adi would be a great advisor given her background in fashion design.

"Have you decided on the type of gown you want or a designer that you like?"

"I haven't seen a dress that I like. So, I have decided to have one custom made. I'm getting ready to contact the three designers whose work is most comparable to my aesthetic.

"That's a good idea to reach out early to a designer. It will ensure that they can have your dress ready in time for your wedding."

"Yes, that is what I was thinking."

"And since you have decided on a custom design, I would like for you to include me on your list of potential designers."

"Adi, but of course, absolutely. Sorry, but I didn't know that you also designed bridal wear. Is this a new line for you?

"No, but it's an area of interest to me. I feel that there is more latitude for creative expression in bridal dresses, making them wearable art, but also functional. My speciality is painting the simulations of embellishments such as beads, crystals, and so forth, on the clothing piece. I do not use those actual materials in the design. I do have a portfolio of sample wedding dresses that I can send to you, if you are interested."

"Yes, please send it to me. I'm excited to see your work."

"Great, I'll email my sketches. Glad that we had this chat. Looking forward to hearing back from you. And there is no pressure for you to choose me. Please, hire the designer who meets your vision for your dress. I mean that. Love you Auntie. Ciao."

"I love you too, Bella. Bye."

Within minutes, Neva was able to click on the link to her niece's online portfolio. After reviewing a few of the sketches, she knew that Adi would be the one to make her dress.

Six weeks later, Adi came to Woodsburne to bring the wedding ensemble that Neva had selected. The fitting took place in Neva's apartment.

As Adi carefully unpacked the two garment bags, Neva paced the floor behind her.

"Take deep breaths, inhale and exhale." Adi instructed her aunt over her shoulder.

The three finished pieces of the ensemble were in the first garment bag. The A-line overskirt, caplet with elbow length flutter sleeves, and a slim belt.

In the second bag was the sample wedding dress. A column shape, tea length dress with a fitted bodice and dramatic bateau neckline which extended across the shoulders.

The V-shaped back bodice ended a few inches above the waistline; and there was an inverted pleat at the bottom of the skirt. The pleat on the final gown will be hand painted in an intricate beaded-like pattern.

The silhouette of the dress is eye-catching from the front and back. The fabric chosen for the wedding dress and overskirt was silk Mikado, in a rich cream color. Silk organza, in light beige, was selected for the caplet.

"Let's get you into the dress first." Adi said, as her aunt took off her short robe.

The dress would need minor alterations at the waist and hips. The front neckline beautifully accentuated Neva's collar bone and shoulders. Around her waist was the slim silver belt made of white crystals. The belt would accentuate the shimmering richness of the cream color in the final dress.

"Okay turn around and look."

"Oh my gosh. The look is stunning, even in this material." Neva said as she looked at herself in the front and back mirrors.

Adi moves the back mirror, which was on wheels, so that Neva could see all sides of herself.

"I love it. You really captured me and the look I wanted: clean lines, simple but elegant." Neva said, as she kept turning to look at herself.

She felt beautiful in the dress but was too self-conscious to say it aloud.

"You look beautiful auntie, simply gorgeous. Now, let's try on the other pieces."

Adi helps her into the caplet which is hand painted to look like it has been embellished with flat backed crystals and sequins.

"This is incredible. You would have to be up close to see that it is not actually real."

Neva couldn't take her eyes away from the garment piece and kept touching it, expecting to feel the crystals.

"With this on, the dress looks completely different. Giving it an haute couture look. Adi, you are incredibly talented."

"Thanks auntie," Adi said demurely. "Next the overskirt to complete the bridal look."

"Wow. I am at a lost for words other than Wow! It looks like a one piece dress."

Neva takes a deep breath as she looks at her reflection in the mirror.

"The look is beyond anything I could have imagined. I feel like royalty. More importantly, my maturity is hinted at, yet the design is modern. The ensemble look is perfect for the church ceremony. And the dress with the belt for the reception."

Neva turns to her niece and takes her hand.

"I don't have the words to thank you for this. The whole outfit is more than I could have hoped for."

"This is how I envisioned you looking on your wedding day. A queen in love." Adi tells her. Overjoyed that her aunt loved the design.

Adi poses a question as she rehangs the caplet and overskirt.

"I know that this is not the usual time to discuss repurposing your wedding attire. But I have some ideas for you. Are you interested in hearing them?"

"Yes, please tell me."

"My idea for the overskirt is to repurpose it into a lining for a silk brocade cocoon jacket. Or it could be made into a kimono jacket if you prefer. What do you think?"

"I absolutely love that idea of using it as a lining for a jacket. Would you dye the material or what?"

"Yes, I would dye the fabric first and then hand screen a custom print design.

"I can imagine it. Do you have any sketches? It could be my signature jacket for going to events connected to my gallery."

"Exactly what I was thinking. And yes, I will send you some sketches after the wedding. I only asked the question to gauge your receptivity to the idea. There is no rush for a decision, we can discuss it anytime that you like."

"Do you have any thoughts about my dress?"

Adi suddenly felt unsure. She did not want to diminish the joy of the moment for her aunt.

"Do you remember Zora? She is Aunt Francine's youngest daughter? They were at Auntie Arizzia's wedding. She is getting married next year, and your dress would be the perfect style for her. Both of you are of similar height, and body shape. However, she can't afford a dress like this, and I can't afford to make one like it for her, even at cost. Our family does not want to understand that I can't create couture designs for them at my expense. Does that make me a bad person?

"No, it doesn't. And I agree with you about not being tagged as the family designer without fair compensation for your work."

"Aunt Neva, I'm so sorry. It is totally inappropriate for me to have brought that up to you. But Zora knows that I am designing your wedding dress and wants me to do the same for her. Without paying me of course. It's not your problem, I'll figure it out. I apologize again for even mentioning it to you." Adi tells her looking distraught.

"That is not a bad idea. Passing it on to a family member who would appreciate it. But let me think about it."

"Of course, you have every right to do what you want with it. And I haven't even discussed it with Zora. I'm sure she would be upset if she knew we were talking about this."

"I'm not saying no. We can have this conversation after my wedding."

"Of course, you are completely right. And again, I'm so sorry. Until now, I didn't realize how much I needed to talk about this with someone else."

"Adi, not a problem. Let's return our attention back to the fitting." Neva said more firmly than she intended.

"I ruined the excitement of this moment for you. I'm so sorry."

Adi is distressed by the turn of the conversation. She had promised herself not to mention anything about the dress until well after the wedding. But Neva had given her an opening and she went for it.

Neva looks over at Adi.

"Can I sit in the dress?"

Adi nods, and they sit at the foot of her bed.

"I am awed by the garments that you designed for me. All the thought and work that you put into creating them. The dress, capelet and overskirt are gorgeous. The way that they complement and enhance each other is a work of art. And the belt is an exquisite statement piece. And I will let you know my decision about the dress when I am ready. But, right now, I want you to know that I love you and will help you in any way that I can."

Tears well in Adi's eyes as she listens. Her impetuousness has been forgiven. She feels proud that Aunt Neva, the fashionista of their family, praised her skills. That meant more to her than the accolades she has recently been receiving from within the fashion industry.

"Thank you, auntie, for your understanding and love. Sometimes I feel so pressured to be all things to all people. And I realize that way of thinking will not help me to succeed in this industry. And also, as challenging as it might be, I need to set boundaries with some family members."

"And I can be your ally. Feel free to use me in that regard." Neva tells her impishly.

"Your support means the world to me. Now, let's get back to the fitting."

The wedding for Neva and Chandler took place five months later. As it turned out, Neva's age was an asset in planning their nuptials. Not being a young bride, she did not have to adhere to any prerequisites for the occasion. The assumption being that their wedding would be a sophisticated affair.

The wedding was a three day event, and took place on Marco Island, Florida. The plan for the three days was: *Day One* - cocktail party and dinner; *Day Two* - Wedding Ceremony and Reception; and *Day Three* - Post-Nuptial Brunch. Mostly family and friends comprised the one hundred sixty invited guests.

A cousin, on Chandler's maternal side of the family, provided the accommodation for the bride and her wedding party. She owned five luxury rental properties on the island. The groom and all other guests were staying at the hotel where the wedding reception would be held.

Neva was a breathtaking bride, radiant on her wedding day. The joy emanating from her belied her age. She carried a bouquet of cream calla lilies, the stems tied with coordinating organza ribbon. Arizzia was her matron of honor, and Chandler's brother, Jack, was his best man.

It had been a long day for the newlyweds when they departed from the reception. They were driven the short distance to the guest house where Neva had been staying.

The house had been cleaned and refreshed for their wedding night. The bridal party had been relocated to the hotel. Arizzia had arranged with the house manager for the delivery of champagne and sandwiches for the couple.

She knew from experience that they would enjoy having food waiting for them. A card was left on the counter to let them know about the food in the refrigerator. They were both famished. Neva had hardly eaten all day. She had been too excited to eat, and only picked at her food during the reception.

They sat in the kitchen to eat, dressed in their wedding attire. Grateful for the thoughtfulness of Arizzia.

"Best sister-in-law ever." Chandler had declared between mouthfuls.

Afterwards, they each went into separate rooms to change out of their formal wear. Each of them wanting to prepare on their own for their wedding night.

After a quick shower, Neva dresses in her evening outfit. A white, one-piece backless bathing suit and short caftan. She also takes the rolled print, from Merjanh, out of its satin pouch. She plans on reading it to Chandler later by the pool.

Leaving the bedroom, she goes to the kitchen. Gathering ice bucket, a bottle of champagne and glasses. She places the print on the kitchen island, not wanting to damage it while taking the wine and drinkware outside. She'll return for it later.

There's a nervous fluttering in her chest as she uses the remote to turn on the flameless candles in the lanterns set around the pool area. She walks over to the deep end of the pool. From that vantage point, she can assess the overall mood setting on the patio. Her final check before returning inside.

Chandler comes into the kitchen, looking for Neva. He sees the print on the counter and picks it up.

He reads it slowly.

"Oh Neva," he said quietly.

He raises his head, looking through the glass doors for her. Suddenly, there is the sound of a body falling into water. In a panic, he races outside and leaps into the pool.

Neva is thrashing around in the eight feet of water, surprised by her fall. Trying to get her bearing. The caftan is billowing around her neck and shoulders, hindering her movements. Chandler grabs hold of her, and calms her down. Then eases her into a back float position. He swims them both back to the shallow end of the pool where they can climb the steps out of the water.

"Note to self, don't leave you unattended by a pool." He tells her teasingly. Patting her back, as she shugs out of the caftan. He guides her to a chair and grabs a towel to drape around her shoulders.

Neva blushes, upset by her unintended entrance into the pool. She lost her footing when dipping her toes into the water to test the temperature. Then got distracted by thoughts of their wedding night.

"So, I'm the younger man, huh." He said, gently drying her hair with another towel.

"Good thing. Otherwise, you and an older man would still be floundering in the water, trying to get out."

Despite herself, Neva laughed heartily.

"I just wanted everything to be perfect."

Chandler stops drying her hair. And comes around to bend down in front of her.

"Everything is perfect, we are here together. And I'm here to love you."

They lock eyes, and Neva murmurs.

"Show me."

About The Author

Caleen J. Mettson is a debut author. She has always been interested in the notion of living an authentic life. More specifically, what are the choices that must be made to live such a life. Through her love of art, Caleen explores this theme in her captivating first novel. Weaving a story that invites readers to reflect on the complex interplay between identity, truth, and the stories that we tell ourselves.

When she is not writing, Caleen enjoys reading and bird watching in her backyard. She resides in North Carolina.

Made in the USA
Columbia, SC
14 December 2024

49168281R00190